Fic   Woolley, Persia
Woo
       Queen of the summer
       stars

19.45   DATE DUE   90-100 S

	FEB 0 8 1996	
AUG 0 5 1993	APR 1 0 1996	
OCT 1 6 1993	OCT 0 7 1997	
NOV 6 1993	JAN 2 8 1998	
DEC 1 5 1993	APR 0 8 1998	
MAR 1 8 1996	APR 2 5 1998	
JAN 0 5 1994	JUN 1 6 1998	
	AUG 2 8 2000	
SEP 3 0 1995	MAR 0 9 2001	
OCT 2 3 1995		
NOV 1 6 1995		

ALSO BY PERSIA WOOLLEY
Child of the Northern Spring

QUEEN *of the* SUMMER STARS

Persia Woolley

Poseidon Press

New York London Toronto Sydney Tokyo Singapore

Poseidon Press
Simon & Schuster Building
Rockefeller Center
1230 Avenue of the Americas
New York, New York 10020

POSEIDON PRESS is a registered trademark
of Simon & Schuster Inc.

POSEIDON PRESS colophon is a trademark
of Simon & Schuster Inc.

Designed by Karolina Harris
Manufactured in the United States of America

10 9 8 7 6 5 4 3 2 1

Library of Congress Cataloging in Publication Data

Woolley, Persia, date.
  Queen of the summer stars/Persia Woolley.
    p.   cm.
    1. Guenevere, Queen (Legendary character)—Fiction. 2. Arthurian
  romances—Adaptations. I. Title.
  PS3573.O68Q44 1990
  813'54—dc20
                                                              90-33441
                                                              CIP

ISBN 0-671-62201-3

To all my mothers - natural, god, in-law, and grand.
And especially to Irene Higman, from whom I learned
how important stepmothering can be.

Characters

HOUSE OF PENDRAGON

Uther: *High King of Britain, father of Arthur*
Igraine: *wife of Uther, mother of Arthur*

Arthur: *King of Logres, High King of Britain*
Guinevere: *Wife of Arthur*

HOUSE OF ORKNEY

Lot: *King of Lothian and the Orkney Isles*
Morgause: *daughter of Igraine, half-sister of Arthur, widow of King Lot*

Gawain
Gaheris
Agravain   *sons of Morgause*
Gareth
Mordred

HOUSE OF NORTHUMBRIA

Urien: *King of Northumbria, husband of Morgan*
Morgan Le Fey: *daughter of Igraine, half-sister to Arthur. High Priestess and Lady of the Lake*

Uwain: *son of Morgan and Urien*

HOUSE OF CORNWALL

Mark: *King of Cornwall*
Isolde: *Mark's child-bride from Ireland*

Tristan: *nephew to Mark*
Dinadan: *Tristan's best friend*

ROUND TABLE FELLOWSHIP

Accolon of Gaul: *Morgan le Fey's lover*
Agricola: *Roman King of Demetia, mentor to Geraint*
Bedivere: *Arthur's foster-brother and lieutenant*
Bors: *cousin of Lancelot*
Cador: *Duke of Cornwall*
Cei: *Arthur's foster-brother and Seneschal of the Realm*
Geraint: *King of Devon*
Lancelot of the Lake: *a Prince of Brittany*
Palomides: *slave-born Arab*
Pelleas: *lover of Ettard*
Pellam: *wounded King of Carbonek*
Pellinore: *Warlord of The Wrekin*

Lamorak: *Pellinore's eldest son*
Perceval: *Pellinore's youngest son*
Ulfin: *Chamberlain to Uther, warrior for Arthur*

Griflet: *son of Ulfin, Master of the Kennels*

WOMEN OF CAMELOT

Augusta: *gossipy lady-in-waiting*
Brigit: *Irish foster-sister to Guinevere*
Brisane: *governess to Elaine of Carbonek*
Elaine of Astolat: *slow-witted lady-in-waiting*
Elaine of Carbonek: *beautiful daughter of Pellam, very much
                        infatuated with Lancelot*
Enid: *sharp-tongued lady-in-waiting*
Ettard: *young companion to Igraine*
Lynette: *daughter of Ground's Keeper in London*
Vinnie: *Roman matron in charge of ladies-in-waiting*

VARIOUS HEADS OF STATE

Vortigern: *earlier tyrant, married Rowena*
Rowena: *daughter of invading Saxon, Hengist*

Cerdic: *their son*

Anastasius: *Emperor in Constantinople*
Clovis: *King of the Franks*

OTHER CHARACTERS

Beaumains: *mysterious student of Lancelot's*
Cathbad: *druid who was Guinevere's childhood teacher*
Dagonet: *Arthur's Court Jester*
Frieda: *Saxon milk-maid, lover of Ulfin*
Gwyn of Neath: *horsebreeder and builder on the Hall on*
Glastonbury's Tor
Illtud: *Prince/warrior who became a monk*

Gildas
Paul Aurelian   *students of Illtud*
Samson

Kevin: *Guinevere's childhood love*
Lucan: *Arthur's Gate Keeper*
Maelgwn: *Guinevere's cousin, King of Gwynedd*
Merlin: *Arthur's tutor and mentor, the Mage of Britain*
Nimue: *Priestess and lover of Merlin*
Ragnell: *leader of nomadic Ancient Ones*
Riderich: *Arthur's bard*
Taliesin: *peasant boy who wants to become a bard*
Wehha the Swede: *leader of East Anglican Federates*
Wihtgar: *Saxon Federate settler*

*Assorted courtiers, pages, musicians, visiting dignitaries and
sprites, according to the reader's imagination*

King
Arthur's
Britain

ORKNEY
ISLES

N

Inverness
Loch Ness
PICTLAND
CALEDONIA
Glen Coe

Loch Lomond
Firth of Forth
Dumbarton Stirling Edinburgh
LOTHIAN

Joyous Gard

The
Mote
RHEGED
Carlisle
NORTHUMBRIA
Appleby
Solway Firth
Ravenglass
York

Irish Sea

Lincoln

GWYNEDD

The Fens
Cambridge
WELSH
KINGDOMS
The Wrekin

EAST
ANGLIA
DEMETIA
Gloucester
Oxford
Carmarthen
London
Caerleon
LOGRES
Silchester
Glastonbury
Winchester
DEVON
Camelot
Portchester
Tintagel
Exeter
The Saxon Shore
CORNWALL
Castle Dore

0   50   100 MILES

0   50   100 KM

Preface

DURING the last half of this century the authors of novels based on the stories of King Arthur have more or less divided into three categories: those who cast the stories as fantasy, those who see them as "women's romance," and those who give them a realistic treatment.

As readers of my first volume, *Child of the Northern Spring,* know, I belong to the last group. Although the characters I'm writing about are superstitious, there are no dragons, no magic swords, no *whooshing* away of islands with a flick of the wrist. There is a place for that kind of sword and sorcery, but it is not in my books.

Nor have I chosen to focus exclusively on the love stories of the famous legend. Like Malory, I prefer to treat them as an integral part of the different characters' development rather than as the main point of the story.

If Arthur and Guinevere lived (and scholars make cases both for and against their actual existence), it would have been during the period following the fall of the Roman Empire—roughly between 450 and 550 A.D. This was a time of tremendous change and upheaval throughout Europe, and nowhere was that more evident than in Britain.

Archaeologically we see a gradual dying out of Roman culture among the Britons—they would eventually be conquered by the vigorous, often brutal Anglo-Saxon settlers. But the struggle for supremacy went back and forth between these two factions for well over a century, during which time there was a brief but major Celtic revival reflected in grave goods, art, and religion. And in the midst of that there seems to have been a noticable peace that lasted for several decades prior to the final Saxon incursions.

It is precisely against this turbulent background that I have set the adventures of the Round Table characters, for legend says that King Arthur led the British forces to victory over the Saxons at the battle of Mt. Badon, after which he reigned for twenty years of peace and prosperity.

While it is with history that I've set the stage, it is from the literature that I've taken the characters, remaining as true to the legends as a realistic approach allows.

The Round Table cast is a fascinating study in human types. Some of the characters have remained pretty much the same over the centuries, such as Tristan, the big young warrior who falls in love with his king's wife, or Palomides, the Arab knight who is accepted for his honor and bravery but always holds himself slightly apart.

Others are more complex and have changed over the centuries as the stories have developed. Gawain, for instance, is the knight of greatest courtesy and honor in the earliest stories. But after the medieval romances introduced the Frenchman Lancelot (he was really a Breton), Gawain's character began to change. Certainly the French versions show him as loutish and hot-tempered, and a decided rake where the women are concerned. I've incorporated both aspects and made them part of Gawain's own growth.

I have also incorporated actual historical figures—Agricola, Geraint, Mark, and Tristan are all considered by scholars to have been real people. And occasionally I've played with archaeological finds, such as the Anastasius Bowl, which was part of the treasure retrieved from the Sutton Hoo ship burial. Although the grave itself dates from the seventh century, it contained a silver bowl clearly marked by a smith during the reign of the Byzantine Emperor Anastasius (491 to 518 A.D.). More than one archaeologist has puzzled over how that elegant bowl came into the possession of the barbaric Swedes who had settled on the edge of East Anglia—and I couldn't resist working backward through the geneologies in order to have Arthur give it to the first king of that East Anglian dynasty.

The historical novelist always faces the problem of anachronism and must make the choice between contemporary readability and historical accuracy. In my case I've opted for readability, or occasionally for tradition. Therefore all the invading Germanic tribes are referred to as Saxons, though the northern settlers were predominantly Angles, and those in the south included Jutes and Franks as well. Since the Britons themselves called them all Saxons, I note it here strictly for academic accuracy. And while the game of chess probably had not reached Britain by 500 A.D., the tradition of Guinevere playing chess with her abductor is so strong, I chose that game rather than the more prosaic draughts, in part because there is so much symbolism connected to the royal pieces of the chess set.

One of the great aspects of the Matter of Britain (as the Round Table stories as a whole are called) lies in the fact that it is a living, viable myth that continues to grow. Each new teller of the tale is indebted in some ways to past versions, and I wish to acknowledge my own debt to Mary Stewart, whose Merlin books continue to be my standard of excellence. Not only have I consciously looked to her for style and approach, but I have also built on her concept of Merlin and Nimue in lifting their relationship out of the typical "gold digger" dynamic it had lingered in so long.

My specific thanks go also to Geoffrey Ashe, whose help and guidance through both the literary and physical landscape verged on the miraculous; to Marion Zimmer Bradley for insights into Morgan le Fey; and to Parke Godwin, who not only allowed me to use the Prydn—a people he created in *Firelord,* but also helped me develop the character of Ragnell.

In the area of research I am particularly grateful to Barbara Childs, who put me in touch with Xenophon's work on horses; Linda Farley of Crossroads Counseling Center for taking the time to educate me in the dynamics of stress following rape; Ted Johanson, who answered my questions on Roman law, and the librarians of the Auburn-Placer County Library for their patience and help in locating odd bits of information on Britain's flora and fauna. As overall godmother to the project, I'd like to thank Marian Jordan.

To all the fans who wrote to ask when this second book would be coming out, to the friends and family who have listened patiently to more about Dark Age Britain than they really wanted to know, and particularly to Pete, who keeps telling me it will all be worth it, goes a great big "I couldn't have done it without you!"

I certainly hope you enjoy it.

Persia Woolley

AUBURN, CALIFORNIA

1986–1989

ONE

The Summons

, Guinevere, wife of King Arthur and High Queen of Britain, dashed around the corner of the chicken coop, arms flying, war-whoop filling my throat. The children of the Court were ranged behind me, shouting gleefully as a half-grown piglet skittered across the inner courtyard of the Mansion. The paving stones were slippery from a morning shower and the squealing shoat skidded into the kitchen doorstep before careening off toward the garden.

"Not again!" I howled, throwing myself on the creature just as a stranger stepped through the door.

With a flurry of bunched muscles and flailing trotters the porker squirted out of my grasp, leaving me red-faced and breathless. Brushing my hair out of my eyes, I looked up to find a small, mud-spattered priest staring down at me in astonishment.

"Your Highness?"

I grinned at the tentative greeting and scrambled back to my feet. Heaven knows what he expected of his High King's wife, but I was what he got.

"What can I do for you, Father?" Beyond us the shoat had wiggled through a hole in the fence, followed by the jubilant youngsters who raced across the vegetable patch. I winced as an entire section of cabbages was demolished.

"I've come from the convent, M'lady . . . where the Queen Mother lies ill. . . ."

Watching the mayhem in the garden, I was only half-listening until I realized his message concerned Igraine. Turning to look at the holy man more closely, I saw for the first time the seriousness of his demeanor. "How ill?" I asked with alarm.

The man's voice was husky. "She's been bedridden for weeks, but it wasn't until yesterday she agreed to notify you."

It was so like Igraine not to make a fuss. Already frail and weak when Arthur and I had married, she'd gracefully declined my suggestion that she stay with us, preferring to return to the convent where she'd retired after Uther's death. She promised to send word if she needed anything, but this was the first time such a message had arrived.

Wiping the mud from my hands, I squinted toward the gate. "Arthur's off fighting the Irish in Wales. It'll take days—maybe weeks—to get the news to him."

"She didn't ask for her son, M'lady. She asked for you."

I paused at that, wondering if the whole world knew that Arthur and his mother avoided each other. If so, the people made no mention of it, for they loved Igraine in her own right and would say nothing to cause her embarrassment. It was part of the unspoken magic that surrounded her.

The priest pursed his lips and studied his hands primly. "There is something she wants to tell you and she refuses to confide it to anyone else. So the sooner you can come . . ."

"Of course," I promised, untieing my apron and wadding it into a ball. "I'll leave immediately. Do you wish to stay here in Silchester, or come with me?"

"I've been on the Road for a day and a half, so the rest would be most welcome."

I nodded and thrust the apron into his hands before heading for the stables.

Ulfin was the old warrior who had been left in charge of the houseguard during Arthur's absence, and he chewed thoughtfully on his lower lip when I told him the news.

"I'll see to everything," he assured me, so I changed into traveling breeches and arranged for Brigit to run the household in my absence while Ulfin gathered a guard of four young men and readied Featherfoot for the journey.

"The lads I've picked are sharp and well trained, M'lady." He frowned fiercely at the buckle as he secured my things behind the saddle. "But I should like to come with you—'twixt Saxon and Irish prowling the woods, there's plenty who would be happy to take the High King's wife hostage while he's away." He made the sign against evil before turning to face me. "I was Chamberlain to King Uther and have known Her Highness from the days before she and Uther were married, so I'd like to be there—in case there's any final service I could provide."

The catch in his voice brought home the realization my mother-in-law might be dying. My eyes brimmed with sudden tears and I turned to Uther's Chamberlain in panic.

Ulfin put his arm around my shoulder and steadied me with a fatherly embrace.

"I feel so helpless." The words squeezed around the lump in my throat. "If only Morgan were here—she's the one versed in healing. Why, I can't be of any use if . . . if. . . ."

"Of course you can." Ulfin's voice was stern and confident. "The Queen Mother's as fond of you as though you were her own daughter, and the chances are she doesn't want to be healed, but eased into death with a loved one near. The sooner we get started, the sooner she'll be comforted."

I nodded mutely, hoping he was right. Birth and death are as much a part of life's tapestry as singing and dancing and gathering up after war, and to avoid them is to avoid being human. But the idea of losing Igraine opened a terrible, sad ache inside me.

We rode silently through the town, past half-ruined houses and empty shops. Like most Roman things, they were only partially used, for the years of decay since the Time of Troubles had taken its toll. I'd never been as comfortable in the stiff, square buildings of the Empire as I was in the thatched roundhouses and wooden halls of my youth, and now the half-deserted town added to the bleakness of my mood. When we passed the outer earthworks and headed down the Road to Bath, I pulled my cape tighter around my shoulders and concentrated on the dearest memories of my mother-in-law.

When we'd first met, she was beautiful and serene—the very embodiment of queenly dignity. I'd stood awestruck before her, a rough northern girl, plain of face and awkward in manner, with no idea what was expected of me.

Used as I was to the freedom of Rheged's mountains and valleys, this marriage was none of my doing. I'd had no desire to learn Latin, or wear dresses, or go south to marry that new High King. Angry, rebellious, foiled in an attempt to run away, I had not gone willingly to my fate. But personal desires are rarely considered in political marriages, and no one seemed to care how I felt about the matter. No one, except Igraine.

She'd come out of retirement to greet her son's bride and shape my future as surely as Merlin shaped Arthur's. I was—and sometimes still am—too outspoken to please most nobles, and my life at the High Court could have been a misery if the Queen Mother hadn't taken me under her wing. During the months after the wedding, when Arthur was off at war, she smoothed my tomboy ways into some semblance of grace, and taught me to look beneath the surface of the people around me. It was then we had become close, and she'd told me any number of stories of her early life. She did not, however, talk about Arthur's origins, or how she herself came to be High Queen, and I lacked the courage—or rudeness—to ask about it.

The common folk claimed Arthur's birth was the result of magic—that Merlin created him to fulfill the prophesy that a great king would rise out of Cornwall and lead the Britons to victory against the Saxon invaders. There were stories of dragons and comets, and mighty spells cast over the fortress at Tintagel. I was sure there was more to the story than legend allowed, and hoped I might understand Arthur better if I could figure out the riddle of his parents.

Igraine was regal and dignified, and always thought of the needs of others, while Uther—by all accounts—had been harsh and abrasive, and was as much feared as Igraine was loved. Indeed, the very fact that they'd become a couple at all seemed a puzzle to many, including me.

Born of the royal line of Cunedda in southern Wales, Igraine would have known a life of ease and luxury but for the shadow of Vortigern, the Wolf; even the established families of the Empire walked cautiously in the days of the tyrant.

Like most British children, I'd listened to the elders tell the stories of Vortigern, who rose to power following the Time of Troubles, after the Legions were taken back to the Continent to support Constantine's bid to become emperor. Seeing Britain left defenseless, our barbaric neighbors—Pict and Irish, Angles and Saxons—rushed to plunder the rich Roman province. But though we begged Rome for help, the reply was an admonition to look to our own defenses because the whole of the Empire was crumbling and there were no legions to spare.

In the chaos that followed, Vortigern had clawed and schemed and murdered his way to supremacy over the other warlords who were carving out kingdoms for themselves. Once in power, he offered to make the Saxons Federates, giving them both land and money if they'd help us fight off the rest of our enemies.

"Invited the sea-wolves right into the sheep-fold, he did," my childhood nurse used to say. "Anyone could see they'd revolt against him sooner or later. By then he'd fallen in love with the Saxon chief's daughter, Rowena . . . stupid old man put aside his British wife to marry the pretty lass with the flaxen hair, and gave her father the kingdom of Kent to seal the bargain! One wonders how he slept at night, knowing the people cursed him for the turncoat he was!"

Indeed, both Vortigern's waking and sleeping were troubled, for there were rumors that Ambrosius Aurelius and Uther Pendragon, the sons of the rightful ruler, were building an army in Brittany, and would one day return to claim their throne. So Vortigern sent his spies everywhere, until fear begot constant suspicion, and tyranny replaced leadership.

"I was eleven when the tyrant's men swept through my father's villa, murdering them all," Igraine had once told me. "If my parents hadn't sent me away with their old friend the Duke of Cornwall the night before, I would have been killed as well, for the tyrant's men spared no one. But instead I grew up in Gorlois's stronghold at Tintagel, as the Duke's ward."

Igraine was very happy there, playing in the meadows at the top of the cliffs while the surf crashed and pounded on all three sides of the headland, and rainbows hung in splendor over the ocean.

I could easily imagine her—a shy, quiet girl, quite unaware of her own startling beauty, who preferred to spend her time with the wild creatures of field and air rather than in the Hall. She soon developed great skill with wild things—rescuing fledglings that fell from nests, and once even healing a fox kit with a badly gashed paw.

"But best of all," she'd confided, "I liked standing beneath the Sacred Oak, safe and secure while the wild wind whipped around me. There was an excitement in it that made my blood sing. . . ."

Gorlois was as magnificently rough-hewn as his fortress, and when she was fifteen, his beautiful young charge agreed to marry the widowed Duke. So they made their vows under the branches of the Sacred Oak, and when their daughters Morgause and Morgan were born, they too were brought there, barely dry from birthing, to be offered to the Old Gods.

And it was at the Oak that Igraine left votive gifts of flowers and bright ribbon when Gorlois went off to join Uther and Ambrosius in their battle to depose Vortigern. By then Igraine had become a young matron, bringing the same care and devotion to the raising of her lively children that she used to lavish on the small wild animals she'd nurtured as a girl.

"I had no interest in going beyond the narrow path that connected Tintagel with the rest of the world," she'd said with a twinkle of wry amusement. "I clung to the safety Gorlois provided, content with the moira the fates had given me—and would have run in terror if anyone had told me someday I would become a queen."

Even after Ambrosius overcame Vortigern and Gorlois returned to Tintagel with wonderful tales of the new High King, Igraine listened with little curiosity. And when her husband tried to get her to go to the High Court with him, she begged to stay in Cornwall, for the idea of leaving Tintagel filled her with dread.

But what was put off that summer became a necessity several winters later when Ambrosius died and his brother Uther Pendragon became High King. There was no escaping the summons to Winchester to swear fealty to the new overlord, and though Igraine tried to persuade her husband to go without her, it was to no avail.

"I served under Uther in battle," Gorlois announced, "and know how volatile his moods can be. I'll not risk calling down the Pendragon's wrath on this house, so we'll go to the King Making despite weather and calendar and the fact that you've no desire to travel."

And that was that. When they departed for the High Court Igraine rode beside her husband, as calm and valiant a partner as anyone could wish, with no outward sign of her inner turmoil.

"It comes," she'd noted, "of being born to a long line of Celtic queens."

I smiled at the memory of her words, for I too had been raised in the tradition of brave and competent women, and knew the litany by heart; it was one of the things that the Queen Mother and I used to joke about.

But I was not sure I could have coped with a man like Uther, and sometimes wondered how much like his father Arthur might turn out to be.

Ulfin was leading us across the broad sweep of the Berkshire downs by now, and the morning showers had turned into real rain as Uther's Chamberlain dropped back to ride next to me.

"There's an inn by the ford, not far ahead. I know the man who runs it, and it's a good place to spend the night," he announced, and I nodded my agreement.

"Tell me, Sir Ulfin—were you with Uther in Brittany, before the invasion?"

"Aye, M'lady. I was raised in their military camp on the Breton shore. My father was a Master Armorer, helping to outfit both warriors and nobles for the invasion to come . . . it took years to ready the army, and by that time I was grown myself. As was Merlin, the young druid who came to join our cause. So I guess you could say I've known them all, from early days on."

"What were they like?" I asked.

Ulfin considered the matter. "Well, it was clear from the beginning that Ambrosius was the one cut out to be king. Thoughtful, almost philosophical, he weighed all aspects of a thing before making a decision. He kept the druid by his side, and after the invasion recognized Merlin as his own son, though born out of wedlock. Between the two of them, they had great plans for Albion." The old warrior paused, letting the ancient name of Britain hang on the air. "Great plans. And perhaps if Ambrosius had lived longer . . . or if Uther had kept Merlin for his own counselor, once he became King . . . but they had a falling out, those two, and Merlin went back to his cave behind Carmarthen.''

"Even before the events at Tintagel?" I prompted, hoping I wasn't asking him to betray any secrets.

"Oh yes. You must remember that Uther was a different stripe of cat from Ambrosius—taut as a bowstring, with action always at his heel, as though he were goaded by a renegade God. It made him a fine leader in battle, but not a favorite among the courtiers—why, the soldiers voted him into the Kingship before the nobles even knew Ambrosius was dead, and many of Ambrosius's followers weren't too happy about it. Some thought Merlin should have been made High King, but the Enchanter was more interested in cosmic things. Uther was relieved to get rid of him, and I wasn't surprised when Merlin left; they were too much like oil and water to work together well.''

The Chamberlain chewed on his bottom lip and shook his head in bemusement.

"After Merlin's departure I tried to take up some of the slack, for no one else had the courage—or affrontery—to advise the Pendragon. I urged him to use the occasion of the King Making to allay the fears of his courtiers. I particularly reminded him that while he was in the field, leading the men to victory, no one cared where he spread his seed, but now that he was High King and must live with the memories and grudges of his nobles, he should be looking for a wife of his own, not raiding the beds of others.

"Lot of good *that* bit of advice did, after he saw Igraine," Ulfin commented ruefully.

"We'd all heard of her before she came to Court, of course, for rumor said she was fair enough to tempt the Gods, and faithful to the Duke as well. Uther joked about the old man who claimed her for his wife. Not meaning any disrespect," the Chamberlain added, making the sign to appease the dead, "but the Pendragon was a randy sort, and likely to say right out what others were thinking quiet to themselves. He hadn't reckoned on Igraine's having a mind of her own, however— or that she might not want him.''

We were coming down the long, sloping side of a down, and the checkered sign of the inn ahead gave promise of a warm welcome.

"It was chancy time for a while, I can tell you," Ulfin concluded. "And I'm glad to say I was the one who convinced Uther to call on

Merlin for help. So it all came well in the end, if not exactly the way anyone expected. But then, you never know how things will go with sorcerers, eh, M'lady?"

By now we'd turned in at the tavern courtyard, and Ulfin had many other things on his mind, so I put aside my curiosity about Arthur's father and went up to the room the innkeeper gave me, away from the noise and smokiness of the pub.

The innkeeper sent up a tray of food, and I ate the savory stew slowly, trying not to think about Igraine lying ill, with nothing ahead but a cold grave. Afterward I got into my sleeping robe and sat by the brazier for a while, staring into the embers and wondering what had really happened at Tintagel. Arthur didn't know, Merlin wouldn't tell, and with Igraine so close to death, it seemed likely the truth would go to the grave with her.

It was late when Ulfin knocked on the door, come to see if I needed anything before we all went to sleep. He took one look at my face and, closing the door behind him, brought me back to the chairs by the fire.

"It will do no good to brood, M'lady—just give you bad dreams and drain you of strength you could give the Queen Mother. Besides," he added, seating himself across from me, "you mustn't think that Her Highness's life was all duty and responsibility. She was full of laughing, lilting ways when she and Uther first ruled the realm. Not, of course, out in public; she was always quiet and regal before her subjects—but when they were in the arms of the family, you might say, she wasn't reserved at all."

A fond smile played over Ulfin's features and he reached up to take a small leather pouch from around his neck.

"Uther'd never met a woman he couldn't bend to his will, but Igraine was different—she wasn't the sort to be intimidated. I've seen her call his bluff and have him end up laughing about it more than once. And for all that they were an unlikely pair, it was well for both Britain and its leader when she became High Queen. That's something I'll always be proud I had a hand in. It was after their wedding that he gave me this. . . ."

The Chamberlain carefully took a golden ring from the little pouch and put in into my hand. "I was thinking that, seeing as how she'll be buried on Christian ground, not next to her husband, Her Highness might want to have something of his to take to the grave."

I looked down at a gold band with a bright design of color around its rim. It was much heavier than the little enamel ring of Mama's that I wore, but the workmanship was very similar.

"Now you just get yourself into bed, M'lady," Ulfin admonished. "I'll call for you in the morning . . . and I don't want to see your eyes all red from crying, either."

I thanked the Chamberlain for his concern, and, after he left, sat staring at the ring and thinking of Ulfin's words. Finally, with a sigh, I blew out the oil lamp and crawled under the fur blankets.

I might not have any better understanding of how Uther and Igraine had come together, but I went to sleep that night imagining her as the bright young Duchess whose beauty and spirit had changed the whole of British history.

TWO

Igraine's Tale

"She wanted so much to see you—God willing, she'll waken long enough to know you're here," the Abbess whispered, hurrying me along a cloistered walk toward Igraine's cell.

A handful of nuns knelt in silent prayer outside the door. The Queen Mother's young companion, Ettard, was with them, and she looked up at me imploringly, as though I had the power to bargain with fate.

The little room smelled of candle wax and sanctity. An older sister, no doubt versed in healing, rose from the stool beside Igraine's cot. Giving me a respectful nod, she came to my side and indicated that the end was expected any time.

I thanked her and moved slowly to the foot of the bed as the nurse tiptoed out.

Arthur's mother lay in a deep sleep, her eyes closed, her breathing shallow. Linen sheets covered the narrow pallet, and her hair, once fabled for its gold, now spread over the pillows in a silver cloud. The wasted body barely showed beneath the rough blanket, and she looked more like a child than a powerful monarch. Yet even drawn and pale, Igraine's features bore the mark of great beauty, and in spite of the dark circles under her eyes, she had a calm and peaceful air. Considering the tumult that had surrounded her life, this serenity in the face of death was all the more touching.

When Igraine had chosen to come live in the convent, she'd left behind all the trappings of her former glory; the cubicle was empty except for the bed and an unpainted wooden chest. A homespun garment hung from a peg by the door, more fitting for a farmer's wife than a great queen.

The tree beyond the unglazed window was filled with willow warblers. They were Igraine's favorite birds and their soft calls and silvery trills filled the air, as though already singing her to the Isle of the Blessed. I looked down at her still form and sobbed aloud.

There was a flicker of movement and the dark eyes opened, assessing my presence at the foot of her bed.

"M'lady . . . oh, M'lady," I cried, rushing to kneel at her side and pressing her cold hand to my cheek.

"Now, now child . . . there's no need to weep. It's enough that you got here in time." She was smiling at me while her fragile fingers tried to wipe away the tears. "Tsch, tsch . . . I didn't send for you to watch you mourn. I'm not afraid of dying, and I've made my confession already, but there's still a matter left undone. Are you listening, child?"

"Of course, M'lady," I gulped. "What can I do?"

"Prop up my pillows, to begin with. I can't talk lying down, and I want to tell you about Uther, and Tintagel."

For a moment I thought she had confused me with a priest, but the old twinkle crept into her eyes and she gave a small laugh.

"There's some things, my dear, which men will never understand— even, or perhaps particularly, men of the cloth. I've made my peace as regards my Christian life, and expect to see the heaven they tell of soon enough; but it's wise to give credit where it's due, and matters that pertain to the Goddess are best shared with one who follows the Old Ways. Besides," she added thoughtfully, "it's a story you'll do well to remember."

So I propped her up on the pillows and settled silently on the stool to listen.

"Gorlois was always a good man; honest and true and gentle," Igraine began. "And I would have done nothing to hurt him, in either word or deed. Perhaps the fear I felt in leaving Tintagel was as much for him as for myself, for while I didn't understand the Goddess yet, I dreaded Her power."

The Roads to Winchester were packed with people hurrying to obey Uther's summons—nobles decked in fur and gold, client kings sur-

rounded by their warriors, even commoners striding along on foot, all
come to see what sort of creature this new Pendragon was. Sunlight
glinted off rooftop and hill, where new snow turned the landscape black
and white, and winter trees stood etched like brooms against the sky.
Even the horses' breath hung in steamy clouds as they passed through
the walls at Southgate's tower.

Igraine's uneasiness was soon replaced by curiosity, for the shy country Duchess had never seen such a gathering before. She even enjoyed
the first evening in the Hall, though the High King himself did not
make an appearance.

Waking at dawn the next morning, she wrapped herself in a long,
dark cloak and tiptoed out of the Hall to go walk among the birches
at the top of the hill, seeking the inner peace such settings always gave
her. It was there she found a young falcon, hunkered in the snow, with
one wing dragging. Slipping her soft glove over the bird's head to quiet
it, she crouched down to examine the pinion.

Suddenly a pair of boots planted themselves between her and the
path back to the Hall—well-made boots of polished leather, with spurs
that spoke of both power and cruelty. For one terrifying moment
Igraine's heart leapt into her throat. Then, like a falcon, she raised her
proud gaze upward to the man who towered over her.

"I had no idea who he was, but as I took in the hawklike features, I
knew he was as wild and untamable as the wind at Tintagel," my
mother-in-law said, her voice vibrant with memory.

The man stared down at the beauty at his feet, surprise leaving him
speechless. And Igraine stared back, noting every detail of his face. It
was only when he raised his hand and she saw the Dragon Ring that
she realized he was the High King.

"Do you always tame raptors, M'lady?" he inquired suddenly, without introduction or greeting.

"Not tame, M'lord, merely heal," she answered, never flinching
under his scrutiny. It was simple response, but it went home to Uther
in a way she had not foreseen. He flushed heavily, and turning abruptly,
strode away.

Igraine felt the same wave of warmth steal through herself, and bundling up the falcon, hastily returned to the Hall. But all the while she was fixing the bird's wing, her mind was on the morning's encounter. Her hands shook and her body ached with confusion and desire.

"I was sure something fearful was going to happen," she murmured, "and that night at the feast I tried every way possible to avoid him."

But the Pendragon prowled the Hall like a wolf circling sheep. He was edgy and feverish, greeting people too loudly and breaking off conversations in mid-sentence. Igraine could feel his presence coming closer and closer, and studiously kept from catching his eye, even accidentally. By the time Uther stood in front of her, he burned with fervor and she stared with equal determination at the floor.

Without a word to Gorlois the High King took her hand and lifted it to his lips. She raised her eyes slowly, unwillingly, and blushed when their gazes met. For a moment she tried to pull her hand free, but Uther refused to let her go, and turned to propose a toast instead.

"To the Duchess Igraine of Cornwall. I pay you this singular honor, oh, Fairest in the Realm, in the hope that you will take kindly to my suit, for rough men such as myself need to be healed by Goddesses like you."

The courtiers were horrified at his presumption, and Igraine writhed with humiliation and anger, sure that everyone could see the passion that warred between them. But she held her head high and accepted the compliment graciously. It was only later, when they were back in their quarters, that she turned to her husband in tears.

"Of course Uther pays attention to you, my dear," Gorlois said reasonably. "He has a fine eye for the ladies, and a roving nature to boot, and if I did not know you so well, I might worry that he'd turn your head a bit. Believe me, our new monarch's interest will shift to some other comely maid before the week is ended, so we'll just wait it out."

But his words only made Igraine more miserable, for she could not tell him that she feared her own desire more than Uther's, and the notion that she was just another woman to be conquered and forgotten cut deep against the quick.

Great, racking sobs began to shake her and nothing Gorlois said could calm her panic. Before long the Duchess was wailing like a sidhe out wandering in the wildwood, pleading hysterically with her husband.

"Take me home, M'lord . . . please, by all the Gods that be, take me away from here, I beg you."

"We'll go directly after the King Making," he promised, hoping to settle the matter, but the distraught woman only moaned more deeply, and in the end he grew frightened for her sanity, so they left as soon as it was light.

"Perhaps," the Queen Mother mused, "Gorlois was right, and if we had stayed, Uther's interest would have flagged."

She began to cough, and her breathing became more labored.

"You shouldn't be talking so much, M'lady . . . you need to save your strength," I admonished her.

"What for?" she wheezed, gesturing toward the water pitcher.

Her hands were too shaky to hold the goblet, but when I raised it to her lips she looked at me over the rim, her eyes crinkling in a half-smile. "The only strength I need is to tell the story straight out, as the Goddess would expect. . . .

"You must understand that I was not intentionally complicit in what happened. Caught in a web of the Old Gods' making, clothed in a moira beyond my comprehension, I was, up to that point, honest and honorable in all that I had done or said. Even after we left, racing for the safety of Cornwall, I hoped to avoid the fate I didn't understand." There was a pause before she added, "No one can outrun the Gods."

They had no sooner settled into Tintagel than a messenger from King Mark of Cornwall arrived. He warned them that Uther had declared Gorlois a traitor for not swearing fealty and was leading an army into Cornwall.

"Mark rides with him, but he wants you to know he will not take arms against you, since you are his own Duke," the courier announced glumly.

Gorlois gave a hollow laugh. "We appreciate His Highness's reassurance. But I don't suppose that means he will take arms *for* me."

Embarrassed, the fellow stumbled through an explanation that Mark didn't want to further upset the High King, but after he had left Gorlois let out a string of oaths, calling the pudgy young King of Cornwall every kind of coward he could think of.

"Ah well, as long as you stay here there's nothing to fear," the grizzled warrior concluded, slinging his cape of black Spanish goathair over his shoulder. "There's no way outside of magic that Tintagel can be taken—even one warrior can hold the path, if necessary. So I'll leave the houseguard under your command and take the rest of the men to Dimilioc to wait for Uther. If he won't listen to reason, he'll have to listen to the song of swords."

Igraine nodded in agreement, but trembled nonetheless.

Gorlois wrapped his solid arms about his wife and she leaned in against him, sheltered and protected in the folds of his fuzzy cloak. He held her tightly, promising to return with word as to how things were going unless Uther had him and his men besieged at the hill-fort. Then he strode away across the Hall and Igraine was alone.

"I do not know how to describe the terror that filled me after Gorlois left," she whispered. "At night I huddled in the middle of our big carved bed, praying for my husband's return. Sometimes during the day I climbed to the top of the rampart, looking down on the gate that guards Tintagel and reminding myself that as long as I stayed on this side, I'd be safe from the forces Uther had unleashed. Yet all the while the booming of the surf at the base of the cliffs was pounding in my blood, and the murmur of the tide over the shingle whispered to my heart. Whenever I remember those days, I think the Goddess Herself had taken up residence in the cave below the fortress, for every moment pulsed with a fierce, primeval power."

On the third night Igraine was so filled with tension that she walked the ramparts under the sparkling stars long after the servants thought she was in bed. A treasure of brilliance lit the western horizon, and the breeze off the water was unusually soft and warm, as though the calendar said June instead of March. The night was dazzling in its beauty, promising birth and renewal, and the young Duchess's mood shifted from dread to delight. Like a flower unfolding, the petals of the

universe opened for her, and she stood in rapture on the edge of the
world.

And then she saw it—a firedrake that came leaping across the sky
like one of the dragons Merlin had prophesied, racing toward her
through the stars. It came out of the depths of beyond and flung itself
earthward in a blaze of glory. Thinking it was going to crash upon
Tintagel, Igraine threw herself against the tower wall.

The meteor fled westward, its light slowly dimming as the fiery head
disappeared over the edge of the horizon. But the Duchess of Cornwall
didn't see its departure, for her attention was riveted on a commotion
at the postern gate.

Hewn into the face of the cliff, the gate guarded the secret escape-
way that led straight from the heart of the fortress. Few people knew
of its existence, much less dared to risk the steep, spray-washed stairs
by night. Yet three hooded figures were demanding entrance and
Igraine watched intently, all but forgetting to breathe.

A sleepy sentry peered into the shadows cast by his guttering torch,
then saluted quickly as the man in the black cloak brushed past him
and entered the gatehouse. The young Duchess gave a cry of relief;
Gorlois had returned. Safety and sanity were coming back to her, and
with a rush of gratitude she ran down the steps and across the garden
to their chamber.

He bounded up the inner stairs two at a time, and she paused in the
doorway, her shadow filling the stairwell as it raced out to meet him.
When he reached the landing she flung herself into his arms.

For one oblivious moment she was wrapped in the cloud of his cape
before he lifted her off her feet and carried her across the threshold,
kicking the door shut behind them.

Maybe it was the spring in his step, or the ease with which he held
her, so light and sure, that gave her warning. Even before he set her
on her feet and stepped back, letting the hood fall away from his face,
Igraine knew this was not her husband. Yet she stared into Uther's eyes
with surprise rather than outrage.

They stood in confrontation for a long, long minute, each silently
probing the other. The High King watched her carefully, knowing that
the longer she delayed in sounding the alarm, the less likely it was she

would do so. And Igraine watched him, appalled and thrilled by the risk he was taking.

At last the Pendragon reached for her wrists and tried to draw her to him.

"What of Gorlois?" she asked, resisting the invitation in spite of her own desire. With a cold will she kept her voice as level as her gaze.

"He sleeps on his field-cot, safe at Dimilioc, M'lady," Uther replied. "I am not here as a victor come to take the widow of my vanquished foe. I am here because you want me as much as I want you, and we are well met as equals."

In spite of the fact that she was trembling visibly, Igraine studied the man before her, gauging the depth of his words, the pride of his tone. Like the red doe that makes no commitment to the stag until he has proven his ability to overtake her, the Duchess stood poised as if for further flight.

Neither of them moved, though her skin tingled where he held her wrists.

"There is a fever that rages between us," Uther whispered, bending close above but not quite touching her. "I am as certain of that as I am of which way the wind blows at sunrise. But you must come to me of your own choice—there shall be no thought of rape between us."

He waited, his lips just short of hers.

Igraine felt the warmth of his breath against her skin, and the flutter of her heart as she stretched on tiptoe to reach his mouth. Passion leapt up within her and in one motion she freed her hands and twined them through his hair, her lips finding his mouth with a kiss as eager as his own. He gathered her up against his body and she wrapped her legs around his waist, hardly even aware when he lowered her to the bed.

"It was a night when I was the Goddess incarnate, and that huge carved bed was my altar," the Queen Mother whispered. "After the first wild need was met, we turned to pillow talk and he told me how Merlin had worked out a plan for invading Tintagel through the postern gate. Somehow the Magician had learned the password for the night, and disguising Ulfin and himself to look like Gorlois's men, led the little group up the secret, cliffside path. But it was the black Spanish cape that was the master stroke—even men on guard can be tricked into seeing what they expect, if one is careful.

Uther was immensely proud of having gotten through the gate, and I marveled at his courage. And later, when he slept and I lay watching him, I knew that for this one night I had been given the trust of a fierce, free thing that must occasionally seek sanctuary or it will beat itself to death. I don't know if that makes any sense to you, Gwen, since you never met him."

"Perhaps," I murmured as Ettard came quietly into the room. She announced that a priest was waiting outside, but the Queen Mother shook her head and Ettard discreetly withdrew.

"Before I forget," Igraine said when the door had closed, "I've left that girl what little property I haven't given to the monks at Tintagel. It should be enough to keep her comfortable, and I'd appreciate it if you'd find a place for her with you. . . . She still talks about the months we spent at Court when you and Arthur were first married, and I'd feel better knowing she was under your protection."

"I'll look after her, M'lady," I promised.

"Good. . . ." Igraine's fingers had taken hold of mine and she gave them a little squeeze.

"There is little else about that night you could not imagine for yourself," she murmured, drawn back again to Tintagel. "I own that I was fully aware Uther was not my spouse, and those who claim that Merlin turned him into such a perfect likeness of Gorlois it fooled even me, credit the Enchanter with more magic than common sense." She smiled wryly. "Can you believe anyone thinking a woman couldn't tell the difference between two men?"

When Ulfin, who had accompanied his king disguised as of one of Gorlois's men, rapped sharply on the door, Uther rose and dressed hastily. Once he slung the black cape over his shoulders, Igraine got up and came to stand in front of him, settling the cloak more firmly and drawing the hood up in case one of the sentries looked too closely at his face.

Staring up at the sharp features and burning eyes, she prepared to say good-bye. This was not a relationship to be woven into everyday life, but a gift from the Gods—a touching beyond time that no human

could gainsay. They were not the first the Goddess had brought together this way, nor would they be the last, but Igraine knew better
than to think it might continue. With deft fingers she traced the line
of his cheek before rising on tiptoe to whisper farewell.

Uther's expression was hard and quick, as though he were already
threading his way past guard and sentry in his bid to leave his enemy's
stronghold undiscovered. But he softened for a moment and promised
he would find some pretext for making an honorable truce with Gorlois.
Then he was gone.

The Duchess returned to bed, too drained to think about the night's
events and too stunned to wonder what kind of child might come of
such a union. She lay across the tangled covers, clutching a pillow in
her arms and drifting on the edge of time until the day should properly
begin.

But dawn brought word that Gorlois had died in a night raid against
the High King's camp, and her household was set buzzing with questions as to how the Duke's spirit could lie with his wife hours after his
death.

Igraine reeled before the news, seeing her world splinter around her.
Sorrow and anger warred through her normally calm nature, and she
stood like a statue in the center of the storm, staring out across the sea
and listening to the cry of the wheeling gulls.

Her daughters crept fearfully into her chamber, clambering onto the
rumpled bed and clinging to each other in terror. At thirteen Morgause
had grown into a handsome girl with the high, ruddy coloring of
Gorlois, though now her face was white and frightened and she whimpered softly. It was ten-year-old Morgan, dark and cunning, who narrowed her green eyes and glared around the room with the fierceness
of a cornered animal.

"Will King Uther make us slaves?" Morgause's voice was barely
audible. "Or will he kill us outright, as he killed Father?"

"I . . . I don't think he'll do either," Igraine answered, trying to sound
more certain than she felt. "And we don't actually know who killed
your father. If he was leading an attack against the King, he was
probably killed in battle by a man attempting to defend himself."

The widow's voice trailed off as her daughters stared at her in
disbelief, refusing to consider Gorlois's death anything but murder.

Morgan's black brows came together in a scowl and she sprang off the bed with the high, unearthly scream of a banshee.

"I can smell him," she shrieked. "Uther, the Roman who calls himself High King . . . he stalks Tintagel like a beast, sating his appetite on our family!"

Igraine gaped at her daughter in astonishment. Could the child have the Sight . . . was it possible she knew who had so recently occupied that bed? Would she see her mother's action as the treacherous betrayal of a good man rather than the fulfilling of the Goddess's demand? And how did Uther himself see it—Uther who had promised to hold the Duke harmless for her sake, or perhaps his own. What mantle of guilt lay on his conscience this day, and how would he rage against this unexpected twist of fate?

Uther Pendragon returned to Tintagel that afternoon, riding in state up the path from the mainland. He brought the body of the fallen Duke home, the black cape draped over the litter.

The Duchess of Cornwall was standing, still and proud, on the dais at the end of the Hall when Uther entered, and his fierce blue glare pinned her to the spot. His spurs struck sparks on the stone floor and the riding crop in his hand flicked rhythmically with each step. He was as haughty and distant as any conquering lord, yet amazingly, he bowed before her in recognition of her bereavement.

"It is with great sorrow and concern that I bring the body of your husband home," the Pendragon began, anger and bitterness sharp in his voice.

The children moved closer to her skirts, terrified by the sight and sound of the man. Igraine looked into his face, seeing behind the severe features the bafflement of a wild thing fighting futilely against the web of fate.

"And now I shall leave you to your grief," the Pendragon announced. "You may bury your lord wherever you see fit, and in whatever manner you choose. But when the two weeks of mourning are over, I shall return to make you my bride, as if I had, in fact, dealt the deathblow to the Duke last night."

Shocked, Igraine watched Uther turn on his heel and leave, looking neither right nor left and never pausing to see if she would accept him. She felt the pent-up rage of the man driving him out and away from the company of others, and she was not surprised to learn later that he had ridden for hours over the moors, killing the horse under him and coming back to his camp on a beast he'd taken from an outlaw he'd met in the wilds. Compassion, whether for himself or others, was not part of Uther's nature; pride and honor and fierceness were more the colors of his armor.

The wedding was held at the end of the fortnight, but it was an occasion marred with grief as much as joy. The girls nurtured an insatiable hatred for their stepfather and their loathing was so great, Igraine feared for their future. So it was with relief as well as heartache that she agreed they both be sent away as soon she and Uther were married.

Morgause was given in early betrothal to King Lot of Lothian and the Orkney Isles, one of the brash young men who squabbled among themselves in the northern kingdoms beyond the Wall. It was a fitting choice, for the girl was high-spirited by nature and might have dominated a more placid man.

Morgan le Fey was sent to a convent in the north to learn the arts of healing, more because the nuns would watch over her well than because of any religious conviction on Igraine's part, for the new High Queen was still Pagan.

"It was not until I realized I had to give up even the child of that night's union that I began to question the Old Gods," the Queen Mother sighed. "To lose all your children, including the one unborn, is a high price for any love, my dear. But Uther refused to consider keeping the baby; at first he argued that people would think it was Gorlois's, conceived as it was so close to the Duke's death. Later it seemed as though he blamed the infant's need to be begotten for entangling us all in that night of passion." She sighed softly. "Perhaps, as Merlin claimed, we were each just pawns doing the Gods' work. Before Arthur was born the Magician came to visit, asking permission to take the infant and raise him himself. I've never been comfortable with the Enchanter, but he kept his word and Arthur grew into a man any woman would be glad to call son." She turned her level, direct gaze on me. "I don't know that he cares to hear it, but if you've a chance, tell him I'm proud of him."

For a minute more she stared into some unseen space, summoning what was left of her strength.

"It was only later, when the remorse and barrenness closed in, that I looked for forgiveness and understanding, and found them in the new Christ." The Queen Mother began to grope for my hands. "It's getting so dark," she murmured, catching hold of my fingers and holding them tightly. "It was never easy, between Uther's wild and stormy nature and the constant demands of being High Queen. At first I hated my new position, quailing inwardly before the crowds and wishing desperately we could retreat to some quiet spot of our own. But a Queen belongs to the people, and I was theirs as much as his. Over the years I grew bolder and not so shy just as he grew less harsh and abrasive. And we ruled well together, of that I'm sure, for he held the Saxon invaders in check and the people prospered."

Igraine was panting now, frowning into the distance at shadows I could not see. Suddenly she tightened her grip.

"I loved him in spite of everything, and in his own way he loved me; like the wind of Tintagel, he brought me life while I brought him calm. But you must understand the price we paid for such a love, Gwen . . . the cost in children who were left motherless too early . . . in personal desires held forfeit to duty . . . in penances paid and raw edges abraded by our own consciences. And yet . . ."

The death rattle struggled in her throat, but she turned her face to me as a blind one does, a sweet smile suffusing her features.

". . . I would do it all over again, tomorrow."

They were her last words, and in the silence that followed, a single warbler's song stole across the room.

THREE

Return to Silchester

We buried Igraine in a simple convent grave, the ring Uther had given Ulfin clasped in her fingers. A profusion of wildflowers filled the meadow beyond the convent wall and I spread a blanket of them over the coffin to break the fall of the clods. It seemed the least I could do for her.

Ettard stood beside me, pale and damp with grief. Her meager possessions were already packed and after the funeral was over we bade the nuns good-bye and prepared to return to Silchester.

I have always hated litters and intended to ride Featherfoot and let Ettard use Igraine's litter by herself. But the pretty girl burst into tears at the idea of being left alone, so I relented and joined her in the swaying box. She grew calmer once we were on the Road, and lapsed into the silence of her sorrow.

Parting the curtains, I stared out over the sea of grass. Drowsy with the hum of bees and the sweet smell of wild thyme, the downs stretched lazily under pale, dreamy clouds. But I saw instead the dark towers of Tintagel and the steps to the postern gate carved into the face of the cliff itself. Like a bit of timeless history or the thing that myths are made of, the destinies Merlin had set in motion swirled in that darkness. . . .

A night of sleet and pelting rain from above, of spray and storm-tossed surf that spumes up from below. Patient as Cronos in midwinter, the

Magician waits for the child to be brought. Warm, bundled against the cold, the infant is handed over, the talisman around his neck the only gift the grieving mother can give him. That, and a name . . . Arthur. Arthur from the Roman family of Artoris; Arthur from the Celtic word for bear; Arthur, from the heavens where Merlin has seen the prophecy.

Within the heart of Wales, small and unimportant, the court of Sir Ector rings with the shouts of boys at play. Racing at breakneck speed along the rides of the woods, swimming in Bala Lake, listening to the tales their seedy tutor tells of bigger worlds and courts of power—the three are brothers in all save blood. Arthur and Bedivere the fosterlings, Cei the Baron's own true born. "Tell us about Merlin, who has hidden the King's son on a magic isle," they beg, never guessing it is the Mage of Britain himself who teaches them.

Uther harries the Saxons, and is harried in return. Ambrosius drove them back to the Saxon Shore, his brother strives to keep them there. Igraine and her husband are well thought of, and no one asks about the child, for Uther has a wild, unruly nature and a sore conscience where Gorlois is concerned. Even as a girl, growing up in Rheged, I'd heard of the Pendragon's temper.

In the north Morgause begins producing sons for King Lot. Gawain, born barely a year after Arthur, Gaheris, and Agravain—firebrands all, as stubborn and headstrong as their parents.

And Morgan, when she is old enough to take the veil, suddenly leaves the convent to marry the King of Northumbria. A Celtic ruler, Urien devoted more time to hunting and cattle raids than to his new wife, and she soon returns to the Old Gods, becoming a druidess in the Sanctuary. When Vivian dies, Morgan is herself named Lady of the Lake. I had seen her once, hidden in the woods at the edge of the Black Lake, performing strange and frightful rites.

. . .

As I had seen King Lot—brawny, boisterous, visiting Rheged in an effort to solicit our support against the young man Merlin had brought forth after Uther died. "Puppet of the Magician—said to be Celtic on his mother's side, but Roman in training, through and through," the King of Orkney thunders, trying to rally our support against the new Pendragon. Yet for all Lot's impressiveness as warrior and leader, the men of Rheged have no wish to join his cause—it is Urien he seeks to elect High King, and our Northumbrian neighbor had too often raided cattle across our border.

So the ancient land of Albion convulses in civil war. The Cumbri, those northern Celts clinging to the Old Ways, roar and howl and fight against the southern Britons who cling with equal stubbornness to the memory of the Empire. And when the Great Battle is over twelve northern kings lie dead, including Lot. Urien surrendered, and later, at the Sanctuary, the Lady of the Lake bestows the sacred Sword of State on Arthur, making him the new High King. I had met him then, as he made his way to the Sanctuary—a young man who seemed more from the land than the nobility . . . an odd candidate for what Merlin called the greatest King in all of Britain's history.

And I, what had I to do with the dreams of an aging sorcerer? Not much, I suspected.

It was Arthur, not Merlin, who picked me to be his Queen. Of all the northern kingdoms, Rheged alone had stood at Arthur's side, and now that he needed to solidify his victory, what better way than to marry a northern princess?

So I had gone to my fate, raging at the moira which sent me south, into the shadow of the ruined Empire.

But Arthur turned out to be far less Roman than I had feared, and easy to love as well, and with the Queen Mother's guidance I've taken my place as his partner with very little trouble. I had much to thank her for, and loved her as dearly as I loved my own mother.

For a moment a vision of Mama rose before me . . . the beautiful, laughing young queen who had given her life for her people as surely as if she had climbed into the Need-fire on Beltane and been offered up as a human sacrifice. Not that the May Day rites include such sacrifices nowadays, but every Celt remembers what lies at the heart of the royal promise—that any true monarch stands between the people and their Gods, willing to bridge the distance with life itself if the two become estranged.

Mama's sacrifice had not been that dramatic, but she had died nonetheless, back when I was barely ten years old.

In her own way, Arthur's mother had also given over her life to the people, for although she had become High Queen because of a personal love for the King, her majesty and greatness of spirit put the needs of her subjects first from then on.

That is, of course, what queens are expected to do, and I counted myself lucky to have two such fine examples before me. It didn't ease the pain of losing Igraine, however, so Ettard and I spent a mournful, silent day in the litter.

On the second morning Igraine's companion began to talk a little between snuffles of grief.

"She was like a mother to me." The girl's voice was light and childish. "Took me in the first day I came to the convent, and me an orphan with neither future nor hope."

I nodded silently, wondering if it was the loss of her own children that had given Igraine a particular talent for comforting motherless youngsters.

With a little encouragement Ettard began to tell me about her early life. Her story was not an uncommon one. Raised on a steading near a river, she was twelve when a high-prowed ship came gliding up the watercourse. The men of her family were away fighting in the Great Battle, so the Saxon pirates made quick work of overpowering the women's defenses.

"I tried to hide in a hayrick while the raiders swarmed over the farm, but no matter how deep I burrowed, I could still hear the screams of my mother and sisters . . . raped and ravaged and finally spitted like sheep for roasting over a fire."

Her voice was flat, as though the memory no longer touched her heart, but the very idea made my stomach turn.

"I might have been killed, too," she went on, "but it was a young man who saw my sleeve poking out from the hay, and he didn't give me to the leader, but kept me for himself in return for my not scream-ing."

Ettard blushed suddenly, having confided more than she had in-tended.

"You poor thing," I consoled her, putting an arm around her shoul-der and letting her snuggle in against me.

"I stayed on after the sea-wolves left," she whimpered, "hiding in the burnt-out husk of the barn by day and foraging for berries and roots at night. The Saxons didn't come back, but as I'd nowhere to go, I would have starved to death. Or frozen in winter. Then, in late autumn, a wandering holy man found me and took me to the convent. I didn't go there to take vows, M'lady," she added hastily, "only to find refuge. My mum raised us all to honor the Old Gods, and the nuns took me in without even asking if I'd been baptized. I don't know what would have happened if they hadn't, for I have no family left in all this world."

She paused and I thought how lost a person is without kin to claim their own. There are few ways for a man to survive alone, with the woods being full of beasts and outlaws and so many of the cities deserted—for a woman it's doubly difficult.

"From now on we'll be your family," I assured her.

Ettard stared up at me, her eyes shining with gratitude. Although I was only a few years her senior, she clearly seemed to view me as her guardian.

As we neared Silchester she plied me with questions about the people she'd met last year, when Arthur and I had wed. Yes, Vinnie, who had come south as my chaperon, was still with us, as was my foster-sister, Brigit. No, Nimue and Merlin were gone, traveling to Lesser Britain on a kind of honeymoon. But both Bedivere and Cei, the foster-brothers from Arthur's early life, were with him in Wales, quelling the last of the Irish insurgence.

"And Morgan le Fey?"

I stiffened. Arthur's half-sister and I were not on the best of terms, for I had accidentally come upon her in the midst of a lovers' tryst and she had flown into a rage, claiming I was no better than the "goody-goody Christians" and would no doubt spread the story of her affair throughout the Court. No amount of reasoning could calm her, even though I too was raised in the tradition of Celtic queens bedding whomever they wished, provided it did no harm to their people. Instead, she and her lover had packed off to her Sanctuary, leaving me to try and explain their absence without revealing what had happened.

Now I glanced at Ettard and said as casually as possible, "I think the Lady of the Lake is too busy teaching the young princes at the Academy to come south." If Igraine's companion knew Morgan was angry at me, she didn't pursue the subject.

"What about Morgause?" The girl was studying my face intently and nodded when I shook my head. "I thought not. She would have come to see her mother if she had been this close. I always wondered why she wasn't at your wedding. . . ."

The implied question hung between us, and I tried to shrug it aside, unwilling that anyone else should know how deeply Arthur hated his other half-sister. "The Orkneys are a long way away," I hedged.

"But Gawain is with the High King still?" Ettard's voice turned eager.

"He'll no doubt be the hero of the summer campaign." I grinned. The Prince of Orkney was coming into his own as a warrior, full of bravery and a bright battle-lust that was the envy of all the other men. Before long the bards would be making songs of glory in his honor.

"What about Silchester? Is it very fancy—more fancy than Sarum?"

"Oh much more," I assured her. "It used to be a wealthy merchant town, so the sewers actually work and the bigger houses still have running water and heated floors."

When we arrived at the Mansion I turned the convent girl over to Vinnie, who greeted her fondly. They had gotten on well enough last summer, so I was confident she was in good hands.

With the harvest coming in and the men due home before long, I had more than enough to keep me busy from dawn to candletime. There was fruit to gather and roots to dig, hay to be secured and cheeses to put by. Working side by side with peasant and servant, I watched the larder grow each day and sighed contentedly before dropping into exhausted sleep each night.

As the summer waned Brigit helped me set up an infirmary in the little Christian church—any war-leader's wife knows that the proud boasts of springtime are paid for in the shattered bodies that come home in autumn. And every evening I prayed fervently that my husband would not be among the casualties this year.

I had the children take turns on the walls, watching for Arthur's return, but it was Griflet who brought the news. He found me repairing, for the hundredth time, the fence around the cabbages, and I whirled in alarm as his horse clattered into the courtyard. The animal was lathered and the boy covered with grime and sweat, but the smile on his face spread from ear to ear as he dismounted.

"The High King wants you to know he'll be home by tomorrow's sunset, and after all these months of foraging, could do with a home-cooked meal."

"Not hurt?" I asked as Ulfin's son dismounted.

"Not a scratch, M'lady—not a scratch!"

With a yelp of glee I flung my arms about him and we danced a wild little jig amid chickens and children while the rest of the household came dashing to see what all the commotion was about.

"There's others that are wounded, some of them right bad," Griflet added breathlessly when we came to a stop. "But the Irish have been driven from southern Wales once and for all, and His Highness is mighty hungry."

"You there," I called to the youngsters, having instantly decided on the menu. "Whoever catches that roaming porker gets an extra helping of dessert. Just bring him around to Cook so she can get started."

Next afternoon the Companions marched down the broad Roman Road with the sun glinting off their spearheads and the horses prancing proudly under the Banner of the Red Dragon.

Brigit and I stood on the ramparts while the crowd gathered by the gates and filled the air with cheers and clapping as they waited for the victorious warriors.

Even from a distance Arthur looked splendid: bronze and ruddy, he carried the pride of his accomplishment with youthful vigor. As he reached the gate he glanced up with that fine, level gaze that marks him so clearly as Igraine's son. I was jumping up and down, waving my scarf and cheering along with the rest, and when he saw me he grinned and gave the Roman "thumbs up" sign before passing under the arch. I turned and raced down the steps, hurrying along the back streets to avoid the crowd as I rushed to the portico of the basilica.

The mob was pressing into the archway of the forum's plaza, clogging the entrance and bringing the royal stallion to a fidgeting halt. The trumpeter had to blow several flourishes before the people parted and by then I'd skinned in the back door and was waiting for the public welcome.

The crowd rippled aside as Arthur made his way toward me. The rest of the Companions were strung out behind him, caught in the crush of people still funneling into the plaza. It was impossible to see who was there and who was not, but at that moment all I cared was that my husband had come home in one piece and was glowing with triumph.

As queen and spokesman for the people I intended to give him the traditional greeting but when a squire hurried forward to hold the warhorse, Arthur leapt from the saddle and bounded up the steps to my side. Without waiting for the time-honored words, he slid one arm around my waist and swung round to salute our subjects, then lifted me off my feet and kissed me soundly as the crowd went wild.

"Now that," he shouted over the uproar, "is more like a welcome home!"

Held firm against the length of his body, I threw my head back and laughed with him, happier than I'd ever been before in my life.

We rode the crest of exhilaration through the joyful public display, and it was only later, after the ritual bath had soaked away the dirt and bruises of the Road, that I told him about Igraine's death. He turned and stared out the window, his face as empty as the twilight sky above the treetops. One hand reached up, unbidden, to touch the amulet he wore around his neck—the charm Igraine had sent with him when she gave him up. Then with a sigh he turned and smiled slightly at me.

"Thank you for going to her—between you and Morgan, I'm sure she had the best of care."

"Morgan wasn't there," I answered, wondering how he thought she could have made the trip from Lakeland to Logres on such short notice.

"Not there? You mean she stayed here and let you go alone?" Suddenly Arthur was standing before me, both hands on my shoulders. "Morgan is here, isn't she? She must be."

When I shook my head he turned away with an oath. "I can't

understand it. The best healer in all of Britain, my own half-sister and High Priestess to the Gods, and she isn't here when I need her. I specifically requested that she join you."

Arthur's voice was sharp with frustration, and he quaffed his wine in a single draft while I bit my lip and looked down at my hands. Apparently Morgan's anger at me had not abated—no doubt she would have been glad to come to his camp, but because he'd asked her to wait here with me, she'd chosen not to respond. And there was no way for me to explain without the whole story coming out, making me the gossiping little snitch she claimed. So I listened in silence to my husband's lament and squirmed inwardly at being caught in such an impasse.

With a sigh Arthur sank down at the long table and stared moodily into his cup. "I was counting on her to save Bedivere."

"Bedivere!" I scrambled over to the bench where Arthur sat, trying to remember if I'd seen the lieutenant in the tumult of greeting just past.

"Aye, Bedivere." Arthur poured himself another goblet of wine, not even noticing when he spilled some. "He fell in the last encounter . . . damn near died on the spot. It took every skill we had to staunch the bleeding, and if it hadn't been for Lance, we wouldn't have gotten him this far."

By now my husband was on his feet, moving restlessly back and forth across the rush-strewn floor. Concern for his best friend overshadowed even the season's victory, and the tension built until he rounded on me sharply.

"Ye Gods, Gwen, what would I do without him?"

It was a cry full of fear and frustration and the unnerving realization of death's nearness. Now that he had brought his men safely home, the war-leader was free to mutter to himself and quake in the face of what had happened. He refilled his goblet and resumed his pacing.

"At least Brigit is at hand," I pointed out. "And where Bedivere is concerned, that should make up for the fact that Morgan isn't looking after him."

"Ummm. . . ." My husband grunted noncommittally. "Don't see how."

I started to point out that Bedivere was in love with my foster-sister and her presence now was bound to cheer him. But Arthur was intent on his own thoughts, so I held my tongue. Besides, love—our own or other people's—was not something he paid much heed to.

"What I'm most afraid of," he growled, "is that Bedivere will just give up. It's a dreadful thing to lose a hand, no matter who you are. But when you're the High King's lieutenant and a superb warrior besides, being left with only a stump could mean the end of everything."

"Or the beginning of something new," I suggested. "Bedivere's far more than your lieutenant; he's been your councilor and confidant for years. Even if he never rides to battle again, surely he'll go on being your best adviser."

"That's true." Arthur tossed off another cup of wine and putting down his cup, stretched noisily. "It was quite a campaign, Gwen . . . quite a campaign."

Igraine once told me that Uther always picked a fight with her on his first night home. She said it was the way he crossed from the outer world where he dominated all others to the inner world where he could drop his own defenses. I watched my husband and wondered how much he would take after his father. I'd never seen a dark, unruly side to Arthur, but that didn't mean it wasn't there.

Fortunately he wanted to share his memories rather than get into a row, so I listened carefully as he recounted the war.

At the onset the remnants of last year's rebels had banded together to meet the Britons in a pitched battle.

"It might have been all over right then," Arthur noted, seating himself at the end of the table. "The Irish wanted to settle the matter according to the Old Way, in single combat between two champions. Stupid business—almost as chancy as Trial by Combat. I wasn't going to hear of it, but Gawain got his dander up—you know how he is when it comes to a challenge. And before I knew it, he was on his way out to meet the Irish champion, Marhaus, in a fight to the death. They went at each other from the cool of the morning until well past noon, with neither one able to get the upper hand. In the end both had to be dragged off the field, exhausted and covered with blood." Arthur shook his head over such folly. "Thank goodness Gawain wasn't badly hurt; he's the best warrior I have!"

After that the enemy had scattered, forcing Arthur to divide his men into independent groups to pursue them.

"We chased them from the Brecon Beacons all the way to the ancient track on Presely Mountain, and from there down into the sea. Half the time my men would go out hunting for dinner and end up in a tangle with the Irish Boar instead." He leaned back, absentmindedly propping a foot on the bench so that I could undo his boot. "Fortunately many of the men seem to be good leaders as well."

When I had finished with the first, Arthur raised the other foot. He continued describing the men who had come to join the Companions, and I listened with only half an ear, wondering how long he would go on talking and if he'd be too tired or drunk for loving. Dropping both boots under the table, I got up and went to stand behind him, rubbing his shoulders while he talked.

"There's one who stands out above all the rest, Gwen," he said with a yawn as I began to tug at his tunic and finally pulled it over his head. "Lancelot—King Ban's son from Brittany. Seems he was educated by the Lady of the Lake at the Sanctuary; studied medicine and science and history as well as warfare and swordplay. Thank heavens he learned his lessons well; he's the one who saved Bedivere on the field."

I folded the tunic thoughtfully and put it on the table. When I was a child Vivian had been the Lady of the Lake, and she had asked that I come live at the Sanctuary to study with the other princelings there, but my parents had refused. If I had gone, no doubt this Lancelot and I would have grown up together. I looked forward to asking him all sorts of questions, for I've always wondered what I had missed.

Behind me Arthur stretched again and I glanced down at his feet, which were still propped on the bench. When he wiggled the toe that poked out of a hole in his sock, I paused to assess the damage, sure there would be a huge pile of mending after a summer of hard wear.

"Got you!" he cried, grabbing me by the waist so unexpectedly that I let out a yip of surprise. He pulled me, laughing and sputtering, down onto his lap.

"You didn't really think I could be all *that* tired, did you?" he teased, holding me firmly.

I giggled and struggled, trying to twist around so that I could face him for a kiss, but we knocked over the chair in our tussling, and then we were making love among the rushes and bracken fronds that covered the floor.

It was a rowdy, boisterous coming together, full of Arthur's usual enthusiasm and directness, and by the time we separated we were both relaxed and happy.

But, I thought ruefully, if we're going to make this a habit, I'd best replace the rushes with a rug.

FOUR

The Fellowship

hen Arthur's men divided up to chase the Irish across Wales, they agreed to rendezvous in Silchester at the autumn equinox. Now the war-bands began to straggle in, anxious for news of comrades and eager to celebrate the end of the campaign.

I met the men as much by accident as by intention, in one case literally bumping into a pair of them when our paths crossed in the barnyard.

"Ohhh!" I sputtered, trying to keep from dropping my basket of eggs, but burst out laughing as I recognized Palomides.

The Arab who had brought the use of stirrups to Arthur gave me a mischievous smile and bowed with a flourish. "Pelleas," he said, turning to his companion, "behold the High Queen."

I looked at the newcomer curiously, for Arthur had said he had the makings of a superb horseman. Thin and awkward, he went down on one knee and began stammering out an apology for not having recognized me.

"That's all right," I assured him. "Palomides mistook me for a page the first time we met."

The Arab and I laughed at the memory while Pelleas gawked in disbelief and when Palomides leaned down to give him a hand, I hurried on to the kitchen.

Next morning, as we were getting out of bed, Arthur announced we should hold a victory celebration. "Something grand, like the reunion at Caerleon. . . ." He was splashing at the water bucket and went on talking as he dried head and face with a towel. "Think you could arrange it for a week from now?"

"Dear man, do you have you any idea how long it takes to put on a feast?" I slipped out of bed and crept up behind him. "Never get it done in time," I declared, yanking the corner of the towel so fiercely that he spun around in surprise.

"Of course you can," he responded, hanging on to the towel in spite of me. "Cei will help you."

And then we were in a tug-of-war, laughing and playing, with all plans for the feast forgotten. So it was midday before I located Arthur's foster-brother.

It was Cei's fine eye for detail that had led Arthur to make him Seneschal of the realm. Many find his sharp tongue unpleasant, particularly when he's collecting taxes from them. But I admire his dedication to Arthur and his ability to ferret out hard-to-locate items amid a hundred ruins and unnamed sources.

He embraced the idea of a feast enthusiastically. "The basilica's not in bad shape, except for the corner where the roof's fallen in. Have to get rid of the owls. . . ." Cei frowned for a minute, then brightened. "You look to the guests, M'lady, and I'll take care of the festivities."

So Silchester became a beehive of activity. Arthur took out daily hunting parties, which kept the warriors occupied and added to Cei's menu at the same time. And in the sewing room the women plied their needles, furiously embroidering each newcomer's name on the pennant that would grace his chair at the feast. These were the symbols of acceptance within the Fellowship, and every man must have one.

Even the Saxon milkmaid Frieda bent her blond head to the task, though her stitches were rough and awkward. "Now you know why I prefer to work in the milk-barn and kennel," she grimaced.

"Macht nicht," I assured her. *"Es iss sehr gut."* Patient as she had been in teaching Arthur and me her language, I could be lenient about her handiwork.

Cook collected all the usual edibles from the countryside while Cei pillaged ancient gardens for such rarities as walnut trees and late-bearing figs.

Two days before the celebration the Seneschal stood before the long table in our work chamber, scowling at a glass bottle with a rag in its neck and a layer of oil floating on the top of the contents. "It's the best to be had under the circumstances," he reported dubiously.

"I'm sure it will be fine." Arthur barely glanced up from the horse-breeding chart. "This is a reunion of rowdy warriors, not elegant nobles—most couldn't tell good wine from bad."

I grinned at that. Having been raised on cider and strong brown ale, I've never developed an appreciation of the vintner's art and can rarely tell the difference between wines, unless one of them is vinegar.

Cei continued to frown at the the bottle, then shrugged, as though resigned that it would have to do. "Shall I set up the Round Table?" he inquired.

"By all means." Arthur's attention was suddenly engaged. "Ever since Merlin's prophecy, the men have talked about the Round Table as though it has a magic of its own." My husband let his glance slip sidewise, sweeping me with the conspiratorial look I love. "Never did meet a Celt who could resist the promise of fame and glory."

I laughed, for Arthur was fond of teasing me about my Celtic heritage, though most all Britons were Celts to begin with, just as later we'd all been proclaimed Roman citizens as well.

"But Arthur," the Magician had said, "will be a king for all Britons; Roman and Celt, Pict and Scot . . . yes, even the Ancient Ones will look to him for justice. And the Knights of the Round Table will become part of a glory that shall be sung for all time."

It was a grand and stirring prophecy—and one we had no notion how to fulfill.

I thought of it again when the British warriors came streaming into the basilica for the feast—men like Geraint and Agricola, who spoke an antique Latin and wore whatever badges of office had been handed down from ancestors honored in the days of the Empire. Mingling with them, equal in courage and stature, were the rough-hewn war-lords who had returned to the earthen forts their ancestors carved out of the hilltops. Heroes in homespun and hides, they've never learned to read or write, but sang and bellowed at each other in the tongue of the Cumbri.

Pellinore of the Wrekin was one such. A warrior dedicated to the pursuit of all the women in the hope of finding the Goddess incarnate, he swaggered into the Hall full of cheer and ale. When I waved a greeting he came forward immediately.

"That's a mighty handsome piece of silk, M'lady," he commented, taking the corner of my Damascus scarf in his big hand. "A fitting touch in such a royal setting—Cei's done a fine job with the old ruin, hasn't he?"

I nodded in agreement, glancing around the room. The basilica had been cleaned and polished; flags and shields hung from the moldering walls, and fresh torches had been placed in ancient sconces. The curved trestles of the Round Table were set out in a circle, each Companion in his designated chair with his men ranged behind him. Servants and children ran errands between the trestles or darted across the open space in the center, and the air hummed with conversation.

I grinned up at Pelli just as he let out a fearsome oath. "Someone's hiding behind that hanging, M'lady," he whispered, drawing his dagger and crouching to leap.

Startled, I turned to look at the large, exotic rug Cei had hung as a backdrop behind us. It's colors were deep and rich, with a central panel of maroon holding a circle of silver stars. I was wondering where the Seneschal had found it when Pelli sprang forward, bellowing his challenge as he flung back the edge.

"Show yourself, skulking swine!"

There was a flurry of feathers and oaths as a pair of indignant owls glared down on the warrior.

"Oh, Pelli, it's just the birds." I laughed as much at Cei's ingenuity as at Pelli's bewilderment, and was glad when the older man roared good-naturedly as well. After Pelli moved away I surveyed the rug more closely, thinking of the bedroom, then turned to look at Arthur.

Rested and relaxed, he leaned back in his carved chair with the deceptive casualness of a seasoned warrior. I'd made him a new scarlet tunic, and the torchlight winked and glimmered on its embroidered trim. Where the sleeves fell back, a king's ransom of golden armbands could be seen reaching all the way up to his elbows, and the official Ring of State graced his hand. In the flickering light the gold-and-garnet dragon seemed to coil around his finger, rich and powerful. Altogether he was a man who wore his kinghood well, and I thought again how lucky I was.

Once the Hall was full the trumpeter coaxed a cascade of notes from his battered horn and a blaze of color whirled into the empty space within the Round Table's heart. I stared at the gyrating figure in mystification, not recognizing the acrobat who had joined our wedding party last year.

"Dagonet came on the campaign," Arthur whispered, leaning over to me. "Did well enough as a foot soldier, but it was his light-hearted antics around the campfire that proved most useful. He's so good at jesting, Gawain dubbed him the Royal Fool."

"Your Highnesses," Dagonet called out, bowing low before us. "May I conduct this feast for you, since the Wizard is off dallying with his lovely spellbinder elsewhere?"

The jester wove a dance of the Companions' recent exploits—miming a swaggering warrior one moment and the dying enemy the next. As the ever-important smith he repaired a bent sword with such gusto he managed to smash his thumb against the imaginary anvil, and even parodied the High King leading the cavalry against the foe, finishing up with a triumphal return to Silchester.

"And all," he cried in conclusion, "all that for the Cause—a prosperous Britain, loyal to King Arthur and safe from the threat of invasion."

I joined in the laughter and clapping when Dagonet took his bow, thinking that a jester could be very handy in reminding the people what we were trying to do.

"And now, my fellow heroes and buffoons," the Fool announced, " 'tis time to pay our respect to Their Highnesses and receive the gifts of treasure due every proud warrior, that it may truly be said that Arthur is the most generous of Kings."

First among the heroes was Gawain. As Dagonet recounted his confrontation with the Irish champion, the Hall filled with applause— the Prince of Orkney may not have bested Marhaus, but he basked in the glory of having fought him to a standstill. When Arthur slid the thickest of the gold bracelets over his hand, Gawain grinned up at us, the impish nature of the boy I'd known in childhood still beaming from his face.

To Cei went an ornate inlaid bracelet, for the Seneschal loved elegance, no matter how old or battered. And a fine golden torque was laid aside for Bedivere, who had given his hand in the service of his King—though the lieutenant was too badly wounded to attend the ceremony, all witnessed how deeply Arthur cared.

So the men came forward to receive their due, to bend the knee, to thank us in their individual ways. Pellinore and Lamorak; Griflet and Geraint and Cador of Cornwall; Palomides and the skinny lad, Pelleas—the names spun out, the rewards were given.

I gasped when Dagonet announced Accolon of Gaul. This was the young warrior who had come to serve Arthur and been seduced by Morgan le Fey instead. Memory of my sister-in-law's anger danced around me—raging little wildcat, hissing and screaming at me in fury. As Accolon approached I wondered whether his presence meant the Lady had gotten over her pique, or that his desire for a warrior's glory was stronger than his love for her.

Bors of Brittany came next, bounding across the space before us and asking leave to present his cousin Lancelot.

I leaned forward, eager to meet the Champion who had been raised at the Sanctuary.

The torches guttered suddenly, and I blinked in consternation; it was Kevin, the first love of my youth, who moved forward and knelt in homage.

Stunned, I stared at the dark head before me. My heart was pounding in my ears and I began to breathe again only after Arthur spoke and the stranger looked up.

This Lancelot had the same triangular face as Kevin, with a broad brow and blue eyes set wide under a shock of black hair. But there the similarity ended, for the newcomer had too many teeth—they gave his mouth a full and sensual look quite unlike Kevin's. And, of course, he wasn't lame as the Irish boy had been.

I glanced down and saw that my knuckles were white from clinging to the arms of the chair.

"My dear," Arthur said warmly, "this is the warrior I told you about; the one who saved Bedivere's life. Lancelot, my Queen, Guinevere."

The hero turned stiffly in my direction, his manner polite but constrained. I smiled, as much from relief as pleasure at meeting him, and waited unsuccessfully for him to smile back.

"Your Highness," he murmured in acknowledgment, but stared right through me the same way the stuffy Christian bishops do. His attitude surprised me, for I am friend as well as Queen to most of the men and used to being treated as such.

"We are much indebted to both your families," Arthur was saying, including Bors in his announcement. "You have always come to our aid when we needed you. So as a token of our appreciation, I give you each a purse of gold coins."

A gasp went through the rest of the Companions—coins have not been seen in Britain for many years now, and the idea of any warrior receiving such a gift was amazing. Clearly it was a mark of the highest esteem, and I hoped it would make our visitor from Brittany unbend a little.

"I did not come to fight beside you for pay, M'lord," Lancelot said, looking at the proffered pouch as though it were something loathsome.

"Of course you didn't," Arthur answered genially. "I know that very well. But even King Ban's son must incur expenses, and I cannot believe that your father would be any less generous to a warrior who served him as well as you've served me."

The stranger continued to hesitate, and Arthur made a show of leaning forward and plopping the bag of money in his hand.

"For goodness' sake, Lance, take the stuff," he urged under his breath. "It's not going to corrupt your commitment, and it will show the others how much I value you."

A sudden smile of comprehension swept over the dark features—its bright flash reminding me again of Kevin—and he nodded gratefully.

"May I strive to be worthy of your trust always," he responded, his voice now rich with life and enthusiasm.

For a moment I thought he would include me in the dazzle of his pleasure, but he rose and turned away without even glancing in my direction. Stung, I stared after him, wondering what sort of manners the Lady had taught at the Sanctuary.

Dagonet was calling Agricola to the fore, and the patrician King of Demetia's glad recognition of my presence made up for the rudeness of King Ban's son. Perhaps, I told myself, the Breton feels shy and ill at ease so far from home.

At the end of the presentations I signaled the servants to bring forth the first of the venison, accompanied by the tuneful lilt of elder pipes and the rumble of a hand drum. A procession of platters was paraded solemnly around the inner circle of the Round Table, each laden with meat or fowl or fruit. All were met with boisterous cheers and exclamations of pleasure, for next to fighting, warriors love feasting best.

After dinner, when Riderich the Bard was tuning his harp, one of the children came pelting across the Hall, the wine in his serving flagon slopping from side to side.

"Whatever are you doing!" Cei cried, horrified at seeing his precious hoard treated so carelessly.

"There's a stranger demanding admission of Lucan the Gate Keeper," the boy shot back. "But the fellow won't leave his weapons outside. He's got a Pictish name and claims he must see the High King immediately."

"Tristan?" Arthur prompted, motioning the lad to approach.

"Maybe." The child scowled uncertainly as Arthur relieved him of the half-empty pitcher and handed it to me. "He's a real tall man, and there's blood all over his shield."

"Tristan," Arthur affirmed, glad that the lanky warrior from Cornwall was whole and alive, for his was the last of the war-bands not accounted for and we'd begun to worry. Giving the boy a pat, Arthur sent him back with the message that the stranger could come in.

It was indeed King Mark's nephew and he had his cohort Dinadan with him. The two men strode into the Hall side by side, Tristan all arms and legs while the smaller, wiry chap trotted along next to him. Many made fun of these Cornish knights because they looked so like a rangy wolfhound and sleek terrier making their rounds together, but I grinned and rose to give them a royal welcome.

Tristan's shield was smeared with the blood of a recent engagement, and his head bore a hasty bandage. A bright red stain was seeping through the linen wrappings on his arm. Yet in spite of this the warrior was in high spirits.

"I bring word of the Irish Champion, Marhaus," he called out gaily. "Thought you'd like to know I sent his head back to his family in a small, wooden box."

A roar of amazement rose from the Companions.

"Took him on in single combat," Tristan went on while Dinadan bowed formally to Arthur and me and tugged at his friend's sleeve until the other warrior followed suit.

"It must have been quite a battle," Arthur noted wryly as Tristan made a cursory bow.

"Oh, it was. Hardest fight of my life . . . so far."

Tris's boyish charm and confidence was infectious and he moved to the center of the gathering, eager to give a full account of the fight.

Whatever other differences his Pictish father had passed on to his son, modesty was not among them. He reeled from point to point in his story, encouraged by a crowd that proffered full goblets and drinking horns at every opportunity. By the time he came to the decapitation, the audience was wild with cheering; it was a virtuoso performance that touched the heart of all the Companions.

All, that is, except Gawain.

When the applause began to fade, the redhead from Orkney leaned forward and called out loudly, "You say you sent Marhaus's head back to Ireland?"

Tristan blinked in surprise and gave a puzzled nod.

"In whose name did you kill him?" Gawain demanded.

"Why, in Arthur's, of course." Tris shook his head slowly. "My uncle let me fight for the High King this year to make up for past absences . . . I've been Arthur's man this whole summer. You know that, Gawain."

"Marhaus was brother to the Irish Queen," Gawain said pointedly, turning to address the now silent Hall. "Well placed and highly thought of, he might have gained the throne someday. Won't they now look to Arthur for vengeance?"

"Well, I don't know . . . maybe, I suppose," Tristan stammered. Clearly he was not used to considering the consequences of his actions and he turned to Arthur uncertainly. "I did do the right thing, didn't I?"

The High King smiled and nodded gravely. "Of course you did, Tris, and you've won our admiration by this display of strength and courage. Marhaus was the finest warrior in Ireland, and an honorable man besides." Arthur paused and looked firmly at Gawain. "I do not think anyone could mistake a life lost in fair combat for a murderous attack which would call for vengeance."

I glanced quickly at the redhead. It was my friend Pellinore who had killed King Lot in the Great Battle, and though Gawain had sworn fealty to Arthur, he harbored a son's hatred for his father's slayer. From time to time Arthur had to remind his nephew that blood-feuds would not be tolerated among the Companions.

Gawain took the message sullenly but left off baiting Tristan, and Arthur went on as though nothing had happened, inviting the two men from Cornwall to stay with us over the winter. Dagonet led them to a pair of empty seats behind the circle of the Round Table while Riderich picked up his harp and turned our attention to the ancient, well-loved stories of prowess and glory.

Looking around the gathering, I thought how much it had grown since that first meeting just last spring. The camaraderie was much the same, the pride and pleasure of men who had fought side by side and were alive to tell the tales. Whether they had come because of Merlin's promise or Arthur's growing reputation as a leader, they were here in all their diversity. Well known and recently met, I scanned their faces and wondered how we would all fit together.

My eyes lingered an extra moment on the dark features of Lancelot, and he looked up, startled, as though I had touched him. He met my gaze briefly, then abruptly looked away.

Whatever the Breton might bring to the Round Table, I didn't think I'd like it.

FIVE

The Lieutenant

o one had been sure, back when Arthur first proposed it, whether mounting our warriors on horseback was a good idea. But in two years the Companions had developed into light, fast-moving cavalry units that were immensely effective against the raid-and-run tactics of our enemies. By now they had honed their skills in the field and were glad of the chance to show off before the townspeople. So everyone in Silchester gathered at the amphitheater on the second day of the celebration—no doubt it was the biggest crowd since the days of Roman circuses.

Lancelot gave a dazzling display of horsemanship and when he was finished he came to join us, sitting down next to Arthur without waiting for an invitation. I complimented him on his riding and received a cold, haughty nod in response before he rested his chin on his hand and commenced studying the activity below.

After a bit he turned to Arthur. "Might be a good idea to hold tournaments of this sort on a regular basis—use them to keep the men and horses in trim over the winter."

Arthur was immediately intrigued and I turned away, furious that this stranger who snubbed me should feel free to counsel my husband like an equal.

"You'd think he was Arthur's lieutenant, the way he's moved into Bedivere's place!" I fumed as Brigit combed out my hair before dinner.

"Perhaps that's as it should be," the Irish girl answered, twisting a sidelock into a wave and pinning it to the mass on the top of my head.

"How can you say that? Bedivere's always been Arthur's right-hand man."

"And now Bedivere himself doesn't have a hand."

"But you said he'd get well!" I rounded on her in dismay.

"He probably won't die, if we can keep gangrene from setting in," she said slowly. "But he's had a close call. He won't be active again for some time, and Arthur needs a lieutenant now."

Brigit nudged me back around. My hair is my best feature, being thick and red-gold in color, and Brigit spent hours keeping it looking nice. Years ago both she and her cousin Kevin had been given to my father as peace hostages by an Irish family immigrating to Rheged. We'd grown up as fosterlings, and I'd come to rely on her wisdom and calmness as time went by. So I mulled over her words while she went on with the coiffure.

Bedivere had been my first and closest friend when I came to Court, just as he had been Arthur's. They'd worked as a team since they were children at Sir Ector's court—Arthur thought up the ideas, and Bedivere made them happen. When I married Arthur they simply included me as a natural third. The three of us spent innumerable hours together, riding out to check horse pastures, exploring ancient hill-forts or lounging around the fire on rainy days, playing draughts and talking about projects that would help the Cause. It never occurred to me it wouldn't always be that way.

Now I was faced with the galling prospect of Arthur having a lieutenant who excluded me so thoroughly I might as well not exist.

"Give this Lancelot a chance," Brigit advised, putting Mama's gold fillet on top of my head. "He'll no doubt bring a fresh eye to things, and while it's bound to be different, it may not be all bad."

I grimaced as she handed me the mirror and she burst out laughing.

"Whatever would I do without you?" I grinned.

"Probably get into no end of trouble," she quipped.

Next morning I went to the infirmary, hoping to find Bedivere awake. His craggy features were sunken and drawn, and his eyelids barely fluttered when I sat down on the stool beside his cot. All the fire and color had drained from him, as though lost in the torrent of blood that had gushed from his wound. From the sweet smell of the poppy I guessed he was sedated, so I made a prayer to the Goddess for him and quietly tiptoed out.

It was clear that Bedivere would be convalescing for some time. I swallowed hard and reminded myself that Arthur needed a working lieutenant and it didn't matter whether I liked him or not.

In the days that followed I ran into Lancelot everywhere—in the Council Chamber, crossing the stableyard, pausing to note particular plants in my garden—his presence was unavoidable. He moved like a cat and proved to be superb with a blade, and I was sorely tempted to ask if he'd learned his technique at the Sanctuary; it was said that in the Old Days the Morrigan, great Goddess of blood-lust and death, had Herself taught heroes the art of war at such a school in the heart of Britain. But Lancelot made such a point of ignoring me, I had no choice but to treat him with equal coldness and keep my questions to myself.

Cei went to live in one of Silchester's finer deserted houses—the Seneschal's love of privacy was well known. The rest of the Companions joined us in the Mansion near the city wall. Large and comfortable, it had been built to house members of the Imperial Post, and since restoration of a messenger service was one of Arthur's dreams, it seemed a fitting place to make our headquarters.

The new men settled into the ways of the Fellowship and their mood was good. Only Gawain was touchy and short-tempered, no doubt still smarting from the knowledge that Tristan had beaten Marhaus when he could not. He sulked as though his honor had been damaged, when in fact it was only his pride that was hurt. As if by tacit agreement, no one brought the subject up.

"At least," Arthur noted, "Tris has the sense to keep out of the way; I gather he spends most of his time at the infirmary with Bedivere."

The tall Cornishman was a fine harper and seemed to enjoy entertaining the invalid. Like all warriors he had a following of young boys but there was one in particular, a scruffy shepherd lad named Taliesin, who idolized Tristan not because of his fierceness as a fighter, but because of his beautiful music.

Taliesin trailed after his hero like a smudged shadow, eager for a chance to carry the small traveling harp, or change a broken string, or oil the satiny wood. He was a quiet lad who watched the world around him intently but rarely spoke. I couldn't tell if he was shy by nature or simply awed at finding himself in the High King's Court.

One morning I came on the boy carefully polishing the harp with my Damascus scarf, which I must have left in the Hall the night before. I was so surprised, I forgot to be angry.

"Sir Tristan says a harp's a living thing, M'lady," Taliesin said reverently, quite oblivious to the fact he had appropriated his Queen's property. "Like a beautiful woman, or a proud god, it needs to be cherished and treated with respect."

I listened to him, fascinated, for his voice was rich and vibrant, and he spoke with a passion quite astounding for one so young. Apparently his love of the subject was powerful enough to overcome his usual reserve.

"Music was created in the Beginning, when there was only the Word, sung by the nymphs of the sacred wells," he went on, jumbling up all manner of religions. "Why, even the Greeks worshiped the Harper because he sings the sun up in the morning, along with the birds and other beasts. And when I have a harp under my fingers, the music takes me everywhere and I become every living thing."

The boy had spun a web of poignancy with his voice, as though striving to express the ineffable. Then just as unexpectedly, his tone changed to that of any other ten-year-old. "Sir Tristan says I'll be a player of songs as well as a bard of history, when I grow up."

Tris came into the room just then, and Taliesin leapt up to greet his mentor. With a bare nod in my direction, the two of them set off to see Bedivere.

I retrieved my scarf, shaking my head in bemusement and wondering who had given the lad the Cumbrian name of Shining Brow.

As the days shortened toward winter, the rituals were all observed—Arthur sacrificed a white bullock on the morning of Samhain to begin the slaughter of those beasts that could not be kept over for lack of forage. By evening the soft pall of smoke from curing fires hung over the meadow, marking the making of jerky, sausage, and hams for the larder.

I hurried on my rounds from spinning room to kitchen, kennel to infirmary. The Irish wolfhounds Brigit's family had given Arthur as a wedding present had grown into great, shaggy beasts. The white bitch, Cabal, would be whelping come spring, so I took her whatever kitchen scraps might be good for her. Her devotion to Arthur was one reason she was being trained as his war-dog; she'd wag her tail politely and deign to accept my gifts but never let me forget that her loyalty was to Arthur, not me.

You and that Breton, I thought testily.

Bedivere grew strong enough to join us in the Mansion, sitting by the hearth and practicing the harp with the use of a gauntlet equipped with hooks to replace his hand. He sometimes spent hours at a time staring into the flames in silence but never, that I heard, complained of his fate. Whenever Brigit was near his mood lightened noticeably, and I watched their quiet courtship happily, for I could not imagine a finer mate for the Irish girl.

But on a gray, drizzly day the world caved in on Arthur's foster-brother and after he told me, I went storming off in search of Brigit.

"Why?" I demanded, finding her folding the comforter at the foot of our bed. "I can't understand why you turned him down."

Startled, my friend turned on me with a look of disbelief. "You can't understand? You, who wanted to run away rather than accept a groom you hadn't chosen? How can you *not* understand?"

The force of her indignation shocked me into silence.

"Gwen, do you think you are the only one with dreams that went unanswered? The only woman who had to put aside her own desires to meet more important needs? Left to myself, I would have stayed in Ireland and gone to live in a convent when my family moved to Rheged . . . I told you that the first day we met. 'Tis the Christ I'll be sworn to, not mortal man, and until the day comes when I can join a house of God, I'll not be encouraging anyone's hopes for marriage, no matter how dear he is!"

She began to sob and bit her lip to hold back the tears. I wrapped my arms around her and held her much as she had held me when I had needed to cry in times past.

"He's a good man," she sighed when the tears abated. "One of the best in the whole world. And I'd give anything to have had him fall in love with someone else. But it matters not whether he's Pagan or Christian, whole or half-crippled . . . I do not want to marry, and it would be unfair to pretend otherwise. I'd be no kind of wife for him or anyone else. Can you understand that?" The look in her eyes was pained and pleading at the same time.

"Shush now . . . of course I understand," I whispered, trying to find words to comfort her. "I just didn't realize how important that dream was to you. I mean . . . Brigit, are you sure you want a convent? I don't remember your talking about it much, and think of all you'd be giving up! Never to have a child, never to hold an infant close, never to be a mother? I cannot imagine such a life."

"Aye, see now." Brigit straightened her shoulders and gave me a small smile. "There's dreams of your own that lie hidden, unspoken as it were. I can't recall you mentioning a longing for children, either, yet there it is, strong and sure, waiting for the day it is fulfilled. And just as you accept your moira to be Queen and wife and mother, so I have accepted mine to be a Bride of Christ. Pray God give us both the patience to wait the unfolding of our fates."

I nodded slowly, beginning to realize that she'd put into words the feelings I had yet to phrase within myself. In the past I'd not thought much about becoming a mother, simply assuming it would follow once I was wed. Now that it wasn't happening, it was a subject that came more often to my mind. I did not, however, mention it to others.

So I conceded Brigit had a point and left off scolding her about Bedivere, though my heart continued to ache for the gentle lieutenant.

It was later, when the storms of March were lashing the land, that I came out of the kitchen and all but tripped over Taliesin. Seated on a stool outside the door, he was plucking out such a mournful tune that I paused to look at him more closely.

"Whatever is the matter, child?" I asked, trying to remember where I'd left my scarf.

The boy gulped and looked up shyly. "It's Sir Tristan, M'lady. His king has sent for him to return to Cornwall, and soon I'll have no teacher."

"Oh, come now, there's still Riderich."

"Aye." Taliesin sighed, "And he's good for learning history and stories that are just spoken. But I want to make songs that are special to the Gods, and for that I need a special teacher."

The boy's discouragement was almost tangible, so I said I'd see what could be arranged and turned my attention to the spice cupboard, wondering why Mark wanted Tristan to come home.

"It seems that after all these years of searching, the King of Cornwall has found a royal family who will give him a child-bride."

Dinadan's announcement took us all by surprise. Mark was a walking monument to self-indulgence—a great mountain of flesh who'd never curbed any of his appetites. His determination to wed a girl on the edge of puberty had been the cause of much comment over the years; the men made jokes about it and the women frowned in empathy for any child so chosen.

Even I had been considered, back when I was barely thirteen years old, but Mark kept a very Christian court and I'd managed to disqualify myself by stressing my Pagan beliefs.

Lancelot was sitting on the other side of the hearth, rubbing tallow into a pair of boots, and he looked up from the shadows. Although I was growing used to his coldness toward me, there were still moments when his similarity to Kevin took me unawares.

"Who is the girl?" he asked.

"Isolde, daughter of the Queen of Ireland and niece of Sir Marhaus." Tris's voice was glum.

"Whew . . ." I let out a whistle, wondering if Mark knew who had killed the Irish Champion.

"I just hope the Irish don't know," Tristan went on with a slow frown. "It's me Mark is sending to fetch the girl for the wedding."

Distaste for the errand was evident on the warrior's face. Tristan wasn't strong on either diplomacy or duplicity, nor was he particularly quick-witted, so I hoped he could take Dinadan along to keep him out of trouble.

"Well," Arthur pointed out, "there's no need to flaunt the fact that you were the one who wielded the sword. The deed was done in my name, after all."

And so the matter was left. But later that night Arthur brought the subject up again as we prepared for bed.

"Even if they realize Tris's role in Marhaus's death, I have a hunch the Irish wouldn't stop this marriage. It makes an ally of Cornwall, and they may hope to turn King Mark against me in the future."

"Could they do that?" I asked, taking the pins and barrettes out of my hair.

"With Mark, who knows?" Arthur sighed and pulled off his boots. "He's probably the least trustworthy ally in the whole of Britain."

I nodded, remembering it was Mark who would not come to his own Duke's aid when Uther had marched on Tintagel.

"We'll miss Tristan sorely," my husband continued. "He's been wonderful in seeing Bedivere through his convalescence. He even suggested that Bedivere go to Rheged to study music with your family's bard. Do you think Edwen would be willing to take on a student?"

The idea had never occurred to me, though everyone said Edwen was the best bard in Britain. Perhaps in his older years he would enjoy teaching others his craft. My father already liked Bedivere, and it seemed certain Gladys and Kaethi and all the rest of the household would take good care of him. If we sent Taliesin with him, the lad could study with Edwen, too, as well as provide the lieutenant with whatever help he needed as he learned to live with his new, hooked hand.

So when the weather lifted and the Roads opened, we said farewell to Tristan and Dinadan, who went south to Cornwall, and sent our two aspiring musicians north to Rheged with messages of love and good wishes for my family.

It was now two years since I'd seen my father and I would have liked to go with Bedivere, but we were expected to attend Mark's wedding at Castle Dore. I settled for sending all the news I could think of, including how well Arthur and I got on. The one thing I couldn't give them was word that I was pregnant; in spite of all our romping, my prayers, and the mistletoe talisman Kaethi had given me, my courses came as regularly as the new moon.

This summer, I told myself . . . this summer I would seek help from the old women who had charms for such things. In the meantime there were preparations to make for the journey to Cornwall, for we planned to leave right after Beltane and take the household with us.

It would be the first royal progress I'd ever organized myself.

SIX

The Invitation

nd, of course, Geraint."

Arthur was studying a map he'd unrolled on the long table as he ticked off the various leaders we'd be stopping to see along the way to Cornwall. Like most monarchs, he found it easier to check on the state of the crops, people, and warriors by visiting the client kings rather than relying on reports. Now he motioned me over.

"You've never been to the south, have you?" When I shook my head he grinned. "Give you a chance to see what the rest of Logres is like—and Devon and Cornwall as well. Here's Mark's country down here, in the west. And over here"—he swept his hand to the southeastern corner of the map—"is the Saxon Shore. Kent—the land Vortigern gave to Hengist as the bride price for Rowena. And Sussex, where Aelle calls himself King. Both of them ruled by Saxon chieftains. But between Cornwall and Sussex there's everything from faded Roman glory to refurbished hill-forts, and a lot of Federate steadings as well. It's the Federates I'd like to reach."

"Why?" I peered at the area where the settlements showed a heavy sprinkling of Saxon names. "They're no better than Vortigern's mercenaries. The only difference is that they were brought in by the Legions instead of the tyrant."

"But it's a difference that counts. Some of those Federates have been here for generations, swearing fealty to British kings all the while. Most have no truck with the raiders who plunder and sneak away. They could hold the key to keeping the invaders out, if I can just make sure who among them is loyal. . . ."

"Ummm," I responded uncertainly. Every British child knows the story of how the Saxons rebelled against Vortigern—and when the Saxons sued for peace, the Britons came unarmed to the Truce Feast, believing they dealt with honorable men. Until Hengist gave the signal, filling the Hall with wild, curdling screams as hidden daggers glinted in the torchlight and plunged into the heart of Britain. Murdered—all our statesmen murdered—each by a Saxon tablemate.

Later Merlin repaired the fallen lintels of Stonehenge, making it a memorial to the slaughtered Celts, but that didn't bring back our leaders, and the murderous Saxons ended up with their own kingdoms. I didn't think of that story when I was dealing with Frieda, in spite of her Saxon background—but I couldn't forget it when thinking of those people as a whole.

Several days later the dairy-maid appeared in our doorway, her face contorted with a sob. Alarmed, I jumped to my feet and rushed to her side.

"My grandfather's been crushed under a wagon," she explained as I led her into the room. "I know we're packing for Cornwall, M'lady, but I'd like to go home for the funeral."

"Of course," I assured her. "Is there anything we can do to help?"

She hesitated, then looked from me to Arthur. "Grandpapa was an ealder—and there's many a Saxon leader who will pay his respects at the funeral pyre. My family would be honored if you would come as well. I'll vouch for your safety," she added, fingering the bone handle of the knife tucked into her belt.

Arthur and I exchanged glances. I knew he was seeing a chance to advance the Cause among the Federates, but I just saw a chance for betrayal. His dream overweighed my caution, however, and we agreed to leave for the Saxon funeral the next morning. But after Frieda left the room, Arthur suggested I should stay in Silchester.

"And sit here patching your breeches while you go off on all the adventures?" I joked, not believing he was serious. So far, in everything but war, we'd worked together side by side and I saw no reason to think that would change. "Besides, I'm better at the language than you are. You'll need me to translate."

Arthur was on his feet, making a slow turn around the room, and he came to a stop at the end of the table.

"Well, I'm thinking I'll take Lance. He's fluent enough in Saxon and between us we'll pretty well know what's going on."

The realization that he honestly did mean to leave me behind brought me to my feet. Not only had that haughty Breton replaced Bedivere, he was threatening to replace me as well. An indignant retort sprang to my tongue.

Arthur saw the look on my face and hastily added, "He and I can fight back to back if it comes to that."

I paused, my reaction deflected by the practicality of his words. I might be his rightful partner and co-ruler, but I couldn't argue I was as good a swordsman as Lancelot. It took the wind out of me, like falling off a horse. Plunking down on the chair without a word, I silently cursed the day they quit teaching women how to handle arms.

Next morning Arthur and Lance left with Frieda; if my husband had any trepidations, he kept them to himself. All I could do was stay home and fret.

It was midday when I went down to the kennels. Arthur had spent many happy hours as a youngster looking after Sir Ector's dogs, and I knew when he made Ulfin's son Griflet the Kennel Master, it was a more important honor than many courtiers might realize. Arthur valued the lad for his ability with the dogs; I valued him for the loyalty and forthrightness he'd inherited from his father.

Griflet wasn't in any better mood than I was. He and Frieda had been sweethearts for the last two years, and he had hoped to accompany her to the funeral.

I knelt down next to him and we watched the puppies tussle in the straw. Cabal was keeping a close eye on both her offspring and me, so I asked Griflet to pick up the runt of the litter and hand it to me. It was gray like its sire and had the same gregarious personality, immediately sinking its milk-teeth into the cuff of my tunic.

"Have you met Frieda's family?" I inquired, hoping the Kennel Master had firsthand knowledge of these people.

"No. She says they would not accept me; that she'd be disowned if she married a foreigner."

He laid an ironic stress on the last word. Like most Britons, it infuriated him that the immigrants call us "foreigners" in our own land. Frieda said it was no more disrespectful than our calling all the new-comers "Saxons" when there were just as many Angles or Jutes or Franks among the Federates as there were people from Saxony. No doubt she had a point, but I still didn't like the implication.

"Does that mean you and Frieda won't be marrying?"

"I don't know, M'lady. She loves me, of that I'm sure . . . and likes being part of the Court as well. But the Saxons are awfully clannish— always talking about the Old Country and keeping in touch with relatives left behind. I daren't push her, for fear she'll leave and go back to her folks entirely."

The lad sighed heavily and ran a finger down the nose of the pup. "I'll be much relieved when she and His Highness are back," he acknowledged.

I couldn't agree more.

During the next four days I went about my chores with a lump of fear lodged just below my heart, and when it was time for the travelers to return, Griflet and I took the dogs out to meet them.

The wolfhounds heard the hoofbeats first and went streaking ahead over the rise. Caesar gamboled about full of wags and enthusiasm, but Cabal was content to take her place at Arthur's side, pacing quietly at the stallion's off-fore leg just as she would when they went into battle.

Frieda had not returned but stayed behind with her family in mourn-ing, though she promised to join us before we left for Cornwall. Grif-let's face mirrored the uneasiness of his heart, and he dropped back to ride in silence next to Lance while Arthur and I pulled ahead.

Featherfoot was prancing and playful, but I kept her on a short rein as my husband peered at me from red-rimmed eyes.

"By Jove, how those barbarians love to drink," he said with a sheep-ish grin. "Spend all their time in the Hall, swilling brews that set you on your ear."

He went on to describe the funeral with its tall pyre and the wind that roared up when the kindling caught—flickers of flame dancing and crackling while women wailed and men rushed forward to fling amulets into the inferno. Spirit and prayer and terrible grief rose on the towering column of smoke, carrying the dead man's soul to the Saxon Gods, who live in the sky rather than under the water as Celtic Gods do.

But what had intrigued Arthur most was not the rites themselves but the man for whom they were held.

"He was neither a warrior or a noble, but an ealder, Gwen—a freeman who'd devoted his life to studying the Saxon Law. Their Law is a living thing that grows as they use it, and he was one of many who define and determine it. He didn't have royal power or great wealth, but you should have seen the number of chieftains who came to pay him tribute!" Arthur shook his head in admiration. "Afterward, in the Mead Hall, Frieda's father welcomed us as special guests, and introduced us around the gathering."

My husband was trying to stifle a smile, like a youngster who is having trouble keeping a secret. I waited expectantly, and after a moment it burst from him.

"We've been invited to visit the Federate leaders in the south this summer. It could lead to all sorts of things: truces and treaties and trade agreements. Maybe even some way to blend these newcomers into the fabric of Britain. It's a wonderful chance to advance the Cause!"

He was full of enthusiasm, but I gave only a dubious nod. As far as I was concerned it was one thing to befriend an individual and quite another to have dealings with the very people who wanted to steal our land.

"What else did you find out about them?" I asked cautiously.

"Well, their women don't sit on the Councils—they bring forth the bowls of mead or ale and serve the men in the Hall, but leave before the serious discussions begin."

"What sort of Council has half the population missing?" I bridled.

Mischief tugged at the corner of Arthur's mouth. "A very timely one. I've been thinking about instigating it here at home. We might get more accomplished without the distraction of the fairer sex."

"Nonesense!" I sputtered, unwilling to let a slick compliment mask an idea that was insulting to the core. Featherfoot tossed her head and snorted as if in agreement, and I laughed. "Fairer sex, my foot. Your head's still full of cobwebs from all that drinking. Beat you to that outcrop," I challenged, seeing a long stretch of verge opening beside the Road ahead.

Never one to turn down a race, Arthur spurred his stallion forward, and then we were flying over the land, laughing and panting and daring each other to keep up. The dogs stretched out beside us, running at full speed. A flock of starlings rose in consternation as we thundered past their copse of ash trees, and by the time we came pounding, windblown and happy, to the walls of Silchester, all thought of the Saxons had been left behind.

It didn't stay that way long.

My old governess, Lavinia, was thrilled at the prospect of the trip. Claiming that nothing impresses barbarians as much as a grand display of pomp and color, she and Ettard set out to refurbish my wardrobe. For years Vinnie had struggled to get me out of breeches and into clothes "befitting my station," and here at last was her grand opportunity. I grinned and left it up to her.

State visits, as well as royal marriages, require the presentation of gifts, and while Vinnie put store in a fancy wardrobe, both Arthur and I had more faith in the gold and silver presents that betoken a rich treasury. But household treasure is not as easily replaced as the golden jewelry kings give to their Champions; every war-lord grows rich from the jewelry stripped off his dead enemies, but few warriors carry hollow-ware into battle. So Arthur had Cei bring all of Silchester's treasure-trove to the mansion, and the three of us went through it together.

There were flagons and goblets, trays and plates, bowls and baskets and boxes of every description. The afternoon sun streamed into the room, highlighting bright enamels and satiny bronzeware, pewter and fine red Samian pottery, inlaid wood and carved ivory. Spread out over table and floor, it was an impressive display that ranged from useful to handsome. There were many things suitable for the Saxon chiefs, "but nothing fit for a king's wedding present," Cei grumbled.

I hauled the last bundle from the bottom of an olive-wood box and, sitting cross-legged on the floor, began folding back the protective sheepskin. A gleam of polished metal winked up at me and I gasped as a beautiful silver piece lay exposed on my lap.

"Ah, yes, the Anastasius Bowl," Cei remarked as I lifted it up. Sunlight sparkled from the fluted ribs that graced its sides, and in the center of the basin a woman's head had been chased into the metal. It was every bit as elegant as the silver tray Agricola had used to serve us peaches, back before we were married.

Arthur bent down to run a finger along the rim. "That Frankish leader, Clovis, sent it to me as a Gift of State when I became King. I'd forgotten all about the thing."

Cei turned the bowl over and pointed to the mark of the silversmith, which indicated it had come from Constantinople. That fact alone made it a gift worthy of any monarch.

"I suspect that Clovis gave it to me as a bribe to keep me from going to King Ban's aid should the Franks launch an attack against Brittany." Arthur grimaced. "It wouldn't work, of course . . . but still I'm loathe to give it to someone like Mark, who might use it to make Clovis feel I had not appreciated his gift. Ye Gods, diplomacy gets tiresome. There's times when I'd gladly trade it all for the life of a peasant!"

I laughed, knowing exactly what he meant. Carefully rewrapping the bowl, I returned it to its box, still wondering what to give Mark and Isolde.

The problem was solved when Agricola insisted on donating his own silver platter to the cause of the Cornish King's marriage.

"But M'lord," I protested, "didn't you tell me that was a wedding present when you yourself got married? Surely you don't want to part with it?"

"Yes, it was. And my wife and I had a fine life together—but I have no interest in marrying again; there's quite enough for me to do as the King of Demetia without taking on a new wife as well. Let's hope the gift will augur as much good fortune and pleasure in Mark's marriage as it did in mine."

His words were light and cheerful, but I was glad that Vinnie wasn't present; she harbored a special fondness for the Roman widower and, I suspected, a secret dream of matrimony.

A messenger was sent to get the tray from Agricola's villa near Gloucester and it arrived the morning before Beltane. I wrapped it carefully in my shearling cape and put it in the willow trunk with my personal possessions for safekeeping.

Frieda returned that day as well, and seemed to be glad to be back at Court. I was relieved not only for Griflet, but for myself, too, as

Brigit had requested permission to go north to the convent over the summer, instead of traveling with the household.

"I won't stay with the sisters permanently—at least, not yet," the Irish girl promised. "But I want to talk with Mother Superior about the future. And you don't really need me on this trip, as the other women can attend you."

Her request made sense, of sorts, and since we had just finished packing the hampers and panniers for the journey, there wasn't time to argue. So I gave her my blessing and turned my attention to the Beltane rites.

The change of seasons is always a chancy time, when both Gods and mortals run the risk of coming face to face. Samhain is by far the most frightening, for in that autumn time ghouls and spirits move abroad and people can be snatched without warning into the Otherworld. Beltane is generally fairer, with its songs and dancing, May Day rites and grand processions as the cows are turned into the pastures for summer. Since everyone must participate at Beltane—young and elder, weak and hardy—a bustle of activity filled the Court.

I found the kitchen in chaos. Enid had dragged out every pot and pan and was surveying the lot with obvious misgivings. Small and dark as a changeling, my lady-in-waiting spent most of her time in the kitchen because Cook was more in need of help than I was. Her brows knit in exasperation as she assessed the remains of the Empire.

"Those old Romans must not have had much of an appetite; aren't any vessels here big enough for a proper frumenty. From the looks of it, they never sacrificed anything bigger than a pigeon!"

I grinned and pointed out that when the Romans became Christian, they'd given up blood sacrifices. "But if anyone knows where a caldron could be found, it would be Cei."

Sure enough, the Seneschal located a battered bronze crater, and before long Enid and Cook were busy mixing up barley kernels and milk and dried fruit for the ceremony.

As the shadows lengthened Ettard and I took the children through the house, making sure that every ember was extinguished in hearth and oven, lantern and brazier—at Beltane one must truly return to the darkness of the days before the Gods. Only then, with the lighting of the Need-fire, can the Gods prove they have not deserted us.

It is a ritual I've taken part in all my life. With every year the memories become richer, layered one over the other like petals of a flower holding a secret in their center. In good years it is a time of high spirits and anticipation, but when plague and pestilence stalk the land the royal promise leaps to mind with the Need-fire spark. Mama had died the day before Beltane, and since the flux was still rampant, my father's life would have been forfeited if the Need-fire hadn't caught. The memory of that terrible fact lies always just beneath my Beltane joy.

This time the bonfire roared to life with a fine, bright blaze, and the people laughed and capered and danced in giddy delight at leaving winter behind. When the flames died into a glowing pile of embers, we all helped pull the frumenty pot up to the coals and I began the circle dance.

Singing and clapping, the women followed after me—snaking back and forth between the glow of fire and the dark of night, doubling round on ourselves—a living spiral in the dance of life bobbing and weaving to the high, piercing notes of Dagonet's pipe.

The men moved in behind, swaying and stamping as they reached out to spin us around. Deeply throbbing, lightly sinuous—together we called the Goddess, woke the land. Great waves of love, of pent-up longing, of glorious release, rose in the voice of the people as the cold constraints of winter dropped away and spring came romping across the fields.

Every shadow whispered hope and invitation, and I was back again in the fire-glow of the Beltane after Kevin left. Now . . . now . . . I prayed, as if the time since his disappearance had not been. If you are ever going to claim me for your own, it must be now!

His face shimmered suddenly before me; dark-eyed and haunting, but without a smile or gladness of any sort. And when I flung my arms out to him, he turned aside with a look of pure contempt.

Confused, blinded by hot tears of hurt and disbelief, I stumbled from the circle. Arthur's arms went around me, swinging me up in an arc so high that my feet left the ground. Flying, soaring, whirling breathlessly in his embrace, I blinked repeatedly, trying to clear my vision until I saw that it was Lancelot who moved silently away from us, not Kevin at all.

The pain and poignancy of that love which was never to be, mixed with the cold hardness of the Breton's scorn, made my heart cry out. Tears ran down my cheeks, mingling with the sweat of fire and dance, and when Arthur steadied me on my feet I answered his kiss with a grateful eagerness that did the Goddess proud.

Just before we consummated our ritual, I commended Kevin to Epona's care, wherever he might be, and once again reminded the Goddess that the moon was full and I was in need of a child.

SEVEN

Discovery

hen the May Day festivities were over we headed off to Cornwall—a cheerful bunch, laughing and joking in the dazzle of spring. After the winter at Silchester everyone looked forward to a change of scene, but for me it held the special promise of getting to know both the land and people.

I rode Shadow, the little white Welsh Mountain mare Arthur had given me as a wedding present, and he was astride his large black stallion. The horses were fit and eager for the Road, tossing their heads and making the bells on their bridles ring. The Banner of the Red Dragon floated above us, while the entire entourage was decked out in their most colorful outfits. Even I was wearing a dress, and Igraine's golden torque encircled my neck. Altogether we made a splendid picture.

Everywhere we went our subjects came out to greet us, cheering in crowds by the gates of towns or saluting us singly from field and farm. They were as curious about me as I was about them and often called out my name as we approached. I waved and saluted them in return, glad to see them friendly and happy.

Other travelers joined us if they were heading south or pulled to the verge of the Road as our party swept past. Peddlers, healers, farmer's wives taking food to market, a band of young adventurers sharing the rigors of travel—I studied their faces closely, wondering about their dreams and hopes.

We were coming through the Mendip Hills when a strange, mournful sound overtook us. It was as many-tongued as a pack of hounds, but muted and softer, like geese flying somewhere in the distance. The great, sky-filling flocks had long since settled down to nest, so I looked to Arthur with a query.

Before he could reply the dogs burst into sight, rounding the shoulder of a hill like a tide of flapping napery spotted with blood. White as linen, every animal had dark red ears.

"Great Gods, it's the Gabriel Hounds," Gawain cried, reaching for his dagger. Lance drew his sword and the wolfhounds froze, hackles raised and bodies taut.

The racing pack divided to pass on either side of us, sending waves of panic through the household as an ear-splitting whistle rent the air. A man on a dun charger came into view, clinging to his galloping mount like a burr to a blanket. He bore down on us, long hair flying and eyes agleam.

Shadow whinnied in terror as the thundering horse reared skyward to avoid crashing into us. For a long moment it danced in the air, front hooves pawing, nostrils flared and eyes rolling, before crashing to a halt barely three paces in front of me. The dogs ceased their yelping and turned back to their master.

"Arthur Pendragon?" the man called, eyeing my husband with a fierce intensity—half mischief, half threat.

"Who asks?" Arthur's hand rested on the hilt of Excalibur.

"Gwyn of Neath," came the quick reply. "Thought I'd find you somewhere in these hills. Welcome to my territory."

"Your territory?" Arthur cocked an eyebrow. "A bit far from southern Wales, aren't you?"

By now our challenger had turned to ride beside us, sending his dogs on ahead. He gave the King a gap-toothed grin and nodded politely to me.

"Neath's just the family holdings—I'm going to Glastonbury to claim the land I liberated from a scoundrel who challenged me at a ford . . . typical braggart, he was. But I've taken to raising hounds and horses, and his land is good pasturage."

From the web of scars on Gwyn's arms I suspected he'd spent more of his life on the battlefield than in either stable or kennel, but perhaps he felt it was time to hang up his shield—older warriors become a liability when their speed drops off.

"Came out to ask if you'd like to stay over," the wildman went on. "I've a hunting lodge not far away—excellent larder and good enough quarters. Been breeding a line of large horses—good for cavalry—and hoped we could discuss bloodlines over ale and meat."

Arthur glanced at the man's mount. A young gelding, he was big and sound, and tall in the bargain; just the sort we needed.

"Heard you're developing a strain of your own," Gwyn continued, eyeing Arthur's stallion as well. "I've a notion to try for a line of blacks. . . ."

Whatever doubts Arthur had disappeared, and by the time we sat down to dinner he and Gwyn had gone over all the mares in the barn and determined which ones might be suitable for breeding with the stallion.

During the meal Gwyn's bard regaled us with stories of the witch of Wookey Hole, who lived in a nearby cave with a pair of goats.

"My da saw her once—face all twisted as she stared into a polished crystal ball," the bard recalled. "Carries the thing at her belt and uses it to make charms."

I was wondering if she might have some spell for fertility when Gwyn spoke up, his dark eyes riveted to my face. "People don't go near her cave, however—there's terrible groans and screams come from that cavern now and then."

I shivered and made the sign against evil and in the firelight caught sight of Lancelot doing the same. He may not have much respect for me, but at least he paid the Gods their due.

"Tomorrow," Gwyn announced with a sudden, toothy grin, "I'll take you through the Gorge. Wonderful place; fairly reeks of the first days of creation."

In the morning we took the path that leads down into a canyon between steep limestone walls. The gray-white stone is ridged like giant columns, seamed with balconies and festooned by vines and trees that cling to every ledge. As we followed the dancing stream deeper into the chasm, the hanging gardens towered over us. I had never seen such naked grandeur at close range and joined the rest of the household in marveling at the strangeness of it—even the arrogant Breton seemed impressed.

Gwyn continued with us to Glastonbury, talking about his plans.

"Have a notion to build a Hall on top of the Tor." Both his tone and the cavalier wave of his hand made it sound like child's play.

I thought of the great hill that rises abruptly above the marshy lake. Nimue, who is a priestess in her own right, says the Mother Goddess has an invisible shrine on the highest level of the Tor. The idea of erecting a home in that holy space seemed cheeky in the extreme, unless Gwyn was himself related to the Gods in some strange way. I studied him surreptitiously, noting the slight stature and gnarled features. He caught my gaze and gave me a broad, knowing wink before I could look away.

Lancelot also watched the fellow with a quizzical interest. Having been raised by the Lady, the Breton was no doubt well versed in the ways of the fey.

Yet when we paused at Glastonbury it was Lancelot who went into the chapel in the vale, stooping slightly to make his way through the low door.

"Would you care to pay your respects as well?" the hermit who tended it asked me. "It's sacred to the Mother, you know."

It seemed odd for a Christian holy man to dedicate this little thatch-and-wattle church to the Goddess who was already worshiped on the hilltop. "The Mother?" I repeated.

"Why, Mary, the Mother of Jesu," came the answer.

I hastily declined the invitation but wondered why Lancelot would want to visit such a place.

"Merlin came and went among the Christians, sharing ideas and asking questions," Arthur reminded me. "Maybe Lance is curious in the same way."

"Maybe," I conceded, thinking it a peculiar trait in a warrior.

We made a detour to inspect a deserted hill-fort above the tiny town of South Cadbury. The fortress was as old as Liddington, and almost as big, for within the ramparts the hill rose and rippled toward a high plateau. The buildings were too ruinous to use, but someone—Arthur thought perhaps it was Uther—had made an effort to refurbish the defensive wall. We pitched camp at the edge of an oak grove that had grown up around the remains of an old Roman temple, and after dinner Arthur and I took our blankets up to the top of the plateau, a little distance from the rest.

The evening was clear, and the sky arched deep and black and glittering with stars above us. We talked softly before sleep, our half-whispered words fluttering away in the darkness as we slipped into silence.

Wrapped in a half dream, the whole of Albion stretched out around me, turning slowly like a lovely lady preening herself from every angle before the mirror of my mind. I saw the golden scarps of Cotswold, the green sea surge of the downs and the giant arches of ancient elegance rising from the steaming swamp of Bath.

Yet the heart of Britain remained hidden, shifting like a rainbow in the mist—even beyond the power and majesty of Cheddar Gorge and the vast watery plain around Glastonbury, there was something dearer, closer to the core of life. Slowly she unveiled it—the homey steading carved from the forest, the cluster of a village, the shepherd's bothy and the shanty of the fisherman. They glimmered in my memory like the faces I had seen on the Road, a prismatic portrait of the people who called me Queen.

Nearby a nightingale called, its sweet, haunting cry piercing the dark.

Between the tiny bird song so close at hand and the vast, echoing spaces within the firmament, stood the human dream. Whether it is for a good harvest or the making of treaties, the return of a love or the prayer for a live birth, every heart moves toward a goal that weaves into the fabric of time, adding threads of gold or coarse wool, twisting, knotting, becoming part of a pattern too big for mortals to comprehend.

I felt the dreams of the people beating softly all around me and knew that I was as committed to them as Arthur was committed to the Cause. It was a deep, stirring realization, and my spirit moved toward wonder while I lay in my husband's arms.

"They call this the Land of Summer," he whispered quietly, as if he feared to wake me. "I guess that makes you my Queen of the Summer Stars."

The words spun round me in a dream of my own, and I smiled to myself, afraid to respond too openly lest he never express something so tender again. It was the closest Arthur had ever come to a term of endearment, and it filled my heart with absolute delight. Someday, I thought drowsily, he might even decide he loved me.

As we rode through the fertile, red-earthed fields around Exeter, Geraint came out to greet us. Although he was younger and less polished than his mentor, Agricola, one could see why Arthur had made him the King of Devon—not only was he a military genius, he had an air of competence mixed with good high spirits.

"Aren't you the dandy!" Arthur exclaimed, admiring the young man's green silk tunic and linen breeches.

"You haven't heard about the trading ship from Byzantium?"

"No!"

The new monarch grinned. "It arrived right after the gales—put into my port at Topsham with a full cargo, including bolts and bolts of silk. The wardrobes of the West Country nobles are now quite resplendent."

The ship had also carried wine and glassware and delicate pottery from the factories on the edge of the Black Sea, as well as a young Greek slave who played haunting melodies on a strange musical instrument. Geraint had bought the lad, and after a sumptuous dinner it was the music of the Pan pipe rather than the stories of the harp that we listened to. There was dancing and clapping and games of chance and skill, and I noticed that the King of Devon flirted with Enid more than a little.

"Proud as those peacocks he keeps in the garden, and twice as handsome," my lady-in-waiting quipped as she helped me get ready for bed. "But he'd be better off thinking less of military glory and more of the kitchen; the room's smoky, the oven doesn't work and there's no paving around the well in the courtyard."

"Perhaps," I suggested, "what he needs is a wife to set his domestic scene right for him."

"A man like that isn't wanting for marriage, just a good manager." Enid slipped my amber-and-ivory necklace into its sheepskin pouch and grinned mischievously. "Still, he does cut a splendid figure."

And Geraint was a splendid host. He showed us through the buildings being repaired, proudly pointing out the marbles that had been rescued from the ruins. On the second day he provided a picnic on the strand, where we all discussed the possibilities of refurbishing the Topsham wharves in order to accommodate trade with merchant ships.

Arthur squinted down the estuary toward the distant Channel. "With London lying in no-man's-land, ungoverned by either Saxon or Briton, we need to develop another port. Someday we may want to resume trading across the Channel."

"What could you possibly send to the Continent?" Enid asked. "Shears for the barbarians?"

Since the hordes that had toppled the Empire were famous for going unshorn, her comment brought a burst of laughter from Geraint. "We could always barter for soap," he suggested. "They may be shaggy louts, but I've heard they're clean."

"So it's soap you're needing?" Enid countered. "Frieda taught us to make that years back . . . I'll give the recipe to your cook."

"You're welcome to stay and make it yourself, if you've a mind." There was a playful challenge in the King of Devon's voice and Enid cocked an eyebrow in reply.

"I'm sure I'd be welcome to do many things, M'lord, but I have no hankering for being a servant. Cooks you can hire, me you cannot."

Gawain, who was fond of bantering with Enid himself, choked on the wine he was swigging, and Arthur had to pound him on the back. The dogs commenced barking uproariously, and everyone was laughing as we stood up and dusted the sand from our clothes. Only Ettard remained silent, staring thoughtfully at the King of Devon—but then, the convent girl was never noted for her sense of humor.

.   .   .

As the time for the wedding approached, Geraint led us out across the vastness of Dartmoor, clearly delighted to show off his new land.

Dartmoor's high plateau is a wild expanse of bog and heath, whipped by wind and scoured by the shadow of clouds. Deserted except for the ponies and deer and a few wild sheep that graze along the edges of deep-cut streams, it whispers of times forgotten . . . strange rocks thrusting upward through thin soil, trees twisted and crabbed by the harsh wind, and the long abandoned remains of huts too small to house humans.

"Homes of the Ancient Ones." Gawain explained, making the sign against the Unknown. "They call themselves the firstborn of the Gods and caper in skins beneath the moon."

I glanced over at the Prince of Orkney, wondering how much he knew about these folk. Kevin had encountered them in Ireland and had taught me to recognize their signs, though they avoid towns and Roads and contact with most mortals.

"Was this where they lived?" I asked.

"More like where they left," Lancelot interjected. "They withdrew when the Legions spread across Albion, and now live in the Hollow Hills with the sidhe. It is not wise, M'lady, to disturb them."

Condescension dripped from the Breton's voice. I started to tell him I already knew a good bit more than most about the creatures that are kin to the fey, but the lieutenant had turned his attention back to Arthur. So I swallowed my words and railed inwardly at the arrogance of the man.

If the heights of Devon's moor are wild and lonely, the spread of Cornwall's land is rich with farms and people. Green fields stretch right to the edge of the sheer coast, and beyond those cliffs the waters of the sea twinkle blue and emerald and sometimes even amethyst.

As we made our way to Castle Dore my mind filled with questions about the young bride. Isolde had been in Cornwall for well over a month, and presumably she and Mark were past the first uncertain days of shyness or infatuation. Each should know if the marriage was ill advised by now. The fact that no one had moved to cancel the wedding indicated that all was well.

Still, I was uneasy . . . Igraine had summed it up years ago: any man who seeks to marry a lass young enough to be his granddaughter is weaving the web of his own heartbreak.

I hoped Mark would not wake up to discover his dream had become a nightmare.

EIGHT

Celtic Sun

"B lessings of the White Christ on you." The King of Cornwall spread his arms in greeting, a smile wreathing his great horse face. "The splendor of my realm is at your disposal—may God give you the appetite to enjoy it."

We had not seen Mark since our wedding feast, and as he came down the steps from his wooden hall I was glad to find him less repulsive than I remembered. He still looked like an overfed ox bedecked with gold and jewels, but his blue silk tunic was clean and his white beard neatly trimmed. Most notable of all, he no longer conveyed the sulky petulance of a spoiled child.

The man had gone to great lengths to make this a memorable occasion and proudly recounted his efforts.

"The only thing I couldn't get was a Roman bishop for the services—they all said it was too far to travel. But I've furnished my priest with new vestments of the best silk, so that makes up for it a little."

I remembered the Byzantine trader with a smile—he seemed to have traded enough shining cloth to stretch from here to Topsham's wharf!

There was no church big enough for the ceremony at Castle Dore, so Mark had a temporary chapel built around a Pagan holy spot, blessing and rededicating it to the new religion. The side walls and back were woven of willow wands laced with flowers and bracken fronds, making a pretty little nook that was open to the audience on the fourth side. The ground was strewn with rose petals so deep they drifted like

snow about the base of the altar, and the whole looked like the handiwork of the fey.

"After all," Mark confided, "a girl only has one wedding, and I want
Isolde's to be perfect."

His tone was positively reverential. I wondered again what this Irish
girl was like. There was much speculation about her among the guests,
but the bride stayed in her chambers the entire day before the wedding,
so we could do little but wait 'til she appeared at the ceremony.

The morning of the wedding came fair and shining, the perfect
beginning for a summer day, and Mark was beside himself with joy as
he showed us to our place. Off to one side a harper played softly, but
a quick glance showed it wasn't Tris. I wanted to ask where the Cornish
hero was, but just then the priest signaled for the ceremony to begin;
with a beneficent smile Mark went to take his place by the altar, and
we turned to catch a first glimpse of the bride.

It was Tristan who led her forth to her nuptials.

Covered from head to foot by yards of sheer white silk, Isolde moved
like a wraith down the aisle that had been cordoned off with purple
ribbons. She clung to the warrior's arm and he narrowed his stride to
keep measure with her tiny steps as he guided her to her groom.
Stopping once, she raised her face to the Champion; for a moment
there was utter silence as he stared down at the hidden features. Then
he patted the hand that clutched his arm and gently urged her forward.

The harper left off strumming when the two of them reached the
altar and the ritual began.

Tris gave the girl away and discreetly withdrew. There was a deal of
praying and vow making, and Mark put a huge gold ring on her delicate
finger when the time came. With a grand flourish the priest pronounced them man and wife and gestured for the King of Cornwall to
unveil his prize.

We all gasped as the silk fell away. Standing before us was an
exquisite beauty with black hair, violet eyes, and alabaster skin. She was
small as well as young and looked not at her groom, but at the audience,
seeming to search for a familiar face among so many strange ones.

Mark enveloped her in a tentative hug and made a gentle effort to
kiss his bride. Isolde adroitly ducked her head forward, receiving his lips
on the top of her hair as though she were his child, not his mate. Yet

the King beamed happily when he presented her to the gathering.

The Cornish people roared their approval, but I turned my gaze away, unable to meet the eyes of the girl who continued to scan the crowd. Although her new husband clearly adored her, there was not a trace of emotion on Isolde's face.

Mark brought her to stand before us.

"Behold the great beauty of Cornwall." His voice rang with pride as she curtsied politely.

"May your marriage be blessed with many children." I tried to make the words light and merry, but my heart plummeted when Isolde looked up—it was clear she had been crying not long before.

How many hours of weeping, I wondered. How many half-formed schemes and frantic dreams of escape had the Irish child spun? If she was this unhappy, why had she not spoken out and demanded return to her homeland? Was it possible they would refuse to take her back? And how could the Queen of Ireland have sent her daughter off to Britain without any assurance that the girl would at least like her royal spouse?

Isolde's maid, Branwen, hovered at the bride's side as though fearful her mistress might collapse.

"Is there anything I can do?" I asked when Isolde turned away. Branwen paused for a moment and it struck me how alike the two young women looked, though Branwen was obviously a little older.

"No," she answered stiffly, "both my cousin and I were raised to honor the duties of a royal marriage."

Ah, yes—even in Ireland one finds those famous Celtic queens!

The feasting lasted well into the night, with bards and acrobats and pipers entertaining between rounds of food and drink. Servants brought forth huge quantities of ducks and geese, dove and partridge. There were fish of every conceivable kind, cooked in a variety of ways—stuffed, steamed, filleted, skewered, roasted, or poached. And the wine was dipped out of two enormous craters that stood in ornate tripods. Cei took a cautious sip, then cocked an eyebrow and raised his goblet in compliment to the bridegroom. It seemed that everyone, except perhaps Isolde, was having a fine time.

I looked about for Tristan, expecting to find him with our Companions. Being so tall, he was normally easy to spot, but this evening he had become invisible.

"Haven't seen him since he and Dinadan tiptoed away during the ceremony," Arthur allowed. "No doubt the two of them are setting up some prank for the revelers."

It seemed a reasonable explanation, and I let out a sigh of relief. Mark's Champion appeared to have come unscathed through the ordeal of fetching the bride from Ireland after all.

When it was time for Isolde to retire to the bedchamber, Branwen put her arm around her cousin's shoulders, gently sheltering her as she led the girl away.

I glanced over at Mark, wondering how he was going to deal with one so young and inexperienced. He read my concern and leaning toward me, whispered, "For a prize like that, one can afford to be patient."

Such sensitivity came as a surprise—perhaps the young girl's enormous husband was developing some consideration for others after all.

Later, as the guests were making their way to their chambers, I grabbed Arthur by the waist and drew him outside, suggesting that we forgo the Lodge in favor of that wonderful bed of rose petals. He gave me a knowing look and, taking my hand, led the way to the deserted chapel.

It was there we found Tristan. He sat hunched with his back to the altar, his head buried in his hands from which a length of white silk hung like a shroud.

Dinadan stood nearby, guarding his friend's privacy.

The lanky warrior's heartbreak was all too clear, so with a nod to Dinadan, Arthur and I quietly slipped away. There were many other spots where we could sleep, but no more appropriate place for Tris to grieve for a love no one even knew he had.

The wedding celebration included a week of games and competitions, hunting and dancing and all manner of entertainments. There was even a tournament.

The Cornish were not familiar with the long, heavy lances our

Companions use, and they responded enthusiastically when Pelleas and Gawain demonstrated a jousting maneuver with them. I was glad to see that the Prince of Orkney had taken the skinny young horseman under his wing and Pelleas was thrilled to have such a famous mentor. Like a cat that responds to stroking, Gawain left off sulking over the Marhaus adventure and now showed himself to be kind and gracious to everyone. Morgause's son could add charm to any occasion, when he felt like it.

Arthur and Mark and Geraint took time to discuss the prospect of reopening the Cornish tin mines. So far the Saxon incursion had not moved as far west as Devon, and now that the Byzantine merchants had found a ready market at Topsham, perhaps Britain could redevelop her tin trade.

Theo, the Goth who had become leader of our fleet, sat in as well, for though he and Mark had no love for each other, the onetime pirate had proved himself adept at keeping marauders from the Bristol Channel. And Agricola volunteered his knowledge of international trade. As kingly councils go, this one was quite productive.

With Arthur thus occupied, Lancelot was left with time to spare. He soon befriended Tristan, who too often sat moping on the sidelines during the festivities. The pair of them went everywhere together. They were the biggest men in the realm, except for Pellinore and his son Lamorak, and so well matched that they filled an entire doorway when they stood side by side.

"Yesterday Griflet and I watched them wrestling," Frieda commented as we combed out the dogs one evening. "Neither was able to best the other. I wouldn't want to tangle with either one of 'em, M'lady . . . no, not at all."

I smiled at her caution, and the fact that the Breton was providing Tris with a way to work out his misery, whether he knew of the other's hopeless love or not.

The new bride appeared to have reconciled herself to her fate and by the third day was sitting in splendor at Mark's side. He cosseted her like a spoiled pet, picking out the best of the wild strawberries from his own plate and putting them on hers. There was something touching about the scene, but it didn't endear the girl to me. She accepted or disdained his offerings with an imperious nod or shake of her pretty head and I wondered what sort of Queen she could possibly grow up to be.

On the last night of feasting Isolde was clearly out of sorts. Toward the end of the meal she stood up from the table and stamped her foot in exasperation.

"Tristan is the only one who can help my headaches," she pouted. "No one else can play the Irish harp I brought with me, and you know how much I need the music for my nerves."

Mark's face was reddening, but as the Hall grew still he smiled calmly at his wife. "Of course the harper may attend you. But you'll have to wait until we've thanked our guests for sharing this occasion with us."

"What do I care about your old guests!" Tears brimmed in those beautiful eyes. "Surely they don't want me to sit here, ill and unhappy, just for protocol's sake."

Mark leaned forward and, saying something the rest of us couldn't hear, got Isolde to sit back down, although she stared petulantly at the plate before her.

A surge of chatter swept the Hall as everyone turned to their neighbor in sudden, animated conversation, embarrassed by the events at the royal table. Seated next to Ettard, Geraint listened politely to some tale or other. I watched them casually, thinking he was the perfect noble: brave in battle, discreet at court, and full of wit as well. The convent girl alternated between simpering coyness and blatant adoration.

Enid walked past their table, tossing off a comment that caught Geraint's fancy, and he gave a laughing response. Predictably, Ettard was not amused, though the King of Devon managed to coax a smile out of her once Enid had gone.

Geraint asked to come with us when he learned we were planning to continue to the Saxon Shore. "I have no Federates in Devon—the line of hill-forts that runs north along the Avon keeps them out of the west. But I'm planning to meet with the men of those forts, and I'd be honored to present them to you."

So we left Castle Dore with a flurry of farewells and good wishes for the Road. Even Isolde put on a cheerful face, giving us a formal thank-you for the splendid silver tray. I only hoped Agricola had been right about its auguring well for the newlyweds.

The fine, gay mood of summer lasted as we made our way along the south coast of Britain like a band of revelers on a long holiday. Riding proud along the high cliffs, we all stuck honey-scented sea pinks in our hair, and sprigs of yellow vetch as well. And where the rivers dropped down to the sea in steep, shaded canyons, we rested amid oak and fern, willow and mosses. Camping beside the green estuaries, we chatted with ferrymen and fisherfolk and shared our fires with other travelers. Dagonet piped up a cheerful tune, and we'd all go skipping along the shingle shore. Arthur doesn't care for dancing, even on ritual occasions, but I whirled, breathless and merry, with everyone else except Lancelot.

At Maiden Castle we met the convocation of war-lords from hill-forts with names like Hod Hill and Castle Ditches and White Sheets. Tough, pugnacious men who were neither as open as Pellinore nor as wild as Gwyn, they had dug into their old fortifications and dared anyone, Saxon or otherwise, to displace them. Yet they accepted Arthur as one of their own, proudly displaying their troops for him and joining in the Council round the fire at night. He listened carefully to their reports of Federate activity and praised them each for being so well informed. I watched them in the fire-glow, thinking of Merlin's promise that Arthur would be King for all Britons.

"Looks to be a fine year," Geraint noted as we came into Dorchester. "Everything quiet along the Saxon Shore, and a good crop in the fields. Why, the Cerne Abbas Giant was even seen dancing on his hillside, which always means a bountiful harvest."

"Dancing?" I queried, remembering Agricola's description of the huge figure cut into the turf on the chalk hill. The Roman noble and his wife had once spent the night sleeping on the Giant, in the hope that it would help them have children. That seemed a chancy pastime if the thing was going to start moving about.

"Oh, yes, M'lady, dancing . . . the fling, I think it was. Or was it a hop-skippety?" The King of Devon cast me a sly look and broke into laughter when I realized he was joking.

Whereas the war-lords were eager to pass on whatever information they had about the barbarians, we found the would-be aristocrats of Dorchester so full of smug complacency as to be practically useless.

"The Federates?" Our Roman hostess scowled at the very word. "We have nothing to do with the likes of them. They're all over Portchester, of course—built their squalid little huts everywhere, both inside and out of the walls. But here they remember their place and don't bother us." She called over a servant—whose blond coloring looked suspiciously Saxon—and carefully surveyed the fruit on the platter he carried. "It's so hard to manage a villa these days, what with the slaves running off three years ago. Ungrateful wretches, I hope the Saxons got them!"

Geraint left us next morning, heading down the Roman Road for Exeter.

"I've come to bid you farewell," the gallant proclaimed, reining in before my ladies. "Can't imagine a lovelier way to start the summer than in the company of the wise, the beautiful, and the Queen. Makes me feel like Paris with the Goddesses who started the Trojan War."

I grinned at his nerve while Ettard dimpled coyly and Enid gave him an arch look. But before she could speak he threw us a kiss and wheeling his horse around, galloped away.

My ladies stared after him, speechless, and I thought how lucky they were—unlike royalty they were free to choose among their suitors for themselves.

Remembering Isolde, I thanked Epona that my own political marriage had proved so fortunate. Arthur was a mate I could love as well as admire; my subjects accepted me with the same generosity of spirit they had afforded Igraine, and the only thing lacking in my life was a child.

When we came in sight of the Cerne Abbas Giant I gaped, open-mouthed, at the white outline of a man standing with his feet apart and club raised for action. The thing takes up most of the hillside.

"Some say it represents Hercules," Agricola reminded me, "though one can see why childless couples come here, too."

Indeed, the Giant's member is outlined, bold and erect for all to admire, and I wondered if sleeping on it really did help couples conceive. When I suggested we try, Arthur actually blushed.

"Seems a bit—uh—public—don't you think?" he stammered. "I mean, it's not as though we're not capable. . . ."

I couldn't help laughing, for goodness knows he didn't need help in his part of our coupling. Finally, after a bit of coaxing, he agreed to climb the hill with me once the rest of the camp had gone to sleep.

Later, as I gazed into the starry blackness above us, I begged the Ancient Powers to make up for whatever it was that kept me from conceiving.

But the Gods turned a deaf ear and my courses continued to come as regularly as the phases of the moon.

A small, nagging doubt had begun to darken my world.

NINE

Saxon Shadows

s we moved into the Saxon Shore the sense of adventure grew all around us. Like the Ancient Ones, the Federates were known more through hearsay than daily life, so the promise of actually meeting some filled me with excitement.

The man who waited at the seventh milestone beyond Portchester was blond, stocky, and not smiling. His hand rested on the throwing axe tucked into his belt, and when we approached he strode into the middle of the Road as though it were his own.

His voice was no more friendly than his face, and he made a quick count of our Companions before checking the device on our banner. "Arthur Pendragon?"

"I am he." Arthur set his shoulders and stared the fellow in the eye.

"I'm Brieda—sent to escort you to M'lord Wihtgar."

Without further word the guide led us into the dark woods and down a dirt track to the watermeadow beside a stream. I'd heard that Saxons prefer settling in the wet lowlands, and Wihtgar seemed to be no exception.

Fields had been cleared, pastures laid out, and a stout wall of logs put up around the small settlement. The palisade was made of whole tree trunks rammed upright in the ground and was very impressive. The Saxons are said to skin their enemies alive and nail the human hides to their palisades as a warning to all others. This one held no such horror, but I shivered when I saw it nonetheless.

"Don't tell me you're afraid? I thought Celtic queens weren't afraid of anything," Arthur teased.

"Of course not, silly. There's no bravery in doing something you don't have sense enough to be scared of," I answered, lifting my chin in mock defiance, and we both laughed.

To my surprise, Lancelot grinned too and I caught a twinkle of appreciation in his eyes before he looked away. It lightened my mood unexpectedly.

A horn hung from a tree at the edge of the clearing, and after Brieda signaled our arrival with it, we approached the steading. A gate swung open, revealing a score of people coming out of huts and barns—mostly blond, mostly tall, and all watching us cautiously. Even the smith at the forge stopped to stare, his stilled hammer creating an eerie silence.

We came to a halt inside the gate, the wolfhounds standing at attention beside our horses. They held their shaggy heads high and the jewels on their bronze collars winked in the sun. A mongrel of the steading gave a warning bark but neither Cabal nor Caesar deigned to notice.

The little crowd of Saxons stood off from us; no one spoke, though there was some nudging and pointing in my direction. I wondered if they had heard as many dreadful things about us as we had about them.

Suddenly a toddler broke away from his mother, gleefully propelling himself toward Cabal. "Bow-wow," he caroled, lurching under her chin. The adults froze, though whether from awe or fear I couldn't tell. The war-dog didn't even blink.

With a snarl the mongrel charged through the crowd, teeth bared in challenge. For a moment I thought the baby would be caught in the chaos of a dog fight, until a Saxon stopped the cur with a well-placed kick.

It broke the tension and a murmur of comment rose around us. When the toddler began to whimper, his mother scooped him up in her arms, and Wihtgar came slamming out of his hall.

"So you are here, British King," the Saxon called out, scanning our party quickly. "I salute your courage."

"And I salute your hospitality." Arthur's tone was positively majestic. "We come in peace, and I assume we shall be free to leave in peace."

Wihtgar nodded and began a speech about the loyalty of the Federates, invoking the years of faithful service his people had given. I took
the opportunity to study the man.

He was solidly built, with graying hair and skin that was weathered
to the tan of leather. An amber talisman hung from the pommel of the
sword at his side, and the edges of his tunic were sewn with bright
braid. Though he was obviously the lord of the place, his boots were
covered with mud from the fields and there was no Roman gentility
in his stance.

On a rise behind him loomed the Mead Hall, the thick planks of its
walls set vertically into the ground. In shape it was rectangular, like
Roman buildings, but not nearly as elegant. A steep, thatched roof
sloped down from the roofbeam, which was carved to the likeness of
a monster, and several sets of antlers graced the doorway in the middle
of the long side. What windows there were were shuttered, not glazed.

A number of huts and hovels clustered around the main building like
piglets around a sow. Squatting under roofs that came almost to the
ground, they seemed too little to be used for anything other than
storage.

"Well, where are your manners, oafs!" Wihtgar had come to the end
of his speech and now turned to his people. "Make the British leader
comfortable. Brieda, see to the horses. Gerta, take the women with you.
And you, Eostre, prepare the wassail for our guests."

The men and women began to mill, still murmuring as they crowded
around me and reached out to touch my mare. Shadow, never the
calmest of animals, tossed her head and tried to back away. Frieda
plowed through the little crowd and, grabbing Shadow's bridle, held
her steady so that I could dismount.

"The people mean you no harm," she whispered. "A white horse is
sacred to them. They want to touch her for good luck."

I didn't relish having my mare pawed over by strangers, but Arthur
was moving away and I was afraid of getting separated from him. As
I turned to run after him a large woman planted herself firmly in front
of me.

From the ornateness of the brooches that were pinned on each
shoulder and the wealth of beads and chains that swagged over her
bosom between them, I surmised she was the chieftain's wife.

She was as broad and sturdy as Wihtgar, with hands that were strong and callused from hard work. I thought of the Roman matron in Dorchester; whatever "place" that latter-day noble thought the Saxons kept, it was clear the Federates defined themselves as keepers of the land.

"The guest bowers are this way," our hostess announced. "You will be quite comfortable."

I sent a last pleading look toward Arthur, but he was already climbing the rise to the Hall and Frieda put a restraining hand on my arm. So while the men disappeared into the main building to eat and drink, I entered the somber world of Saxon women.

The "bowers" were the outbuildings I'd noticed. There were sheds and shanties for everything from spinning and weaving to leatherwork, and they were not only dark and stuffy but also cramped. Our sleeping quarters were somewhat bigger and more comfortable, with benches for beds and raised wooden floors that were warmer than the stone and tile pavements I was used to. Pelts and skins were piled in the corners, and I suspected it would be a cozy retreat when winter came.

Once I was settled Frieda led us to the kitchen where the Saxon women waited while their men were in the Hall. They studied us openly, eyes widening as they saw Igraine's gold torque. Even my dress was a cause of wonder, and Vinnie basked happily in the reflected glory of Saxon admiration.

After I was seated on a stool by the oven, the chieftain's wife introduced her household, coming at last to her youngest daughter.

"Eostre." The pride of motherhood made Gerta's deep voice richer. "She is our Cup-bearer in the Hall."

The girl was well named, shining in this dark firmament like the Goddess of Spring. Her pale hair hung in long braids, and when she curtsied I thought of Rowena, that famous Saxon beauty who had become the wife of Vortigern. It was said the old tyrant fell in love with her as she knelt to offer him the wassail bowl. I wondered what had happened to her when Ambrosius defeated her husband—no one ever spoke of her after that.

When the presentations were over the evening filled with women's chatter. Although they spoke some form of dialect, I could follow the gist of the conversation, most of which was about children. Everyone seemed to have produced offspring, and some complained of having more than they could manage. All I wanted was one, and I chafed at the unfairness of it, wondering what I had done to displease the Gods.

We left Wihtgar's holding the next day with much cheering and a friendly farewell, for the men had enjoyed the visit much more than I did. Arthur assured these people that their rights would be upheld and grievances listened to, and they affirmed their loyalty in return. I had found it a colossal waste of time, but my husband was satisfied.

Wihtgar sent Brieda along as our guide through the Weald, that ancient forest where the Romans smelted so much iron that great mounds of slag were left behind. Now it was dotted with isolated Saxon settlements. We were hosted by men with names like Stuf and Maegla, and each new steading was much the same as the last—Arthur was successful in the Hall, I was miserable among the women.

When we were on the Road the Companions rode ahead and behind the women, just in case of adversity, and Lance took his place beside Arthur. I tried to stay with them for a while—the Road being more than wide enough—but the Breton confined his comments to Arthur and left me out entirely. The responsiveness I had glimpsed at the Saxon gate seemed never to be repeated.

Finally I dropped back to ride by myself, glaring at Lancelot's back. When he first came I'd thought he might be shy and stiff with all women, but I'd seen him chat with Enid many times, laughing and easy. And he never indulged in the cryptic glances or private joking one generally finds between warriors who are lovers. So it appeared his hostility was aimed at me and me alone. I couldn't care less about that, I told myself, if only he didn't monopolize so much of Arthur's time.

Excluded from my husband's side during the day and relegated to the Federate kitchens at night, my world grew small and dim. I longed for the light, lilting mood of Cornwall and found instead the earnestness of Saxon life. Tough, determined immigrants who had arrived with nothing other than what they could carry, they were obsessed with wresting a future from the thick forests of Britain, and one felt their determination on every hand. By the time we reached London I was far less frightened of the Federates than bored by them, and even though I tried to be polite, I looked forward to the familiar comforts of a Roman town.

But Britain's Imperial City was little better than the Federate camps; with trade and transport gone, it had lost its reason for being. Blocks of statuary had been used to fill the breeches in the towered walls, leaving them patched and motley. The docks they overlooked were deserted and the famous bridge that spans the Thames would scarcely support the weight of a farmer's cart. We rode single file along the side where the strongest timbers lay, wary of those places where the wood was rotten. Even the City gates were useless, being propped half-open across the roadway.

Coming to a halt before the arch, Lance called out to the boy on guard. "Arthur Pendragon, High King of Britain, requests permission to enter the City of London."

The lad peered at us curiously, then disappeared from his perch and returned, some minutes later, with a churchman who was hastily adjusting his vestments.

"Your Highness." It was the Archbishop who had married us at Sarum, and he gave me a curt nod before turning to smile on Arthur. "You do us great honor, though we're not prepared for a royal visit. I myself live in one wing of the Imperial Palace—if you don't mind sharing it, we'll try to make you comfortable."

Arthur thanked him and we were soon following him through the half-deserted streets.

The people who watched our progress were an odd mixture: descendents of Roman administrators, Britons driven from Sussex when the barbarian Aelle took power, and a scattering of Saxons whose huts now leaned against the walls of ruined mansions. A straggle of them accompanied us to the Imperial Palace.

That old place was in an appalling state of disrepair, and the fine park that had once surrounded it was overgrown by every sort of bramble and weed. I tried not to let my distaste show and worked alongside the Grounds Keeper and his family to clear a courtyard room where we could host the Federates. At least I would be able to sit at my husband's side during the Feast.

"Not this time, Gwen." Arthur concentrated on lacing his boots. "Wouldn't want to do anything that would unsettle our guests."

"What are you talking about?" I flared, thoroughly sick of considering the Saxons. "These people are no better than the ones who slaughtered the Celts, and you're worried about unsettling them? Have you gone mad?"

"It's precisely because of past treachery I don't want you there," he said evenly. Reaching for the top of his boot, he slid the handle of a dagger up to where I could see it. "This time if they start something, we'll be prepared. But you should be with their women—they'll be expecting you, as hostess."

I sagged against the doorjamb, cranky and weary and hating the idea of another night among the barbarians.

"Last stop, my dear," he added cheerfully, taking up the crown the Christians had given him. "After this it's heading for Caerleon and the Round Table gathering." He planted the crown rakishly over one eyebrow and grinned at me. "I'm thinking it's time we get back to our own."

Arthur has the kind of confident charm that makes people eager to follow him, and not even I was proof against it. So I smiled tiredly, reaching up to straighten the golden band and wishing him luck with our guests.

"Don't wait up," he admonished. "You know how late the Saxons like to drink."

And then he was heading for the Feast and I made my way to the kitchen, tired and cross and thoroughly miserable.

"The foreign queen looks sad," a Saxon servant said, not realizing that I understood. I bridled at the word *foreign* and bit my lip to keep from giving her a piece of my mind. Both servants and slaves in this new-comer's culture had rights by law, and though this woman wore the thrall collar of a slave, I fully suspected they would call me to account if I boxed her ears. So I folded my hands and stared down at Mama's ring, wondering if she'd ever had to exercise this kind of patience.

"From her figure, I'd say she's never had a child." The woman appraised me from top to bottom. "Someone should take her to the wicca out in Westminster's swamp."

"And just what does this wicca do?" I demanded angrily.

"Makes charms, and potions; calls up spirits and quickens the empty womb," came the staunch reply. If the Saxon was surprised to hear me speak her language, she didn't show it. "I could take you there . . . for a price, that is," she added, narrowing her eyes.

"How much?"

She scanned me more carefully this time, her gaze finally settling on Mama's enamel ring. I tried to tuck that hand into my pocket, but the Saxon reached out a stubby finger.

"The ring . . . the many-colored ring. That's all; surely a petty price to pay for a child of your own."

I hesitated, wondering if she would understand that this was a special gift, a token of love from a parent now long dead.

"It will pay for the meeting with the wicca as well . . . we'll not ask more," the servant went on, greed making her willing to bargain.

I tried to weigh the two, the tie from the past against the hope for the future, but there was no way to equate them.

"I'll take you out there now, before the sun sets . . . the day of a full moon is the best time," the woman coaxed. "And within the next month you'll conceive. Imagine, trading a little cold ring for a warm cradle and cheerful hearth."

Still I paused, and she came closer, hissing in my ear. "But must make it now, so as to be back before the men are ready for bedding. And then, when you lie with your lord tonight, you'll know you'll be giving him a child of his own."

It was a skillful argument, and in the end I agreed to the trade. Frieda was called over to witness the contract, then went to fetch my cloak.

We slipped out the western gate of the City and found a path along the riverbank. On the higher ground the trees were old and gnarled, but as we neared the swamp they gave way to stands of willow and tufts of reed.

The air was heavy at the end of the day, like thick honey, and fat, fleshy lilies floated on waters that reeked of rot. Our guide threaded a path between puddles and backwaters, where unseen things plopped into the stinking soup as we approached. Once I felt something squishy underfoot that wriggled silently away in the dark waters.

My skin began to crawl. What if this wicca wasn't a woman at all, but one of the hideous creatures the Saxons tell about around the fire? A horrid goblin, perhaps, or a were-creature, half beast, half human, that feeds on unsuspecting souls? The British sprites and spirits are generally bright and mischievous, but the sulky, bad-tempered creatures of the Saxon Otherworld are dark and ugly and thoroughly frightening.

By the time the shape of a hut rose out of the mists I wanted to bolt and run—only Frieda's hand on my arm stopped me.

I stumbled across the doorstep into a chaotic mix of smells, but as my eyes adjusted to the gloom, it was clear the place was neat and tidy, if crammed with jars and bags, hanging herbs and stacks of folded packets.

The hag who greeted us was blind in one eye and deaf to boot. She leaned so close to hear my request, I could count the hairs on the end of her nose. When Frieda and our guide had explained the bargain, the old woman shooed them outside, then turned to face me directly.

"Is it an easy delivery you want," she croaked, scrutinizing me with her one good eye, "or barrenness you wish to cure?"

"Delivery," I blurted out, refusing even to consider the other idea. "I need the assurance of a safe delivery."

The crone nodded thoughtfully, but that rheumy eye continued to peer at me. One scrawny finger scrabbled loosely against the air and at last, muttering to herself, she turned to the shelf of herbs behind her.

The last light of the sun glowed beyond a window paned with horn. A fly had gotten caught in a cobweb in its corner and buzzed noisily in an effort to escape.

The old woman's attention shifted to the sound; quick as lightning she captured the thing and held it prisoner in her fist while pulling the stopper out of a glass bottle. With a flick of the wrist she loosed the fly into the container and replaced the stopper. I could see the creature crawling over the desiccated bodies of similar captives, long since dead and dry.

"Everything's got a place in nature's pharmacy," the wicca admonished, grinning gleefully as she put the bottle back on the shelf. "Barrenness, you said," she went on, reaching for the leathery remains of a flattened toad.

"No, no, good woman," I burst out. "Just a safe delivery, that's all I need."

"Come now, child! Can't deliver what hasn't been spawned," she chided. "You trying to tell me you've conceived before but couldn't carry it full term?"

Hot, angry tears sprang to my eyes, and I wanted to shout at the old fool that she was wrong. I wasn't barren, I wasn't! But my need for the potion overrode my frustration, so I blinked hard and held my tongue.

"There, you see," she confirmed with a nod. "It's barrenness we need to find a cure for."

The woman puttered about at her workbench, pounding and crumbling bits of stuff into the mortar. Everything that went into it was dried and black or brown, sometimes crisp and sometimes lumpy, but all of it noxious. As a last precaution she added what she said was the wool of a bat, then filled the mortar with hot wine from a pan by the hearth and set it aside to steep. Seating herself on a stool next to the fire, the crone stared into the embers, musing as much to herself as to me.

"What if your moira doesn't include children? Many another queen has found her duties as a monarch more than enough to fill her time."

I started, wondering how she knew my rank, for neither I nor my companions had mentioned my name or title, and the dark cape didn't reflect my royal status.

"Ah, well." The wicca sighed with a cackle that might have been a laugh. "Arthur's son will keep you more than busy, my dear, so don't you fret."

The hair on my nape rose like a dog's; suddenly I wished I'd never sought help from this creature who knew too much. A fine, uneasy sweat broke out over my whole body.

" 'Tis no doubt well-enough done," she mumbled, sticking her finger into the brew and stirring it about. "Now you just drink it down, and see if that won't fix the problem."

I wrapped both hands around the warm bowl of the mortar and taking a deep breath, closed my eyes and began to gulp the mixture— past experience had taught me that the recipes for fertility were more often revolting than pleasant, and best gotten down as quickly as possible. But before I had drained the contents my throat closed and my stomach rebelled. I lowered the vessel slowly, willing the potion to stay down as long as possible.

The wicca snuffled and snorted by her hearth, and when I was convinced I wasn't going to vomit, I opened my eyes and found she had gone to sleep.

I stared at her closely, wondering if she was really the Goddess in her hag aspect. Saxon or Cumbri or Roman Briton, all old women draw closer to the Ancient Deity, no matter what name they call Her by. I searched for some sign of divinity, but all I found was a toothless crone whose fingers twitched as she snored by the fire.

Finally, clutching my cloak around me like a cocoon, I stole out the door and bumped into Frieda. That poor girl looked as frightened as I felt, and together with our guide we fled back to the gathering in London.

Ironically, between the mead that Arthur had drunk and the nausea the potion left me with, neither of us felt like making love that night. But I went to sleep convinced the experience had been worth it, for it had not escaped me that the witch had promised that Arthur and I would raise a son.

TEN

The Poisoning

rthur was hopping up and down, trying to pull his legging over one foot while balancing on the other.

"Treaties, truces, and rights of trade," he crowed. "Even more than I hoped for, Gwen. Why, some, like Wehha the Swede, have promised to join me in fighting the raiders, if need be. Do you realize what that means for the future?"

I nodded feebly, hard-pressed not to burst into tears. My belly ached from the brew I had drunk and my heart hurt each time I saw the bare spot on my finger where Mama's ring should have been. I knew Arthur had every reason to be jubilant, but at the moment I was too miserable to manage more than a smile.

Fortunately he was so excited by the new developments, he didn't question my indisposition. It was just as well—for some reason I didn't want to explain about the wicca.

We left London that afternoon. Everyone else was in high spirits, so I sat my horse regally and tried not to moan. The aches and pains moved slowly through my body, and by the time we reached Caerleon I had begun to perk up, knowing that Brigit would be waiting to greet us.

"King Mark made quite a fuss over the silver tray, and the Saxons were all impressed with our pomp and presents," I reported as she helped me unpack the lavish wardrobe. But when I told her the story

of the wicca, she looked at me with growing horror. "Mostly I'm sorry
I didn't see more of London—I'd like to go back sometime when I'm
feeling better," I concluded.

"God listen to the child!" My Irish friend hastily made the sign of
the cross. "They almost succeed in poisoning her and she talks about
going back. You should be thankful the Good Lord watches over you
. . . though He must be hard-pressed at times."

I grinned at that, suddenly very, very glad to be home.

Brigit's own summer had been less adventurous, but as she spoke of
life at the convent a serenity came into her voice that reminded me
of Igraine. I reached out and put my hand on her arm, interrupting her.

"It really is the right thing for you, isn't it?"

She looked up, half-glowing with an inner conviction, half-worried
about how I would react. We stared into each other's eyes, the whole
of our lives' caring summed in that long, searching gaze. A smile of
relief began to fill her face.

"Yes, Gwen . . . it really is."

"Then go with God," I whispered, looking away before my sorrow
at losing her could spoil it.

"Well, I won't be leaving quite yet—I'd like to stay with you through
the winter, or even until the baby comes, assuming the wicca's potion
works."

We threw our arms around each other then, laughing and crying at
the same time, and I blessed whatever Gods were responsible for having
given me so loyal a friend.

Since there had been no military victories to celebrate, Arthur decided to hold a tournament for the autumn gathering in Caerleon.
That tidy little town, tucked in a loop of the river Usk, had long
since taken the Pendragon to its heart; it was here he'd been crowned
king and here he'd stopped the Irish invasion. The town itself is full
of the stone walls and arches the Empire's engineers loved to make,
but the people are Cumbri to the core, and they welcomed us with
music and fanfares and great waves of cheering. Even the dancing
bear was brought out, and I wondered if it remembered when we
were here two years ago.

During the next few days the war-lords and heroes of the Round Table came streaming down the Road. Since the Fellowship was made up of hardy warriors more interested in gaming and gambling and wenching than courtly surroundings, most of them pitched their tents in the meadows.

King Urien arrived with his troops all wearing the badge of the Raven, while Cador, the Duke of Cornwall, made camp across the greensward from him. Men of the same generation, who'd been blooded warriors before Arthur was even born, there was a camaraderie of respect between them. It occurred to me that although Urien had led the northern kings in the civil war against Arthur and Cador was Gorlois's son and therefore had ample reason to resent Uther's heir, Arthur had won both men over so thoroughly that they were among our strongest allies.

Pelli had other business to attend to—no doubt involving a woman—but Lamorak brought the Wrekin contingent and they mixed with the men who lived with us—Gawain and his brother Gaheris, Palomides, Pelleas, Lancelot, and the rest. Added to these were strangers come to compete for a place in Arthur's cavalry, or just to enjoy the show.

The only guest I worried about was Morgan. We had invited her, of course, not only because of her position as High Priestess, but because Arthur was fonder of her than any other of his immediate family. Even the accidental mention of Morgause's name was enough to unleash an unreasonable anger in him, and both he and Igraine had suffered a kind of confused shyness toward each other. But he trusted Morgan. It was Morgan who had welcomed him after the Great Battle and acted as his spiritual mentor when he made a retreat at her Sanctuary. It was Morgan who encouraged him to accept the High Kingship and gave him the Sacred Sword Excalibur in a ceremony before the Kings of the Cumbri. So the idea of not including her at a High Court celebration was unthinkable. I just hoped that by now she and I could meet as friends—if she was willing to overlook her vexation with me, I'd forgive her for not coming to Bedivere's aid.

Morgan's arrival must have been impressive, for Enid burst into my room without even knocking. "The Lady of the Lake is here, M'lady, with a whole cadre of druids and men-at-arms!" Her voice mirrored her astonishment. "She wants to see you at the portico."

I took a deep breath and went to greet my sister-in-law.

The portico was full of people—women in white robes fluttering like butterflies, armed bodyguards standing at attention, and peasants begging to be allowed access to the High Priestess. Morgan herself was hidden by her devotees, so it was her lieutenant who left the group and strode toward me.

He was as barrel-chested and big-shouldered as a blacksmith, but something had crippled his legs so that they never grew in proportion to the rest of him. Dressed in a green livery, with breeches and high boots specially tailored to fit his stunted legs, his bizarre appearance gave him an ominous air.

The dwarf stared right through me as he approached. I studied his face, broad-cheeked and flat-nosed, and found it to be as closed to scrutiny as his mistress's was. Whatever went on behind those masks of power was well hidden from the world.

"Her Royal Highness, Queen Morgan le Fey, Co-ruler of Northumbria and High Priestess of the Old Gods," the dwarf announced, his deep voice filling the room.

Arthur's sister emerged from her entourage. Petite as she was, she moved with an absolute air of authority. An elegant golden coronet bearing the symbol of the Goddess held her black hair in place and the chill of her sea-green glance silenced everyone it fell on. She glided across the distance between us, inky shadows trailing in the sweep of her black cloak. Its richly embroidered border contained signs and symbols of the Goddess—I had no doubt a number of spells had been worked into their stitching, for Morgan was famous both as a needle-woman and a shamaness. I watched her approach, thinking she was also a master at making the grand entrance.

But when I stepped forward, arms extended for a kinsman's embrace, my sister-in-law drew back. I was left standing there, stupidly reaching out to empty space.

"I understand you've been to see a Saxon wicca," Morgan spat at me, ignoring my stammered welcome. "That was very ill advised, Guinevere—a stupid action, even for a girl of your limited background. The

Old Gods are jealous of their power, and do not take lightly to such foolishness. I will not sanction the results of your little excursion, whatever they may be. Now if you'll have a servant show me to my quarters . . ."

I stared at her, shocked in spite of myself. It had never occurred to me she would hear of my trip to Westminster, or take umbrage at it.

A long silence spun out between us while I searched her face for some sign that she might listen to my explanation. Finding none, I turned away and asked Enid to escort the High Priestess to her chambers. Without a word the group trailed off after their leader and I wondered how on earth we'd get through the next five days. . . . If only Igraine were here!

The tournament began next morning. Cei had erected an awning over the reviewing stand at the amphitheater, its bright colors adding to the gaiety of pennants and fluttering banners. Not only was it a festive touch, it was useful as well since the day turned unseasonably warm and by noontime everyone was sweltering.

I ordered the wine brought out and filled the hodgepodge of goblets myself. They ranged from glass to pottery, with a few stout pewter vessels and an occasional silver chalice, the last of some fine set long since lost or stolen. Ettard took the trays around to the nobles, and when she was done there were still three full goblets, two of them silver and one pewter.

The joust we were watching was long fought and hard won, for the horsemen were exceptionally well matched. A young man from Northumbria had come to court for the first time and was now acquitting himself marvelously. When he managed to unseat Palomides the audience rose to give the newcomer a standing ovation.

The victor dismounted and helped the Arab Companion to his feet, then made his way across the arena to where we sat. His hair was matted and he was covered with sweat, but pride glowed from his face when he bowed before his sovereigns.

I reached over and handed him one of the silver chalices, and passing the other to Arthur, raised the pewter goblet in a toast to the young man.

The crowd loved it, and after offering thanks to the Christian God the boy downed the drink in one long quaff. If I'd known he was that thirsty, I'd have given him water instead.

The lad held the chalice for an extra minute, examining the decorations that graced its rim. On a whim I called out for him to keep it—he deserved special recognition, and the vessel was a fitting gift.

The stranger went down on one knee with a simple thank-you and, wiping his mouth with the back of his hand, rose and started across the arena toward his horse.

I grinned as I watched him go, glad that the fame of the Fellowship was attracting such promising young men. At this rate we would have Champions of the Round Table living in every kingdom of Britain.

The boy stopped midway across the arena. Throwing up both arms, he suddenly swung round with a sweeping motion and started to run back toward us. There was something wild and giddy in his movements, and a jumble of words poured from his mouth—half-coherent praises for Arthur, half exclamations of savage glee. From the corner of my eye I saw Lancelot spur his horse across the arena to intercept the now hysterical stranger at the foot of our stand.

Staggering in the last few yards of his dash, the boy faltered, his arms flailing frantically. The Breton's horse shied, white-eyed and snorting, as the youngster plunged forward beneath its hooves, collapsing like a broken doll. The silver chalice rolled free of his grasp.

Lancelot leapt from his saddle and began peering into the lad's eyes, prying open his mouth and trying to read the pulse in his neck. But the stranger thrashed about so violently not even the big Breton could hold him still.

Jumping free, Arthur's lieutenant picked up the goblet and examined it carefully before bringing it up to his nose.

Silence had descended on the throng, and after one long, terrible minute, Lancelot lifted his eyes to me.

"It reeks of hemlock," he announced, never shifting his gaze. "It would seem the boy has been poisoned."

His words stole the color from the autumn day and I sat down abruptly, shaking my head in disbelief.

Arthur was leaning over the balustrade and Lance climbed up to join us, proffering the chalice as evidence. The High King sniffed it, then handed the thing to me with a grimace. Sure enough, a faint mousy smell lingered in the bottom of the cup, and I turned away, sickened.

The boy was in full convulsions, screaming and writhing on the ground. Morgan's dwarf was beside him, shooing people away while the High Priestess knelt above the youngster's head, trying to press something under his nose. I had not seen my sister-in-law in the audience, but blessed her presence and prayed that the Gods would give her the power to cure the lad. A pall was already spreading over our festival—if the boy died, the fear of murder could tear the Round Table apart.

We went on with the Feast that evening in spite of the disaster. It was clear that the Companions were deeply shaken by the day's events; standing in small, murmuring groups, they fell silent and kept their eyes downcast as we took our places at the Round Table. At my suggestion Dagonet called down a special blessing on the stricken guest before we started eating.

Morgan arrived midway through the second course and made her way to the center of the circle.

"The boy is dead." Her voice carried throughout the Hall, freezing it suddenly to silence. "Foully murdered, probably by someone who thought the fancy chalice was the King's own. There was no time to save him, just as there would have been no time to save Arthur, if he had been the one to drink the brew."

No one moved.

"I would say," the High Priestess went on, her green eyes narrowing, "that it was treachery gone astray, and we are lucky that the High King is still alive. For that we should thank the Gods, and pray the culprit be found and punished quickly."

A gasp ran through the gathering as the threat to their king became clear.

"Is there any way to tell who did this thing?" Arthur asked, his normally sunny voice gone dark.

"I saw no more than anyone else at the amphitheater." Morgan paused, waiting for the warriors to grow still again. "The Queen arranged for the goblets to be brought, poured out the wine for everyone, and later handed the chalice to the young man. That is all I know."

My breath caught in my throat. The bones of what she reported were true—I had poured the wine, and I had given the boy his death;

everyone had seen that. Yet Morgan was somehow implying that there was a connection between me and the poison, and the tension in the Hall became ominous. Caesar was lying at my feet and he raised his head, disturbed by the mood around us.

I looked more closely at my sister-in-law. She stood in the center of attention, black hair unbound and falling to her hips, heavy enameled armbands glimmering into view when she raised her arms and the sleeves of her white druid's robe fell back. She was the picture of divine aloofness—her expression betraying no emotion and her voice remaining absolutely neutral. No one would guess she carried a personal resentment toward me. My skin began to prickle.

"Are you making an accusation?" I demanded, the question bursting out without my volition.

Morgan studied some spot midway between herself and Arthur.

"Of course not," she said carefully. "I would never imply such a thing. Why, to plot to kill one's own husband, who is also the High King, would be a crime that cries to the heavens for vengeance."

She paused again, letting the idea sink in, then elaborately turned to face me. I cursed my unruly tongue as my stomach began to churn and the prickles on my skin turned to ice.

"No, I do not want to believe you capable of that sort of cunning." Morgan sighed and smiled sadly as though pondering some hidden sorrow she was loathe to make public. "Besides, whether you appreciate it or not, I love you as a sister and cannot imagine you'd turn without cause on my brother Arthur."

Her words were as smooth as silk, yet beneath the honeyed tone there was a noose, and I could feel it tightening around my neck.

The Companions debated this new development in hushed tones, then fell silent as a young man rose and asked permission to speak.

"I am Cadwaladr, cousin to the one who is dead." His voice filled with anguish. "I demand that the King charge whoever brought death to my kinsman with murder."

The words echoed through the Hall and Caesar dropped his muzzle back to his paws with a sigh.

Shocked, Arthur turned the full weight of his majesty on the lad.

"Are you accusing the Queen?"

The boy gulped, glanced over at Morgan, and then nodded. "We all saw her give him the goblet, and whether it was meant for him or for you, a death followed."

I could swear the fellow had been coached.

Arthur stared at him in disbelief, bafflement and anger beginning to war across his face.

Morgan raised her hands as though making a pronouncement from the Gods. "Such a charge requires the Queen's name be cleared in a Trial by Combat."

Arthur and I both caught our breath, horrified at the idea an antique ritual could supplant logic and justice.

"The Old Ways are very specific about removing a stain from the reputation of a queen, for she is the voice of the people, and must be trustworthy in all things." The High Priestess's voice was full of pious regret.

Arthur glanced at the men of the Round Table. They sat as though made of stone, some meeting his eyes, some not, but none so much as shifting in their seats. At last the High King directed his attention to the supplicant before us.

"Are you, Cadwaladr, willing to meet the Queen's Champion at dawn tomorrow in a Trial by Combat?"

The boy, so recently bereaved, now found himself challenged by the very King he'd hoped to serve, and he quailed noticeably.

"Either agree to carry your accusation to the field, or withdraw it," Arthur thundered.

Stammering, the lad consented to the Trial, and Arthur swung back to our warriors.

"Well now, which of you will volunteer to champion the Queen?"

There was an awful silence, and my stomach tied itself in knots.

Arthur's fingers curled into a fist, and he slammed that hand into the palm of the other, cracking the knuckles as he did so.

"I don't see how anyone could think Guinevere guilty of such a thing," he bellowed, his voice rough with indignation. "She is a loyal wife, a true companion, a trustworthy counselor, and a fine Queen. Every one of you here has benefited from her caring and concern, and I am ashamed that you would impugn her honor in this fashion."

He paused to glare at each Companion. I dared not look at them but stared only at my husband. When his gaze had swept the Hall he turned directly to me and reached for his goblet. Tossing the contents on the floor, he held it out for me to refill.

I leaned forward to do so, suddenly reminded that I had filled his cup on the occasion of our first meeting. Now, as then, I smiled at him gratefully.

He raised the goblet, and proposing a toast to me, drained it completely and turned the chalice upside down as proof of his trust.

But still the Companions were silent.

"Very well." His voice was stern and measured. "I appoint Lancelot of the Lake to champion the Queen's cause tomorrow. Should he be beaten and killed, it will be proof of Guinevere's guilt; should he prevail, she will be considered cleared of all charges."

Arthur looked slowly around the circle, daring anyone to take umbrage with his order, and the knot in my stomach threatened to bring up my dinner on the spot. Under the table I gave my husband's thigh a pat, then excused myself and fled to my room, stopping at the courtyard drain only long enough to lose my food.

Brigit held my head and fetched a drink of water from the fountain. When we reached the royal apartment she bundled me up in the down comforter as my teeth began to chatter and my hands turned cold.

It gave promise of being a long and terrible night.

ELEVEN

Accusations

organ stood before me, laughing to herself as she lifted the infant from my arms. "Will not sanction, sanction, sanction it," she cooed, dandling my dream child over an abyss.

I whimpered and the Lady turned on me with a hiss. "Shush—you'll waken it; see how it cries to heaven for vengeance." She capered on the edge of the chasm, threatening to drop my baby.

Sobbing, I lunged for it, twisted in the void, saw the young man writhing below, drawing me down . . . down into the darkness. . . .

Brigit's arms were around me, holding me, rocking me just as Mama used to when I had nightmares as a youngster. She was humming snatches of the lullaby that Mama used to sing, that Kevin crooned the night we escaped from the Black Lake. I gasped for air, for waking . . . and found the memory of possible death in the morning. Awake or asleep, terror lurked everywhere.

"Sir Lancelot wishes to see you."

Ettard's words filled my ears but their message escaped me. Drowsily I thought about Arthur's choice of the arrogant Breton to defend me. Clearly he was the most reliable of the Champions, even if he did scorn me with silence. And now, through some strange twist, our moiras had become entwined, making us each central to the life—or death—of the other. His death in the Trial would bring about my death, too, and by surviving himself, he would guarantee my own continued life. It seemed an odd partnership for people who didn't like each other.

"He's requesting a personal audience," the convent girl repeated. "And asks that it be private."

I struggled to full wakefulness and saw Brigit's eyebrows lift.

"There's no need to worry about propriety where Lancelot and I are concerned," I assured her. "You know we barely tolerate each other."

The nausea returned as I sat up, and I patted Brigit's hand. It was she who had suggested that my upset stomach might be caused by pregnancy, if the wicca's charm had worked.

That was the one bright hope in this otherwise horrible night, and I clung to it fiercely while Brigit combed out my hair and Ettard helped me into a robe. The irony that I was finally harboring a new life at a time when my own was in danger did not escape me.

A waning moon was scudding through the clouds and I paused to stare up at at the poor, lopsided thing, wondering what Arthur's lieutenant would say.

Perhaps, since both our futures depended on his prowess tomorrow, he was coming to offer a word of encouragement. That would be a kindness I'd appreciate right now. Or even better, he might be gracious enough to apologize for his past rudeness and agree to end our hostilities.

If that's the case, I told the moon, I'll meet him halfway.

When I was settled in my chair and the door opened, I turned toward it expectantly, a smile of appreciation already on my lips.

Lancelot entered without a word and planted himself midway across the room. In the dim light of the lamp I couldn't read his expression, but his manner was quiet as he folded his arms and waited for my women to leave.

"Since I am going to be championing you in a few hours," he began, once we were alone, "there is something I wish you to know."

I leaned forward, trying to gauge his mood as the moon limped out from behind her clouds and cast a cold light across his face. For the first time I saw the fierce anger burning in his eyes. It was so startling, I recoiled as from a blow.

"I may die in that combat, M'lady, and if that happens, I don't want to go to my grave with you thinking I willingly defended you. Oh, I'll fight as well as I know how, but only because Arthur has commanded it . . . you haven't duped me as easily as you have the rest."

Stunned, I stared speechlessly at the man, waiting for him to explain. But he stood his ground in silence, dark and immutable. Used to Arthur's pacing in times of crisis, Lancelot's stillness made me nervous and I rose to my feet.

"What do you mean, 'duped'?" I snapped.

He gave a snort. "You forget, I was raised in the Sanctuary of the Goddess. I know how the Celts harbor grudges—and that many see Arthur as an interloper. The Lady may have gotten them to accept him as their High King, but I have no doubt there are some who would like to see him dead."

He paused, his tone so calm and assured I could hardly believe he was speaking of treason.

"Whether you are an assassin trained for the job from the beginning, or the unwitting pawn of others, the fact remains that you had both the means and opportunity to concoct that poison and give it to your husband."

"I beg your pardon!" I stalked across the room, stung by his accusation. Rounding on him suddenly, I demanded, "Whatever are you talking about?"

"About your consorting with the old hags in the woods. And about your visit to a Saxon wicca—a creature who may well want Arthur dead," he shot back.

His mention of the wicca caught me totally off guard. I was shocked on the one hand that my private business was being held up to ridicule and enraged on the other that he so easily assumed my actions were motivated by treachery. Added to that was his damnably smug conviction that he was right. Outrage began to rise in me.

"You're right, I met with the wicca," I retorted, striding to the opposite end of the room. "And I've practiced all manner of rites and done all sorts of things, both with my husband and alone."

The force of my indignation brought me back, and I began to circle my accuser like an animal. My voice was low and measured, and I moved around him as I spoke, so that he had to turn constantly to face me.

"Not only that, I have been present when vile potions were brewed, and drunk the wretched things down when every sense in body and mind rejected them. I've done all that, and more. And would do it again," I added, stressing every word carefully, "if it would insure a child for Arthur."

Coming to a stop, I pulled myself up as tall as possible and met the Breton's gaze eye to eye.

"Can you, my fine fellow, say you would do as much for your King?"

Dumbfounded, the lieutenant stared back at me, his eyes wide with astonishment.

By now a flaming pride was coursing through me. No pompous newcomer from Brittany was going to cast doubt on *my* motives, much less my loyalty to Arthur. I had every right to have the man thrown in irons—except that I needed him to fight for me on the morrow!

The ludicrousness of the situation struck home and I would have laughed aloud, but the room was beginning to spin and the last thing I remember was Lancelot reaching to break my fall as the floor rushed up to claim me.

I came to sometime in the night, rising from a dreamless place to see Arthur sitting on the edge of the bed. Still half-asleep, I wondered why he looked so worried. I wanted to reach out and take him in my arms, but when he saw I was awake he brushed a broad hand across my brow.

"Brigit says you've lost a lot of blood, and must stay quiet."

The words made no sense, and I frowned up at him, confused. "Blood?"

The Irish girl was beside me then, and as Arthur rose she settled into his spot.

"Your flow is much heavier than usual," she said gently. "But whatever caused the first gushing has passed, and a few days on beef broth and bed rest should see you well again."

Suddenly memory flooded back—the accusations, the trial, the fact that I might be pregnant. Or might have *been* pregnant.

"You mean . . ." The words wouldn't come out, and I looked hastily from Brigit to Arthur. I had not yet told him, so he couldn't know how cruel this news was.

Brigit's nod confirmed my fear.

"And the Trial?" I whispered.

"It will be held in about three hours." Arthur sighed deeply. "Lance asked me to assure you he'll do his best."

My eyes filled with unshed tears—sorrow, pain, hope, fear—they were all there. I turned my face away, not wanting to weep in Arthur's presence.

Brigit rose quietly, leaning over to straighten the pillows and smooth the blankets. "Time you get some sleep, M'lady. And you too, M'lord. You'll both need all the strength you've got come morning."

Arthur mumbled something about staying in the other room, then came over to the bed and wished me an awkward good-night. I wanted to cry out, to beg him to hold me safe until dawn, to let the tangle of misery all pour out. But instead of lifting me in his arms, my husband took my hands in his own and stared silently into my face. Then with a gulp he dropped my fingers and headed for the door.

I stared after him, knowing it was not the first time in life I'd had no one to turn to, but that didn't help. Looking down at the bare spot where Mama's ring used to be, I tried to think what she would do in such a plight. Probably get a good night's rest, I thought wryly as the tears broke loose and I began to sob.

At sunrise Lancelot rode forth and did battle with the boy who had voiced the charges Morgan whipped up against me. The lad proved to be as competent as his cousin on horseback, but Lance's skill with the sword gave him the edge on foot. Before the dew was dry on the grasses Arthur's lieutenant had the stranger pinned to the ground, and suggested he retract the accusation of murder in exchange for his life. Fortunately the youngster had the sense to accept the offer.

I was grateful Lance gave him the option; at least I wouldn't be held accountable for two deaths in this wretched affair.

Minding Brigit's instructions, I stayed in bed for the next two days. It gave me a chance to think about what had happened.

Whether I had miscarried or not was uncertain—but even if I had, it was but a poignant result of the greater crisis.

Lance's fear that I would bring death to the High King explained a good deal of his behavior. Hopefully he'd look on me with less suspicion now, and recognizing that we were each dedicated to Arthur, we might eventually become friends.

The fact that none of the other warriors had come to my aid was harder to understand. Clearly they'd been scared and confused at the start of the Feast, even before the boy had died. Perhaps they had already heard about the wicca and misunderstood my motives just as Lancelot had. That didn't make sense, since Brigit and Frieda were the only others who knew . . . and Morgan.

I lay back among the pillows with a sigh. How many times had I made excuses for Morgan? In her own way she was as beautiful and passionate as Igraine, and she gloried in being the High Priestess with the absolute conviction that she was the favorite of the Gods. Everyone in Britain stood in awe of her, and the first time I met her, I'd been filled with dread and terror.

But Morgan was also a woman prone to wild mood swings, able to go from charming graciousness to temper tantrums or cold arrogance in remarkably short order. I had tried to make allowances for that, hoping that her rage at me would diminish as her affair with Accolon cooled. But now it seemed she bore me a grudge far deeper than the discovery of her liaison.

Perhaps she resented my being so close to Igraine, when she was not. Or maybe she could not forget that if it weren't for Arthur, she and Urien could have been High King and Queen. Whatever her reasons, it was obvious that while I'd been trying to mend a family spat, Morgan had become my deadly enemy.

Not that I thought she'd planted the poison—Morgan had helped put Arthur on the throne, so she would surely not want to kill him. But making use of the moment is one of her specialties, and her rush to place the blame on me could hardly be denied. I didn't like the idea, but if Lancelot had failed in the Trial, both he and I would be dead by now—because of Morgan.

On the afternoon of the second day I pushed aside Brigit's cluckings and dressed for Court; there were a few matters I wished to take up with the Lady of the Lake.

. . .

"Left yesterday," Cook said, scowling at the fish she was scaling. "And no word to the kitchen, even. Her whole party gone—poof—like magic."

Cook flipped the fish over and attacked the other side, her irritation making the silver scales scatter in the sunlight. I turned away, my anger with my sister-in-law flashing in much the same way.

Come into my Court, would she, and snub me dead upon our meeting? Play on innuendos and fear to charge me with murder, and build the net so skillfully that not even the High King could stop it? And after threatening both my honor and my life, disappear before she's called to account . . . gone, just like that—poof—leaving the commoners to marvel over her magic.

Venomous bitch, I thought, heading for the room with the long table where Arthur and I ran the realm. At least it was clear that my husband hadn't been fooled. Bless him, he might be guarded and obtuse about expressions of love, but he'd rallied to my cause in a way that left no question of his belief in me.

Lance and Arthur were studying one of Merlin's scrolls when I came in, and both gave me a welcoming smile. It was the first time Lance had greeted me with anything other than disdain.

"I think I owe you an apology, M'lady," the Breton said, moving toward me.

"I owe you a great deal more," I replied, extending my hand as I crossed the room.

"We both do," Arthur interrupted, taking both my hand and Lancelot's and bringing them together with his own. "So much so that from now on Lance will be known as the Queen's Champion. It is an honor he earned in the arena of the Trial."

There was much relief in Arthur's voice, as though the tension between his lieutenant and his wife had been obvious even to him, and now he was glad things were resolved.

For a moment the three of us stood there, laughing and beaming at each other, and then Arthur let us go and we all moved toward the table.

"Well," Lance mused, "the Combat satisfied the Old Ways and left the courtiers feeling that something had been done about a needless death. Fortunately neither my opponent nor I suffered more than a few bruises, though I was sorry to see the lad go home; we could have used him among the Companions."

"But it didn't solve the question of who put the poison in the cup, or why," I pointed out, pulling up a stool and sitting down across from them.

"That's what we've just been discussing." Arthur rolled up the scroll and slid the lead guard up its threads to keep the thing closed. "Seems one of Urien's pages saw someone fiddle with the goblets while Ettard was talking with Gawain. The fellow wore no badge, but with so many strangers at the tournament, the page didn't think much of it. He did notice a scar that ran from the man's cheek to his chin, but that's about all."

Arthur looked over at me with a nod. "I've told the Companions to keep an eye out for him, but doubt they'll turn up much—many warriors are scarred that way. Besides, every king has enemies, so I'm not going to waste time worrying over this one. What bothers me most is how easily the concept of justice was swept aside in favor of the Old Ways."

He turned from the table and began to move about the room. "Trial by Combat, indeed! Doesn't do anything to find the culprit. And it certainly makes a mockery of things when guilt is decided by who has the most powerful Champion in the arena. We've got to reinstate the concept of justice based on law and responsibility. It's the only way to keep civilization alive."

"You might begin by telling that to Morgan," I suggested.

"Oh, she couldn't agree more," Arthur said blithely. "We had a long talk after you left the feast. She was devastated about the misunderstanding over my message to come to Silchester at the end of the Irish campaign—thought she was supposed to wait for further confirmation, which of course she never got. And she was heartsick at having to order the Trial by Combat; Morgan doesn't approve of such ordeals herself. But considering the mood of the crowd when they realized the poison was meant for me . . . well, it was the best she could do to keep the mob from taking action right then. I told her we were both most grateful."

I jumped to my feet with an oath. "Grateful, my foot! That woman made everyone think I was guilty of *murder,* Arthur. For two years she's brooded over a wrong she's afraid I might commit against her, and it's gotten all twisted up into plots and schemes and false accusations . . ."

My jaw went closed with a snap. I was standing directly in front of my husband, staring up into his face. But instead of understanding and concern, I found the same closed mask his sister habitually wore.

Arthur moved away from me, heading back to the table where Lance was discreetly studying the map.

"She told me how you've taken a dislike to her, Gwen; undermining her position among the women whenever possible. I think, considering your attitude, that she's been most forgiving and helpful. I don't want to hear any more about it, but I suggest you try to find some way to make amends."

I stared at his back, a torrent of words held in check by Lancelot's presence. My face was hot with embarrassment that Arthur and I were having our first quarrel in front of an audience.

Furious, I turned on my heel and left, striding through the curtains without a backward glance.

In the Hall I ran into Pelleas and Gawain, and it took little urging to get them to escort me on a ride. Before long we were racing over the hills, letting the clean air of the countryside sweep away the musty, mousy smell of Morgan's scheming.

But next time, I vowed . . . next time I'll be prepared. The Lady of the Lake wouldn't find me such an easy target again.

TWELVE

The Wise Ones

"Ye Gods, Gwen, if the barbaric Saxons can accept a code of rules to live by, surely the Britons can do the same!" Arthur's voice was sharp with frustration. Ever since the Trial by Combat he had been exploring the idea of a universal legal system, but the client Kings were wary and balked at the idea.

"I'm not talking about bringing back all of the old Roman system," he grumbled. "Just reinstating a basic level of justice that can be counted on throughout the realm. That was one of the Empire's great strengths, and it would do more to unite Britain than anything else I can think of."

"Ah, but that's the rub," Lance interjected. "The client Kings are afraid of anything that doesn't increase their own power . . . half of them are barely hanging on to their subjects' loyalty as it is." His voice slid into a parody of King Mark. "If we accept this nonsense about the High King's justice, next thing you know the people will start calling the Pendragon 'Emperor,' and then where will we be?"

Lance mimicked the portly Cornish leader so perfectly that both Arthur and I burst out laughing.

We were coming up from the beach at Newport, riding three abreast on our way back to Caerleon where we were going to spend the winter. Cei was busy procuring supplies and organizing our men into work parties to help clear the Roads or repair weirs, while Gawain kept the warriors in fighting trim. Arthur and I concentrated on matters of state, and generally asked Lancelot to sit in with us.

I stole a look at the Breton. As the fall ripened he had become much more relaxed with me, and we moved into the same kind of working threesome Bedivere and Arthur and I had known. Together we spent hours talking and laughing and arguing as we winnowed a host of new ideas for the Cause, though none of us realized we were sowing the seeds of a harvest far greater than our present dreams.

Since the weather was mild, we visited the nearby client Kings along the southern coast of Wales. This was the land of Igraine's birth, a place of soft green hills and winding valleys, rimmed with sandy beaches and dotted with cities not yet deserted and dying.

The people were a wonderfully exotic lot, retaining colorful scraps of past luxury whether they lived in old villas or rough-hewn steadings. As yet untouched by the Saxon plague, their harbors were still visited by Mediterranean ships. The aristocrats sent their children to the Continent to be educated, and some even rode about in contraptions called carriages.

Agricola had such a conveyance and had let me ride in it on the trip south to marry Arthur. Now that we were staying so near Demetia, he put it entirely at my disposal. Far lighter than a farm wagon, when the team was at full gallop we whisked over the paved Road like a cloud across the morning sky. All my childhood dreams of being a warrior rose up around me, and I'd imagine I was Boadicea in her wicker war-chariot, leading British troops into battle. If it wasn't for the fact that Arthur would have teased me unmercifully about it, I would have asked if we couldn't get one to keep with us always.

"You're right handy with a pair, M'lady," the war-lord Poulentis exclaimed the day Arthur let me handle the horses on the way out to the hill-fort at Dinas Powys. Our host stood in the midst of an unpaved court, his swordbelt worked in the Byzantine manner and a necklace of Egyptian glass beads circling his neck, though his homespun trews were ragged and patched.

"Can't say as how I've a taste for such frippery," he added, grinning good-naturedly at the vehicle. "Or fancy houses with plaster and murals. Drystone walls were good enough for my ancestors—they're good enough for me."

Poulentis led the way into his small, rugged Hall and gestured toward the hearth at the far end of the oval where haunches of pork crisped and sizzled on the spit. "I'm more in need of a sty for my new pigs than a carriage for my vanity."

I laughed with pleasure, taking in the familiar sight of guests seated around the open fire. Sparrows and mice rustled in the thick thatch of the roof, and for a moment it felt as though I were home again in Rheged.

"You do know Illtud, don't you?" Our host asked as an impressive gray-haired gentleman rose to his feet at our approach. He had a majestic air not common in those who wear the simple robes of a Christian monk and I tried to remember where I'd seen him before.

"He's Igraine's cousin," Poulentis whispered as the newcomer greeted Arthur with a kinsman's embrace. "Used to rule this whole area."

It came back then, the memory of the man who had been a powerful Prince and fine warrior but chose to renounce it all in favor of the Church.

"M'lady." Illtud smiled easily at me as we sat down. "I hear that you and my young cousin are doing fine things in Logres. The peasants prosper, the shores are safe, and Britain no longer bleeds with internal feuds." He helped himself to a chunk of bread and turned to Arthur. "That trip along the Saxon Shore seems to have solidified your presence among the Federates. What's your biggest concern at the moment?"

"Communication," Arthur responded, obviously as impressed as I was by Illtud's knowledge of our affairs. "I'm developing a royal messenger network, but it takes time."

The monk chewed thoughtfully. "Have you thought about using beacons? The Romans built a lot of signal towers in the north, of course, but you have the natural geography to help you here."

Arthur put down his drinking horn and turned his full attention on the holy man. Illtud cleared a space on the table and moved the wine flagon to the center, then lined up the enamel salt bowl and a wooden trencher as he talked.

"From the rampart here at Dinas Powys you can see Brent Knoll in Somerset. Beyond that is Glastonbury Tor, and from there one can see both north and south with equal ease. Of course," the monk added, "you might have some problem with that old scoundrel Gwyn—I hear he's appropriating the Tor for himself, and may not be cooperative about a beacon."

Arthur grinned. "Gwyn and I have an understanding—and a mutual venture in horsebreeding."

"Ah, so you've already encountered your fey neighbor?" Illtud's laugh was very gentle for a man so big. "Well, if you decide you'd like to have a western stable here, my estate at Llantwit is at your disposal. You could bring your foals for training, and rest the seasoned horses after campaigning. Be good for my students, also—they need a little grounding in practical matters. We've more than enough wandering hermits burning with zeal for the Christ; what we need now are priests who can help the people on an everyday level, with education and medicine and better ways of farming. It comes a little hard to some of the boys," he added wryly. "Youngsters like Samson and Paul Aurelian get awfully carried away with the Spirit; even Gildas turns more toward books than working with the laity."

I started at the last name, for I'd known Caw's son in my child-hood—had, in fact, rejected his proposal of marriage. I didn't realize he had joined a monastery here in south Wales, however.

"Now then, what are you going to do with this Round Table of yours?" Illtud asked.

Arthur stared at him blankly. "Do with it, Cousin?"

"Yes, do with it. To have developed a fighting force such as your cavalry; to have bound them to you in the Fellowship which is now becoming famous; to have gotten them to lay aside family feuds in order to follow you . . . all these things are commendable. Well-nigh impossible, I would have said, knowing how touchy the Celts can be. Surely you aren't going to stop there?"

I wondered what Arthur was going to answer, but just then Poulentis turned to me, noting that the fine ceramic finger bowl the servant proffered was a new acquisition. I studied it carefully, intrigued by the decoration of leopards that chased each other along its clay curves.

"The spotted cat of Anglesey?" I joked, remembering the story of Palug's sons who took pity on a speckled kitten that had washed up on their shore, only to have it grow up into a ferocious beast that prowled their woods.

"That creature gets bigger and fiercer as time goes by." Poulentis laughed good-naturedly.

"So you don't believe it's the descendent of a leopard escaped from one of the Roman circuses? Maybe it came from Maelgwn's menagerie?"

"Menagerie indeed." The war-lord's face went hard with disgust. "King Maelgwn is a braggart who will embroider any detail to make his Court seem more exotic. Recently he's been boasting that new brute of a dog he's so proud of came from the Otherworld. Named it Dormarth—Death's Door. Next thing you know he'll be claiming to keep dragons and griffins as everyday pets!"

Poulentis's assessment of my cousin was heartening. It was a relief to know that others found him as vainglorious and arrogant as I did. My dealings with Maelgwn had been very unpleasant; before I married Arthur he'd tried to force himself on me, and when I'd blackened his eye in the struggle, he claimed he'd been hit by a whore.

The memory sent a shiver across my shoulders—part loathing, part fear because Maelgwn had sworn to get revenge for my rebuff. I'd never mentioned the incident to Arthur lest it provoke strife that we could ill afford, for we needed the King of Gwynedd as a northern ally. But the very thought of the man was unsettling, so I turned the conversation to the pigs Poulentis was raising. Pleased to talk about his own pet project, our host began describing the animals he'd just gotten from Pembrokeshire and the subject of my cousin was forgotten.

It was when we neared Carmarthen that people began asking about Merlin—he'd been raised nearby, and now that he and Nimue had been gone for more than two years, there was both curiosity and speculation about the Magician's whereabouts.

"I happen to know," the miller confided, "that the Wizard has returned to that cave he calls home, but is keeping his presence a secret."

"Really?" I tried to turn my amusement into amazement; Merlin would hardly come back to Britain without informing Arthur.

"Absolutely." The man nodded with certainty. "From time to time his page rides down from the hills and passes by my mill on the way to town for supplies."

"Whatever would a Magician need with supplies?" I queried, remembering that Merlin never missed an opportunity to reinforce the idea that both he and his powers were supernatural. It was, he'd explained to Arthur, one way to keep the High King's enemies off balance.

"More like the supplies are for the page," the miller answered shrewdly. "An enchanter doesn't need other than a fern-seed for invisibility and a dream to weave into substance."

I grinned at the man's pride in being so clever and let the matter drop. But two days later, while Arthur and Agricola took the carriage out to survey a section of Demetia's Roads, Griflet and I rode up the path toward the Sorcerer's cave.

It was nearing midwinter, but the day was full of that soft sunshine that sometimes warms the marrow of an aged year. The dogs ranged through the woods beside the trail and Featherfoot seemed as glad of a chance to go adventuring as I was—it put me in mind of the years in Rheged.

Once past the stream by the mill Griflet looked around nervously. "Do you think the Wizard will be home, M'lady?" The Kennel Master's brow was furrowed with apprehension, and he crossed himself quickly when a doe bounded unexpectedly across our path. "They say Merlin's cave is made of crystal that leaps with color in the flicker of a torch, and strange music drifts up from its depths—that's where he sees things not meant for human sight. Do you think, M'lady, that he'll expect us to enter it?"

I grinned at Ulfin's son and suggested that he should stay outside with the horses. In truth I had no desire to go into the Sorcerer's world either, for Merlin and I had never been friends, but I was very fond of Nimue and wanted to determine that they really were back before telling Arthur about the rumor.

It was the dogs who found the turnoff from the path, rounding a hawthorn hedge and leading us to the edge of a meadow. A single pony watched from the lean-to built into the lee of the hill and nickered as we approached. I called the dogs to heel lest they frighten the animal while Griflet took a long look around.

Bounded on all sides by the forest, the broad breast of the hill was open to both sky and wind. A ledge of gray rock protruded from beneath the long, low opening of the cave's entrance and the green of ferns indicated a spring close by. The rockwork was free of debris and a pilgrim's cup rested in the niche above the pooled water.

Something shadowy moved within the cave and Griflet watched it intently as I dismounted and bent to fill the cup. I made a show of pouring out an oblation for the Gods so that whoever guarded the cave could see we came in peace.

"Gwenhwyvaer. . . ."

The sound was clear and unmistakable, and the hair on my arms began to lift. Twice before I had heard the Goddess speak, and now She was calling me specifically by my ancient name.

"White Shadow of the North, well come to Merlin's home."

I turned slowly, staring up at the figure that moved into the light of day. She had the form of Nimue, albeit now dressed in the breeches and tunic of a page rather than the white robe of a priestess, but her eyes were huge and black with the presence of the Goddess.

Griflet dismounted and we sank to our knees as the Mother of us all came forward. Earth and sky trembled at Her approach, and I closed my eyes tightly before she laid Her hands on our heads in blessing.

"Why are you crying, child?" The voice was deep and vibrant, echoing with the Otherworld.

"Barren. . . ." I whispered. "I . . . I can't have children."

"Of course you can—and will—in the fullness of time."

It must have seemed a small thing to the Goddess, for She spoke lightly, as though reassuring a child. The dread that had crept into my thoughts in recent months tattered and dissolved under the spell of her assurance. Waves of relief flooded through me, and I lifted my face toward Her, still careful to keep my eyes shut. One does not stare into the naked visage of any deity.

Slowly Her hands moved from my temples, across my eyelids, and down my cheeks. When She withdrew her touch and I finally opened my eyes, it was Nimue who looked down at me. She was every bit as young and beautiful as I remembered, and I was delighted she had returned.

"It is good to see you in such fine health, M'lady," the priestess said, her voice shrinking back to its normal size.

Griflet rose to his feet and busied himself with the dogs and horses. I noticed that in spite of the fact that he was Christian, he had accepted her blessing without a fuss and smiled shyly at Nimue when she greeted him.

The priestess was silent as we made our way across the meadow, but when we reached the ledge of the cave she gestured to a stump that had been placed among the boulders. "No need to go in. The sun has warmed the rocks and the view is lovely today."

She seated herself tailor-fashion on the ledge while I perched on the wooden seat, silently relieved that any encounters with Merlin would take place in the open.

"When did you two get back? And why haven't you come to Court? We heard you went to see Clovis—are the Franks really as barbaric as they say?"

My questions tumbled out in a flood, but the priestess stared out over the vale for a long time before she answered.

"Merlin's not with me, Gwen. I've come back alone . . . to get things ready . . . so he can join me later." Her voice was uncertain until she suddenly turned to me with a smile. "All of Europe talks about the warriors of Arthur's Round Table. Every Champion wants to join the Fellowship and follow the owner of Excalibur into great battles. Is it true he's routed every enemy he's gone against?"

"That's just rumor; mostly he's been able to make truces," I countered, remembering that long ago the Wizard had promised Arthur's fame as King and peacemaker would outlive his reputation as a warrior. "Whatever has kept Merlin in Brittany?"

Nimue's face stiffened and she turned away, her voice sinking to a whisper.

"I have given my oath not to speak of that."

I looked at my friend more closely, searching the face of the girl who had dared to love the timeless Magician. When she first came to Court she'd been a doire, the holy keeper of a sacred well. And though I later learned she had studied with Morgan—who had grown uneasy with her powers and driven her away—there had always been an innocence about her that I trusted.

Now she was changed. Although she spoke with the same gentleness as before, there was something brittle and unyielding in her manner, like the shell of a crab, and it hid, or protected, the innocence I remembered. Even her voice was different—cold and constrained— and I had no choice but to honor her promise not to discuss Merlin's absence.

So we talked of other things—of Igraine's death, and King Mark's marriage, Morgan's effort to blame me for the young man's murder and Lance's saving my life in the Trial by Combat. The priestess listened gravely to that story and asked if I'd spoken with Morgan since. When I told her no, she nodded thoughtfully to herself but made no comment.

For her part, Nimue told me of the places she and the Enchanter had visited together, of the university at Bordeaux where Merlin was much in demand as a teacher of natural science, and of Marseilles where traders from all over the world tie up at the docks and goods from China are bartered for Baltic amber or Spanish oranges.

Her voice warmed as we talked, and by the time I rose to leave she had promised to send word as soon as the Enchanter arrived, in return for my swearing not to reveal her presence in Britain to anyone, even Arthur.

"The people would begin to hound me with entreaties for themselves or questions about the Magician, and I'm not ready for that yet," she said softly.

So I gave her my word, still wondering what had changed her so.

We walked down to where Griflet waited with the horses, and I gave her a farewell hug. The doire trembled as though on the verge of tears but abruptly began to perform the Blessing for the Road.

"Remember to have patience," she admonished as I mounted Featherfoot. "This is the springtime of your reign, and you and Arthur have splendid work to do in the kingdom yet. There'll be time for raising children later."

I smiled at that, touched and reassured. Merlin, the Great Mage of Britain, had respected her gifts enough to make her the Goddess of his old age, so if Nimue said we would have children, I was content.

When Griflet and I reached the screen of hawthorns I looked back to wave a farewell. The doire stood on her cave ledge, alone and proud, like the first woman of all time. But instead of watching us she was looking up at the sky, searching for something beyond human ken.

It was only later, when winter was waning, that the threads of our encounters began to weave into the moira of the future.

Arthur and Lance and I were strolling along the beach at Newport while the dogs snuffled through the seaweed and the gulls wheeled overhead.

"The people and the warriors will follow any suggestion I make," Arthur mused. "If I tell them we need a code of law, they'll accept it. It's the leaders I can't convince. There's got to be an answer—Merlin would have one, I'm sure, if I could only ask him."

My husband paused to pick up a shell, hefted it for a moment in his hand, then let it drop. I wanted to tell him that Merlin was on his way, that the doire had come back and was preparing the cave, but a promise to Nimue was a promise to the Goddess, and I dared not break it. Instead, I turned Arthur's own thought into a question.

"If you could talk to Merlin, what would he suggest?"

"Oh, I don't know. Probably something similar to the Round Table . . . membership as an honor reserved for only a few . . . those who agreed to follow a certain code . . ."

He stopped, suddenly engrossed in thought, and Lancelot voiced the idea that had come to all our minds at once.

"Why can't the political leaders be included at the Round Table?"

The question hung in the air, bright as a thrush's song, and Arthur turned to us, an exuberant grin spreading across his face.

"Of course! We'll *use* the Round Table, just as Illtud suggested. Merlin promised the warriors glory when they were starved for it; we'll do the same for the nobles, but instead of fame in battle, we'll offer them glory in their Courts. By giving them membership in the Round Table, we'll extend the mantle of our fame over them—provide them a special aura of excellence . . . and a code of law, as well."

He turned to me, full of questions. "Can we do it? Can we make the High Court so admirable, so exciting, so colorful, that every other chieftain will want to be part of it?"

"I don't see why not." I laughed, swept up by his vision. "With you and the Cause to build on, Cei's talent for pomp and Lance's cavalry tournaments for the warriors, the Pendragon's Court could become the envy of the whole world."

I was half jesting, but my husband was absolutely serious, so I hastily amended, "Or at least from here to Constantinople."

Arthur's doubts vanished. "We'll begin this summer. I'll convene a meeting of all the leaders of the realm and fairly dazzle them with magnificence—give them a chance to see what the Round Table could be, and whet their appetite to join."

He threw back his head in a wonderful laugh while Lance and I joined in, and all three of us went spinning and gamboling along the edge of the surf like puppies chasing their own tails.

So word was sent from the summer Isles of Scilly to the windswept heights of Pictland that the leaders were invited to attend a Round Table Council in London. There would be feasting and tournaments, games and dancing, and all manner of festivities—all to be presented with as much elegance and panache as we could muster.

"Nothing mandatory, you understand," Arthur declared, pressing the Dragon Seal on the bottom of the proclamation. "We'll make them *want* to be part of the splendor—as Merlin used to say, first you catch your horse, then you break it."

Vinnie was delighted, as it meant further use for the fancy wardrobe she'd created, and Cei set about making his plans and organizing the feasts. As for the guests, whether they knew it or not, Arthur was going to draw them back from the edge of anarchy and make Britain the last western outpost of civilization.

In the midst of our preparations Brigit asked permission to go to her convent. It was now well into spring, and there was no baby to wait for, so I had no reason to keep her with me. By now I was more used to the idea of her leaving and was able to send her off with my best wishes—and a silent request to the Old Gods to keep an eye on her, just in case the Christian God forgot.

It was well she chose to go when she did, for I was too busy to mourn her departure. Everyone was full of plans and excitement, and I had never seen Arthur so happy; he was convinced the change in the Round Table was the most important decision of his career.

In that he was right, for our lives would never be the same again.

THIRTEEN

London

e left Caerleon on a warm spring day with townspeople and farmers all coming to see us off, bringing food and good wishes for the Road as though we were part of their family rather than royal rulers. Everywhere one heard the bright banter of parting friends mixed with the whispered farewells of lovers, for it had been a good winter for the heart as well as the mind.

The pub-master's daughter presented Gawain with a drinking horn she had carved and rimmed with silver. He was clearly pleased by the gift and drank a toast to her, but later I saw her crying and hoped that the Orkney Prince had not been encouraging dreams he couldn't fulfill. He might be an easy man to love, but an unwise one to plan on, and I wasn't sure she was old enough to recognize the difference.

A clutch of girls had pooled their talents to make Lamorak a purse to hang from his belt and teased him about finding a fortune to fill it with; the dyer's children tied garlands of flowers around the wolfhounds' necks and gave Dagonet a nosegay as well; even Cei was wearing a bright new ring upon the little finger of his left hand. But when I asked him about it, the Seneschal scowled fiercely and turned away. I was sorry, for I had hoped it betokened a romance of some kind; Arthur's tax collector was a man too often full of gloomy moods and a bright, sunny love would do him no end of good.

But if Cei was taciturn and secretive, the people of London were open and friendly, thrilled that we were going to hold the Round Table in their city. They lined the Road to the double gates and leaned over the parapet of the walls to shower us with flowers and goodwill.

Lynette, the daughter of the Grounds Keeper, appointed herself my escort as we went through the Imperial Palace. "My family did the best they could, Your Highness." She grinned up at me, her ten-year old face smudged with dirt. "You wouldn't believe the stuff we carted out of this place."

With a sweep of her hand she indicated the most cavernous room I'd ever seen—the mosaic floors were pocked with holes where fire pits had been dug, the walls were sooty from years of smoking torches, and the jumble of furniture piled in corners only made it seem more deserted. Still, I had no doubt Cei would find a way to turn it into a splendid Hall.

"Come see the Park," Lynette begged. "We cleared out the brambles and even replanted the old garden."

Sure enough, though the farther corners of the grounds were still festooned with ivy and bindweed, there were cabbage and turnips, new lettuce and fresh beets, all thriving in well-laid beds. Sage and thyme and rosemary clustered near the broken fountain while banks of marigolds filled in the basins. A stand of foxglove lifted thick lavender flowers along a path to the orchard.

"And behold, what used to be the Bishop's cherries!" Mischief lurked in Lynette's eyes as she pointed to an enormous old tree. "Fusty old man prized them pretty high, setting boys to scare away the birds and not letting anyone else have any. But when we heard you were coming, my father declared this was a royal garden and no one but you could pick from it—so all the cherries are yours alone."

I couldn't help grinning at the thought of the churchman losing his precious fruit to the Queen he pretended didn't exist.

Lynette chattered away in between pointing out medlar and pear, apple and mulberry, then suddenly turned serious. "My father says the city council will ask His Highness to make London part of Logres—do you think he'll accept?"

I smiled at the child's candor but sidestepped the answer by assuring her Arthur would consider any idea brought before him this summer.

The people of London were as determined to state their case as Lynette had been bold in asking, and several mornings later Arthur looked at me ruefully over breakfast.

"It appears we're going to be King and Queen of London," he allowed, munching thoughtfully on a bannock. "Taking it under our protection isn't a bad idea. The camps I regarrisoned after the Lincoln campaign are well placed to guard the likely routes of attack. And London itself acts as a wedge between the Saxons to the north and those of Kent and Sussex—keeps them from joining forces. Besides, the people are so eager for a leader, I'm loath to throw them back to the limbo of the last decades."

"Doesn't seem we have much choice." I grinned. "Bedraggled they may be, but they're certainly determined to have us."

Arthur nodded and popped the last of the bannock in his mouth, then rose and gestured for me to follow. "Let's go take a look at the pavilion Lance is putting up by the ruins of Caesar's Tower."

He strode off before I was even on my feet, and I had to lift my skirts and run down the corridor to catch up with him. The heavy robes of state were not meant for keeping up with the likes of Arthur.

A flock of ravens rose, croaking, from their roosts as we approached the Tower. Judging from the size of the nests amid the broken walls, the birds had long since claimed the spot for their own. They wheeled and soared overhead in amazing acrobatics, and I watched their antics with delight as the Breton joined us.

"Sacred to the Old God Bran." Lancelot gestured to the knoll on which both ruins and tents now stood. "This is where they buried his head, to protect Britain from invasion. I wonder if the Romans knew that when they built this tower?"

Arthur and I laughed at the irony, but I paused to make a hasty prayer—after all the work that had gone into preparing for this gathering, I hoped Bran could tell the difference between Saxon raiders and invited Federates.

One after another the leaders streamed through London's gates, their presence announced by the newly appointed Town Crier. He marched before them, ringing a bell and calling out name and rank so that the people in the streets would know what royalty they were beholding. It also gave us warning that another guest was about to be presented at the Palace.

We housed the nobility wherever we could find room for them—mostly in the pavilions or better-preserved stone structures. The rest crowded into inns and taverns, and the warriors slept in the Park.

A few of the monarchs could not attend—my cousin Maelgwn because his wife was ill, and King Mark—who didn't like to travel anyhow—used his new bride as an excuse to stay home. He sent Tristan and Dinadan as his emissaries, however, and we welcomed them gladly.

My father could not come because of his own ill health, but he sent Bedivere, and there were boisterous greetings all around. The lieutenant had regained his strength and humor and was now quite adept at the use of his hooked hand. When I told him that Brigit had gone to the convent, he nodded with a gentle smile. "May all the Gods bless her," he responded.

Urien came to greet us and announced that Morgan sent her regrets. "She's very busy, you know, what with so many Irish bringing in the new faith."

I studied the King of Northumbria, wondering if he knew about his wife's hostility toward me. I suspected he was a man who preferred not to look below the surface of things—a life full of horses and warriors, hunting and feasting, seemed to suit him wonderfully, and I was certain he would avoid anything that could disrupt it. At least Morgan's absence meant one less problem for me—I had quite enough to think about already.

Many of the leaders brought sons or daughters to stay with us—the boys to study under Lancelot or Palomides, the girls to serve as ladies-in-waiting for me. It strengthened our ties with the parents but also meant I was responsible for a growing bevy of young women. I turned them over to Vinnie, trusting that the matron's diligence as a governess would keep them out of trouble, and out of my way.

Vinnie reinstated the practice of afternoon tea, serving herbal brews and biscuits at the end of the day much as Igraine had when she was High Queen. It's a nice custom and I joined my ladies for this whenever I could find the time.

Glancing about the room, I was surprised at how many there were and how few I recognized—girls from the north of Wales who had inherited the same plain face and apricot hair I have; sturdy youngsters from the dales and moors of the Pennines; and the delicate flowers of Cornwall's steadings. Only Enid and Frieda were missing—they were too busy helping me run the Court to think of themselves as ladies-in-waiting.

"Oh, dear," Vinnie sputtered as another newcomer curtsied before me. "I told Elaine to close her bodice with that brooch, not use it as an ornament in her hair!"

This was the girl from Astolat, and I stared at her curiously. Her father, Bernard, had described her as pious and shy, and in need of a mother since her own had died some years ago. But where I expected a timid, backward child, this maid was a full-grown woman with a startling look of abandon—her wild, tumbling tresses fell forward over the half-open bodice, and she moved with a languorous, provocative grace. Yet her eyes were downcast, and she drifted away with the demure air of one untouched by the world.

"I don't know what to do with her." The matron sighed, carefully pouring me the first cup of tea. "She's not deaf, for she starts if one claps one's hands. But she goes about in that distracted way, as though listening to voices others cannot hear. It's enough to give one goose bumps."

"If you ask me," Augusta volunteered, "she's not all right in the head." The Roman girl from a midland villa stretched out a manicured hand for a biscuit, and Vinnie sharply reminded her to serve me first.

"Will there be a Beltane celebration at Court next year?" Augusta inquired, smoothly changing the subject as she extended the tray toward me. "Some say the High King keeps a Christian Court, and others not."

"We allow all people to worship whatever Gods they choose. Bishops and druids, saints and priestesses are all welcome at our Court," I responded, carefully not looking at Vinnie. The matron had long since given up trying to convert me, but she had a strong distrust of druids and their ancient powers.

"Beltane is my favorite time," Augusta allowed, and several girls giggled because so many romances begin at the spring bonfire. The midland beauty soon brought the conversation around to romantic gossip and began teasing Ettard about Pelleas's obvious interest in her.

"I suppose he's nice enough." The convent girl shrugged as she pulled apart a biscuit and drizzled honey on the pieces. "But he's terribly poor, and awfully common compared to Gawain or Lancelot. Now that the Queen Mother left me land of my own, I must consider my station."

Augusta snickered at such pretensions.

"No, I mean it," Ettard persisted. "I'm not interested in any man who is not at least of Champion status."

I was tempted to remind her that she'd been a homeless waif herself once, but her tone was threatening to become whiny, so I bit my tongue and looked at Elaine instead, thinking the girl from Astolat was not the only one with a poor grasp of reality.

Augusta had led the conversation around to favorite heroes, and although everyone admitted to flirting with Lamorak, it was Lancelot who was considered the most romantically mysterious.

"You know him best, M'lady," Ettard said suddenly. "What is the Breton really like?"

The question caught me by surprise, and I paused, wondering what to say. Lance was funny and tender, clever and serious, and had a wicked little way of looking at me as though there were a marvelous secret only the two of us shared. He could lift my spirits with a glance, as he had at Wihtgar's gate, or be so preoccupied with an inner problem that he didn't even hear my voice. He was, I realized, the most fascinating man I knew—but I had no intention of saying so to my ladies.

"The Breton is too hardworking and dedicated to Arthur to pay much mind to romance," I responded, hoping it sounded less pompous than it felt.

There was a murmur of bemusement and the conversation moved on, but the definition of Lancelot stayed in my mind.

As the time to begin the festivities drew near both Arthur and I watched for Merlin, hoping he would make one of his remarkable appearances. Not only would it be splendid to show him what we had done with his idea, it would put an end to the questions about his whereabouts which were circulating even here. But neither the Magician nor Nimue came.

On the morning of the first day I climbed to the top of the riverbank wall. It was the only place where I could get away from what had become a constant commotion in the Palace, and I looked out over the Thames with a sigh of relief.

The Londoners had repaired the Roman bridge and a steady stream of country folk flowed through the gates, drawn by curiosity about the High King's presence. Even the water teemed with boats—rafts and dugouts as well as wood-planked vessels of all sorts. A barge tied up at the wharf, putting ashore two peddlers and a man carrying an eye doctor's case, while a farm boy hoisted crates of fowl onto the landing. Cei stepped forward to claim the squawking birds, followed by a whole parade of pages who hauled them away to the cooking area.

A group of Federates had rowed down the Thames, and the man standing in the prow of the lead boat was being hailed by a blond girl at the end of the wharf. It was Frieda, come to greet her father, who was honoring us in return for Arthur's paying our respects at the ealderman's pyre. The Saxon was a big man, and the joy that spread across his face when he saw his daughter showed clearly how much he prized her.

Turmoil suddenly erupted at the Colchester gate where a band of barbarians were demanding entrance. Once inside the walls they marched down the street in primitive splendor, led by a slave who held aloft an iron rod topped with a fan of feathers and fluttering ribbons. Next came the chamberlain carrying a large whetstone as though it were some sort of scepter. The leader himself was garbed in wolfskins and strutted proudly at the head of his war-band while the women and children followed in silence.

The Town Crier was announcing Wehha the Swede of East Anglia, so I turned and bolted down the steps, barely making it to the Palace in time to take my place next to Arthur before the entourage entered the refurbished Hall. As they walked the length of the room I adjusted my skirts and patted my hair into place—being elegant takes a lot more time than I would have guessed.

"You like my standard?" Wehha demanded, gesturing to the metal staff with its outlandish topknot. "Good as any Roman tufa, no?"

Arthur pronounced it "amazing" while I struggled to keep a straight face; the idea that someone so clearly barbaric should aspire to the trappings of Imperial insignias struck me as wonderfully funny.

Arthur explained that the Swede and his party were invited to a feast next evening.

"And we look forward to honoring your wife," I announced, augmenting my limited Swedish with bits of Saxon and Latin. "When we are your guests, we follow your ways. Now you are my guest, you follow mine."

The man from East Anglia stared at me in disbelief, then turned to Arthur, clearly expecting my invitation to be overruled.

"It is as the High Queen says," my husband assured him. "In our Court women are given full voice and equal respect."

"Such nonsense," the barbarian muttered. "Surely the Romans didn't teach you that."

"No," I retorted, "it has been the way in Britain since before the Legions came."

There was much head shaking as his delegation went off with Cei, and Arthur gave me a sidewise glance. "I just hope he can get through it without a domestic insurrection."

"I just hope we can get through it at all." I grinned, wondering what insanity had made us take on such a venture.

The actual week sped by in snips and snatches of color—the kitchen was in superb form, serving up oysters and eels and fishes of all kinds from the river, birds and game and field greens from every garden and farm around. Each night there were different specialties—snails from a villa in Cirencester where the Romans once raised them just for such feasts, or fruits picked fresh from the royal garden—I did not see the Bishop's expression when the cherries were served. Wine and cider, beer and ale, were in abundance, and there was even a flask or two of the Irish waters of life, though that was not widely circulated. Altogether Cei had outdone himself.

Wehha's wife was miserable, staring at her hands all evening long and barely looking up when I tried to welcome her in her own language. After the first night I told her she could stay home, for it was clear she was as upset at being included in a Feast as I had been at being excluded.

Elaine of Astolat caused a noticeable stir the first time she ambled across the inner circle of the Round Table to pour our wine. More than one appreciative male turned to follow her progress and even Arthur's attention was caught.

A soft, inviting smile lingered on her lips as she filled our goblets, though she kept her eyes downcast and never actually looked at us.

Arthur turned to me with a low whistle. "Wherever did she come from?" he inquired, and when I told him, he shook his head slowly. "I just hope she doesn't invite more trouble than she can handle."

The girl moved on, quite oblivious to the stir she was causing. Lance had taken a lily from the bouquet near his plate but left off examining the curved petals in order to raise his glass when Elaine reached for it. Their fingers touched inadvertently.

The Maid looked up, startled as a dreamer suddenly waking. She stared at the Breton for a long minute, and a blush swept up her throat and across her face. Filling Lance's goblet, she handed it back to him. He smiled and gave her the flower in return.

Without a word she put the lily into the neckline of her dress, fixing it carefully so that it was cradled between her breasts, then drifted on to the next trestle.

"I think you've just made a conquest," I teased.

"Oh, Lord, I hope not." The lieutenant sighed. "I certainly didn't mean to."

During the days Lance's tournaments more than satisfied the military men, while Bedivere temporarily resumed his place at Arthur's side, playing the diplomat to the nobles. Most were local magistrates and descendents of Roman tribunes who had risen to power when the Legions left. These were men better equipped for negotiation than confrontation, the remnants of the old bureaucracy that we were trying to woo into the fold. Arthur and Bedivere met with them singly or in groups, entertaining them as lavishly as possible and always coming round to discussing the Round Table. Many of them were flattered at the idea of being allied with us, and the Fellowship that once numbered barely two score threatened to grow to upward of a hundred.

Tristan spent most of his time in the Park, sleeping off too much wine or playing sad songs on his harp. I came across him toward the end of the week when I went to gather mint for the dinner that night. The gangly warrior was sitting on a broken column, staring into space. When I inquired how things were in Cornwall, he just gave me a doleful look.

"Is it that bad?" I asked Dinadan after Tris took up his harp and moved to a bench under the far willow where he was half-hidden from the rest of the world.

"Aye," sighed his comrade. "And not just for him, I'm afraid, M'lady." I lifted an eyebrow in silent inquiry, and Dinadan continued. "Perhaps if I'd gone to Ireland with him to fetch the lass, things might have been different. You know he's not very . . . sophisticated, shall we say. And he'd never thought much about women before, except to pass the night with occasionally. Now he can't seem to think of anything but that girl, and then it's with grief and pain and stolen delight. I canna' see how they can take pleasure in their meetings, considering what import the Christians put on fidelity."

"Then his love is not one-sided?"

"Would that it were, M'lady! The little minx eggs him on, until he's half-crazy with desire and jealousy."

"Oh, dear," I murmured, beginning to understand why Tristan was so downcast.

"The girl comes from Pagan royalty." Dinadan shrugged woefully. "The rights of a Celtic queen are natural to her thinking, and though she pays lip service to her husband's White Christ, she doesn't understand why the idea of her bedding Tris should make the old King so upset."

"Mark knows?"

"Not exactly; he's so happy with his pretty little toy, he doesn't want to see what's going on. But if he should catch them together . . . I canna' say where this trouble could end." The wiry fellow shook his head despondently and heaved a big sigh, then took his leave as I went back to picking mint.

But Tristan was not the only one pining for love, it seemed. Lance found himself followed everywhere by the soft, inviting shadow of Elaine. She went through the garden daily, looking for lily blossoms, and when she found one she'd tuck it between her breasts and stroll down to the tournament grounds in search of the Breton.

If he was there, she'd settle herself near his things, like a faithful dog guarding its master's possessions. When he came, hot and sweaty from the field, she waited patiently until he gathered up his equipment and came back to the Palace. Each day she offered to carry something, and each day he thanked her kindly but declined the invitation, at which point she would fall in behind him and whoever else he was with, trailing along silently in the wake of her idol.

If she didn't find Lance at the tournaments, Elaine would move slowly and methodically through the town, searching doggedly among the vendors' stalls or scanning the tables of the temporary *biergartens* the Saxons had set up. As far as anyone knew, she never uttered a word.

"Frankly, she makes me uncomfortable," Lance said one evening. "The child's so unwitting, she shouldn't be wandering about alone that way. Catcalls and invitations follow her everywhere, and if I were you, Gwen, I'd have Lavinia keep a tighter rein on her for her own sake."

I nodded, thinking no doubt the Breton was right—as soon as the Round Table was over, I'd sit down with Vinnie and we'd decide what to do.

But trouble came on the last day of festivities, before I had a chance to talk with the matron. Suddenly Elaine's father was standing before me, wringing his hands in despair.

"Raped," Bernard howled. "If it wasn't for Lancelot, my daughter would have been raped, right here in King Arthur's Court. Surely that is no way for the Companions to behave; I can't imagine that the King would countenance such a thing!"

I hastened to agree, though Bernard wasn't listening.

"She's always been a good girl. A devout child, faithful about going to Mass. Only shy . . . very, very shy. And trusting."

Lance and Arthur arrived, and my husband came immediately to the distraught father. "They were drifters, Sir, not men of the Round Table after all. The one Lance captured says they'd come into London hoping to cadge some food and work. I assume," he added, turning to me, "that the girl is recovering?"

I nodded, assuring him that Vinnie had found her more frightened than hurt. "But"—I looked firmly at Bernard—"I suggest you get a chaperone for the girl."

"I'll do more than that." Bernard was pounding one hand into the palm of the other. "I'll take her back to Astolat and put her in the tower on my island until a wedding is arranged."

"That sounds like punishment instead of protection," I blurted out, shocked by his reaction.

"Not at all. I love my daughter and want to see that she's safe. Elaine is used to spending long hours alone; I don't think she'll mind. Certainly"—he cast a sidewise look at Lancelot—"it's better than having her trail after a man who doesn't appreciate her. I won't have her made fun of, or worse yet, used like a trollop for a bit of sport. She's a good girl, a devout girl . . . just shy." His jaw snapped shut and he glared around the room pugnaciously, as though daring anyone to say otherwise.

So the balding widower took his ripe and luscious daughter home. I felt immensely sorry for the poor girl, shut up in the narrow confines of an island tower, and hoped she was too dull-witted to understand what was happening to her.

The Round Table concluded that day, having achieved everything Arthur wanted, and afterward Urien invited us to visit him in York.

"As I recall," Arthur said casually when the last of the guests were gone and it was just the two of us alone foraging for a supper of leftovers in the kitchen, "I promised you a trip through Britain as a wedding present. Seems to me this is a good time to do it, now that the southern Federates are in hand. What do you think?" He cocked an eyebrow in my direction and I flew into his arms, thrilled that he hadn't forgotten. "Nothing fancy," he cautioned, "but a swing up through the north, and then perhaps a visit with your father."

"An adventure of our own, without the whole household?" I queried, and he looked down at me with a grin.

"All our very own."

There was nothing else he could have suggested that would make me happier. Next day I packed all the fancy clothes away and sent them with Vinnie and the young women to the villa at Cunetio—after the experience with Elaine, I wasn't about to take a flock of girls I didn't even know into strange territory.

Arthur had Palomides take the new recruits to Silchester for training, and by the time we moved out through Bishopgate I was once more back to breeches and tunic, with only Enid and Frieda in attendance and a heart full of romantic hopes.

FOURTEEN

The Attack

e traveled at a good clip. I would rather have had Featherfoot under me, as Shadow was prone to being skittish, but this northern expedition hadn't been planned when we left Caerleon. At least the beautiful white mare had a smooth and easy gait.

The forest beyond London was dark and primitive, full of ancient hornbeams and giant oaks that were threatening to engulf even the wide Roman Road.

Arthur gestured toward it. "The Legions used to cut the brush as far back as a bowshot on either side so no one could lay an ambush. If we're going to make it safe for trade and travel and the royal messengers, we'll have to find some way to keep the verges clear."

Lance agreed, and we were shortly into a discussion of other matters of state as well—the progress of building beacons from Somerset through the Welsh Marches, the question of Aelle's willingness to stay within the borders of Sussex in the south, and what was happening among the barbarians north of London.

"The camps to the east have reported little activity," Arthur noted. "But this would be a good time to check with them."

So we moved up the valleys of the Lea River and the Stour, staying at the outposts Ambrosius had set up in the buffer strip after he drove the Saxons back into East Anglia.

It was my first encounter with the frontier soldiers—neither hero nor

Champion, these were the men whose daily presence made our kingdom safer. Sharing gruel from a leather cooking bag suspended over the coals of an open pit, I watched my husband talk with them. Men and boys, young and ambitious or worn and weathered, sometimes wise and often scarred, they were all delighted to have a leader who could hunker down with them beside the campfire, asking about horses, supplies, and the activities of the locals who had pledged themselves as Federates. So far the reports indicated nothing unusual.

From Cambridge we followed the Roman Road along the Fens, skirting that flat, misty world of water and silt ridge, reed bed and sedge grass. By day it shimmered green and silver, with here and there a glimpse of moss and marsh fern beneath scrub oak and willow, and occasionally I caught sight of tall purple loosestrife spires or the blue flash of a kingfisher where the water ran clear in its twisting, shifting channels.

But at sunset the Fens presented another face—gray and flat as winter, mournfully drained of color, they lay wet and waiting under the huge sky as the dying sun colored the clouds, reddened to the shade of blood, and rushed downward in a crimson flood until the flat, endless marsh spread beneath reeking heaven like a great, gouted wound that would not stop bleeding.

I shivered at the omen and made the sign against evil.

Thankfully Lincoln lies beyond the waterland, and the men of the garrison greeted us with high spirits and glad cheers.

"Anything out of the ordinary? Large influx of barbarians, for instance?" Arthur inquired over dinner that night.

"There's a constant trickle of immigrants, M'lord." The young Briton in charge of the garrison bore the Roman name of Tiberius and wore a swordbelt fastened by an ornate Saxon buckle. I marveled at the odd mixture of old and new, foreign and familiar blended into an unconscious whole as he speared another piece of meat from the common pot. "Most all of them are little groups of people claiming to be relatives of people already here—every time I see Old Colgrin on market day he's got another cousin with him. If they keep bringing 'family' over at this rate, there won't be any Saxons left on the Continent!"

Arthur chewed thoughtfully, the firelight highlighting his frown. "But no word of war-bands? No specific leader who is calling men to him?"

Tiberius shook his head. "Not so far as we've heard, Sir. Each group is ready to fight for its own survival, of course, but they all claim to be loyal to your Crown. If I catch wind of anything amiss, will let you know immediately."

"You do that, lad." The High King relaxed. "It's fellows like you I count on," he added, giving the young man a clap on the back as they both stood up. Tiberius beamed under the approval.

"It wouldn't hurt to put on a exhibition of horsemanship while we're here," Lance suggested and received an approving nod.

The cavalry display was attended by troops and townspeople alike, a mixture of ruddy Britons and clusters of big, blond Saxons. I watched them covertly, hoping they would return to their kindred with awesome tales of our mounted warriors.

When we left the city everyone turned out to bid us farewell, the troops drawn up smartly as though for inspection, the civilians shouting and waving cheerfully, seemingly glad to be under the Pendragon's protection.

We took the ferry across the Humber to Brough and made camp on the far side of the ridge beyond the estuary. It seemed impossible to get Arthur's attention while we were on the Road—even at night he was thinking and talking and planning for restoration of the land, and my dream of a romantic tryst threatened to be lost in the crush of practicalities. My women may have been left behind, but Arthur's Cause was always with us.

So this night I suggested we have our tent set up in a secluded spot separate from the rest of the camp. He raised an eyebrow in surprise, then grinned in agreement. It might not be as private as the chambers Urien would give us in York, but the three Companions who came with us would provide a shield from the usual demands that are made on a popular king. At least we could have a little time alone.

The glade was screened by trees but open to the sky, with a giant oak looming to one side. We picketed the horses nearby and set our tent on the other edge of the greensward, where the full moon soon bathed it in pale light.

When we were lying in each other's arms, spent from the first onrush of passion, I ran my fingers through the hair on Arthur's chest. He was sleepy and content—eyes closed and jawline softened. For the first time in many months I could see the boyish, vulnerable side of him. A deep welling of tenderness and love crowded my heart.

"It's been a long time," I whispered.

"Hmmm. . . ." His response was noncommittal, and I wondered what he thought I meant. "Seems as though everything's been happening at once," he mumbled. "I'm still sorting through the possibilities opened up by the London Round Table. Why, Gwen, do you realize we've established diplomatic contact with more different tribes than anyone before us, except perhaps the Romans?"

His jaw was getting firm again, the mind starting to reengage.

"And do you realize," I countered, running my fingers along the bridge of his nose and smoothing out the creases between his brows, "how much I love you?"

It was the first time I had told him such a thing, and I waited hopefully for his reaction.

The silence that came between us grew longer and heavier with each breath.

"Mhhh," he said finally, heaving a sleepy sigh and turning over on his side.

Drat! I thought, mentally kicking myself. Arthur always shied from emotional exchanges—even nice ones—and you would have thought that by now I would know better than to try and coax him into one. Instead of bringing us closer, my admission had only made him more guarded.

With a sigh of my own I turned on my side so that we touched at shoulder, rump and feet, and silently vowed never to bring the subject up again. I had no doubt my husband held me in high regard and I told myself it was better to have caring actions in silence than pretty promises left unfulfilled by a more loquacious lover. So I put aside my dreams of romance and, yawning fully, went to sleep.

. . .

"Saxons!"

Cei's warning wakened us just before dawn. "Five of them in the lead—riding up from the Humber, heading directly for us."

Arthur leapt up from the blankets, taut as a bowstring as he reached for his mail shirt. There was a rustle of link on link when he slipped it over his head, and I knelt to secure his swordbelt in place. Light from the setting moon streamed through the open tent flap, glinting off the gold and jewels of Excalibur's hilt, and I prayed the Sacred Sword would even the odds of our four against the five barbarians. Once the baldric was buckled Arthur put his hand on my head.

"Best you get away from here, lass. I'll have Lance take you to the main camp."

"Nonsense," I retorted. "I've always wanted to be a warrior."

I was rummaging among the bedding, pulling Arthur's green cloak free. I'd made it as a wedding present, and though it hadn't originally been intended as a war-cape, the necessary padding had been added when it became clear that Arthur would always be in danger.

"Besides," I noted, holding up the cape, "I'd rather be with you so I can see what's happening."

"Then by the Gods, stay out of sight; you know how Saxons treat captured women." Arthur's voice was curt as he slung the cape over his shoulders. I thought of Ettard's family and shivered.

He left without another word as a strange horse neighed nervously in the distance. I held my breath, praying none of our mounts would break the silence that had descended on the camp.

No doubt Cei was already with the animals, for even the untrained Shadow remained quiet. I climbed into my breeches and tunic and, piling my hair up under a knotted wool cap, crept out of the tent. With my lanky build and plain features I'd been mistaken for a squire more than once—if I didn't call attention to myself, I could at least see how our fortunes were going.

To the east the sky was barely lightening while the last of the moonlight struck the clearing slantwise, making dark shadows of our men as they prepared for battle. Each moved with a lean, measured grace, making neither sound nor unnecessary motion. Arthur mounted first, followed by Gawain and Lance—Cei was already astride his war-horse.

My stomach tightened as hoofbeats marked the approach of the Saxons. They were letting their animals pick out the path, totally unaware of our presence—with any luck they would ride right into camp, and we could capture them without bloodshed.

Suddenly Shadow let out a ringing whinny, and a string of oaths exploded in the darkness on both sides. The Saxons were just breaking through the screen of trees between us and the path as Cei sent his horse rocketing toward them with savage, silent intent.

Something hard met something soft, followed by an awful, gurgling sound, and sweat broke out all over my skin.

In the melee that followed there was no way to tell one man from another. Wrenching moans and the gut-piercing ring of blade on blade echoed through the trees while the smell of blood splattered the air. The horses milled amid screams and curses; a large, unfamiliar animal loomed in front of me, and with sudden terror I realized the circular white shape that floated in the gloom above it was the shield of a barbarian.

The man yanked his steed aside to avoid getting tangled in the tent ropes just as I broke from them and I heard his oath of surprise as he saw me. I ran headlong for dark shadow of the giant oak, intending to climb into the safety of its branches—anything to get away from the carnage that now flowed everywhere.

The invader's horse came pounding after me, shaking the ground with his hooves as I raced for my life into a soft, dreamy world where everything moved with great deliberation and a hundred thoughts registered with each stride. I wondered why I'd never asked Arthur how he'd gotten that scar on his shoulder, and if Taliesin was progressing well with his music, and what barbarian would get Igraine's golden torque if I didn't survive this attack.

The tree rose before me, but to my horror the lowest branch was well above my reach, and though I jumped for it, I missed and fell, panting, to the ground.

Cei was howling imprecations and the horse behind me snorted violently, rearing suddenly as I tried to roll out of the way. The rider let out one last, rattling scream and fell from its back. Terrified, the warhorse wheeled away as Cei planted a spear upright through the invader's chest. The ash pole glimmered palely in the early light.

Thankfully the fellow was silent, though there were others moaning and writhing in the bloody dawn.

Then all at once it became very quiet. Cleansing as clear water, an absolute stillness bathed the world while the sun rose on the blood-soaked turf of our camp.

No one moved for the longest time, though someone was sobbing with a great racking sorrow. Through blinding tears I gazed around the clearing, searching out one after another of our men. Cei was cleaning his spear with long handfuls of grass, his mouth set in grim silence. Gawain hacked viciously at something in the grass and began to caper in a wild, drunken dance of glee and terror, singing and crying as he brandished the head of his enemy by the hair. Lance knelt beside a fallen foe, his hands moving gently over the man's face, slowly closing the eyelids. It might have been the tender caress of a lover, and I wondered what the Breton felt in such moments of awful triumph.

Only Arthur was not in sight, and I bolted from my hiding spot, driven by the fear that he'd been killed.

"Gwen!" His voice came sharply through my panic, and as I turned toward the sound he reached my side, gathering me up in his arms. The momentum of his rush carried us both forward into the center of the clearing.

"Thank heavens!" he rasped. "I couldn't find you . . . I thought . . ."

I flung my arms around him and buried my head in his shoulder, hearing the sobs muffle against his cape. The shining exaltation of life triumphant in the face of so much death coursed through us as he carried me into our tent and dropped the flap closed.

It was then, in the wild, fierce mating that followed, that Arthur spoke his love of me for the first, and almost only, time.

"These were guides, sent to meet a small landing party." Cei gestured wearily toward the five corpses. "The rest surrendered without a fuss. Gawain has them under guard in the main camp." Arthur's foster-brother looked drawn and pale in the early light, and he favored one arm.

"Are you wounded?" I asked, remembering that he had dealt with two of the enemy single-handed.

"Wrenched, not slashed," he answered curtly.

"You're much to be commended." I looked directly into Cei's cold, guarded eyes. "I would not have seen this day's sun but for your bravery, and want you to know I appreciate it. Any woman you claim as mate can be proud of your courage."

He stared at me without responding, then turned his face away. Evidently it was not a compliment that pleased him, though I had meant only the best by it.

Arthur was packing up and the Seneschal hastened off to the main camp without even glancing in my direction again.

As we neared York the Road filled up with people bringing the mid-summer harvest to a fair. We marched among them, keeping the Saxons prisoners under guard. That motley group included more women and children than men, and most of them were grieving silently for their dead. I suspected we had encountered a clan of immigrants rather than a fierce war party and hoped they wouldn't all be treated as marauders.

"Don't let their appearance fool you," Urien warned over dinner that night. Since there had been Federates living in or near York for many years, Urien knew their ways well. "The barbarians don't need special warriors. Oh, they have a few Champions—men called berserk-ers who make a ritual of warfare and work themselves into a frenzy of blood-lust before battle—but most of their troops come from the land. Every freeman farmer is a trained fighter; at any moment he can put down his plow and take up his weapon. Not a bad system. Each supports himself and his family, *and* defends his lands and lord if they are threatened. Much more efficient than this," he added, gesturing to the British warriors who lounged at the tables of his Hall with nothing else to do.

"I'll give your captives a patch of land, and let them shelter with the other Federates if they'll swear fealty," the older man suggested as he upended his cup. "They rarely give me any trouble, except for that batch up on the coast causing mischief around Yeaverling—settlements so spread out in that area, one can't protect them all. But my local Saxons are hardworking and cooperative, and pay their taxes in mead and bread. Here," he added, pulling off a portion of the loaf in front of him and depositing it on my plate. "Made of a grain they brought with them—grows on the poorest soil—they call it rye."

I looked at the dense, grayish stuff and when I took a tentative bite my nose caught the pungent tang even before my tongue did. It had none of the lightness of wheat bread, but I tried it with a slab of cheese and found it pleasant. Between soap and their law and this new sour bread, the barbarians were bringing all sorts of interesting things to Britain.

Our conversation moved round to news of the west which, according to Urien, had also had a prosperous year.

"The Irish are coming in droves," he announced, turning to me. "Your father says they are mainly following Fergus into Strathclyde, though there's various families in Rheged as well. The one by Morecambe Bay has developed a thriving business in dogs like yours."

He nodded toward Caesar and Cabal, and I grinned to myself. Those would be Brigit's kin, trading away puppies as fast as their wolfhounds could produce them.

"At least the Irish have ceased raiding." Urien chucked a bone to his terriers by the hearth-fire. "Maelgwn is holding the north of Wales secure, and there's little influx except in holy men further south. Saddest news out of Wales is poor old Pellam. That wound of his still won't heal, and his kingdom is languishing because of it. Horrible business when a monarch is cut down by his own sword."

The King of Northumbria made the sign against evil, and we all followed suit. The story of the Fisher King strikes dread in the hearts of all British leaders, for a king who is not whole and healthy brings plague and pestilence upon his land. And when the cause of his disablement is his own weapon, there is little chance that he will recover. For years now Pellam had clung to life, neither sound enough to recover nor brave enough to make the royal sacrifice. The whole ghastly thing echoed of punishment by the Gods, and I wondered why the Lady of the Lake had not gone to his aid.

"Pellam's Christian," Urien observed, "and will have nothing to do with the Old Ways. It's a wonder he survives at all."

The conversation soon drifted round to reminiscences, and Urien's bard began retelling stories of Arthur's early exploits in the area, when he had helped Urien drive the barbarians back to the coast. Cador of Cornwall had gained much glory in that campaign, and I turned to watch him and his son, Constantine. The younger warrior was a strapping fellow somewhat older than Arthur and as ruddy and rawboned as his father. But Cador had grown gray and grizzled now—I suspected he looked much as his father, Gorlois, would have when Igraine married him. Between the song of the bard and the look of the man, the bravery of past generations wove into a comforting present.

Since so many people had come to the city for the fair, Urien used the occasion to have the leading Federates meet with the group we had captured. They in turn promised Arthur they would stand surety for the newcomers' loyalty.

A fine ceremony was held at the center of the Market, where all could witness the High King's leniency. Arthur gave each captive freedom, along with a bag of barley so they not be an unfair burden on their sponsors, and everyone seemed pleased with the arrangement.

That afternoon I prowled through the old Imperial city, exploring what had once been the northern capital of Britain. The huts and shops that have grown up higgledy-piggledy within the fortress are as colorful and exciting as those at Chester. A multitude of alleys and shortcuts wound between them; "snickleways" threading past stalls and arcades, giving onto hidden courts where flowers run riot in the lee of a wall or bakers put fresh scones and pot-pies on their windowsills to cool.

I paused by a stall at the end of one such meander, my attention caught by a pair of tiny fur slippers. The soft moleskin promised to keep a toddler's feet warm, and I picked one up, marveling at their smallness.

"Fit for a royal bairn," the woman said, carefully drawing a length of linen thread through her block of beeswax. When I looked up, surprised, she grinned. "The whole country knows where you and His Highness are these days, M'lady . . . and we're right glad to be hosting you, at that."

She carefully threaded the smallest bone bodkin I'd ever seen, then picked up another piece of work and began the painstaking process of stitching the furs together, chatting comfortably. "Between your visit and the fair, it's a good time for all of us. Every Champion in your party must have come to trade for goods in the Market. In fact," she added nonchalantly, "I'd be happy to give you the little pair of booties as a thank-you."

It was a casual offer, made without innuendo or intent to hurt. From her tone one would guess she'd birthed half a dozen infants such as the one who slept in the cradle nearby and no doubt thought it the most natural thing in the world. A blind, black jealousy swept over me, and I looked away hastily.

Unfairly or not, I resented the bounty of her womb when mine lay fallow and I had to fight not to lash out at her in pain and anger.

The baby fretted drowsily, and the woman set the cradle to rocking with her foot, her hands still busy with the pelts. "Once you and the High King settle down, you'll be raising young'uns of your own. I'd be honored if you'd accept these as a token of our respect."

She spoke with the commonsense conviction of any farmwife, as though the idea of my not becoming a mother had never occurred to her. Suddenly my own in-turning misery seemed twisted and warped. I looked at her and smiled, grateful for the vote of confidence. When she handed me the booties I was sure it was a sign of good luck.

On the last day of our visit Urien feasted us on the terrace of his Imperial Palace. A pleasant breeze was softening the heat, and I sat back, rested and comfortable, watching a flock of birds that rose, circled, and returned again and again to a spot behind the kitchen. When I finally asked about them it was Uwain, Urien's son, who answered with a laugh.

"Pigeons, from the cote. We feed them all year long, and if there are unexpected guests, Cook just nips out and grabs an extra bird for the pot."

It seemed a splendid idea, and I stowed it away for future use as Uwain moved off to talk with the rest of the guests. Watching him go, it occurred to me that he would soon become a warrior. As he joined a group of Companions there was laughter and joking, and I smiled when Gawain slung his arm around his younger cousin and gave him a good-natured hug.

At the end of the meal Tristan came over to speak with Arthur, asking permission to leave our party and go to Morgan's Sanctuary.

"There's something I need to consult her about," the lanky Cornish-man explained. "And Uwain has said he'll guide me, as he planned to visit his mother anyway."

Arthur readily gave his permission, and it was only later that I began to wonder why a Christian knight would seek help from the High Priestess. I asked Arthur if he had any idea, but the contradiction had not occurred to him.

So when we left York and headed up Dere Street to the Wall, it was without the Harper. But the more I thought about it, the more peculiar the whole matter seemed, and by the time we reached Corbridge I was distinctly uncomfortable—whatever Tris needed, I suspected the Lady would not give it to him.

FIFTEEN

The Stuff of Dreams

t Corbridge we stayed at the inn of the woman who had made my down comforter. She was bashful about hosting the High King's party, so I tried to put her at ease after dinner by telling her how much Arthur and I enjoyed the quilt. The woman bobbed her head in pleasure, then asked hopefully if Palomides was with us.

"He had to stay at Silchester to train the new recruits," I explained, only then remembering that she had helped him when he was a child.

"Strange little tyke he was." She paused in the midst of sweeping the crumbs from the tabletop. "His master claimed he was an Arab, born into slavery. All I knew was the boy was too young to look out for himself when his owner died. So I was relieved that my sister was glad to take him, what with her being without children . . . 'tis a lucky thing when a barren woman finds a child in need of mothering, don't you think?"

"You haven't seen him since then?" I queried, shying from the subject of infertility. "He's grown into one of the finest horsemen in Britain. In fact, it was Palomides who brought us the use of the stirrup."

"Well, fancy that." The good women was pleased he had won renown, although it was clear she had no idea what a stirrup was. Perhaps she'd never see the canvas and leather loops we now sew on all our saddles.

"I often wondered what would happen to the boy," our hostess went on, carefully adjusting the rush-light in its stand. "Different he was, and not just in skin color. I always felt he was destined for something else—travel, maybe, or the life of a monk."

I'd never thought about the Arab's future, other than to suppose he'd marry. Certainly he had a charming way with the ladies, and it seemed unlikely he'd become a hermit. But he was often quiet and thoughtful when others were laughing boisterously, and perhaps that denoted deeper dreams than the rest of us knew. He was, in that way, much like Lancelot.

"You have ample reason to be proud of him," I told her, and was rewarded with a shy smile.

We crossed the Wall and made our way into the round, windswept hills known as the Cheviots. As we were passing an old Roman camp, the Road was blocked by a flock of sheep being driven back to the fold by a family who now lived within the crumbled walls. The shepherds approached us with a mixture of hope and fear, explaining that a band of barbarians had been raiding their flocks all spring.

"We're peaceable men, Your Highness—used to fighting wolves and weather, not raiders. Perhaps you and your warriors . . ."

Arthur nodded quickly and after a hasty conference with Lance and Gawain, allowed that the Companions would root out the bandits while I and my women stayed with the shepherd's family.

"This time I'll not have you in the midst of things," my husband announced firmly, as though expecting me to protest.

I was more than happy to comply—since the experience at the Humber I had neither the curiosity nor the desire to take part in battle again. I even wished Arthur didn't have to, but a king who doesn't lead his men in combat doesn't stay king for long, so I gave him an extra hug and asked the Gods to protect him.

The shepherdess was a small, wizened woman whose bright eyes devoured everything they spied. Leading us into the room the helpers used as a communal sleeping quarters, she apologized for the lack of refinement. "With the weather so mild they won't mind sleeping out, Your Highness, but I haven't time to make it more fancy. We start shearing tomorrow, and outside of lambing, it's the busiest time of the year. But you'll find the room cozy enough and safe, even if it is plain."

I thanked the woman and not wanting to be an imposition, asked her to let me help in some way. So the next morning, after a breakfast of thick, creamy oatmeal, she suggested I take a pair of salve pots down to the men.

I'd never seen shearing—in Rheged we gather our wool from bush and bramble where the Soway sheep have rubbed it off, for they are far wilder than the animals of the Cheviots. I watched, fascinated, as the men washed the animals first, then used a pair of metal shears to divest each animal of its entire fleece, much as a mother peels off the clothes of a youngster.

Sheep are smelly beasts, and I've hated the odor of raw wool since I was young. Now I stood in a cloud of it, holding the ointment jars handy for the men. It seems even the smallest wound under a heavy fleece gets infested with maggots that literally eat the sheep alive, so a mixture of broom buds and lanolin had to be daubed on every sore.

As the shearing progressed the sight of those fat, white worms wriggling blindly in the pink flesh turned my stomach, and I barely had time to put down the salve pots and run to the stream before I was sick.

"Best you help me in the kitchen," the shepherd's wife suggested as I stammered out my apologies. "There's plenty to be done there."

But the next morning I found the new fleeces had been laid out in the kitchen overnight, and the noxious smell hung like a fog over them, making my gorge rise again. I bolted through the door just in time.

The shepherdess set me and my women gathering bilberries well away from the sheep that day, and I felt much better in the fresh air—though I began to pray Arthur would return soon.

On the third morning I avoided both the fleeces and the kitchen entirely, yet once more I found myself bent double beside the stream, retching violently. When the fit was past the shepherd's wife put a cool cloth to my forehead and bade me sit beside her on a stump.

"When did you last bleed, girl?" Her tone was gentle, but she was watching me closely.

"Uhhh . . ." I looked out over the little pool where the sheep were washed, trying to remember. "With the new moon."

"New moon last week, or last month?"

"Not last week . . . are we that far into the new cycle?" The words were all the way out of my mouth before the implication hit home.

"The moon I saw last night was midway to being full again." The shepherdess's eyes crinkled with laughter. "I'd say you've been so preoccupied with other things, you haven't noticed that you're pregnant. I'll wager that once you're away from the fleeces, your mornings will be more comfortable, and you'll have a perfectly normal pregnancy."

The words streamed over me like a warm bath, bringing a joyous flood of laughter and tears. I threw my arms around the old crone, letting her rock me in a motherly embrace; in those few minutes she was Igraine and Mama and Brigit all in one, and my thanks to the Goddess welled up in a great surge of pride and triumph and gratitude.

At last I was going to become a mother.

Arthur and the Companions returned two days later, tired, dirty, and immensely pleased with themselves.

The shepherdess insisted that just as sheep needed washing, so did men, and after the biggest caldron in camp was filled and a fire built under it, the Companions waited patiently for their turn behind the blanket screen to make themselves fit again.

Arthur was full of excitement about the foray and began relating his news while the bathwater heated.

"Tracked the villains over to the coast, to a great rock that juts out above the sea," he announced, shedding his tunic and scratching vigorously. "Then swept down the shore. The villages were quiet enough, but we burned out three camps where raiders had dug in. I don't think there'll be much problem for a while." He nodded appreciatively toward his men. "Best warriors one could want. Gawain has taught Pelleas well; he's a real demon with the sword now. And Lamorak is coming along splendidly. We brought the whole area under control without any losses to ourselves, and left with oaths of loyalty from the settlers, too."

I looked at my husband—even sweaty and grimy he radiated a mixture of childish glee and adult satisfaction. Merlin had taught him well how to use diplomacy and logic, but what he loves best is the shaping of his dream with his bare hands. This last week had provided just that, and he was as thrilled about it as I was about being pregnant. Though I wanted to tell him my own news, this was clearly neither the time nor the place.

"Had to leave Lance behind, however." Arthur was pulling off his boots, and I looked up, startled. "We ended up at the mouth of the Coquet River, where it lets into the North Sea. Pretty little valley and a miniature estuary as well. Something about it quite captivated the Breton, so I gave it to him as his own; be a good idea to have a Round Table presence up here anyway."

The idea of Lance leaving the Court came as a total surprise. Most of the unmarried Companions lived with us unless, like Geraint or Agricola, they had kingdoms of their own. Even Gawain, though he would likely be chosen king of both Edinburgh and the Orkney Isles when his mother died, showed no desire to take up residence anywhere but with us. Not only would it be a strange break in custom to have the Breton living elsewhere, we would miss him considerably. Perhaps, I told myself, he would only go there occasionally.

"Lance wanted to tidy things up . . . and get acquainted with the locals. I noticed the blacksmith has a comely daughter." Arthur chuck-led, and I wondered how much that had to do with the Champion's interest in the place. Maybe his moira was leading him toward romance after all.

Once they had washed, the men ate heartily and tumbled into bed. Arthur was too tired to give me more than a sleepy goodnight, so I lay beside him and hugged the secret of the pregnancy to myself. It would keep until we had a quiet moment alone when we could explore our pleasure together.

But privacy is hard to come by on the Road, and by the time we reached the Pentland Hills I still had not confided my news. The morning sickness evaporated as soon as we left the sheepfold, but my courses hadn't returned and I was growing confident that the shepherd-ess had been right.

The very knowledge of it filled me with splendor—rich and ripening as the harvest around us, I savored my secret with inner delight. Com-ing out of the forest near Edinburgh, we flushed a doe and her fawn who paused to stare at our entourage before bounding away—gazing into her large, liquid eyes I saluted her, mother to mother, before she led her youngster to safety. Staring up at the evening star, I let my senses move out across the land—drifting on the soft breeze, delighting in the cluckings of a duck calling her brood together in the twilight, taking the smell of new-mown hay as perfume for my soul. Never before had I been so content, so much part of the spiral dance.

Whenever I came across the little moleskin booties in my luggage, my fingers strayed lovingly across the fur while I wondered about the child who would wear them.

Tristan and Lance met on the Road and caught up with us just as we were settling in for the night outside of Edinburgh.

"Why on earth are you perched up here when there's a perfectly good fort over there?" Tris demanded, gesturing toward the settlement across the ravine. He was as puzzled as the rest of us by Arthur's insistence on staying on this plateau instead of making use of the hospitality below.

I suspected Arthur's refusal to enter Edinburgh stemmed from his aversion to his sister Morgause—even though she was safely away in the Orkneys, my husband would not go near her citadel.

"No need to enter the town," Arthur growled as he pronged a chunk of salmon from the spit. "I can review the troops up here just as well." It was the answer he'd given everyone, and now he changed the subject. "How was your visit with Morgan?"

Tristan stared at his feet, hands hanging limp at his sides. Despondency was plain on his face. "I went to see about having a spell lifted . . . but the Lady says that since I've become a Christian, she cannot help me." He heaved a great sigh before turning to me. "She sent you a lady-in-waiting, however. The woman wanted to freshen up before being presented, so I left her with Enid."

My back stiffened and I struggled to keep suspicion out of my voice. "Why would Morgan do that?"

"Don't know." Tristan shrugged, too immersed in his own misery to care. As he moved toward the cooking fire, Lance stepped forward to greet us.

"All quiet at Warkworth," the Breton reported, a smile lighting his features. He was as jubilant as Tristan was morose. "No more sign of raiders, but I organized a guard for the place, just in case."

"And the pretty girl?" I asked.

"Girl?" His blank response could hardly have been feigned. "I don't recall any girl—but it's a marvelous spot for a retreat."

Enthusiasm welled up in him, and after he'd gotten some food he returned to the subject, pulling up a camp stool and describing Warkworth between bites of food.

"It's a wonderful place, Gwen. There's a deserted steading on a knoll in the bend of the river. The gardens are well laid out, the orchards are sound—if overgrown—and the Hall was already being repaired when I left. It will be beautiful next spring; a joyful garden. Everyone needs a haven of some kind, a little spot of beauty well away from blood and chaos," he added softly.

I nodded, remembering Arthur's promise that we would someday have such a place of our own. Perhaps once he knew we had a family coming . . .

A stern voice shattered my daydream. "The High Priestess sends her regards."

Morgan's woman stepped forward. She was thin and lanky as a piece of jerky, and I disliked her on sight.

"Velen, Your Highness. I've been a midwife for thirty years, and have brought my medicines with me. Now that you're pregnant, the Lady wishes me to look out for you."

"Pregnant?" The word leapt out of Arthur's mouth like a frog, and Lance turned to stare at me with equal surprise.

I glared at the woman, furious that she'd spoiled my chance to tell Arthur alone.

"Is it true?" Lance inquired, and when I nodded his face lit up with a wonderful smile. "Oh, Gwen, I'm so glad for you."

The sparkle in his eyes was full of pleasure and joy, very like an echo of my own feelings at the shepherdess's words, and I started to grin from ear to ear.

But Arthur just stared at me. "Are you sure?" he asked cautiously.

"Well, uh . . . yes," I stammered, wishing desperately that we weren't surrounded by the Companions. "It's been a little over two months now, and still no sign of bleeding."

I had expected Arthur to be pleased and happy about the news, and his hesitancy startled me. Peering at him more closely, I wondered if he was one of those men who are so frightened at the prospect of childbirth, they miss the joy of pregnancy. I wanted to laugh and take him in my arms, reassuring him I would be fine, and then hear how proud and glad he was, once the shock wore off. But in the circumstances all I could do was beam at him.

"When will it be born?" he inquired, still stunned.

"March." Velen spoke with such authority, one would think it was her child, not mine. "And M'lady must be very quiet and cautious between now and then."

"Nonsense," I retorted, waving her away. "I've never felt better in all my life. Healthy as the proverbial horse, and outside of a craving for oysters, nothing much else has changed."

By now Arthur had his wits about him, and he cast me one of those sidewise looks. "I should have guessed," he chuckled. "There's been an endless stream of yellow-skirted fishwives climbing this hill, filling the air with their hawker's song and their pockets with trinkets—all to supply the royal needs!"

Lancelot was looking back and forth between Arthur and me, and he threw back his head with a fine, free laugh.

"A bairn for the two of you—'tis the best news I've heard yet!" he exclaimed. "And a wonderful way to end the summer."

Gawain and Pelleas had drifted into the group, drawn by the sound of mirth. Gawain clapped Arthur soundly on the back and teased him about being a staunch fellow in bed as well as battle.

"Be that as it may," Morgan's lady cut in, "Her Highness must not indulge in whims like oysters—might harm the child. And no more traipsing about the countryside, either. What she needs is a warm room and a place to settle into."

"That's easily enough arranged," Arthur announced. "We'll be wintering over at Stirling and can snug down there through the spring."

"You know I'd be pleased to host you here." Gawain gestured expansively toward his city, but Arthur stopped him with a firm shake of his head.

"Stirling it is," the King averred.

The Prince of Orkney and Lothian sagged like a scarecrow with the stuffing pulled out, obviously hurt at such a curt dismissal of his invitation.

Tristan had been sitting, silent, on the sidelines, taking no notice of our celebration. Arthur turned to him. "I hope you're free to come north with us—I'll be meeting with Scots and Picts and could use a good translator."

A log in the campfire crumbled suddenly, and in the leaping light I saw Gawain lift his head, his eyes bright with resentment.

"I'll come, if you want me," Tristan answered, not much cheered.

"Of course we want you," Arthur assured him. "With my Queen pregnant and my best men around me, it promises to be a fine winter . . . fine indeed."

His tone was so full, and his smile so broad, all my doubts about his reaction to the pregnancy disappeared, and a heady, buoyant happiness folded around me. Neither Gawain's sulkiness nor Tristan's sorrow could dampen my spirits.

Glancing around the circle, my eyes met Lance's and we smiled in unison, each glad for the other. His pleasure in finding Warkworth was every bit as deep as my glory in being pregnant, and together we reveled in sharing the joy.

It seemed that any number of dreams were, at last, coming true.

SIXTEEN

Stirling

ill you look at the luxury of it!" Enid gasped, delighted to be staying in a real Hall after weeks in military camps and half ruins.

Large and well built, it reminded me of my childhood home at Appleby—a Great Hall big enough to accommodate major Councils, with second-floor lofts for sleeping and spinning, and both kitchen and servants' quarters tucked into their own wing. Even the columns that supported loft and roof were similar—carved with vines and leaves and full of peeping, spritely faces peering out to see what mortals did.

I grinned, glad to know both pregnancy and birth would be accomplished in such a cheering, homey place.

But while we reveled in the domestic amenities, Arthur was pleased by its geographic location. The great rock at Stirling juts out of swamp and waterside just at the point where the Highlands come down from the north to be met by the Ochil Hills on one side and the Campsie Fells on the other. Like a stopper in the neck of a funnel, the fort overlooks the long, flat, valleys that separate the rugged ranges to the north, while to the east the river Forth spreads out into its firth. From here Arthur could make forays throughout central Scotland, secure in the knowledge that no one could advance on Stirling without being seen well in advance by the sentries on the walls.

Once we were settled I suggested to Arthur that we send Velen back to the Sanctuary, but he not only refused that notion, he insisted that

I thank Morgan for providing me with a midwife. So the woman stayed, nagging and fussing about everything I did, and the only place I could escape her was on the ramparts. Fortunately the magnificent view and sense of space always lifted my spirits.

Staring north along the valley floors at the farms and pastures that quilt the edges of the slow, looping river . . . peering up at the mountain scarps where ancient forests embroider dark memories on the autumn wind . . . watching the mist rise from the rust and golden landscape while the far-off honking of geese signals the return of winter on the estuary . . . at such times I would marvel at the mystery of Being and wrap it around the little life that was growing within my womb.

I was on the parapet the day the nomads came marching down from the north. Singing and clapping and half dancing as they walked along, they numbered less than a dozen—small, dark people decked out in piebald furs and heavy jewelry who followed rather than led a handful of reindeer. There was a fair commotion when they were challenged by the guard at the gate, but he let them through, and Enid came to fetch me, announcing the newcomers expected an audience. Arthur and Lance were off meeting with the Caledonian chieftains in the mountains to the west, so it fell to me to handle whatever came up.

Someone routed Tristan out of bed to act as interpreter, and when I reached the Hall Tris was grumbling like a bear who's been wakened too early in the spring. "I have no idea what she wants. Whatever tongue she speaks, it isn't Pictish," he mumbled.

A girl standing at the head of the delegation mimicked the Cornish warrior's yawn, and the rest of her party giggled. They were as weathered as if they'd never lived under a roof, and the men glanced about the Hall uneasily. But the saucy young woman faced me across this impasse of languages with a fine bravado.

"She's a Gern-y-fhain . . . hereditary leader of the Prydn," Gawain called out, making his way across the Hall without looking at Tristan.

He began an animated conversation with the girl; both spoke as much with their hands as their voices, and at one point the redhead from the Orkneys all but collapsed in laughter, which sent the Prydn into gales of merriment of their own.

"Her name is Ragnell," Gawain reported, "and she brings her people and animals south for the winter pasturage. She also wants you to know she comes from a long line of famous gerns."

I smiled inwardly, amused that even in the north the tradition of powerful queens was passed from generation to generation. Looking at the outlandish creature, I wondered if I seemed as ludicrous to her as she did to me.

Ragnell caught my gaze and gave me a regal nod of recognition. I returned the gesture with equal solemnity, and then suddenly we both burst out laughing.

"She says the tall-folk have put up fences across her pasture, M'lady," Gawain explained. "All people need pasturage, so she's willing to share with you, within reason. But fencing off what the Mother made for everyone is selfish and . . . and not acceptable," he added with chagrin.

"What would she have me do, tear down the fences and let our horses run loose?"

Gawain cast me a quick look, then turned back to the nomads. By now the smell of their poorly tanned pelts was beginning to pervade the room, and one of the men took to scratching himself industriously—no doubt the warmth of the indoors had made his lice more active.

"She is willing to allow you your fences, provided you allow her the use of the water," Gawain explained after another animated exchange. "She wants you to divert the stream so as to form a pond outside the fence."

I stared at the gern in astonishment, wondering what on earth I was doing bargaining with this impish creature—I suspected that the men would have made short work of her request, shooing her away to find pasturage somewhere else.

"I know the area she's speaking of," Gawain interjected. "It's out by the barrows, beyond the henge with the white pebbles. Her men and I can dig that diversion in three days' time." There was a sudden flurry of exchanges between Gawain and Ragnell, and after much coaxing he turned back to me. "She also says she'll give you a charm for a safe delivery."

My eyebrows shot up in surprise because the pregnancy didn't even show yet. She grinned at me and adroitly sidestepping Gawain, ran up the steps to where I sat in the carved chair and laid her hands on my belly.

"May thy wealth be gloriously healthy," Gawain translated as Ragnell intoned her blessing. "She herself has born two bairn, though only one lives."

At such close range the smell of the girl was overpowering, and the dirt crusted around her fingernails was appalling. But when she looked up from her chant her dark eyes were large and loving, as when I'd seen the Goddess in Nimue, and for all that I didn't understand her language, her message was clear.

For a bare moment we were sisters in the hand of the Mother. Then caution returned, and she backed away from me even as I smiled and thanked her for the blessing and promised her her water.

With that they were gone, running and skipping out of the Court like acrobats on a holiday, though I suspected it was more from relief at escaping this encounter than their own high spirits. Whatever they thought of this meeting, I was deeply touched by their Queen.

Everyone who had seen them go through the courtyard came crowding into the Hall, curious as to who these strangers were.

"Prydn . . . fairy-folk . . . the Ancient Ones who call themselves the firstborn children of the Gods," Gawain announced. "There weren't any Prydn in the Orkneys by the time I was born, but my governess had grown up with one of their changelings who'd been left on her family's doorstep one deadly winter. They have a saying—'Better to lose a child to a warm hearth than bury thy wealth in the cold heath.' "

Surprise and uneasiness stirred through the household at the realization that we'd just hosted a people one step away from the Otherworld. But while many of the courtiers made the sign of the cross or that against evil, I was filled with admiration for Ragnell's courage in coming to Court and asking that I redress what she had perceived as a wrong.

"Ugh." Velen sniffed with disdain. "How could you let her touch you, Your Highness? Why, the whole Hall reeks of their smell."

I was tempted to say I knew cleaner queens who were far more dangerous than this little wildcat, but I held my tongue.

. . .

At the end of the week Gawain came back from his irrigation project, cocky and cheerful and bearing a gift from the gern.

"Ragnell gathered them herself," he announced, carefully handing over a half-dozen white quartz pebbles. "From the base of the Standing Stones. She says they are gifts of the Great Mother because they reflect the light of the moon."

He made the sign against evil while I stared curiously at the small, sharp-edged rocks. "They scatter them around the stones," he explained, as though that cleared up the mystery.

I might not understand what she used them for, but the gern's gift pleased me, and I asked Gawain to convey my thanks if he saw her again.

"Oh, we'll be meeting." He shook his head in admiration. "Wonderful woman, that! More spunk and spit than any I've yet met in the south . . . with the possible exception of Your Highness," he added quickly. "Can't remember when I've had such a good time."

And with that he swaggered from the room, shoulders swinging and good humor fairly pouring off him.

"Whatever did you put in this stuff?" I asked Velen with a grimace. The brew Morgan's lady gave me daily had taken on a decidedly different taste.

"It's a new herb," the midwife said smoothly. "After the third month new medicines must be added to the tonic."

I watched her carefully, thinking for the hundredth time that I didn't like her but had no way of dismissing her without getting into a row with Arthur. Maybe I could send her away and pretend she'd decided I didn't need her after all. But that idea made me even crosser; who was Morgan to force me into tarnishing my honor with a lie?

It was a fine autumn morning—the sort when the vales ring with the bellowing of stags and squirrels begin to search for warm places to sleep the winter through—altogether much too nice to let it be spoiled by Morgan's lackey. So without another word I marched down to the stable and took Shadow out for our usual ride to the Crag, a pinnacle little more than a mile away.

The wind blew fresh and smelled of snow, but the leaves of the birches still spangled like golden coins against the darker green of the wildwood, and I smiled in spite of the chill. My mare was edgy and full of twitches, moving her ears constantly and snorting at any shadow on the path, and I kept up a steady stream of reassurances to her.

It was only when we'd reached the top of the Crag that I saw the clouds, low and heavy and driven by the wind. My stomach tightened suddenly, and I turned back toward home; no doubt we would reach the fort before the storm, but I was beginning to feel uneasy and had no desire to linger.

Nausea struck on the way back, and I pushed Shadow to a faster trot, wanting to get to my chambers as quickly as possible. No matter what Arthur said, I wasn't going to take any more of Morgan's "special medicines"; in fact, I'd send Velen away as soon as I could find her.

A gust of wind lifted Shadow's mane and sent a flurry of dead leaves across the path, uncovering a stoat, which raced for cover. The silly mare shied violently and for the first time in years I found myself unseated. By the time I overcame my surprise Shadow was out of sight, well on her way to the stable.

Cursing roundly, I got to my feet, a rush of pain rising with me. The twisting, turning ache was tying my midsection in knots. I managed to lean against a tree, waiting for the cramping to subside before I began to walk home. When it didn't abate, I staggered blindly forward until a crippling pang doubled me over and I ended up crawling on hands and knees along the path.

This was more than the shock of falling off my horse, and I started to cry with fear and frustration.

How could I have been so gullible as to have accepted medicine from Morgan? Now, with the child's life in jeopardy, my own stupidity seemed enormous, and I sobbed in fury and disgust with myself as well as the High Priestess. Even the Gods must have heard my imprecations, for when I could crawl no farther I gave Them a tongue-lashing that all but blistered my mouth.

The party from the fort came for me as soon as they saw Shadow was riderless, but though they carried me home on a litter and put me into the comfort of a bed, it was too late. After three long hours writhing in pain and rage, I lay exhausted and the child was no more.

Enid sat beside me, trying in her crisp way to give me solace, but it was Ragnell who reached across the abyss of my misery and eased my heart.

Gawain brought the Prydn Queen through the side door of my chamber, and she stood looking down on me, great tears of grief streaking her face. I didn't know when she'd lost her own babe, or how, but such details were unimportant. She perched on the bed next to me, put both hands on my temples, and slowly, softly, began to croon. I closed my eyes, letting her fingers draw away the misery of my soul.

The wordless lament wove a shelter around us—a lullaby of sorrow sung by every mother who has ever mourned. Together we cried for the whole of humankind, born to dream of eternities, waking to find the grave. Slowly, gradually, my anguish was absorbed by that of generations past and made more bearable with this sharing.

Once, just before going to sleep, I reached for Ragnell's hand and kissed it in gratitude before putting it back to my temple. If ever there was an act of compassion, it was hers.

I slept the day and night around, and both Ragnell and Velen were gone by the time Arthur arrived. He burst into the room looking wild-eyed and windblown and let out a bellow you could hear a mile away.

"For goodness' sake, Gwen, whatever possessed you to go riding when you were that far along?"

"Riding?" I flared, sitting up in bed and wondering how he could be angry at a time like this. "I've been riding every day since I was old enough to walk! It wasn't the ride that did it, Arthur; it was that awful medicine Morgan sent. I knew I shouldn't be drinking those potions, I don't care what your sister said!"

"Now let's not start that." Arthur threw his gloves on the table and asked Enid to fetch him something hot. I'd never seen him so riled, as though some sea of emotion had broken through his floodgates. He rounded on me with a howl. "Morgan's got no reason to do us harm, and your constant suspicion is unseemly and not worthy of my wife."

"Unseemly? How seemly is it for you to come raging in here full of

accusations instead of sorrow when we've just lost a child, Arthur
. . . a child?"

The word stuck in my throat, choking me with tears, and I turned
my face away hastily. A huge emptiness was opening within me, threatening to swallow my whole life.

Arthur's temper had cooled, and he came over to sit beside me on
the bed, putting his hands on my shoulders. "Of course I'm sorry
. . . but they told me you might not survive. . . ."

Listening to the silence that followed, I thought how little I understood this man; his own child dead, and he felt not grief but anger.

"Gwen," he said firmly, still holding me at arm's distance, "there's
something you must understand. I don't care whether we have children
or not, but I do care if you live or die."

The shock of his words went through me like a blade, slicing and
numbing at the same time.

"I'm happy with our life as it is, lass—can't see that a child would
be anything other than a bother. I was pleased about this pregnancy
because you wanted it so much, but since kingship isn't hereditary, it
doesn't matter to me if we have a child or not—and there's more than
enough children born already."

His voice had gone cold and hard-edged, and an expression of bitter
disgust fled across his features, making a mockery of the man I knew.

I stared at him in disbelief. Raving one minute and turned to ice the
next—for the first time I truly saw him as Uther's son.

He released my shoulders and getting to his feet, began to pace the
room. The grimness had left his face, but neither of us spoke; I couldn't
put my confusion into words, and he seemed to prefer the silence.

Although I was weak and a bit shaky, there had been no hemorrhag-
ing, so when Enid returned with a tray I rose and joined my husband
at the table, trying to lessen the distance that was growing between us.

As he finished his soup he began to tell me about the lairds of those
bristling mountains to the west; fierce, proud war-lords who could see
the advantages of being associated with the Pendragon as long as he
didn't threaten their independence.

"Hueil's is the only faction that won't meet with us, and if Lance
hasn't won them over by the time I get back, we'll give up for the
winter and come home."

I nodded, still not knowing what to say to this man who had become a stranger in less than an hour's time.

"I'd best be returning to the camp," he allowed, rising and looking down at me. "Just wanted to make sure you were all right."

I longed to find some shelter in his embrace, to feel the whole of him between me and that cold, sad emptiness, but there was no invitation on his part, so I sat silent, unable to move, and he patted my shoulder.

"Best you get some rest, lass."

And then he was striding toward the Hall, and I remained where I was, staring bleakly into space.

Perhaps I had never known him at all. Perhaps we never would share the same feelings, the same hopes or dreams or fears or pain. Perhaps, in the final analysis, Britain was the only child we'd ever have. Someday I'd be proud of that, I knew, but right now the thought just left me numb.

Slowly, silently, I stood up and made my way back to bed.

SEVENTEEN

The Loathly Lady

"A h, Gwen, she makes a bright day beautiful, and a dark mood bearable." Gawain sighed as he stared at Ragnell with such open admiration I couldn't help but smile.

The nomad Queen was moving among her reindeer. Dressed in coarse wool and old pelts, she blended so closely with her animals one could believe she had the art of becoming invisible—only a cluster of brilliant blue kingfisher feathers tucked in her hair gave her away.

Reindeer are fractious as goats and just as unpredictable. They pressed their broad cowlike noses forward when Ragnell scratched them behind the ears but jumped nimbly away if she moved suddenly.

The gern turned her head to sniff the wind, and Gawain laughed. "You know what she does, first thing in the morning? Crawls out of that pile of skins she calls a bed and starts snuffling like a bear digging under a rotten log. Only she's digging in the air. Afterward she pops back under the covers and tells me where the snow has fallen, and if the deer are grazing near or far, and what the 'tall-folk' are having for breakfast in Stirling. I hear how they make fun of her at Court, but there isn't one of us who couldn't learn something from her and her kind."

I nodded in agreement. This young leader of the Ancient Ones— whom the courtiers called "the loathly lady"—romped through their midst with magnificent indifference. Head high, she was a picture of honest pride in spite of the snickers and grimaces that dogged her heels.

It was a quality I admired and began to apply in my own life, for Arthur had returned to Stirling full of plans for the Caledonians, and the subject of children lay dead between us. So, like Ragnell, I held my head high and went on about my duties, hoping neither Arthur nor the world would know how deep the hurt had gone.

Winter came with an abundance of feasts and festivals; the fort was comfortable and the forests full of boar and deer. The men hunted during the day and at night there was singing and gaming and story-telling in the Hall.

Various Caledonian chieftains came to meet with Arthur. They brought food for the table and musicians for the Hall, and the nights rang with the thrum and echo of skirling bagpipes. It was swirling, rampant music that made the blood stir for battle and lifted the head with resolve, until one warrior after another put down the crossed swords and, driven by the wild sounds, leapt and capered between the blades.

Afterward, when the swords were put up, the country dances began. I loved the intricate toe-and-heel patterns that give physical shape to the music, and though Arthur wouldn't join me, I found a willing partner in Lancelot. We spent many an evening whirling through the Hall as it filled with the lively skip of dancers and the whip of pleated tartans.

The affair between Gawain and Ragnell grew into a tempestuous passion that flared explosively between them. Arthur's nephew spent more and more time in the shadow of the barrows where the Prydn had their camp, and some at Court began to worry that the Champion would get trapped in their fey ways. It is well known that when mortals are tempted across the threshold of those Hollow Hills, they rarely return.

"My wife thinks the Prince is under a spell and doesn't see what an ugly scamp that creature is," a local laird confided. "But I'll wager she turns into a lovely lass at bedtime; you know how changeable the fairy-folk can be."

I suspected it was less a question of physical beauty than spiritual affinity that drew Ragnell and Gawain together. Raised in the man-nered, painted Court of his mother, the Prince of Orkney seemed to be reveling in the freedom he found with the homely nomad Queen.

Like a pair of wolves unwilling to be tamed, their spitfire energy fused in a savage partnership. Nor did it seem that either one cared a whit about what the courtiers might say.

So I was surprised when Gawain brought the gern to my chambers and asked if I could find a dress for her—he wanted to present her at the Hall and feared the others would ridicule her native clothes.

I stared in dismay at Ragnell. When she stood on tiptoe she came barely up to Gawain's chest, and since Gawain and I are of an equal height, I was at a loss as to what I had that might fit her. But Enid was quick with a needle, and she added a panel to one of my tunics, turning it into a full-length gown for the Prydn Queen. It was not exactly elegant, but it would serve for her debut at Court.

Remembering her generosity of spirit when I lost the child, I laid out my jewelry for Ragnell to choose from, but she wrinkled her nose in disdain.

Gawain laughed. "I fancy she'd prefer to dazzle them with her own treasure."

And dazzle she did. There was a gasp of amazement when she and Morgause's son appeared at the Hall that night, and I had a hard time keeping from grinning as they walked the length of the room to give us a formal greeting. Gawain was defiantly wearing the rough tunic and cape of skins that Prydn men use, and Ragnell had covered herself with gold; gold braided into torques, beaten into bands, strung as beads or sewn to edgings as bangles. No doubt it was fairy treasure from within the Hollow Hills, and it made her glimmer in the fire-glow like a tiny, primitive Goddess.

Gawain had coached her well, and she gave me a mischievous look as she made a full curtsy. I reached out my hand and squeezed her fingers lightly as she rose. For a moment I felt them tremble and knew her poise was more facade than confidence.

Later that evening one of the war-lords who had drunk too much became suggestively familiar with the gern. Ragnell turned on him so rapidly that he had no chance to raise his guard, and her nails left a set of bloody furrows down his face.

Gawain jumped to his feet, dirk drawn and manner challenging. The nomad had more than defended herself, but after the drunken lout backed down, she stepped forward and spat in his face, no doubt thinking that one insult deserved another.

A murmur of disapproval ran through the Hall and Ragnell let out a string of invective, though I couldn't tell whether it was meant for the boorish war-lord or the Court as a whole.

Gawain slung some comment at her, and then suddenly the two of them were at it, yelling and hollering like banshees at Samhain. The Prydn Queen stamped her feet in frustration and sidestepping her lover, advanced upon my chair. In a movement that was half wriggle, half ripping, she tore off the tunic and with the briefest nod, stepped out of the tatters and turned toward the door.

Clad only in her jewelry, she passed by Gawain with the utmost dignity, as though he didn't exist. He threw out his arm to stop her, and with a flick of her wrist, so quick it could have been that of a thief, she snagged the fur cape he was wearing and, slinging it over one shoulder, marched out of the Hall.

With a yell Gawain disappeared after her, and the Court erupted with laughter. But I sat silent, aching for both of them.

Ragnell never came back, and while Gawain continued to divide his time between the Prydn and the Court, it soon becme obvious the redhead was caught between conflicting loyalties. He would sit, gloomy and miserable, with us, clearly longing for the open fields and his love. Yet after several days at their camp, he'd come back to Court, sad and angry, but relieved to be home.

I watched him fret within the trap of his moira, but when I brought the subject up he growled like a hound with a sore paw, so I let it be.

The winter progressed, and for every three lairds who came to meet the High King, two left willing to talk about truces and trade agreements. Scrap by scrap Arthur was stitching together a unified Britain, and he was so filled with his own dream, he didn't notice his nephew's plight.

One March morning a Pictish envoy appeared, coming up the Forth in a sturdy dugout. He was a brawny fellow with ornate tattoos on his arms and across his cheeks, and though he stayed only long enough to deliver his message to Arthur, the household was full of gossip about him when I returned from riding.

"The paths and tracks from the Highlands are still frozen, so he sailed along the coast." Arthur shook his head in admiration. "I swear those Picts are half seals, they're that at home in the water! Maelchon, the leader at Inverness, has invited us to join him for the Gathering in the Great Glen at midsummer. He sent along a present for you as well—seems they're full of admiration for the warrior queen who fought the Saxons so bravely at Humberside."

I laughed; it always amuses me how quickly news of royal activity travels—and how often it is wrong. Next they'd be saying that I had been the hero of that battle instead of Cei.

Arthur let a sleek, slippery necklace of silver flow into my palm. It had the look of slinking water, and I stared at it, fascinated, while he explained it was a token of their highest esteem. I would wear it with pride at Inverness this summer.

As the weather warmed we began to hear that Hueil, son of Caw and brother of that same Gildas who was studying with the monk Illtud, was trying to gather enough men to force us to retreat back beyond the Wall.

So Arthur and the Companions fought a series of skirmishes through the great forest before Hueil's men scattered across the Trossachs at the end of May. Lance volunteered to stay behind to round them up while we were attending the midsummer rite in Pictland. It was an offer Arthur much appreciated.

The day we were to leave, I climbed to the top of the rampart for a last look at the view I had loved so well and found Gawain leaning morosely against the parapet. He was holding one of Ragnell's hair ornaments between his fingers and barely acknowledged my greeting.

"Gone!" The Orkney Prince glared out toward the north as though his very anger could stop her. "Gone back to the summer pastures without even a farewell."

"Are you going after her?" I asked, and immediately regretted it.

"What good would it do?" He sighed heavily and turned to look me full in the face. The misery of his loss was written clear across his countenance, all bravado and bluff gone.

"She was the world to me, Gwen . . . but Arthur and the Companions are my family." He swallowed heavily and glanced away. "The very night after my father died in the Great Battle, my mother tried to make

me swear I'd take revenge on Arthur . . . even though I had already
surrendered and given him my oath. Being newly widowed, she was
distraught—misspoke herself in her grief, no doubt. But she is an
ardent woman; beautiful and powerful, and you cross her at your own
peril. When I refused her request she cursed me . . . cursed me and
struck my name from the family."

Morgause's son wrestled silently with the memory, then shuddered. "That's when I turned to Arthur and made his Cause my
Cause. He's all the family I can call upon, Gwen, and I could never
forsake him." There was a long pause, followed by a deep sob. "I
told Ragnell she needn't live at Court, that we could meet somewhere in between. . . ."

Gawain turned his back to me and leaned, stiff-armed, against the
parapet, elbows locked and head drooping. This was no time to point
out that the gern could no more forsake her people than he could his,
so I simply put my hands on his shoulders and tried to massage the
tension from the knotted muscles. When he'd relaxed a bit I gave him
a fond pat and went back downstairs, leaving him staring moodily at
the bright feathers his love had left behind.

The conversation had at least given me some insight into Morgause.
I wondered if she still harbored that fierce rage against Arthur, or if,
as Gawain said, she had been crazed by grief when she tried to set her
son against her brother. Certainly in the years since, she had shown no
enmity toward us and had let her sons come to Court as they reached
the age to become pages. I hoped that time had dulled her pain and
would draw the sting from Arthur's bitterness as well.

When we headed into the Highlands it was Tristan who rode at the
front with Arthur and myself since Lance was pursuing Hueil's men to
the west. Gawain preferred to ride alone, surrounding himself in deep,
brooding silence.

Scotland is a rugged land, full of quick, drenching showers and a
multitude of rainbows. The Romans had not brought their Roads this
far north, so we picked our way through primitive pine forests and
camped in the high meadows under the Grampian peaks.

We heard the Picts long before we saw them. At night the high trill

of their flutes danced from one hidden glen to another, broken only at
the lakeshores by a wild, demonic laughter that made my skin crawl.
Even after I learned it was the courting call of a black-throated diving
bird, the eerie sound still made me shiver.

The people began to show themselves in shy, scattered gatherings
beside the strange carved boulders they use to denote boundaries. With
great sobriety they watched our procession pass and rarely said a word.
Only occasionally did we stay at a leader's fort, but even there we were
met with curiosity rather than enthusiasm. While they were not hos-
tile, there was no cheering and glad welcome such as I was used to in
the south.

By the time we approached Inverness the days had grown long and
the twilights lasted well on to midnight. It was then that Gawain asked
permission to search the high pastures for Ragnell.

"I need to have it out with her once and for all," he growled, the
last of his hope warming his voice. "But I'll meet you at the pass of
Glen Coe in a fortnight, no matter what the result of our talk is."

I eyed my friend anxiously—he'd become a man consumed by a love
he could neither claim nor let go of, and it was burning him alive.
Perhaps this was the only way for him to resolve his moira, but I made
an extra little prayer for him, unable to see any resolution that would
not involve pain.

The Pictish leader Maelchon proved to be a gracious host, but his sister
was a lean, haughty woman who gestured scornfully toward the cleft
in the mountains where the lake lay black and silent in the gloaming.
"The annual gathering for the lairds to hold Council, settle disputes,
and drive a herd of cattle into the water to appease the Gods." She
nodded toward the scatter of cooking fires that lit the long banks of
the Loch. "Every year Himself and I get rowed down the length of it
to receive their allegiance. Not that it means much; those brigands
would as soon slit our throats as not."

I was appalled by her attitude, for she acted as though she were the
King's consort yet spoke with total derision about their subjects. Pity
the king and people who must be under her sway.

"Has he no wife?" I asked Tristan.

"He does, but it doesn't matter. Among the Picts it's the men who rule, but they count the bloodline through the mother, so the sister's son is considered first in line for the throne. If she's a powerful woman, she dominates the Court." The Harper shrugged. "That's why I have no standing here, for all that my father was a Pictish king himself."

Next morning we were escorted with great ceremony to a flotilla of boats and dugouts, barges and canoes that were assembled at the head of the Loch. The royal barge was swagged with awnings and pennants, each held to its post by the bleached skull of a stag. The eye sockets of these relics were filled with flowers, while a set of antlers, covered with beaten gold, topped the center pole of the royal pavilion. A scatter of thick fur throws covered the wooden benches on which we sat. There was a constant roll of drums, no doubt to help the oarsmen as well as signal our approach to those along the shore, and the bright notes of the flutes shimmered over the water as we got under way.

Loch Ness is as deep and strange as the Lady's Black Lake in Rheged. Powerful mysteries lie sleeping beneath the surface of the dark water that extends like a long narrow gash between the jagged mountains. This day the clouds were running like sheep across the sun, changing the mood from light to shadow in the blink of an eye.

Whenever our barge approached a clearing on the rocky shore, barons and warriors, craftsmen and husbanders rushed to the water's edge, dancing and singing in salute as we went by.

"They wish to perform a special ceremony with the High King," Tristan reported when we stepped off the barge at the far end of the lake. So I moved aside to watch as a holy man came out of the crowd and bowed low before Arthur.

The shaman was wearing the skin of a stag, its face covering his, its antlers rearing up from his head much like the pictures I've seen of the great Horned One, Cernunnos. He shook a wooden rod with great vehemence, carving the air in Z-shaped strokes. It was clear that he was calling down the spirit of the God into his own mortal being, for like all shape-changers he would soon become one with his deity.

The stag-priest danced and spun in place while a young apprentice shook whispering rattles and put pinch after pinch of resin into a small brazier at his feet. An acrid smoke rose from the embers, and the acolyte fanned it into a cloud around Arthur as the stag-priest stamped his feet excitedly.

Then suddenly all was silent as the boy handed Arthur a bronze mirror much like the one I have from Mama, only this one had a soft leather cover attached to the polished surface.

"Close your eyes," Tristan translated, and when Arthur's lids were shut the stag-priest lifted the bronze disk before my husband's face and folded the covering back from the mirror. A new cloud darkened the sun as Arthur opened his eyes and looked directly at the reflection.

Anger flashed across his features, and for a moment I thought he would fling the thing to the ground. But though his jaw tensed and his eyes narrowed, Arthur held his gaze steady and didn't move.

The shaman was peering intently at the High King through the eye holes in the deer's face, and with a sudden, wild cry he began to prance in a circle around Arthur, bowing and strutting and showing off the majesty of his saber-pointed antlers. My husband stood, resolute and unmoving, in the center of that wild dance. No matter how close the sweep of the mighty horns came, he neither flinched nor looked away from what the mirror revealed, though he paled noticeably in the process.

With a final grand whirl the stag-priest snatched the mirror from Arthur's grasp and, bowing deeply, turned to present him to the murmuring crowd. They broke into applause as the shaman backed away, and Arthur reached out to me, pulling me back to his side. His fingers were cold as ice, and sweat was glistening on his skin, but we stood together before the assembled Picts with regal calm.

The rest of the night was devoted to eating and merrymaking, cavorting around huge bonfires and hailing the Gods of mountaintop and hidden stream. The Picts are famous for their heather beer, which so captivated Cei that he offered to trade his best gold bracelet for the recipe. But the brewer laughed and allowed that it was part of the tribal treasure and therefore not for sale. That was a pity, for to this day no one has been able to duplicate that tasty brew, though I suspect Cei has spent some time trying.

Later I watched Arthur in the fire-glow, wondering what he had seen in the mirror that had shaken him so deeply and wishing I could have gotten a peek, too. Perhaps it held the key as to why he was so guarded and brusque at exactly those times where warmth and gentle sharing should be possible. I loved him dearly in spite of the distance that lay between us, but one could watch him with the dogs and see more tender concern than he would ever allow another human. It was a puzzle that I had no answer for, and I finally told myself to leave it be. There was no point in making myself unhappy over something I couldn't change.

So we progressed down the Great Glen, with feasting and festivities each night and a wide variety of people bringing us gifts each day. There were walrus-tusk charms with pictures scratched on them; thick, solid cloaks with peaked hoods; and more of the beautiful silver chains.

Toward the end of our journey an old woman gave me the handful of fern fronds. "For Merlin. We hoped the Mage would come with you, though rumor says that wench has put an end to him."

"Oh, no," I corrected her. "No, the Enchanter is in Brittany."

The crone looked at me skeptically. "The Ancient Ones see everything, and they say the doire lives in Merlin's Cave, alone. They saw her this last Beltane. I'll wager she tricked that daft old man into giving her all his secrets, then got rid of him."

I shook my head adamantly, and she laughed. "Sorcerer or not, he's still a man, and a mortal one at that."

With a stiff glance she stalked away, and I noticed those around her threw their hands across their eyes lest she put a hex on them. A chill slid down my spine—what if she knew something we did not? What if Merlin was, in fact, dead?

At the end of the fortnight we camped in the broad swath of Glen Coe pass, where the mountains are flung about like building blocks left scattered in a nursery by young Gods. It's an awesome place, full of deep, brooding shadows, and I kept checking over my shoulder for what might be just out of sight.

"Gawain said he'd be here, no matter what," I reminded Arthur as he stared out across the rain-drenched landscape.

"Surely he isn't thinking about staying with the gern?" The tent was too small for pacing, so my husband chewed on the ends of his mustache and scowled.

"I don't know . . . maybe," I answered, wondering how much Gawain had confided to Arthur.

"If he hasn't arrived by tomorrow morning, we'll have to go on without him." Arthur turned away from the tent flap. "Can't think what's gotten into him; be good for him to find a wife and settle down."

It seemed to me that he'd done just that, but being Gawain she wasn't any ordinary woman, and neither one of them wanted to settle down.

The next day was full of the crystal clarity that so often follows a storm, and the granite slabs and dancing streams fairly sparkled in the air. There was no sign of the Orkney Prince, however, so we packed up in a leisurely fashion and headed south.

The majesty of Glen Coe was more beautiful than forbidding in this light, and even Rannoch Moor, that strange bog that covers the high vale under barren peaks, was awash with color. It looked like a carpet of feathers, though I knew it was no doubt treacherous—one misstep could mean the loss of man or horse.

"There he is!" Arthur cried, suddenly pointing across the Moor.

The distant form of a horseman was just visible a long way off. He slouched in the saddle, letting his mount pick its way among the tufted tussocks of the bog. Between the danger of the land and the distance involved, it would take him all day to catch up with us, so we pitched the tents and raised the banner high as a signal that we were waiting for him.

Gawain made it into camp at sunset, just as the mists were rising over the vale. We rushed out to greet him in the dying light, and I gasped at the sight as he dismounted.

Morgause's son looked more like a madman than a famous warrior— unkempt and soaking wet from rain and mist, his cheeks were stubbled and his eyes hollow and red-rimmed. But worst of all were the scratches across his face, as bad as those borne by the drunken Scot who'd accosted Ragnell at Stirling.

"Well come, nephew," Arthur said gently, his tone softer than I had ever heard before. "Are you hungry?"

Gawain nodded. "Been tiptoeing through that bog since sunup." His answer was civil enough, but he avoided meeting my eyes.

"Come on down to the fire," Arthur suggested, slinging his arm around Gawain's shoulder and giving him a pat. "Cei's got together a pot of soup that'll warm you good and proper."

The Orkney Prince nodded a silent assent, and Arthur turned him away as a sheepdog herds an errant lamb. Together they went stumping off into the grayness in search of the male camaraderie that would hearten Gawain more than anything else. With a sigh I went back to the tent and got ready for bed.

Gawain never spoke Ragnell's name again, and whatever he may have told Arthur about those scratches was not passed on to me. By the time we had made our way out of the Highlands the scratches on Gawain's face had begun to heal. But the scars on his heart were harder to see, for he masked his wound with a flinty resolution.

I just hoped he had not turned his face from love forever.

EIGHTEEN

Of Mortal Men

he northern half of Loch Lomond is every bit as steep and narrow as the Highland glens, and as we rode along it I began to wonder if we'd ever reach the Lowlands. Then suddenly the landscape opened up and the loch spread out in a shimmer of summer blue before us. It was like stepping through a door into another world, and I cried out with pleasure at the sight.

Tree-capped islands lay scattered across the dappled water, and when we made camp that night a wee slip of a moon was hanging pale in the silver sky, just as it had over Windermere on the last night before I left home to marry Arthur. That was four years past, and the very idea of seeing Kaethi and Rhufon and Gladys again filled me with excitement. But most of all I looked forward to visiting with my father.

It had been hard for him to ask me to accept a political liaison in place of a love marriage, and I'd not gone to it gracefully. Yet even though Arthur and I did not share the romance that had been the mark of my parents' union, we had a good partnership and a reliable, if unspoken, love. Many another queen has prayed for less.

Now I would have a chance to tell my father how well this marriage had turned out.

"'Tis Himself I'm looking for."

The good-natured demand rolled through camp before the breakfast

fire was even started. The voice was familiar, but the lilt was decidedly
Caledonian, so I buried my head in the pillow, content to let the sentry
take care it.

"Lance, I'm over here!" Arthur sat up abruptly and started to swing
his feet to the floor as the flap of our tent flew open and the Breton
appeared.

He was whippet lean and brown as a berry, but his hair was cut in
the page-boy fashion of the Picts and a full black beard covered the
lower portion of his face.

"By Jove," Arthur swore admiringly, "never could get mine to grow
like that."

"Only way to protect against the midges." Lance grinned, dropping
the accent and striding to the foot of our camp bed.

"What news?" Arthur was getting right to the point. I expected him
to pull on his breeches and take Lance out of the tent, but they became
so engrossed in trading information, neither noticed it was an awkward
place to hold a conference. There was nothing for it but that I pull the
covers up around my chin and sit up as well.

I watched the two of them: Arthur so ruddy and outgoing, Lance
so dark and private. They'd grown into the best of friends and a fine
working team, complementing each other much as the two different
natures of Loch Lomond combine to form a magnificent whole.

"The last of Hueil's men are holed up on the islands in the lake,"
Lance announced. "Can't do much about them in the summer, what
with ducks and fish so easy to hand. But come the winter snows, I'll
starve them out. That is," he added, "if you want me to stay here. I
gather there's some sort of activity in the south, so perhaps I should
come with you. . . ."

"What sort of activity?" Arthur tensed beside me.

"I'm not sure," the Breton responded, his blue eyes darkening as he
frowned. "Morgan le Fey came up to Dumbarton and made a trip out
to see me in early June. She didn't actually say there was trouble
brewing, but asked if I'd heard of a man named Cerdic. I assumed he
was a Celt, with a name like that, but it seems he's the leader of a Saxon
party that came ashore near Portchester. She didn't have any details,
but this might be serious." Lance glanced over at me with a smile. "You
know how she can imply things without saying them straight out.

Actually, she was less worried about an invasion than about Merlin—claims he's met with foul play at the hands of the doire."

I nodded slowly, wondering if that's where the Pictish crone had gotten the idea. If so, Morgan must be spreading the rumor everywhere.

"I made friends with one of Ragnell's men last winter." Lance turned back to Arthur. "They heard Merlin's promise that you would be the King of *all* Britons, and Ragnell has vouched for your integrity. She says you are the leader who was foretold as coming to earth on a comet—it's an old prophecy of theirs."

I remembered Igraine, terrified by the firedrake on the night Arthur was conceived, and marveled at the patterns of Fate.

"At any rate, word has gone out that you can be trusted," Lance was explaining. "So I asked them to find out what they could about Cerdic. It seems he's not only landed in the south, he goes by the title of 'King of the Britons.' "

Arthur let out a low whistle. "What sort of reception has he gotten among the Federates?"

Lance shook his head. "That's unclear. I only got this last information yesterday, and was debating whether I should leave Hueil for another time and ride north to find you when I saw your campfire last night."

"Could be just another Saxon deciding to swagger a bit as he settles in." Arthur reached absently for his breeches.

"Could be," Lance agreed. "Though that doesn't explain his Celtic name, or why he's laying claim to all of Britain . . . they usually only style themselves King among their own folk."

Arthur pondered the news in silence, then busied himself with getting dressed. "Well, let's have a look at Hueil's summer havens," he suggested cheerfully.

So the two of them went off to the lakeshore while I snuggled back under the covers. Here we'd finally gotten out of the Highlands into more familiar country, and already the Saxon problem was plaguing us.

There was one more Court to visit before we reached Rheged, and we rode down to Fergus's stronghold with good weather and high spirits unfurled like the Banner above us. Whatever threat this Cerdic posed, Arthur was determined to finish carrying word of the Cause to the north.

The Gods must have used the whole of Scotland for a playground, for at Dumbarton they left a rounded chunk of mountain right in the midst of a tidal marsh. The citadel on top of it is virtually impregnable—one can see in every direction for miles around, and thousands of water birds rise, screeching and flapping in alarm, the moment anyone approaches. They swirled and cried and banked around us, churning the air with their wings until we were surrounded by a froth of feathers. No one could creep up on Fergus undetected.

I had not seen the exiled Irish King since I had accompanied my father on a state visit as a girl. The dialect came back readily enough, but I was surprised at how much else had changed. Fergus and his people were carving an entire kingdom out of marsh and islands and steadings cleared in the forest; what was once the wilderness of Pict and bear was rapidly becoming the kingdom of Dal Riada.

"A bit grander than the steading where I first entertained you," our host said expansively as he gestured about his Hall. It was full of color and banter and the warmth of friendship. The embers in the fire pit glowed in the center of the room, while cooks and pages and serving children turned the spits or stirred the contents of caldrons that hung from long chains attached to the beams. The dogs moved from table to table, sniffing out scraps and rushing to snap up the bones their masters tossed aside. There was laughter and raucous tales, and later we'd have harping and story-telling and all the bragging of warriors; it is always this way among the Celts, whether they be Irish or British or Breton.

After the trestles were cleared Tristan took out his Irish harp and a murmur of appreciation ran through Fergus's men.

"Watch this," Arthur whispered before speaking to our host in a voice loud enough to carry over the whole Hall.

"M'lord, I ask leave to introduce a fine new musician from among the tribes to the north. He and the Cornish harper will fill your ears with wonder, and weave in song the kind of alliance we are establishing with the Round Table."

There was a rustle of curiosity as a young Pict brought forth his flute and nodding shyly to both me and Fergus, took his place beside Tristan. For the rest of the evening the two of them treated us to folksongs and melodies rather than history and sagas. The lilting tunes and charming words, devoid of battle-lust and lore, touched the hearts of all who heard them. Perhaps Taliesin was right to claim that music is a gift from the Gods.

"Oh, M'lady, but he's beautiful!" Fergus's plump daughter murmured as she stared across the fire-glow at Lancelot.

I glanced over at the Breton, feeling my heart rise at the sight of him. In actuality Lancelot of the Lake was anything but handsome; his brow was too broad, his chin too narrow, his mouth too full, even his hands too elegant for the usual warrior. Yet he never failed to capture female attention, even though he didn't court it. No matter how often I tried to analyze why women reacted to him as they did, I always gave up. He was simply Lance, and by now I was so accustomed to his presence I rarely remembered that he used to remind me of Kevin.

That realization made me pause. I had always thought of change as something sudden, something brought on by definite actions such as battles won or lives ended. Now it seemed there was another kind that worked so gradually we weren't even aware of it—a whole new world of ideas and friendships that slowly supplanted the old, like new shoots growing out of a fallen log.

If that was so, one might think we are all in a state of flux, always on the edge of "becoming" something else. I shook my head, for I liked the world as I knew it and did not want to accept the notion that everything changes.

When the meeting at Dumbarton was over Lance headed back to Loch Lomond with the promise he'd join us at Caerleon once Hueil's forces surrendered. In the meantime we turned toward Rheged and my home.

A spatter of summer showers accompanied us, and as we crested the last ridge and looked out over the city of Carlisle a rainbow arched beyond the big stone bridge that carries the Road across the river Eden.

My spirit rose like a lark at the sight. As a youngster I had disliked Carlisle considerably, finding its Roman center, solid fort, and formal houses far too disciplined to suit my soul. Now I stared at them fondly, remembering the hours Kevin and I had spent at the stables in Stanwix; the sight of my father leading home the victorious warriors who had fought at the side of the young Pendragon; and later, my first encounter with Arthur himself.

The Square by the fountain was packed with summer merchants, bright and noisy and full of gossip. They turned to stare in awe as our party approached, then parted with a ripple of recognition and greetings.

"It's Guinevere and the King," someone cried as people came running out of stores and kitchens to stare as we rode past. I smiled and waved and wished them all a good day, proud to be returning to them in such splendor.

The gatekeeper at the big house by the river scanned my beaming face with consternation. "You haven't heard, M'lady?" he asked, even before I dismounted.

"Heard what?"

"His Highness . . . your father . . ."

"What about him?" I pulled Shadow's head around so the man could approach and not yell out his news across the threshold.

"King Leodegrance lies dying at Appleby. Or at least that was the news yesterday."

My fingers froze on the reins and Shadow tossed her head wildly. The gatekeeper reached out and grabbed her bridle as I turned to Arthur in disbelief.

"How far away is Appleby?" my husband asked.

"A long day's ride," the man answered.

Arthur looked back at me. "It's coming on to nightfall, Gwen. We'd best stay over and leave first thing in the morning; I'll send a messenger to say we're coming."

I nodded, unable to speak. No doubt it was a reasonable decision, though all I could think of was the need to reach my father's side.

"Here, let's get you inside." Arthur reached up to help me from the saddle.

"There's so much we've never said," I whispered. "He can't die . . . not yet, not before I tell him. . . ."

Arthur put his arms around me, silent but reassuring, and I began to sob as we moved into the house.

That night was filled with horrible dreams—ominous and frightful, they carried my father silently beyond the shore while I struggled— vainly, hopelessly—against the ebbing tide until an insistent pounding on the door woke me and Arthur called out softly "Who is it?"

"Pelleas. I caught a young beggar who slipped past the sentry— claims he has to see you immediately. He gave me a brooch that will identify him."

I wrapped the covers closer about my shoulders, terrified that this was a messenger come to say my father was already dead. But the brooch Pelleas handed Arthur didn't look like any I'd seen before—red and gold and dragon-shaped, it gleamed in the lantern shine.

"I'll see him," Arthur responded, hastily fishing about for his clothes as the skinny horseman turned back to the hallway. "It's Merlin's brooch; the one Ambrosius gave him. Can't imagine why he didn't just come in. After all this time you'd think he'd dispense with theatrics."

I struggled into my robe as a flood of hope surged through me. Maybe the Magician could save my father.

The lad Pelleas brought in was dirty and ragged, with a twisted body and hunched back. Both Arthur and I stared at him in silence; it was an extraordinary effort even for a master shape-changer. The boy gave no sign of recognition as he made his way across the room and knelt before the High King.

"What's all this nonsense?" Arthur sputtered, uring the Magician up off his knees. "Come now, old friend, enough is enough."

"Oh, no, M'lord, I'm not who you think. But I have urgent news, for your ears alone." The hunchback sent a quick glance toward Pelleas who was guarding the door, knife at the ready in case this was some sort of treachery against the King.

Arthur was staring fixedly at the messenger. "If you aren't Merlin, what are you doing with his brooch?" he demanded.

Without a word the newcomer turned and looked to me.

"Nimue!" I cried.

The priestess nodded slowly and straightened into her more usual form.

"Merlin said it would guarantee me the right to see you," she explained, turning back to Arthur and taking the pin from his hand.

"I came to warn you about an invasion at Portchester—by a group who have come to conquer, not simply raid and run."

"How do you know this?" Arthur watched her suspiciously.

"I've seen them; counted the ships; talked with the wenches who service the warriors."

"Where is Merlin? Why didn't he come himself?" Arthur's voice had an accusing edge, as though he believed the rumors that Nimue had betrayed the Mage.

"He sleeps in a Crystal Cave," she said levelly, with another flick of an eyelid in Pelleas's direction. "He sent me to protect you until such time as he rejoins us."

"You must be chilled to the bone," I interrupted, and asked Pelleas to fetch some heated wine from the kitchen. He paused long enough to get Arthur's nod of approval, then left the chamber as Arthur pulled up a chair for the doire.

"In the Glass Castle, on the Isle of the Blessed?" Arthur was using the Cumbrian terms for death.

Nimue was silent for a long minute before answering.

"Merlin knew he was dying at the first Round Table. The wasting illness had been eating him for some time, and nothing he or I did could stop it. It's why we went to Brittany . . . so that no one at Court would see him weak and feeble. And he made me promise to tell no one but you two, lest your enemies grow bold in the knowledge that the Sorcerer no longer protects your reign."

She reached out and took both our hands, though whether for her own comfort or ours was unclear.

"He died in my arms on May Day, beneath a flowering of hawthorn, in that wood they call Broceliande. It was at dawn, with the sky full of gladness and the anthem of birds all around . . . when the moment came, the whole of the Universe paused, and for just a heartbeat all was silent, all was still, in honor of his passing."

A similar silence descended over us, and Arthur swallowed hard against it. Nimue's voice was steady and her touch light, though she stared into a world we could not see. The grief she had struggled with at the cave was well worn through, but an immense sadness engulfed her.

"I brought the body back to Bardsey Island, because he said he was fond of it. I . . . I wasn't ready to face the Court, so settled into the cave at Carmarthen where I was close enough to reach you, in case you needed my help. Merlin taught me all he could, and though I may not cast the same shadow of fear over your enemies, I'll always come to your aid if you need me. However," she concluded, looking at each of us, "we'll have to decide on a story for the people—I swore they'd never know that Merlin the Sorcerer is dead."

"Anything we tell them is going to have holes in it," Arthur sighed, the news of his mentor's death making his voice husky. Tears began to glisten in his eyes and it dawned on me that we were both facing the demise of a loved one.

Pelleas came into the room with a steaming wine-pitcher and goblets. Arthur turned away, and Nimue, the most composed of the three of us, moved smoothly over to the young Companion.

"I'll take that," she said, relieving Pelleas of the tray. "Do you want some, too?"

Pelleas, never brash or forthright, nodded shyly. Even in rages Nimue possessed a wonderful poise; like Igraine, no matter what the Fates called on her to do, she would be equal to the task.

Once we were all served she turned to Arthur. "I think you should head south as fast as possible—before Cerdic rallies too many people to his cause."

"*His* cause?" Arthur barked. "The man claims my title and flaunts a Celtic name while leading Saxon sea-wolves. What sort of 'cause' is that?"

"In his eyes, a very good one." Nimue took a deep breath and let it out slowly. "Remember Vortigern's young Saxon wife, Rowena? Once the tyrant married her, he had to stake his future on the Federates. He even went so far as to declare himself to be one of them—'I am a Gewis!'—making their cause his cause. When Ambrosius deposed him, the Saxons had a double reason to spirit his widow back to the Continent; not only was she of their own blood, her child was the son of the British High King. The boy was nine years old at the time, and his name was Cerdic."

"My God," Pelleas whispered, hastily crossing himself as Arthur's eyebrows lifted in surprise.

"So now he claims royal blood through his father's line, and the loyalty of his troops through his mother's." Nimue grimaced. "It's a neat bit of political genealogy."

"And casts me as the usurper." Arthur nodded, brow furrowed and jaw set. "Besides being clever, what sort of man is he?"

"Nearing forty—tough, experienced, and very good at rallying people to his side. He's brought several warrior sons with him, though the youngest, Cynric, is barely old enough to be a squire. I think he hopes to found a dynasty."

Arthur had begun to pace. "And the Federates? How many of them have joined him?"

"So far the danger is contained in the south. The older families along the Thames are still loyal to you, and most of the Fen people as well, while the northern Saxons are too disorganized themselves to help anyone else. Neither Octha of Kent nor Aelle of Sussex have committed themselves, waiting to see what sort of support this new-comer commands—but the landholders of the Weald such as Wihtgar and Maegla and Stuf have thrown their lot in with Cerdic's."

The names brought a sinking feeling to my stomach, for they were the very leaders who had hosted us on the Saxon Shore.

"And they are picking up others on their march to Winchester."

"Winchester?" Arthur exclaimed, suddenly freezing. "Have they taken the town?"

Nimue shook her head. "Not yet."

Arthur was scowling fiercely, everything else save Cerdic forgotten. "If he winters over in Winchester, in the spring his men will be fresh for an assault on the Goring Gap, with the chance to march on London. . . . From there, if he gains the support of the Federates along the Thames, he could drive a Saxon wedge clear across Logres to the Severn plain. . . ."

All thought of Merlin and my father's dying had disappeared from Arthur's world. Here, in the very moment when we both balanced on the edge of the abyss, stripped naked before the specter of death, the Gods were striking us asunder. If ever we had a right to cling together, a need to console each other, it was now. I needed him as never before, and suspected he needed me as well.

Yet Britain needed him, too, and I turned away, stifling a sob as he

ordered Pelleas to waken Gawain and set up a small room for a conference. There was nothing I could do but stand by and watch as Arthur
prepared for war.

Engrossed in my own thoughts, I jumped when Nimue pressed a
mug of something warm into my hands. "It will help you rest," she
whispered. "Arthur doesn't need you at the conference, and I'll wake
you before he leaves."

I started to argue with her, but Arthur was already out the door, so
I drank the potion gratefully and flung myself into a deep and dreamless
sleep.

The sky was going gray before the dawn, and in the willows along the
river the warblers began to sing. I stood before my husband, shivering
in the nippy air.

"I'm taking Cabal, but Griflet and Caesar stay with you. At Appleby
you'll have Bedivere and your father's men to protect you." Arthur
glanced around the room, checking for things he didn't want to leave
behind. "Did you and your father discuss what would happen to
Rheged after his death?"

"We agreed Urien could stand for Regent until such time as I have
children," I answered numbly. "That was part of the treaty you had
us sign at the end of the Great Battle, remember? The one that stopped
the border raids."

My husband paused to look directly at me, then cleared his throat.
"Aye, and important it was, too; the rest of the Cumbri followed suit
because of your father. Do tell him"—his voice dipped slightly—"how
grateful I have always been for that."

I nodded miserably, and then his arms were around me and we clung
together like children in the shadow of night. Visions of Saxon traitors
and hawthorn blossoms and a great man lying dead in a cave somewhere swirled all around us.

"Ah, lass," Arthur whispered into my hair, "it's time we found that
place to build our own retreat, and leave off traipsing about the land.
I've a bellyful of strangers' ways and diplomacy, and would like nothing
better than to choose a place to call home and settle in for a while."

It was such an unexpected sentiment, I stood very still, wondering if I was hearing him right.

"I'll send for you as soon as I've put this Cerdic in his place." He stepped back, holding me at arm's length. "This is one of the safest spots you could be, with nary a barbarian for leagues around. I'll leave Maelgwn in Gwynedd to keep the Irish from sneaking in the back door while I'm busy with the Saxons—but the rest of the Kings will follow me. Now give us a smile," he commanded as Nimue arrived with word that the men were ready to leave.

"I'm going with you," she announced, coming to stand before us in her beggar-boy guise. "I promised Merlin to look after you, whether you want it or not."

"Well," Arthur answered cautiously, "I'm much obliged."

He moved to the door and pausing to look back at me, gave me the "thumbs up" sign. I answered him in kind, and for a moment we grinned. Then he turned on his heel and left.

Nimue's arms went around me, and I clung to her as I had once clung to Brigit—frightened, exhausted, and desperate for some kind of reassurance.

"The bards will call this one of his great victories," the doire said, stroking my hair as she led me toward the bed. "He's wearing the cape you made him . . . the one with the symbols of the Goddess, and no harm will come to him."

Her voice carried the same conviction that Merlin's had whenever he spoke of Arthur. But when I was under the covers and she had turned to go, I asked if she couldn't give some similar assurance about my father.

Nimue hesitated only a moment. "Remember, Gwen, your husband will live," was all that she could offer.

NINETEEN

The Funeral

e were halfway to Appleby when I saw Bedivere galloping toward us. The tone of his greeting told me my father had already died.

"Yesterday afternoon," he confirmed, his voice full of compassion as he reined in next to me. "We heard you were as close as Dumbarton, but he couldn't last any longer."

The words came from across a great gulf, as if they pertained to something else entirely. Tears congealed into a lump in my throat, blocking any sound I might have made. I thanked him with a nod and stared straight ahead as we continued down the Stainmore.

Among the best roads the Romans ever built, it stretched bright and friendly through my memory. It was here that Mama and my father had laughed and raced and loved, back before death stole her and my little brother away. Those were the days when Kaethi taught me of the Old Gods who lived in trees and sacred groves, and I spent every free moment down at the stables with Rhufon, learning as much as I could about the horses until Mama discovered it and banished me to the weaving room.

The breeze that whispered around me now carried voices of that bygone time. I blinked in the summer sun, convinced that if I turned quickly enough, I'd find my family all come back again, making the noisy, cheerful trips between forts and roundhouses and moldering Roman towns. Surely this talk of death was just another bad dream.

But the household members who greeted me at Appleby were already in deep mourning. I accepted their condolences with a silent nod and turned toward the double doors of the Great Hall.

"He was very proud of you, Gwen." Bedivere's voice was hushed as he stood next to me, his good hand at my elbow should I need support. "He talked about you often, and asked me to make sure you received the Ring of State."

I stared down at the heavy golden band Arthur's foster-brother put in my palm but saw instead the small enamel ring of Mama's that my father had given me when I left to go marry Arthur. My fingers closed on the vision without a word as Bedivere and I made our way silently through the doors.

The room was empty and hushed, and far smaller than I remembered. But the shadows under the lofts still offered a quiet spot to exchange secrets, and the carved pillars still rose proudly to the high-pitched roof, though now the faces that peered out from the twining vines wept as we passed slowly under their gaze.

My father's body lay in state on a bier set up beyond the fire pit. I looked down at the weathered face, wondering once more where the life and warmth and spirit of living goes when it forsakes the human husk.

He had not changed much in the years since I'd been gone; his beard was a little grayer, but the furrows of pain from crippling arthritis had been deep-carved almost since I could remember. I stared at the knobby, twisted hands and reached out to touch the little finger where he used to wear Mama's ring.

"I lost it in a good cause," I whispered, hoping he'd understand.

And then I was sitting at a table, going over the funeral plans with Bedivere, leaving Enid to take care of my ladies and thinking how fortunate I was to have a loving household to help me through this time.

"Oh, Missy," Gladys exclaimed when I came into the kitchen. Her red hands and stolid frame were just as I remembered, and she threw her arms around me in a hug as though I were still a child living at home.

" 'Tis a delight to have you back again, and a shame that it's at such a time," she blubbered before pulling back and looking me thoroughly up and down. "The High King's cook seems to feed you well enough. Or maybe you just quit growing up, and decided to fill out."

I smiled in spite of my grief, for she hadn't changed a bit, and her brusque tones and common sense were as bracing as ever. Even her kitchen was as it had been when I left—bannocks baking on the griddle stone, a haunch turning on the spit. Over by the door a scullery maid scrubbed the paving stones. I clung gratefully to the familiar, unchanging warmth of it.

"But you've no little ones?"

Typically, Gladys went right to the point, and I winced as I shook my head.

"Well," she acknowledged, pursing her lips as she sampled the soup in the pot, "we'll fix you some simples to take care of that."

You and all the rest of the world, I thought wearily.

"If only Kaethi were still alive, she'd have a recipe for you."

"She's also gone?"

My knees buckled, and I sank onto the stool by the churn. Kaethi had been the mentor of my childhood, the tart voice of reason that pointed out the foibles of mankind and taught me not to take myself too seriously. I paled with the knowledge that she was no longer here.

"Oh, Missy, I thought surely you would have heard. She died in her sleep last winter."

I looked away, angry and hurt that the Gods should store up so many losses to lay on me at once. "And Rhufon?" I asked, daring the Fates to take him away as well.

"Ah, the Horse Master's still alive, but he got kicked by a dray horse that was being shod, and hasn't been right in the head since. He sits in the sun most any warm afternoon and mutters away to your mother, or Nonny . . . sometimes he talks to you as well."

I sighed, suddenly very tired and alone; without father or husband or even Kaethi's insights, I'd have to convince the people to accept Urien as Regent by myself. It would mean tact and diplomacy, and a good deal more confidence than I presently possessed. I wasn't sure I could accomplish it.

"Of course you can, child. Why do you think we raised you as we did?" The memory of Kaethi's high, birdlike voice came to me as clearly as the splashing of the scullery girl, and I squared my shoulders with an inward sigh.

A Celtic Queen does what has to be done.

The intricate dance of diplomacy began even before the funeral was held. I sat in Mama's carved chair a slight distance from my father's bier and received the nobles of the nearby lands with quiet solemnity. I hoped they took it as a newfound dignity rather than the exhaustion it really was.

Uwain came in his father's place since Urien had joined Arthur in his march against Cerdic. The boy was awfully young to represent a kingdom as powerful as Northumbria, but I suspected my people would find him less offensive than his parent—Urien had regularly raided our borders before Arthur instigated the truce, and not a few of our men had lost limbs and relatives trying to keep our rapacious neighbor out. Old warriors have long memories, so I was relieved it was the son and not the father who came for the funeral.

Fergus of Dal Riada was too busy fighting the Picts to go south with Arthur, but he came to pay homage to my father, as did many of the smaller leaders from the splintered kingdoms beyond the Wall.

My cousin Maelgwn arrived as well—Arthur had said he would leave him in Gwynedd to guard our flank. The man moved suavely across the Hall, accompanied by richly garbed nobles and a huge black dog—probably the beast named Dormarth that Poulentis had mentioned.

The Welsh King was effusive in his condolences. He went down on one knee before my chair, his voice full of honey and sympathy. The sunlight tangled in his graying hair, giving him a distinguished look as he lifted my hand to his lips. One would have thought we were the best of friends, and I wondered if he knew how much I detested him. Certainly he must remember the black eye I'd given him, but my icy greeting didn't remove the smile from his face.

"How sad your father didn't get to see you again," he purred. "He would be much impressed, I'm sure. Why, I remember you as a freckle-faced youngster, and would never guess that you'd become such a beautiful woman."

A stony silence hung between us. I am fully aware that I'm nowhere near the beauty that Mama was; trustworthy, quick-witted, competent—these are the words they use to describe me. Maelgwn's attempt to appeal to a vanity I'd never developed struck me as one more indication of his deviousness.

I pulled my hands free of his grasp and called for Bedivere to join me. Hopefully my cousin would take the hint and leave me alone.

"Who will be selected to rule Rheged, now that your father cannot?" Maelgwn persisted, ignoring my rudeness.

"No one," I snapped. "The people will no doubt approve Urien as Regent until such time as my own offspring are old enough to stand for the monarchy."

For a moment my unctuous relative was caught off balance.

"But surely, as kin to your mother, my own line should be considered."

"It was." I leaned ramrod straight against the back of the royal chair and looked my opponent squarely in the eye. "But both my father and I agreed that a Regency under Urien was more desirable."

"Well, perhaps I can change your mind, fair lady," Maelgwn responded, the cold edge of anger glinting under his words.

We were poised like a pair of swordsmen who have crossed blades down to the hilt, each weighing when and how to jump free of the stalemate. I refused to look away, and at last he blinked and stepped back out of the sunlight.

Bedivere moved in beside me, ostensibly to explain who would lead my father's stallion in the procession the next day. I rose from my chair and walked away with the lieutenant, dismissing Maelgwn without so much as a glance.

"He could cause no end of trouble," the lieutenant warned under his breath, and I nodded silently. It was clear I must put my own imprint on the future of Rheged as soon as possible.

I spent that evening at the stables, reminiscing with Rhufon—who faded in and out of the present like a winter tree wrapping itself in mists—and getting acquainted with the man who had become the new Horse Master.

Some of the new animals eyed me cautiously, but I found fond welcome from the horses I'd known all my life. My father's stallion nickered and blew against my shoulder, butting me impatiently as though annoyed that I should smell so familiar but not be the one for whom he waited. He was a tall horse, even for a Shire, and more high-strung than most. I could not remember anyone other than my father having ridden him, save perhaps Rhufon. It wasn't clear how much this was due to my father's pride in the animal and how much stemmed from the unruly nature of the stallion himself. But we had a long talk, that horse and I, and I went to bed feeling more confident about the morrow.

Before the funeral I tugged on a pair of breeches and simple tunic instead of a dress and, leaving my hair to hang long and free in filial mourning, rummaged through several chests until I found my father's crown. Planting it firmly on my head, I turned and marched down to the stables.

There had been a summer shower in the night, as though the heavens were shedding the tears that I could not, but the day itself bloomed bright and clear. As the entourage formed up, I brought my father's stallion from the barn.

When the solemn drumbeat started, it was I, Guinevere, who walked with the riderless animal behind his master's body.

A murmur of surprise ran through the Court, but the horse and I kept stately pace with the rumbling drum, looking neither to left nor right. I've often suspected that animals know full well what happens in their human masters' lives, and this morning the fractious stallion moved with a slow, deliberate purpose as though grieving for the King who would not ride again.

My father's coffin had long been ready, and it was lowered softly into the grave beside his love's. Mama had died unexpectedly and been buried hastily in a hollow log. Now the earth cradled them both, the one so young and vibrant, the other so bent with sorrow and pain. I hoped that Mama's spirit still lingered on the Isle of the Blessed, to receive my father when he arrived.

As we were coming back from the cemetery the wind rose up. The stallion tossed his head nervously and began to pull against the lead. I soothed him a bit with my voice, but his ears twitched constantly.

Within minutes the billowing white clouds of morning had taken on the purple-gray of a Pennine storm, lying heavy on the green fells like a sullen bruise. When the first crack of thunder rolled over us, the stallion shied sideways, and I turned toward him so abruptly the crown started to slip on my hair.

Grabbing it before it fell, I swung up into the saddle and pulled the trembling stallion's head to one side. He swung in circles, dancing against the rein, and I held him with knee and thigh as I lifted the crown and saluted the people with it.

A shocked gasp met my action, but after a moment's uneasiness the crowd began to cheer. The horse calmed underneath me, his frightened, white-eyed look giving way to spirited pride. I held the mood of both the stallion and the people by sheer force of will and prayed that nothing else untoward would confront us.

By the time we climbed the hill to Appleby's Hall, the stallion was prancing with pent-up energy but no longer threatened to break away, and the throng was chanting my name. It may not have been the most traditional return from a royal burial, but I did not think my father would have minded; certainly I had made it clear that I intended to claim the daughter's right to rule in her father's stead.

I handed the reins over to the groom, telling him to turn the horse out to pasture so he could run as long and hard as he wanted. The boy nodded briskly, and I watched the two of them move away, wishing I too could escape the confines of protocol and statesmanship.

The idea of dealing with Maelgwn at the feast that night was purely repulsive, but Edwen the Bard came to my rescue, filling the Hall with tales about the bravery and dedication of the King we had just buried.

In spite of his warped and twisted frame, my father was a king of majesty, as much committed to his people as Mama was. On the night after her death we had all left this Hall, sick and fever-racked, trudging through the rain to the Sacred Hill for the Need-fire lighting. Moaning in the dark, the ring of dancers begged for surcease of the plague, the rebirth of warmth and light, the promise of life renewed. When the tinder refused to catch, they cried for my father's life in an effort to placate the Gods. It was then I had seen him dancing amid the crackling flames. Hunched and crippled and wrapped in smoke, he capered wildly in the heart of that inferno, seeming to fulfill the royal promise.

Even now as an adult, though I understand he only thrust the burning brand into the dry heart of the pyre, the picture of him silhouetted in that blaze is seared on my heart.

In the midst of his eulogy Edwen crumpled over his harp, convulsed with grief for the leader he had served so long. Bedivere rushed to his side and after helping him to the bench beside the pillar, sat down on the Harper's stool and took up the instrument. That night the one-handed lieutenant created such a lay for my father as to make the whole of Britain proud.

Yet still I could not cry. By the time the evening was over I was drowning in unshed tears and left the Hall in silence, brushing aside Maelgwn's offer to see me to my chambers with a contemptuous glance.

"I shall look forward to hosting you in return, M'lady," my cousin said next morning, bowing ostentatiously as he prepared to depart for Gwynedd. "Perhaps next spring?"

I stared hard at the man, weighing his words for hidden meaning—something in the invitation made me uneasy. Yet no matter how repulsive I found him as a person, we needed him as an ally. So in spite of my misgivings I murmured a vague, "Perhaps," and bade him a formal farewell.

Word came sporadically from the south—*of Arthur gathering a growing army; war-lords and nobles, archers and slingers and cavalry Champions, all joining forces. Of Geraint and Cador rushing to Silchester, meeting with Urien and Agricola as the High King arrives. Most of the might of Britain moves to protect the Goring Gap, rallying under the Banner of the Red Dragon.*

Terrifying reports of Saxons pour out of steading and village—Octha and Aelle lead their armies forth from Kent and Sussex, joining the Federates of the Weald to cast their lot with this new leader who claims he is one of their own. Villas are torched, Britons enslaved, as the ranks of would-be conquerors swell behind the white horsetail standards of Cerdic.

Arthur draws his forces together, but even though it is still high summer, he provides no battle, no chance for glory and loot. Instead, he sets the men to digging storage pits at Silchester, preparing to winter over. In the south Winchester is lost to Cerdic—what was once a British enclave surrounded by a mixture of British and Federates is now a Saxon center. On the hills the men of Kent and Sussex set up camp.

Neither leader moves against the other, but each hunkers down, waiting to see who makes the first mistake.

I heard the news and shivered. With the whole of winter to improve his position, Cerdic would no doubt make Winchester a base from which to launch an attack toward London. There seemed little chance that Arthur could stop the process; given the number of warrior-farmers the Saxons had called up, our forces were badly outnumbered. If the Gods resented our efforts at unifying Britain, Cerdic was the perfect tool with which to punish us.

Stuck so far away in the north, unable to help or even hear what was happening from day to day, I turned all my attention to matters closer to hand. My own position in Rheged must be solidified and the question of Urien's Regency settled. It kept me busy during the day. But every night I prayed long and hard to the Goddess, begging Her to protect Arthur and the Cause, lest the next royal funeral be for my husband.

TWENTY

Rheged

ith Bedivere's help I took my Court of women and a few of my father's warriors from one end of the Lake District to the other, holding Councils, settling disputes, and reviewing the war-bands. Everywhere we went I introduced Uwain and encouraged the people to accept his father as Regent in my stead.

Uwain proved to be an excellent emissary, and the warriors, most of whom had known me since I was a child, supported me readily enough. I was glad they had never followed the Roman pattern of looking askance at women in power.

The commoners greeted me with a mixture of fondness and timidity, uncertain as to what was proper now that I was High Queen. I let the distance stand, maintaining the separate dignity of a ruler, although a part of me wanted to cry out, "For goodness' sake, I'm still the Cumbrian girl that grew up among you."

So I assumed my new role, keeping all personal feelings firmly under control and promising myself that when the pressures of queenhood lessened, I'd have time to laugh and cry freely once more.

Taliesin and Edwen were in my party as well, and I was pleased to discover the bard had taken an interest in the homely shepherd lad.

"Wonderful pupil, that," Edwen noted one evening when we met for dinner. The boy was sitting at the Harper's stool, carefully tuning his instrument, but a rotting, fetid odor seemed to radiate from him. Edwen grimaced and sent him out to get cleaned up, then turned back with an apology. "He's spent the day helping to make gut strings, M'lady—nasty, smelly job, and I suppose he didn't realize how rank he'd become."

"And his music?"

"Ah, he's eager and quick to learn! About manners and Court life as well as the art of the harp. Someday he'll be the finest bard in Britain—and one you can be proud of. Granted, there's something strange about him . . . he'll sit all morning rapt in silence, listening to things the rest of us cannot hear. Or puzzle for hours over tales of the old Gods, as though to unlock some ancient secret. I sometimes wonder if he's a changeling, he's that fey."

Edwen made the sign against evil lest the Gods think he was being blasphemous, and I nodded thoughtfully. If Taliesin was a fairy child, perhaps his strange name had come with him when he was left in a human cradle.

The boy became less shy with me as our progress continued. He was interested in all the magical places of Rheged, and I found myself telling him about the Standing Stones above Keswick, or the Roman fort at Hardknott Pass. He was fascinated with my description of the Lady's Sanctuary and even begged me to let him go to Eskdale and the Black Lake when we reached Ravenglass.

After Morgan's intervention during my pregnancy, I had no intention of allowing her to stir up further trouble, so I looked specifically at Taliesin when I ordered that no one, save Uwain, was to seek out the High Priestess on this trip.

Naturally I would not stand between Uwain and his mother and was not surprised when he came to see me about visiting her.

"Perhaps I can enlist her help in getting my father approved as Regent," he offered, eyes alight with enthusiasm. "She's so devoted to the Old Gods, I know she often seems preoccupied. But she's always interested in matters of state—and she may have further news about what is happening in the south," he added hopefully.

But Uwain's bright spirit was dimmed by the time he returned from the Sanctuary, and when I asked him about it, he shook his head and sighed awkwardly. "My mother is sometimes . . . difficult." The young man looked away shyly. "I didn't even get to the subject of Cerdic and the High King, Your Highness. I mean, I thought she would be pleased with my father's becoming Regent of Rheged; it makes good sense, since her Sanctuary is here. But for some reason she flew into a rage at the idea. You must remember, M'lady, that she's used to commanding the very air around us—thunder and lightning and the comings and goings of the seasons, as well as mere mortals. So she can get very short-tempered if things aren't going as she intends. Yesterday she stormed around her chamber, calling the Gods to witness that she had not been consulted about Urien's Regency and therefore would not condone it . . . so I avoided all other mention of the Court."

It seemed an odd reaction from Morgan, and I was sorry she had no news of Arthur. But the picture of her impotent rage amused me; apparently the woman truly believed she had the right to give or withhold approval of every project that dealt with my husband.

Uwain was clearly troubled by his mother's behavior, and I thought how awkward it must be to have Morgan for a parent. Smiling gently, I thanked him for his effort.

The lad was said to be excellent with animals, and on a hunch I took him down to the stables because Shadow's mouth had shown signs of soreness that morning. He handled the high-strung animal very well, and when I left he was concocting a brew of black current leaves with which to wash her lips and gums. It worked so well, I later put him in charge of looking after the health of all the horses as a way of showing my confidence in him.

Even without Morgan's help the people proved willing to accept Urien as their Regent, and by the time we reached Carlisle fully two-thirds of Rheged was behind me. All that remained was a brief trip along the northern coast of the Solway Firth.

But the first night at Carlisle Griflet came racing into the Hall, pointing frantically southward and crying, "Fire! Fire on Signal Hill! The beacon is lit."

Jagged points of orange flame shimmered and died, only to flare up again in the darkness, and my heart began to race; clearly there had been some sort of confrontation. After decoding the pattern, Bedivere assured me that our forces had been victorious, but confirmation of the details would have to wait for word from the High King himself.

I moved nervously through the next days, praying to the Goddess at night and on occasion even going to Mass with Vinnie—Igraine had suggested I remember the Church if I ever needed peace, so I tried it now. Somehow it didn't help.

The messenger arrived on the fifth day. His horse came to a halt, head down and sides heaving, but the man gave me a grin as he dismounted and turned the animal over to Griflet.

"A magnificent battle, Your Highness. A fine British victory."

"And the King?" I asked, feeling my knees weaken.

"King Arthur is unhurt, though there was terrible carnage. Begging your pardon, M'lady, I could tell you better if I had something to drink."

"Of course," I responded, leading him to the kitchen and drawing a tankard of ale. Between swigs and belches, the fellow spun out his tale.

"We sat in Silchester while the harvest ripened around us. His Highness forbade anyone to go near Winchester, so we assumed there would be no battle until spring. But when the Saxons in the camps around Winchester saw we weren't going to attack, they began to remember the fields at home that needed harvesting. And gradually, one after another, they drifted away, heading back to their steadings in Kent and Sussex."

I burst out laughing for the first time in months. The realization that Arthur had taken the very thing that made the Saxons strong and used it to their detriment filled me with both admiration and joy. Our enemy might be able to call up a bigger army with their farmer-warriors, but our men wouldn't up and pack off when haying time came round!

The messenger clearly didn't understand my reaction, and he watched me nervously as he continued.

"Cerdic had been concentrating on his fortifications, relying on the outlying camps to provide him with food. Now with the buffer forces gone, he could see that he might be besieged after all, so he set his men to foraging for winter supplies. He even grew desperate enough to lead hunting expeditions himself. It was then that King Arthur led us out of Silchester, silently, in the dark of night. When the sun came up we were between Cerdic's camp and his fortress. The battle that followed was awful—hundreds of men slaughtered in the first charge. Don't let anyone ever tell you the Saxons are cowards, M'lady . . . more like terriers who will die with their teeth clamped on their opponent even while their brains are being bashed in."

I shuddered, and the fellow brightened quickly. "The Britons were splendid. Cador and Urien reliable as always, and Lamorak fired by the battle-lust almost as much as Gawain. But the undisputed hero was the High King himself. Riding at the fore, with that great white dog always at his side, he slew the Saxons to the left and right. And all the time wearing the sign of the Holy Mother on his shoulder."

The man crossed himself piously while I stared in astonishment—he seemed to have mistaken the symbols of the Goddess on Arthur's war-cape for some sort of Christian sign. But I was so glad to hear that my husband was safe, I didn't correct the error. Silently giving thanks to the Morrigan, I included the White Christ's mother as well; one does not stint where Goddesses are concerned.

"It was a fine battle, that put an end to Cerdic's plans," the messenger concluded.

"Then Cerdic and his sons are dead?" I asked.

"Well, no, Ma'am. They slipped away in the confusion—at least we didn't find them among prisoners or bodies. They probably headed northeast, for the safety of the Fens."

A rabbit scampered over my grave at mention of the Fens, that immense flat waterland, steeped in the sunset's blood. Shrouded in mists, ruled by a dead moon the color of whey, it teemed with a secret life of its own. And hidden in its heart, beyond our reach or knowledge, our most powerful enemy would no doubt continue to plot our destruction.

The messenger was grinning broadly, so proud of the victory that he overlooked the danger I saw too well. I thanked him for news of the battle and resolutely put my mind to other things.

We held the last of our Councils just before Samhain, and after the Blood Month festival I brought my Court back to the Mote for winter.

Of all the places I love in Rheged, this is second only to Appleby. Situated at the juncture where the narrow, turbulent Rough Firth joins the Solway, the settlement grew up on the hillside next to a huge blunt rock that noses out of the slope of Criffel's pine-clad ridge. If Cheddar Gorge reminded Gwyn of the first day of creation, the Mote always made me think of man's first home—bold and magnificent as it stands guard over the gleaming firths, safe and homey in its clustered round houses with their heavy thatched roofs.

As a child I loved to sit on the high, flat top of the rock, watching the black-headed gulls bank and glide below and staring at the waters that swirled around its feet. Sometimes they are multishades of blue, subtle and lovely, but at other times they roil, heavy and gray, with tides that twist and pull against each other.

It is fitting that the Rough should be both beautiful and frightening, for it is the path that runs directly to the Otherworld. Nonny used to say the mottled shadows that flee over the water's face were the mark of spirits coming and going between lives, and if you weren't careful, they would draw you down to Annwn, that Otherworld Hall where Arwn Himself holds court among the dead.

"I could take a coracle out into the current," Taliesin mused one morning as we gathered winkles from the rocks along the shore. The waters were swishing and whispering in their flight up the narrow channel, and he paused to stare along their path. "I'd creep into the Glass Castle when Arwn wasn't looking, and drink from the sacred caldron of inspiration. . . ."

"You and Gwion," I teased, remembering the story of the lad who found himself in no end of trouble because of Ceridwen's caldron of knowledge. But the boy called Shining Brow was staring off into space as though he hadn't heard, so I went back to the winkles.

The Irish jeweler who set up his shop at the Mote does some of the best work in the realm, and I wanted to commission him to make a series of rondels for the horse bridles. They were to be a gift to the Companions, and both Bedivere and I were at the man's workshop discussing the project when Frieda burst through the door, panting and breathless.

"M'lady! The boy, the changeling, took a boat out onto the water, and it capsized. You can see his body floating beyond the quicksand bank, and it's drifting toward a whirlpool!"

"Annwn, indeed!" I swore, rushing out to see.

Sure enough, Taliesin's lifeless form bobbed up and down in the turbulent waters. Bedivere was already running down to the shore, and as a horrified crowd gathered, the one-handed lieutenant grabbed fishing spear and net and pushed one of the little boats out into the current. He moved so quickly, using the hook on his leather gauntlet in place of his missing fingers, one almost forgot his disadvantage. Within minutes he had snagged the boy's tunic and, pulling him into the boat, brought him back to the shore where we had gathered.

Soaked to the skin himself, Bedivere worked over the inert figure, determined to bring the changeling back to life. An immense amount of water streamed from the boy's mouth before he began to cough and sputter on his own and Bedivere turned the rescue effort over to someone else.

"I thought he'd never come to," the Champion admitted after we'd stripped the lad of his sopping clothes and bundled him into bed.

The lieutenant's teeth had begun to chatter, so I gave him a steaming mug of the brew Enid had made for Taliesin and led him to a seat by the brazier. He let me towel his hair dry and drape a quilt over his shoulders.

"It was a brave thing you did, M'lord." I came round to stare into his angular face with love and admiration. "You're a fine man, Sir Bedivere of the Round Table—one of the best. And you'd make a good father as well. Have you no thought of marriage and a son of your own?"

"Ah, Gwen, you know I've already given my love to one lady; I can't very well take it back now and give it to another," he replied slowly.

"Just because Brigit didn't want to marry doesn't mean you can't find someone else to love and share your life with," I pointed out.

"No . . . I suppose not. But I don't want any other woman than Brigit, any more than I'd serve any other King than Arthur. That's just the way things are."

It was said so simply I couldn't argue with it. Yet it was such a waste. Bedivere had always been a kind of Pied Piper for children—they trailed after him in droves, anxious to learn from him, eager to emulate him. Like Lance, he always had time to stop and listen to a question, explain an easier way of doing something, or, as he had today, risk his own safety to rescue one in trouble. It seemed a pity that such men were willing to spend their lives alone when they'd make such good fathers.

"At least"—he grinned good-naturedly—"Taliesin will live to sing another song."

So we laughed and left it at that. Afterward there were some who said Bedivere should have let the Gods have their way, for when he was recovered the lad told endless tales of having invaded Annwn's Hall in search of the sacred vessel. I found his stories amusing and sometimes fancied I saw the strange light around his head that graces those who've been to the Otherworld. Perhaps in that way his name had been prophetic.

Spring came early that year. The curlews moved inland to their nesting sights while the rooks played in the air, tumbling and falling like acrobats above the trees. Great flocks of swans and geese filled the skies, leaving the Solway for their northern haunts, and in the grasses the high squeak of field mice said the earth was warming again. I watched the Scales rise in the evening sky and knew Arthur would be seeing them as well, so I moved the Court to Penrith in order to be closer when he sent for us.

The knowledge that I would soon be rejoining my husband brought a great lift of spirits, and when I went out to count the sheep at the in-by, my heart was soaring.

The young lambs gamboled across the green, bouncing and bounding as effortlessly as small clouds. They delighted in running and chasing each other, leaping about on springy legs until, suddenly lost, they began bleating so pitifully that it all but broke your heart. And once the ewe was found, such gladness of greeting, such nuzzling and happiness! Butting against the mother's udder, each lambkin would fall to its knees, tail whirling in delight as it searched for the comfort of the teat.

"Just like all young'uns," the shepherd said, grinning.

I watched the game played out over and over again—frolic, fear, loss, and the delight of reassurance when mother and child were reunited—and for the first time since Stirling knew I was ready to carry another child. The realization came with absolute certainty, and I laughed aloud with joy.

This time there would be no medicine from Morgan, no worry about conception or health, not even consternation over Arthur's attitude. I was sure and confident about the outcome as never before and convinced that once it was born Arthur would come to love his bairn. So I waved good-bye to the shepherd when the count was done and headed back to Court with a new purpose in mind.

Bedivere was busy stowing food into a saddlebag when I came into the kitchen, and he related the news a messenger had brought while I was out. Arthur had been making his headquarters at Liddington, the enormous hill-fort that guards the Roman Road where it crosses the Ridgeway. But with the arrival of good weather he'd decided to refortify the hill-fort at South Cadbury, where we had camped under the summer stars. It was a good location for permanent headquarters but wouldn't be habitable for a while yet.

"He's asked me to join him, to help lay out the buildings," Bedivere explained.

I snorted, wondering if there was anything Bedivere couldn't be— warrior, diplomat, bard, and now engineer.

"Why don't I come with you?" I asked, handing him the last of the jerky.

"Because you have a court to move." Bedivere closed the top on his miniature larder. "A single horseman can make better time than an entire entourage. I think Arthur will be sending for you soon, however—perhaps a week or two after Beltane."

That made sense, so I resigned myself with a sigh; after managing on my own these last eight months, I could be patient for another fortnight.

"When are you leaving?"

"As soon as I get my clothes together."

"Ah, the joys of being a free agent." I grinned, and Bedivere laughed.

"Tired of being Queen already?"

"Ready to be a woman for a change," I shot back, and he lifted one eyebrow.

"I'll tell Arthur," he promised, slinging the saddlebag onto his shoulder.

"You might also tell him that his Queen has had enough of the north, and looks forward to returning to the civilized south," I added as we walked down to the stables. I knew the comment would make Arthur laugh.

Bedivere gave me a grin and a wave as he left, and I turned my attention to the Beltane preparations, for May Day was coming shortly.

Griflet would take care of the Need-fire, and in the morning the May Queen would lead us all in the procession to turn the cows onto the summer pastures. Both humans and animals would be decked with garlands, and the sound of conch and cowbell, pipe and drum would welcome in Dame Summer.

With my new resolve toward motherhood, I had a very personal interest in seeing that all went well, both for the land's fertility and my own.

TWENTY-ONE

May Day

"ut M'lady, with Bedivere gone and most of the men sleeping off their carousing, there'll only be Uwain and myself, plus a couple of pages to accompany you." Griflet was frowning in the Need-fire's light, convinced the best way to protect his Queen was to have her stay home.

"Nonsense," I chided him good-naturedly. "What could possibly happen to us on May Day morn? It won't take that long, and we'll be back in plenty of time for the crowning of the May Queen."

The garlands of cowslips and kingcups, early roses and ivy leaves, had been plaited during the last few days, but I wanted to pick my own hawthorn blossoms from the magical thorn tree I remembered from childhood. "Mayflowers are part of the tradition," I reminded the Kennel Master.

"Aye," he sighed. "But there's hawthorn hedges everywhere— couldn't you use one closer? I don't feel comfortable traveling so far afield with the King gone and all."

"Well, I don't feel comfortable about not having a child, either." I lowered my voice and fixed Griflet with a conspiratorial gaze. "The flowers I collect tomorrow morning will help in that."

I counted on the young warrior being reluctant to argue with his Queen about such a personal matter, and when he blushed and looked away I knew the argument was won.

"My women and I will be at the stables come dawn," I concluded cheerfully, turning back to the dancing before he could say anything further.

The eastern sky was just coming to color as we started out. We headed south toward a small, hidden glen in the midst of the forest where the ancient thorn tree had been drifted in blossoms in the years past. It's a secret place with a holy well nearby, and I was counting on the presence of the Water Goddess to assure my future dreams.

The tree stood at the center of a glade, its thick trunk fluted like a column. In the early light the clouds of flowers glowed ghostly white, and it exhaled the sweet, dear scent of May Days past.

My women and I joined hands in a circle around it, softly chanting the Goddess's blessing, calling the sun up through a golden dawn. Sweetly and gravely we began the small prayers and innocent steps of the dance. Light-footed, with arms slowly unfurling like the tender stalks of an early fern, we turned into the sunlight—warming, tingling, opening as the light of day flowed over us until we hopped and skipped and pranced with pride, full of the rich laughter of our own flowering.

It was a beautiful celebration, calling forth the deep, thrilling unity of womankind, and when I dropped to the greensward my ladies-in-waiting showered me with clusters of mayflowers plucked from the tree. Soft as feathers—delicately touched by a tiny speck of red at the base of each petal, with little golden crowns in their centers—they filled my lap, caught in my hair, overflowed onto the grass. There were so many of them that when I was back astride Shadow I had to make an apron of my cape in order to carry them all.

During the entire time our escorts had remained on their horses like sentries at the edge of the clearing, vigilant in protecting us and our rites. The beauty of the morning still enthralled us as we headed home, and we filled the air with May Day songs and laughter—not even Griflet's nervousness could dampen the mood.

It was where the path from the streamside meets the Road that the bandits swept down upon us.

In the lead, Uwain barely had time to yell a warning before the brigands surrounded us.

"Go for help!" Griflet commanded him as the women begin to scream.

The Kennel Master's sword flashes free, his horse swinging sideways across the path in an effort to protect me. Three of the bandits surround him—a brutish arm lifts and slashes downward, its swordblade slicing through the air.

Shadow shies in panic as time comes unhinged, and everything takes on a slow and languid look. Sound and color roar over me: Griflet tumbling from his horse, head bloodied, mouth open. His young body floats through the air before settling onto the ground beneath the horses' hooves. Sobs and curses and the crunch of broken bones wash over me, mingling with the fragrance of the hawthorn flowers still clutched in my arms.

A horse goes down, flailing wildly. For a moment our assailants' onrush is checked as they are forced to veer around it. A gap opens, and I crouch forward, screaming for Shadow to bolt through it, but the frightened animal only jibs sideways. I wish vainly that I had Featherfoot under me—even my father's stallion, headstrong as he was, would be better than this silly mare.

In the midst of the melee Enid wrestles valiantly with a hefty warrior who is intent on reaching me. Her bravery makes me suddenly ashamed—I would have turned and run while others risked their lives for mine. My fear becomes anger, and I lash the brigand with my riding crop until, at last, he veers from my lady-in-waiting to me.

"Unhand my people," I demanded, glaring at the fellow. My voice came deep and furious. "I'm the High Queen of Britain, and I command you to call off your men."

"Good to know we've got the right one," the bandit jeered, grabbing Shadow's bridle. His face was half-hidden by a helmet, but Maelgwn's badge was newly sewn on the shoulder of his tunic.

"Just wait 'til my cousin hears of this," I yelled over the racket. "He'll make you pay for such insolence."

"It's he who will pay." The wretch lifted his head with a laugh. " 'Wherever you can find her' . . . those were his orders."

The words echoed and reechoed in my head as he pulled Shadow away from the fracas, dragging us off the path into the forest. "I've got the prize," he bellowed to his companions.

Swearing by all the Gods I knew, I hauled back on the reins in an effort to break free until my poor mare reared and twisted violently under the conflicting pressures.

"Enough of that," the leader growled, raising his balled fist in threat. "I'd as soon deliver you to my lord unconscious as not."

There was no doubt he meant it. By now the rest of his men had left the path and fanned out around us. My captor snatched the reins from my hands, and we moved smartly into the wildwood.

Stunned, I slumped in the saddle, sullen and silent. At least the brutal attack was over; the last I heard was the voice of a page calling Griflet's name before the curtain of trees cut off all contact with the real world and I faced the nightmare alone.

The harvest of mayflowers was still in my arms, and with the barest movement of my fingers I began dropping them a few at a time as we went along. I dared not look back to see whether they were catching on the brush or falling to the trail but hoped their unexpected presence within this dark and foreboding forest would mark the way for anyone who came looking for me.

We rode without comment or discussion of routes. The ruffians obviously knew where we were, but even if I could escape, I would be hopelessly lost and easily recaptured.

Eventually we reached a camp where a pair of guards greeted us with crude enthusiasm and several suggestive gestures. The tenor of their remarks reminded me that Saxons are not the only ones who rape and pillage. I glared at them imperiously, thinking royal dignity is cold comfort when you need quick action to turn the tide of things.

They allowed me to dismount, but as my hands were being tied behind me Shadow suddenly broke free and streaked off through the forest. It brought a muttering of oaths, though no one bothered to go after her.

A blindfold was dropped over my eyes, but I managed to spit on the bully in front of me before the cloth was jerked tight. Someone cuffed me in retaliation, landing a punch on my shoulder that wrenched it backward violently. Under the edge of the blindfold I could make out the boots of a man in front of me, and with a rage and strength I didn't know I had, I brought my knee up hard and fast.

The howl of pain said my aim had been excellent.

"Vicious bitch," snarled another, knocking me to the ground with a blow to the ribs and unbuckling his belt. "I'll teach you to have some manners, I will."

"Oh, no, you won't!" The leader interceded as I lay gasping for breath amid stabbing fits of pain. "Maelgwn said unharmed. We're to bring her to him in good form and fit condition." A snigger of knowing laughter was abruptly cut off. "I intend to earn the price he offered, and I'll lop off arm or ear or any other member of any man who comes too close to M'lady here. Is that clear?"

There was a shuffling of feet, and then I was being wrapped in some kind of rug, like a caterpillar in a cocoon. With a bit of tugging they got me hoisted over the back of a horse, my head hanging down on one side, my legs on the other. Between the stifling confines of the rug and the pounding in my head and ears, it was a struggle just to breathe, much less keep track of where we might be going.

Time, which had slowed so noticeably during the battle, now collapsed entirely. There was no way to know how long the journey lasted. On the one hand I was glad we traveled at no more than a rapid walk; a trot would have been torture in that position. But it meant the trip took that much longer, and time ceased to have any measurement.

At first I prayed to every God I could think of, but when I had exhausted all divine possibilities my mind moved to other things: whether Griflet had been killed, how long it would take for Uwain to round up a search party, and if anyone else had recognized Maelgwn's badge on the ruffians.

It seemed a senseless thing for my cousin to do. Perhaps he planned to hold me for ransom or call on the old tradition that he who gains the Queen gains the kingdom. I didn't think that likely, for the people loved Arthur, and it was doubtful that they would accept Maelgwn in his stead.

There were no stops for food or camp or comfort, just endless journeying to my unknown destiny. Whether I slept or fainted, I couldn't tell, but I came awake thirsty and aching. My anger had long

since evaporated, and caution began to take its place as I tried to weigh
what options lay ahead. It was clear that I could not gain my freedom
by either regal command or sheer physical strength. Whatever was
going to happen, I'd have to keep my wits about me.

Our route lay well away from the bustle of town or Court, and we
encountered no one else along the way. Eventually there was a pause
and some sort of exchange, then the horses' hooves drummed hollowly
on something wooden.

"Got a carpet for His Highness," the leader called out as our party
came to a stop. "I'll deliver it in person."

Slung over the ruffian's shoulder, I was taken to an inner chamber
and dumped, none too gently, on the floor. Cold air flowed over my
skin as the rug was untied, and the glow of a lantern stabbed painfully
against my eyes after the long darkness. I kept my lids slitted against
its glare and tried to assess my situation before admitting I was con-
scious.

"She's all right, ain't she?" a woman queried. "Your life won't be
worth much if she's been hurt."

"Of course she's not hurt," the ruffian grunted. "Ask her yourself;
she'll tell you we didn't do her no harm. All she needs is cleaning up."

He grabbed my shoulder and shook me roughly, and I groaned aloud
with the pain as my eyes flew open.

"There—what did I tell you?" he announced.

It was the first time I'd had a chance to see his face clearly, with the
long scar that ran down and across his cheek. Many men have such
marks, but I remembered the description of the man who had put
poison in the goblet at Caerleon. I studied him carefully, thinking I'd
do well to commit his face to memory.

"I'll be going," he muttered, straightening up quickly. "Tell the
King to send the gold to my apartment tonight."

The matron nodded, and when he was through the door she carefully
slid the bolt on a Roman lock before turning to face me.

"Let's have a look at Arthur's uppity Queen," she sneered, reaching
out toward the tangled mop of hair that surrounded my face. Her hands
were calloused and rough, more used to manual labor than needlecraft
in a Queen's chambers, and I guessed that she might even be unknown
to the rest of the Court.

"Please, Mother," I begged, catching her hand in my own and giving her the best title of respect I could think of, "where am I?"

"You don't know?" She paused to stare at me more closely. I prayed she'd find something in my countenance that would move her to pity, but instead she let out a mirthless laugh. "Let's just call it His Highness's love nest," she smirked.

"Maelgwn?" I took the comb from her hands and attempted to unsnarl my hair myself.

"Of course Maelgwn. Who else would it be?"

I nodded, anger at the confirmation of my suspicions bringing a hundred tart words to mind.

The crone was pouring water into a basin and began squeezing a fresh sponge in it. Obviously my prison had been furnished with an eye to comfort and class.

"Does he plan to hold me a political hostage or ask for ransom?" I had to fight to keep my voice even.

"That's between you and His Highness, I'm sure." The woman's tone was prim as she discarded my filthy dress. Insisting that I get into a tin tub, she set about bathing my shoulders. The water was only tepid, but I suspected half my shivering came from renewed rage.

When I'd been thoroughly scrubbed down and rubbed with scented lotions, the matron brought forth a blue gown and held it up for my approval. "Silk, it is," she averred, turning it this way and that so the fabric gleamed in the lamplight. "Not even the High King's wife gets a chance to wear silk every day."

I was tempted to tell her I'd wear sackcloth if it would get me out of here, but caution bridled my tongue and I put on the garment without comment. A girdle of tapestry work was added, as well as a necklace of pearls. After she'd put a jeweled diadem on my head, my warden stepped back to admire her handiwork.

She pronounced it "right fine" and turned her attention to laying out a table and chairs by the brazier. A tray of cold food was arranged for my pleasure, and when I was seated before it she tidied up the rest of the room and began plumping the pillows of the bed.

I had no appetite, though it must have been days since I'd eaten. But I toyed with a drumstick and, under the guise of watching the woman work, scrutinized my prison.

The appointments of the chamber were sumptuous, with fresh rushes strewn about the floor and a foot-rug of thick fleece placed carefully beside the bed. The room was clearly furnished for pleasure, but it offered little or no obvious means of escape. The windows were narrow and had firmly bolted shutters across them. There was only the one door, and it was both solid and well set in a stout wooden jamb. Nor was there closet or anteroom in which to hide; an olivewood chest stood against one wall, but I suspected it was too small to be of much help. A brazier, gaming table, and chairs made up the rest of the furniture. And the bed.

I glanced hastily away from that, not willing to believe all this effort was meant to culminate between its sheets. Surely Maelgwn didn't think I could be intimidated into bedding with him or bribed with fancy clothes and heady luxury.

Maybe it was all a ploy to throw me off balance; certainly the mixture of physical brutality one minute and elegant attention the next made little sense. After a bit I quit trying to sort it out and decided that two could play at such a game—quite possibly I could draw my opponent into revealing himself by using his own tactics.

"What are we waiting for?" I inquired of the matron, yawning slightly behind my hand as though thoroughly bored.

"Why, His Highness," came the reply.

I rose and stared down into the coals of the brazier, then strolled slowly around the room while the woman cleared the table. "You'd think he'd have left me something to do."

With a petulant sigh I drifted to the chest, idly lifting its lid. It was impossible to see how deep it was, or if it was empty, for there was a shallow tray on top that held a chess set and heavy, inlaid board.

On impulse I took the game and laid it out on the table by the brazier. Behind me I heard the woman put down the chest lid, but I willed myself not to turn around to see what else she was doing. In no way was I going to show I was disturbed by my captive status.

When the board was set up I settled back to wait, exhaustion tugging at the edge of my mind while the Fates spun out the future. Perhaps I even nodded a bit, for I jumped when a loud banging sent my jailer running to the door.

There was an exchange of passwords, and then the door swung open and the King of Gwynedd came into the room, the devil-dog Dormarth pacing at his side. It brought me fully awake and doubly alert.

I looked up slowly, languidly turning one of the chess pieces between my fingers. With a gracious nod of my head I acknowledged his presence, almost, but not quite, smiling.

"Good heavens, Cousin," I greeted him archly, "whatever kept you so long?"

TWENTY-TWO

Maelgwn

aelgwn stopped just inside the doorway, wary as a man who is moving into enemy territory, uncertain where the ambushes lie.

He had changed in the months since my father's funeral; the self-assured fellow with whom I had traded barbs was hard-edged and taut now, his face drawn and eyes glittering. The black tunic he wore was trimmed with beaver, the embroidery on his belt was worked with golden thread, and he bore himself with an air of casual elegance. But the constant motion of his eyes from one spot to another betrayed his nervous tension. In contrast, the huge dog at his side was still, solid, and immobile. I wasn't sure which I feared more.

"I hope you brought the wine flagon," I said, gesturing for him to be seated. "The cellars of Gwynedd's King are famous throughout the realm, and I've been looking forward to testing their reputation."

Conceit and self-satisfaction can leave a person vulnerable, so I counted on flattery and the fact that he was probably unaware of how little I care for wine. "Perhaps," I added, dragging my memory for a name from Cei's inventory, "you have one of those pleasant whites from der Pfalz?"

"Not with me." My cousin remained by the threshold—at least the man had enough respect for me to be cautious. "If I'd known it would please you, I'd have had it set by. I'll personally pick out a bottle for tomorrow night." The shadow of a smile played around his mouth, though the eyes stayed cold and calculating.

"The wine's of no great importance." I shrugged and looked down at the board, cursing the fact that I wouldn't be able to get him drunk.

Maelgwn dismissed the matron and made some final arrangement with the guard before closing the door and replacing the lock. I tried not to flinch at the sound.

"That's a marvelous dog, by the way . . . and not a breed I've seen before." I eyed the animal with what I hoped looked like admiration. Its short, sleek coat was shiny black, its build muscular and lean—and I judged that if it stood on its hind legs, it would be as tall as any man. It regarded me in return, its eyes red and glowing, and I was the one who blinked and looked away.

My cousin smiled and motioning Dormarth to lie down in front of the door, crossed the room to the table where I sat. He did not, however, say anything.

"I've heard you have a fabulous menagerie," I went on, praying I didn't sound like a babbling fool. "They say it's quite remarkable—that you have peacocks and monkeys, and even a leopard."

With a laugh Maelgwn seated himself, obviously pleased that his reputation for collecting exotic things was so widespread.

"Not quite a leopard," he said deprecatingly. "It was a cheetah ordered from an Egyptian circus owner in Cairo when it was a kit. But the ship foundered just before making harbor at Degannwy, and the animal was lost."

I was surprised he'd not heard of Palug's sons and the spotted cat they'd rescued on the shore of Anglesey but decided not to ask about it; if his subjects chose to withhold news from him, I saw no reason to tell him myself.

"Which color do you wish to play?" He leaned casually over the chessboard and picked up a pawn, at the same time trying to see down the front of my dress. I looked away hastily lest revulsion show too plainly on my face.

"Why don't I take white?" was the best I could manage.

So I played the opening gambit and for the next little while we each concentrated on the game—it mirrored life too closely to be ignored. When I managed to evade an elaborate trap we both sat back, and I heaved a sigh.

"Maybe there's other activities that would entertain you more?" he asked, grasping my hand before I had a chance to tuck it in my lap.

I looked up to find him staring directly at me. He began stroking my palm and when I closed my fist into a ball, he insinuated his forefinger into the tunnel of my curled fingers, moving it in and out methodically.

It was such a disgusting gesture, I flung my fingers open again and wiped my palm against my dress.

"And how fares your wife, Cousin?" The question came out from behind clenched teeth as I glared at him.

"You haven't heard? The doctors at Degannwy say it is but a matter of days now. In fact, the messenger may well be on his way here with the news that I'm a free man and therefore able to remarry. Surely," he added, pushing his face close to mine, "you must have guessed that was why I sent for you?"

I recoiled and leapt to my feet so quickly that the table was upset; whatever hope I had of being held safe in return for ransom had just been dispelled.

The inlaid board fell to the floor with a clatter, sending the pieces scattering. Dormarth growled a warning, so I turned and stalked to the far end of the room, trying not to panic.

Maelgwn stood up as well, and I could hear him behind me. I was trying to get as far away from the dog as possible and only too late realized the danger of being cornered.

"And just what do you expect of me?" I challenged, whirling to face him in an effort to brazen it out.

"You minx, you know full well what I want." It was half snarl, half leer, and so naked in its intent all hope of avoidance was lost.

I tried to dart past him, but he flung out his arms, catching me on the bad shoulder and throwing me off balance. Before I could scramble clear he had me backed against the wall, his arms extended on either side to keep me from wriggling away.

"If you'll leave that high-handed Pendragon and come to me," he purred, "Rheged and Gwynedd combined would make a fine, rich kingdom—a place to found a dynasty. . . ."

It was such a ludicrous idea, I all but laughed aloud. Harsh words of rebuttal leapt to mind, but by then his lips were brushing against my skin and he began to push me against the wall.

I tried to squirm away or at least get enough space so I could bring my knee up, but there was no room between us, and he was careful to stand with his thighs together. The best I could do was draw my hands in under my chin and raise the barrier of both elbows against his chest while I struggled to turn my face away from his mouth.

He slid his arms around me and holding me pinned against his body, began to edge us across the room. I screamed and kicked as we reeled toward the bed like a top, entwined in a wild, flailing embrace.

My feet went out from under me and we sprawled half on the bed, half on the floor. His grip loosened a fraction and I threw all my weight to one side. Rolling free, I watched as he scrambled to a crouch, then did the same myself.

We circled each other as warriors sometimes do in battle, panting and sweating with tension. I cast about with one hand for some kind of weapon, though my eyes never left his face. At last my fingers, brushing across the floor, came in contact with the heavy chessboard.

I pulled it to me, gauging its weight and balance to see if it would serve best on edge as a cleaver or upright before me as a shield. My one consolation was that Maelgwn wasn't armed; perhaps he'd thought it too risky to bring a knife within my range.

The fact that I now had a weapon made him more cautious, and he straightened up slowly, watching me intently the entire time.

"Do you think for one minute that you can change the outcome of what will happen here?" he asked. "There's no one to help you, no-where for you to go, and I'm quite prepared to wait out your silly pride; you can't stay crouching like that all night. Both you and I know I'll bed you, and that is that." He spoke with a scornful smile and deliberately turning his back to me, walked to the bed.

My ribs and shoulder hurt, my back ached miserably, and somewhere inside a giddy, uncontrollable laugh began to take form. The picture of my feral attitude in the face of his calm certainty struck me as hysterically funny, and I had to bite my lip to keep from laughing aloud.

With great nonchalance I also straightened up and, holding the chessboard flat in front of me, slowly turned away from him. With great care I paused for five heartbeats, then suddenly whipped around, losing the board like a plate sent sailing across a green during midsummer games.

Startled, Maelgwn barely had time to fling his arm up and duck his head—but for that, the board would have put a massive dent in his skull. Instead, he rose unscathed and my laughter broke free, filling the room with an eerie, terrible sound.

He lunged for me, surprise and rage burning in his face. The back of his hand smashed against my cheek, jarring my teeth and making my vision blur. The laughing stopped abruptly. But when he leaned over to tear open the front of my dress, his ear came within range and I clamped my teeth on it.

With my nose buried in his hair, I had to gasp for breath around the gristly mass in my mouth, but I clung to the thing like a terrier while blood spattered everywhere and my attacker howled in pain.

He left off pawing at my dress and tried to shake me bodily, but that only made his ear hurt more. Blows to my head were futile for the same reason. Finally he doubled up his fist and hit me as hard as possible in the stomach.

The air rushed out of my lungs and I lost my grip, gasping frantically for breath and doubled over in pain. Unable to defend myself any longer, I slid to the floor.

Blackness whirled softly over me—numbness, darkness, a snuffling, grunting sound that mingled with the blue light of something suffocating me. . . . I came to with the skirt of my dress over my head and my attacker rooting between my legs with urgent intent. I felt the pushing of his member and writhed away as he sought to force it home—twisted, kicked, clawed at the fabric prison, desperate to reach his face, his arms, any place I could inflict damage. But the silk only got more tangled, and in spite of my struggles he finally attained his goal.

He was not a large man but the pain and revulsion of violation sent waves of nausea through me. I groaned and howled and screamed between retches, but to no avail; apparently the guard had been forewarned, and the dog stayed at the door.

It occurred to me that when Maelgwn was done it would be over, and for a bit I tried to move in consort with him, hoping to bring him to climax and finish. But though he mauled and pawed me, sweating and straining and grunting between pants of breath, there seemed no surcease.

Dear Goddess, I prayed, get this beast through his stupid rutting and off of me.

But the Mother must have been attending to other things, for there came no help, and eventually I lay limp across the bed, spraddled and moaning and utterly exhausted. And still he kept going.

No doubt there were moments now when I could have pushed free of him, had I been able to muster the strength and hope from within. But something had happened; I was no longer pinned beneath the bulk of the man but saw the scene as from a distance, looking down on a pitiful parody of the loving union and thinking what unconscionable creatures humans can be.

From the far-off safety of detachment I told myself it was not I he was touching; only the flesh, not the spirit, was subjugated to his will. Let the monster hump and groan and wallow in the trough he was plowing between my thighs; what had that to do with me?

My spirit moved, cool and clean as a mountain pool, in realms he would never know. I closed my eyes and drifted out of consciousness.

"Gwen?"

The word came softly, gently, across vast stretches of time. It was repeated over and over, rounding on the air—calling, guiding, cradling me in its sound. Slowly it gathered my spirit in, drawing me back to existence, to a body that ached and throbbed and moaned with pain.

"Gwen . . . Gwen . . . can you hear me?"

The voice was familiar, running soft and sure, like the hand that brushed the hair back from my face, as much a caress as a gesture of concern. I nodded without opening my eyes, wondering vaguely what Lancelot was doing in my dream.

"Gwen, love, we have to get you out of here. Can you walk?"

"Don't know," I mumbled, the effort raising a searing pain in my ribs. I wanted to tell him I'd try, but all that came out was a whimper.

"Well, I can carry you if it comes to that."

His arms were around me already, holding and cuddling and protecting me against something dreadful that lurked just over the edge of wakefulness. The dream was threatening to become a nightmare, and I tried to avoid it by turning in to his embrace.

But the terror persisted—just beyond memory, diffuse and ugly and having something to do with my cousin.

"Where's Maelgwn?" My voice was weak and frightened and as hushed as Lance's own.

"Posting back to Degannwy. His party almost ran me over at the gate, riding as though the Hounds of the Wild Hunt were on his trail. Must be awfully important to have drawn him out at midnight in such a rush."

Probably his wife's death, I thought fuzzily, then wondered how I knew she was dying. Horrible half memories floated up to consciousness; disjointed bits of detail paraded behind my closed eyelids like a grotesque pageant until the physical pain in my body blotted them all out.

I was shivering so hard my teeth chattered. Lance drew his cloak around us both and began rocking gently as I snuggled in against his warmth. For the moment there was safety, there was protection, there was a kindred soul willing to stand beside me and help ward off my pain. The very idea was unbelievable.

"We must leave soon," he whispered. "My horse is in the copse of birches where I hid when Maelgwn's entourage thundered over the bridge. There's a coracle beached by the side of the lodge; we can take it back across the water. Just stay down and quiet under my cape, and let me do the talking if anyone challenges us."

"But there's a guard at my door."

Both mind and vision were blurring in and out of focus, and I wondered how Lance had gotten in without seeing him. More and more things were getting tangled in this weird delirium.

Arthur's lieutenant swallowed hard and turned his head away.

"Some deaths can't be helped," he answered. "I only wish it had been Maelgwn himself."

The outrage of his tone left no room for reply, so I gritted my teeth and struggled to my feet. My body was stiff and sore, but no bones seemed broken except perhaps the ribs, judging from the constant pain in my chest.

With the Breton's help I made it slowly to the door.

A torch flickered in its bracket, casting shadows across the main room of a hunting lodge where the walls were hung with horns and antlers and a pair of bearskins flanked the door. I saw the sentry's feet as we crept past the place where Lance had dragged the body and mentally made the sign against evil.

There was no moon, so we slipped the coracle into the stream without even casting a shadow and made for a clump of rushes beyond sight of the guards on the bridge.

The cold lapping of the water sharpened my senses, though my mind still moved with the languid calm of one in a trance. The undefined nightmare was following us even across the water, and I shied from thinking of it. It was enough to concentrate on escape.

Our luck held and Lance's horse remained silent as we approached through the trees. Lifting me to the saddle, Lance swung up behind and gathered me in his arms. Within minutes we were well away from the hunting lodge and heading for the Road.

"How did you know where I was?" I asked numbly as we left the trees behind and the horse lengthened out into a long trot beside open fields.

"I was going south to join Arthur, and met Uwain posting back to Penrith with the news. He led me to where the ambush took place; from there the trail of flowers showed where you'd entered the forest, and there were enough in your party to make the tracking easy."

I nodded, only half understanding what he said, though a shower of hawthorn blossoms seemed to be falling around us. My mind reeled when I tried to make more sense of it, and my teeth began to chatter again.

"There, now, you just relax," Lance murmured, settling me back against his chest. He started to croon the little melodies one sings to a frightened bairn, and I moved closer in the shelter of his embrace, suddenly very, very tired and glad to give over control to someone else.

The tears began without my even knowing, starting in little runnels that brimmed silently from a pool of sorrow welling up in my heart. Nestling my head against the Breton's shoulder, I let the flood of anguish pour out while the stars glimmered around us and the horse moved as smoothly as though gliding over glass.

I cried for the loss of my father, of Kaethi, of the child at Stirling and Igraine in the convent; for those I had known and loved, and those, like the guard at the hunting lodge, whom I had cause to fear or hate.

There were even tears for Mama, now so long gone, and for the Irish boy who had once carried me through a starlit night himself, oh so many years ago.

Gone and lost, every one, and only I left to mourn them, here in the magical safety of Lancelot's care. Their faces rose before me, floating in the starlight like the stuff of dandelions wafting on a summer breeze. They lifted and fell while Lance's voice spun out around us, keeping fear and remembrance beyond that web of sound. Sometimes he sang, but more often he talked as Kevin had talked, proclaiming his love and promising to take me to Tara to be his Queen. Even in my fever state it seemed an odd thing for the Breton to do, and I pulled back slightly, trying to see his expression.

It was then, searching the face that was silhouetted against the light of the stars, that I found my young love had come back to claim me after all.

A rush of sweetness, of hope and surprise and unimaginable joy, flooded through me, wakening the bright high happiness that had been so long asleep. I was a girl again, and free, riding on the clean wild wind of the northern fells even as I was held safe and protected within his arms.

He looked down at me with a depth of tenderness that flowed over me without words. And when the flash of his smile filled the night, my heart leapt in wonder that he, too, cherished the love that had never been spoken aloud. The world began to spin wildly.

With his free hand he pressed my head back against his shoulder, kissing my hair and crooning softly. It was a gesture of infinite gentleness and care, and my soul was dazzled with rapture as I drifted out of consciousness for good.

TWENTY-THREE

The Convent

he next fortnight was spent wandering in a delirium of terrifying nightmares and poignantly beautiful dreams.

Everyone I knew gathered in that twilight: Mama and Kevin, Brigit and Nonny, and the spinning mistress Vida. There were people from the Court as well; Arthur himself came and went in my delusions, though it was Lance who was at my bedside whenever I awoke.

Once I lay and watched the Breton through half-opened eyes when he didn't know I had returned to consciousness. He was reading from a scroll, head bent in concentration, dark hair falling forward. He had shaved his beard, revealing again the rich sensual mouth, fascinating in its fullness. After a bit he raised his head to stare off into space, pensive, mysterious, seeking something of the spirit no one else was privy to.

Fragmented memories of riding through the night glimmered at the edge of consciousness, evanescent as any dream, without beginning or end—but I had no idea whether they were scraps of fantasy or based on a real event. Still, somewhere inside me beauty and amazement stirred like a splendid bird that starts in its sleep, then fluffs up its feathers and becomes quiet again. I drifted back to my fever-world with a smile.

Another time I asked where Arthur was, and the lieutenant frowned and said something about a terrible battle. I tried to stay awake—tried to learn where and against whom—but the world dissolved around me, and I was lost in delirium again.

After that the nightmares turned murderous, full of danger and despair. Powerless against the force of them, I fled from scene to scene, *stumbling at last upon a broad, flat plain where two full armies stand ready for combat. In the space between them a pair of ghostly Champions struggle, one with sword, the other with spear. Though they stalk each other with deadly determination, neither makes a sound.*

Horror crept through me as I watched, unable to sway the outcome, incapable of turning away. *Finally, in a spurt of blood and gore, I see the one skewered through the belly by the other's spear—feel the searing pain, hear the death rattle as blood and entrails and life pour from him. Convulsing in his last throes, his back arches and he twists slowly into the light. The hope and visions that once filled his eyes now flickered out and his mouth fell open in a silent scream as he reached across the void to me.*

"Arthur! Arthur!" I came to shrieking, sitting bolt upright as a cold, clammy sweat enveloped me.

"Shh, shh now . . . it's all right . . . it's only a bad dream." Lance was at my bedside immediately and I flung my arms around him, sobbing uncontrollably.

"Arthur's safe, Gwen. Safe. Do you hear me? . . . He's no longer in danger."

"Then where is he?" I wailed, clinging to the lieutenant. "Why isn't he here?"

"Because he's rounding up Saxons in the south." Lance's voice was firm and reasonable, giving solid credence to his words. "The battle of Mt. Badon was a crucial victory, and he dares not leave the final cleaning-up half-done."

It sounded logical enough and the pounding of my heart began to slow. I peered cautiously at the world that was coming into focus beyond the safety of the Breton's arms.

It was a small, sparsely furnished room, much like Igraine's at the convent. Sunlight poured through the open window and spilled down the whitewashed walls. Sparrows were rustling in the thatch, and the murmur of doves cooing in a nearby courtyard drifted through the casement. Compared with the shadowy realms I had been wandering in, this was light and life itself.

The presence of the Breton was also reassuring; he would not be here if Arthur was in danger somewhere else. I ran my hand along his arm experimentally, feeling the strength of the muscle, the fine fur of hair. It was very real to the touch and didn't evaporate the way things in dreams do. With a sigh I leaned my head against his chest, then groaned aloud as a stabbing pain shot through my back.

"Brigit says you must stay quiet," Lance admonished, easing me down among the pillows. "She says the infection may still be present."

"Brigit? Where are we?"

"In her convent. I brought you here because of her skill as a healer. Lavinia should be arriving soon, and Nimue, too."

He paused, and I smiled weakly, glad to have so many dear friends near. It did not occur to me to ask why there was a need for healing.

"I promised to tell Brigit when you woke up," Lance went on. "She'll be no end of pleased."

I watched the Breton leave, feeling that light, free headiness that comes after a long illness, when you know you are going to live but have not yet taken up the daily struggle. Still, my buoyancy of spirit was tempered by something . . . something dreadful and sickening that lurked beyond my ken and threatened to overwhelm me. Turning my face to the wall, I prayed for Brigit's quick arrival, for I did not want to face that something by myself.

Sleep must have reclaimed me, for when I next opened my eyes Brigit was there, sitting in the glow of an oil lamp, silently saying her evening prayers. I watched her quietly, marveling at the air of composure and gentle contentment that radiated from her. For all that I would have liked to see her marry Bedivere and raise a family, I couldn't deny that she looked happy and fulfilled here.

"It really was the right decision for you, wasn't it?" I asked when she glanced over at me.

"Aye." She gave me a fond smile and tucking a wayward strand of hair under her veil, came to sit on the bed. "To accept your moira is half the battle won. Now, tell me how you feel."

We slid into the old ways of banter and shared confidences as though we'd never been apart. She pulled back the covers, and when I rolled over on my side she poked around my back, asking if it hurt.

"A little sore, but not really painful. What happened, Brigit? Why am I here? I can't sort out the memories. . . ."

"You've been terribly sick . . . so sick we thought we'd lose you. Sometimes that happens after rape."

The word clove the air in two, quivering like an arrow just struck home. I froze as half-remembered fears became a certainty.

"Maelgwn . . . that bastard Maelgwn." I groaned, feeling my gorge rise as memory flooded in. "Oh, heavens, what happened to Griflet? Is he alive? And my women?"

Brigit hastily put her hand on my arm. "Lance says Griflet didn't die, nor were the other women hurt. It was you they wanted."

"Griflet warned me . . . dear Gods, he didn't want to take us on that outing." A dreadful, cold numbness settled over me as pictures of the abduction and rape marched relentlessly through my head. My voice went hollow, and the words came forth without any feeling at all—like a distant, detached report of something that had nothing to do with me. "I should never have tried to outbluff Maelgwn. If only I'd been more . . . more sensible. Less arrogant. I should have watched my tongue. . . ."

Every moment of contact with my cousin loomed before me, each full of ghastly portent, each blindly ignored. I recounted them while Brigit sat silent, perhaps knowing that I had to be cleansed of the memory before I could begin to live again.

The bells for chapel rang somewhere in the night, but she stayed beside me, listening, talking, sometimes just holding me while I stared bleakly into the past. By the time dawn was breaking I lay exhausted, wrung out with remembering and ready for sleep. The work of healing was only just begun, but at least it was a start.

The next day Vinnie arrived in grand style, having been carried from the villa at Cunetio in Igraine's litter. The plump little widow swept into my cubicle insisting that she be given the room next to mine. Lance, who had occupied it until then, graciously gave over, and my old governess set about "putting things to rights" as though I were a child in her charge again.

Nothing escaped her notice: a novice was sent off to a local farm to make arrangements for a daily pot of chicken soup with which to augment the convent's simple fare; there were muttered prayers and imprecations as the bundle of herbs someone had tied to my bedpost was replaced by a bowl of holy water which Vinnie sprinkled on me three times daily. And she fussed over me like a robin trying to feed a cuckoo chick.

Nimue's arrival was as quiet as Vinnie's had been noisy; she simply walked into my cell one morning while the nuns were at Mass. Lance greeted her kindly enough, then excused himself in order to leave us alone.

"Like old times," I noted, gingerly sitting up to give her a hug of welcome. "Remember the days at Sarum, before the wedding?"

The doire smiled but hastened to explain that she couldn't stay long. "Arthur sent me to make sure you're fully healed before asking you to travel. And I wanted to see for myself how badly you've been hurt. Judging from what Brigit tells me, you've had excellent care and are making a strong recovery."

I nodded, relieved that Arthur was so fully apprised of the situation and touched by his concern.

Nimue examined me thoroughly and sat down on the bed while I readjusted my clothes. She pronounced me essentially cured—the bleeding and discharge had stopped, the pain had gone. That was no more than I could have deduced, and when she continued to stare at me, I faced her calmly and demanded to know what else there might be.

The doire took both my hands in her own and looked fully into my eyes as she spoke. "Gwen, if infections like this don't kill her, they leave a woman barren. It's unlikely you'll ever get pregnant again."

The words hit like a blunted sword, bruising deeply without breaking the surface. My eyes skittered from one corner of the room to another, not even registering what they looked on, and my voice seemed to have deserted me entirely.

"Are you certain?" I whispered.

"No," she answered, looking down at our hands. "With this sort of thing, one is never certain. I can only tell you what has happened before."

For a long minute the numbness that had imprisoned me of late began to waver, then suddenly gave way to a sea-surge howl of fear and anger—fear of Maelgwn, anger at the irony that now, when the hope of motherhood had grown strong again, it should be dealt this final blow. There are reasons why people grow bitter toward the Gods.

"Does Arthur know?" I asked when my sobbing subsided.

Nimue shook her head. "I wasn't sure, not having spoken with Brigit. Besides, I thought you would prefer to tell him yourself."

I bit my lip and looked away. At least I was luckier than some, for Arthur was unlikely to berate me for this failure. He'd made it very clear he had no dreams of raising sons or any desire to watch daughters grow and bloom. But I winced at the thought of our coming together again. The idea of bed left me feeling numb and chilled, and while I had no doubt he'd continue to recognize me as his Queen, an inner, nagging voice whispered that he'd see me as unclean, defiled, unworthy. Perhaps that was why he had not come after me himself.

Nimue's voice cut across my thoughts. "Arthur received word of your abduction the day after he learned the barbarians were preparing a coordinated assault—Saxons from both the north and south, coming together under Cerdic's leadership. There was no way the High King could rescue you and stand firm against them at the same time." She smiled at me gently. "If it's any consolation, the victory at Mt. Badon was final and complete; Cerdic is dead, and the might of the barbarians is broken. Right now Arthur is rounding up Federates and invaders alike—finishing the job once and for all. It's a tremendous relief to him to know the Queen's Champion is at your side; with Lance to look after you, he knows you're safe."

The doire's explanation allayed some of my fears; one doesn't ask history to pause while you attend to personal matters. But there was still the question of how my people would view me—how much did they know of the rape, and how would they react to my return?

"The news of your abduction spread rapidly, Gwen . . . after all, you are their Queen. Many of them are outraged, and all worry for you, pray for you, demand revenge for you. Arthur himself has been racing around like a madman, popping up in the most unexpected places and riding like a fiend all along the Saxon Shore. That wild-man, Gwyn, keeps up with him, and even manages to calm him down a bit, but many of the people say they are both in danger of becoming demons.

"Naturally there are some who applaud his behavior, wanting him to take vengeance on all who have harried the Britons in the past. Others say he's taking out his anger on the Saxons because he dares not go after the man who stole you." The doire sighed and stood up. "Stories like that spread as quickly as the notion that I lured Merlin into giving me his magic, then used it to dispose of him."

I gasped, sorry she'd heard Morgan's wretched gossip. "Why don't you refute it?" I asked.

"And let the whole world know that Merlin is dead and Arthur lacks his protection? No, I promised that would never happen, that as long as Arthur lives the people will believe he is guided by the Mage, even from a distance." She shrugged slightly with resignation. "So my name is a little sullied; only those who want to think evil of our relationship will believe it."

Once more the power and gracefulness of my young friend impressed me, and I put my hand over hers in sympathy; at least between us the truth was known.

The next few weeks were quiet and restorative; Brigit stopped in whenever her duties as a nun allowed and continued to sleep each night in my room, just as she had when we were youngsters. If I cried out in dreams, she'd talk me awake and help me wrestle with both fear and grief. Eventually my terror turned to anger where Maelgwn was concerned. In moments of blind hate I imagined him flayed alive, slowly and painfully, in the Saxon manner, or watched as Arthur dismembered him a limb at a time. But I was still haunted by the fever image of Arthur dying in combat and quailed at the idea that it might come about through the defense of my honor. So I put aside that problem and let the growing beauty of the country summer heal my spirit.

When I was able to leave the bed Vinnie sat with me for hours by the window while we worked on embroidery and in the afternoons shared tea with anyone who'd come. After she'd moved in, Lance had more time to himself, though occasionally he joined us for tea and always came to see me early in the morning while the women were at Mass. Sometimes he brought a flower or reported on the antics of a trio of hedge sparrows that often flitted through the garden, and we laughed and talked about all manner of light-hearted things. Neither of us referred to Maelgwn or to our dash for freedom in that star-scattered night.

I puzzled over it when he wasn't there, trying to sort out what had truly happened and what were only fever dreams. It seemed possible my memories were more of Kevin than of Lance, though I'd have sworn the Breton had showered me with such an outpouring of love and tenderness that even in retrospect the wild, sweet joy of it brought tears welling to my eyes.

Yet once Lance had gotten over his initial distrust of me, there had never been anything in his voice or look that indicated more than a normal devotion to his monarch. And though I watched him closely now, there was no hint that he harbored a personal love only so much danger would lead him to disclose.

There was no way to ask him about it, for I'd certainly look the fool if I was mistaken, so I put aside those thoughts as well and tried to concentrate on other things.

"A gift of the season," Lance said one morning as he handed me the discarded shell of a hedge sparrow's egg he'd found in the garden.

I looked down at the little sky-blue cup. The Breton had tucked a bit of green moss inside, and on it rested a single delicate star-petaled blossom of pink purselane. I grinned at him with delight—there was no one who could take my mind off terrors as well as he could.

"Just got further word from Arthur," he announced, smiling in return. "He says to tell you he prays daily for your rapid recovery."

I laughed at that; Arthur praying for aught but the unity of Britain was tantamount to my preferring to live in Roman houses; perhaps I was not the only one changing, after all.

"Bedivere's gone to London," Lance went on, moving over to the window. "Arthur wants to hold a victory feast there, and has started rebuilding Caesar's Tower for the occasion." The lieutenant leaned against the window ledge and casually scanned the hills beyond the garden. Caught in the shadow play of light and leaves, he looked exactly like Kevin, and I wondered again what had really happened during that night's ride.

"There's been no end of fuss about a skull the workmen found when they were digging around the foundations," he went on, unaware of my scrutiny. "The druids claim it's the head of Bran, buried there to protect Britain from invasion—they see the High King's uncovering it as the worst of heresies. Arthur just shrugs, saying it's wiser to rely on our own strength of arms to repel invaders than to count on Gods long dead and gone. Unfortunately that doesn't sit well with the druids."

"I guess it wouldn't." I grimaced. The Roman Christians are uneasy with us because we don't condemn the Old Ways or convert to theirs. Now the Pagans were in danger of feeling slighted because of a flip, if practical, remark made out of hand.

"Not only that, the messenger says Arthur has had the Saxons thrown in chains and irons, and marches them before him as slaves."

"Slaves?" The idea brought me up short. My father had never allowed slavery in Rheged, and it hadn't occurred to me that Arthur might resort to such a thing in Logres.

"So the messenger claimed." Lancelot shook his head. "Who knows what's really happening? With all the atrocities I've heard laid at the Saxon doorstep, it may be more wishful thinking on the part of the commoners than an actual policy by Arthur. Still, it's clear that he's been acting strangely since your misadventure."

I nodded—between insulting the Pagans and chasing all over the countryside enslaving Saxons, it looked as though Arthur were going to get us into no end of trouble if I didn't return pretty soon.

"When can we join him?" I asked.

"How does next week sound?"

Lance turned to look at me. There was something boyishly eager in his expression, and it dawned on me that he'd been away from Court even longer than I had. Perhaps he missed it, too.

"Griflet's supposed to be well enough to join us by week's end, and Agricola suggested Arthur meet us at his villa near Gloucester . . . that is," he added, coming over to my chair and staring down at me, "if you feel up to it."

I heard the concern in his voice, saw the care in his eyes. Blue and shimmery as the sea off Cornwall, they sought and held my own with a steady, even gaze.

"If you're not ready to go out and face the world yet, I'll not be trying to force you."

I stared back at him, loath to give up the sweet security and peace of these few weeks, hating the idea of facing curious crowds and crude gossip. My knees felt weak at the prospect, and I wanted to cry out, "Not yet, not yet." But something warned me not to stay here, either.

"It is time I get on with the business of being Arthur's wife," I said firmly, still looking into the depths of Lance's eyes.

My words had been chosen as much for my own benefit as his.

"Very well, M'lady," he answered, and the smile he gave me was full of love as well as respect.

My breath stuck in my throat, and I looked away hastily. It was clear my memory of the rescue was not all fever-inspired.

TWENTY-FOUR

Triumph

here's my wife?"

Arthur's voice carried throughout the villa, and I froze, held silent in the grip of a nameless fear.

I'd ridden down from the convent in the litter, for when Griflet brought Shadow forward so I could mount her, I'd taken one look at the pretty mare and burst into tears. I couldn't blame her for my cousin's actions, but neither could I bring myself to ride her again.

During the journey an unreasoning terror settled over my heart, coloring every thought. By the time we turned up the cypress-lined drive of Agricola's estate I didn't know which I dreaded more—finally facing Arthur or not meeting him at all. I was actually relieved to discover he hadn't arrived yet and set to work unpacking my things with a single-mindedness of purpose, as if by not thinking about it I could avoid the moment entirely.

Now that he was here, I was petrified.

"Hie there, girl, have you gone deaf?" he called again, his voice full of summer laughter. Not only was there no hint of reproach, it rang with eagerness, and a wave of relief washed through me.

Dropping the dress I was holding, I raced down the corridor, straight into his arms.

We came together in a tumbling hug of welcome that reminded me my ribs had only recently healed. And then he pulled back and was looking down at me, half frowning.

"Whatever made you go out alone that way? And right into your enemy's territory?" The teasing in his tone drove all rebuke from the words.

"I wasn't alone; there was Griflet and Uwain and a guard of young boys—plus all the women as well. And Penrith's a fair piece from the Gwynedd border. Whoever taught you geography, anyhow?" I quipped in return.

Arthur grinned at that and scooped me up in another hug, obviously glad to see me.

Dinner that night was a family affair, with the closest of Companions and my women from the northern trip. Frieda brought in Caesar, who gave me a welcome that rivaled Arthur's for sheer exuberance.

"But where's Cabal?" I asked, glancing about the room in search of the white wolfhound.

A look of pain crossed Arthur's face. "The Saxons got her at Mt. Badon. Saved my life at Winchester, she did—and took two men with her at Badon, but gone now, nonetheless."

A pang of regret went through me, and I realized that much had happened to Arthur during this last year that I knew nothing about.

When the tables were cleared Palomides came forward to present a bouquet of posies and a little speech of welcome on behalf of the Companions. It made for a delightful homecoming, and I was much relieved that no one mentioned my recent misadventure.

But after dinner, in the privacy of our chamber, a terrible awkwardness came between Arthur and me. He moved slowly and thoughtfully about the room behind me while I sat at my dressing table brushing out my hair. I heard the straw in the mattress rustle when he came to rest on the edge of the bed.

"Are you all right? Nimue said a long illness . . . a dreadful illness, if the truth be told. Are you completely well?" Something in his tone was too casual, as though he were struggling not to show how much it mattered.

I took a deep breath and turned slowly to face him. He had to be told sometime.

"They say most women who have that kind of sickness die . . . and if they live, they're barren for the rest of their lives. It's possible we won't have any children at all, now."

The words hung on the air like banners gone slack and lifeless.

"And you're not pregnant by Maelgwn?"

"Of course not!" What with being so sick and bleeding so much, I had not even thought of that possibility. "I would tell you if I were," I affirmed, in case he had any doubt.

"Good."

Arthur leaned back with a sigh, and I went to join him on the bed. The very idea that the man who had stolen the High King's wife might impregnate her when the King had not implied a further, more personal insult. And it opened an area I had not even thought of, having always assumed it was my lack that kept me from conceiving. I cast a quick glance at my husband, wondering if he'd been blaming himself all this time.

He put his arm around my shoulder. "I told you before, I'm content enough without children. If you miss raising youngsters, there's plenty around that could use some looking after—just don't bring them into our personal life."

And that was it. The worst news I could imagine had been delivered and accepted with equanimity. I snuggled in against him gratefully, idly playing with the cord that laced his shirt.

"Do you know where Maelgwn is now?" he inquired.

I shook my head and concentrated on the cord. "Must we talk about it? I'd rather just put it all behind us."

"It won't be behind *me* until the man is dead." Arthur's tone was one of cold fury. "I cannot let him live."

The lacing tangled under my fingers as I realized that for Arthur it was not just my honor, but his own in jeopardy. I glanced up at his face and saw his features contorted in the death scream of my nightmare. My eyes blinked and the image faded, but panic filled me nonetheless.

I didn't want to tell Arthur about the vision, and my mind raced to find an excuse for not confronting Maelgwn. "We can't afford personal vendettas, can we? Killing Maelgwn could make an enemy of the Cumbri, and with the Irish always threatening, they need to know how highly we respect their allegiance."

"And what will they think if I don't take action? That I can't take care of my own wife? That I've gone cold and uninterested as a husband? Or that you went with him willingly, as rumor would have it?"

"Arthur, how can you say that!" Shocked, I sat upright and stared at him suspiciously. "What rumor?"

"Oh, just stories. Of course I didn't believe them." He turned away glumly. "But Morgan says there's a servant woman who claims she saw you all decked out in silk and fancies, playing chess and chiding your cousin for not coming for you sooner."

My face went hot with anger and it was all I could do to keep from laying a curse on my sister-in-law on the spot. I could just imagine her hastening to her dear brother's side in order to fill his head with poison about me.

"And what else does the Lady of the Lake say?" I tried, without success, to keep the acid out of my voice.

"That she swore the woman to silence and is doing everything she can to counteract the tale." Arthur was on his feet again, this time pacing quickly around the room. "She's also trying to work out some form of apology and reparation where Maelgwn is concerned; perhaps some ritual to take place later . . . though that isn't going to carry much weight with most of the northern lairds."

He came to a stop beside the dressing table and stared unseeingly at the items spread for my toilet. Suddenly his fist slammed down, making the mirror and comb jump with the impact. Some of the little jars fell over, spilling their contents.

"You know I have to follow up this victory—the Saxon matter can't wait. But the longer Maelgwn goes unpunished, the more people will question my manhood. And war-lords won't follow a leader they have doubts about."

"So what would you do . . . go to war against your own ally?" Anger over Morgan's manipulation made my voice more sarcastic than I meant, and Arthur responded in kind.

"What kind of ally rapes my wife?" he snapped, resuming his pacing.

I swallowed hard, wondering what on earth was happening. "Ah, love, why are we going at each other this way?" I rose to intercept his circuit of the room and planting myself directly in front of him, put my arms around his neck. "Surely we can find a retribution for Maelgwn that doesn't lose the men of the north or add more killing to the slaughters behind us. But for this evening can't we put aside the problems of ruling and make this a proper homecoming, like that between any man and wife?"

Arthur ducked his head sheepishly, looking as chagrined as I felt. Sliding his hands down along the small of my back, he asked shyly, "Are you ready for bedding? Nimue said—that is, she thought—it might take some time before you felt like it, and I should let you set the pace of desire."

Bless you, my sister, I thought silently.

"Well, I'm not sure. . . ." I lifted up on tiptoe to kiss him. "But if we take it slowly and gently, I can let you know if it's painful."

So we bedded, but it was a cautious, restrained coupling with both of us remote and distant rather than close and loving.

He was unusually wakeful afterward and began to talk about turning the recent victory over the Saxons into a lasting peace.

"By making slaves of them?" I asked, and this time it was Arthur who was shocked.

"I enslave no man!" he insisted. "Wherever did you hear such a thing?"

"From the messenger who came to the convent—he said you took them from their steadings in shackles."

"Well, he was partially right," my husband acknowledged. "I put the hostages in chains to keep track of them. And Cerdic's son, Cynric, will remain a royal hostage so other Federates can't rally around him. But I'm not sure what to do with the rest . . . something that will assure we won't have future rebellions."

His voice was weary, but he began a description of the campaign he'd just won, and I listened attentively, like the best of war-leaders' wives.

"Actually it wasn't a single battle, but a series of engagements," Arthur explained. "I suppose the Saxons call it the Battle of Mt. Badon because it hinged on the hill-fort above the town of Badon—the fortress we call Liddington."

It had all started in early spring, when Tiberius sent word from Lincoln that something was afoot in the north. Colgrin and his cousins had ceased coming to market, although there were no signs of plague or devastation to explain their absence. Nimue—and common sense—told Arthur to call up the members of the Round Table, so he put everyone on alert for when the weather warmed.

Then Wehha the Swede reported that Saxon ships had been sighted sailing up the Wash, and men were gathering in the vicinity of Spalding. Cerdic seemed to be rallying the Fen people with reinforcements and promising to lead them out of the swamp and onto the rich midland farms of Logres.

"Even the northern Saxons heard his call, massing in war-gear and coming down the Icknield Way in wave after wave," Arthur explained, using the folds in the comforter to create a rough map. "It was obvious that Aelle and Octha would join in, coming north in order to rendez-vous at the Goring Gap. Once in the Thames valley, if they could convince the other Federates to rise with them, the combined forces could sweep clear to Gloucester. It would divide the British holdings in half, and give the Saxons control of all major Roads and ports on each side of the realm. That's what I would have done, if I were Cerdic."

Arthur sent Cador and his son Constantine to Oxford so as to block any Saxon advance along the Thames. Geraint and his men moved to the hill-forts along the Avon with orders to keep the southern Saxons from heading west but not to interfere if they were marching north. Meanwhile, Arthur set up his headquarters at Liddington.

"I had every intention of forcing the issue in the Thames valley, and the barbarians marched right into it," he said proudly.

Watching my husband as he spun out the story of his victory, I saw things that were not apparent even as recently as last summer. His manner was more marked by determination than enthusiasm and his voice was firm and solid now that the dream was becoming real. Here indeed was a King to guide Britain's destiny.

Cador and Constantine stopped the Saxons at Oxford, chasing them back down the Thames to Abbingdon, where they ran smack into waves of new forces marching west. It was at that point that Arthur rushed through the Goring Gap, catching the barbarians from behind.

"The battles were terrible—bloody skirmishes with little groups, and milling, awful slaughters where the Saxons were massed without proper leadership, for once Cerdic and his sons died the Saxon command broke apart. That's when I took his youngest son captive.

"After we had beaten them, I turned back to Liddington, only to find Aelle, late in joining the march to the Gap, had captured my own headquarters—took no prisoners, but killed every man and boy outright. When I heard that, I sent for Geraint to help me lay siege, and on the third day I recaptured the hill-fort with a direct assault. I paid them back in kind, which made it a grim and bloody business, and one the Saxons will not forget for years to come."

I winced and closed my eyes as Arthur told off the names of the Companions who were dead or wounded, and when he came to Ulfin I couldn't keep from sobbing.

"Uther's Chamberlain was a fine man," Arthur allowed. "And his son Griflet is as brave and loyal as the father was. Any leader is fortunate to have such men in their Court."

I nodded slowly, trying to wipe the tears from my cheeks.

" 'Tis enough of such talk," Arthur announced in a quick change of mood. "We've busy times ahead. The people are longing to see for themselves that their Queen is healthy and sound, and a splendid entrance into London seems the best way to satisfy them. So get out your fanciest dresses, lass, and put on every bit of gold we can dredge from the treasury. I intend to impress them all—Briton and Federate, Cumbri and Pict—with the power and majesty of Arthur Pendragon. And," he added with a mischievous smile, "I want the world to see that you're safe in my care again."

I let out a yip when he nuzzled at the nape of my neck, and then we were laughing and romping together, the awkwardness of our earlier mating dispelled by the return of our usual banter.

At long last I was home.

The question of the Saxon hostages caused all sorts of controversy. Arthur had taken one man from each steading, and we didn't have the resources to keep and feed such a multitude indefinitely.

"I say we kill them all off," Gawain growled. "Or sell them into slavery as they sell Britons when they catch them."

"Absolutely." Gaheris nodded, following the lead of his older brother.

"String them up on crosses, like the Romans used to," chimed in a young man I had yet to meet. His grisly suggestion was made with such relish, I paused to look at him more closely. He was handsome enough, but had eyes that stared brazenly at the world, coldly assessing it in relation to his own desires. Whoever he was, I didn't think I was going to like him.

"Agravain," Arthur told me later. "The third of Lot's sons. Leave it to Morgause to breed such a viper."

It was the first time I'd heard Arthur speak casually of his older sister, and it surprised me.

"Gawain's no viper," I countered.

"No . . . but no thanks to his mother." We were putting the rondels I'd brought from the Mote onto the bridles for the Companions, and Arthur smiled suddenly. "Gawain may be hotheaded and impulsive, but I'd put my life in his hands any day. There's that to be said for Celtic loyalty."

I wondered if Arthur knew Morgause had disowned her son but hesitated to talk about her directly. So I polished a bit of red enamel until it glistened and turned the subject to the captive Saxons instead. "What *are* you going to do with the hostages?"

"Bedivere suggested I send Cynric to our foster-father in Wales. Sir Ector's Court is far enough away, no one will try to rescue the boy— and I know myself Ector's a good man for raising young'uns." Arthur sighed. "As for the others, I gathered them up right after the summer crop was sown. If they don't get back to the fields, we'll have famine throughout the Saxon Shore." He paused, the rondels forgotten. "Cei has studied the barbarians for years, and he says they honor their oath to their overlord above all else. The mistake I made was treating them as political groups rather than dealing with them individually. Now Cei suggests that I have each man swear loyalty to me before his shackles are struck off. Oh, I know," he went on hastily, "it means hours, maybe even days, in the arena, making peace man by man. But I can't afford to keep them all in prison and I do need to extract fealty from them. By the time the oath swearing's over, hopefully everyone will have recognized the fairness and justness of the Pendragon. What do you think?"

I put down my polishing cloth with a grin. "Sounds like Bedivere's advice to me, years ago . . . whenever possible astound your friends and baffle your enemies."

"If Cei has anything to do with it, we'll astound 'em all," my husband added cheerfully. "He's arranged for us to sail down the Thames, all the way to London. There's as many British as Federate settlements along the way, which gives us a chance to impress everyone. It should be as good a show as the Picts put on at Loch Ness."

People have lived beside the Thames since time began, so travel and trade and visiting along the watercourse was commonplace. But this was the first time anyone could remember a progress for victorious royalty, and news of our plans swept through the valley like a fleeting Scottish rainbow.

On the morning of our departure a summer mist lay low on the water. It reminded me of the fogs that druids cast in order to confound their enemies, and I wondered if the Gods had sent it as a sign that they were blessing our efforts after all, for it added no end of mystery to our presence.

At the head of the fleet a captured longboat glided silently through the vapor, its carved prow rising into the sunlight like a water monster come to life. The Banner of the Red Dragon fluttered above Bedivere, who stood solemnly tolling a handbell as the captive Saxons plied their oars.

Behind him sat a drummer, a piper, and a man with an ancient war-horn—one of those curved aurochs horns rimmed with silver whose notes stir the blood of men going into battle. The deep, belling sound floated over the water, mixing with the pulse of the hand drum and the clear, plaintive whistle of the pipe. It brought people running from farm and field, out of houses and through town gates, to watch, fascinated, as we approached.

Next came the barges, looming through the mists like ghost ships, each filled with Saxon hostages. In the center farmer-warriors stood beside chain-mailed champions and local ealders, while at their feet lay the wounded, their bandages and splints giving them the look of broken toys clumsily repaired. All were in chains.

It was an uncanny sight, like something from a dream, and neither the hostages nor the people on the riverbank called out, but each observed the other in silence.

On either side of the river a long procession of Companions kept pace with the barges. Led by Gawain and Gaheris, Pelleas and Lancelot, Pellinore and Cador, each was decked out in the best of raiment, and the metal on their armor had been polished until it gleamed. Every bridle bore the red-and-brass rondels we'd given them.

Surrounded by the jingle of bits and clop of hooves, the Companions paid no heed to the people gathered along the path but kept a formal dignity as befits remarkable men. Between the majesty of the parading Champions and the waterborn proof of Arthur's victory, the crowds were filled with awe by the time our craft came into view.

Cei had commandeered a large Saxon vessel and built a high platform at the beam end. Here we sat, robed and crowned and surrounded by pillows and furs and all manner of richness. Gay colors and silk hangings festooned the canopy that provided shade, and a range of pennants fluttered above the water of our wake.

Below us the leaders of the Federate rebels sat manacled to galley oars. They wore the regalia of their rank—brooches and bright bracelets of gold, belt buckles worked in cunning ways, and necklaces studded with garnets. Yet for all their wealth they sweated grimly as they rowed the Pendragon to his triumph—a lesson without words for every observer.

So we made our way by meadow and farmland, past hanging forests and the relics of Roman towns, and through the broad, beautiful sweep of the Goring Gap. All along the way the people stared at us in astonishment. Many fell to their knees in homage, some crossed themselves, and others made the sign against evil—but all watched our passage with amazement.

We nodded soberly to those who gave us a silent salute and occasionally raised our clasped hands so that everyone could see both King and Queen were there to serve them. I hoped it would help counteract Morgan's gossip; the last thing we needed was for people to believe I had been in collusion with my abductor.

· · ·

"What's this?" I asked as we came to a sizable island in the middle of the river.

"Astolat," Arthur replied. "You remember Bernard, don't you?"

"And Elaine." I nodded, scanning the little crowd along the shore for sight of the widower and his voluptuous daughter. The father was quickly found, standing athwart one of several skiffs that were tied to a makeshift dock, but the girl was nowhere to be seen.

A tall stone tower was barely visible above the trees. In the shadow of the topmost window stood a lonely figure, her long hair unbound and tangled around her head. She peered cautiously at the procession of Champions moving along the riverbank as though afraid of both seeing and being seen, and I wondered if the enforced solitude had completely unstrung her mind. My heart went out to her.

Suddenly Elaine moved forward and stepping into the sunlight, leaned out over the window ledge.

I waved to her, but her attention was riveted on the procession; though she held a weaving shuttle in one hand and a hank of yellow floss in the other, both loom and bodkin were forgotten as she stared raptly downstream.

There was something uncanny in her strange, intense stare, and once more I wished her father could understand that imprisonment would not cure her "shyness." With a sigh for human nature I put the subject aside and promptly forgot her. Later I would have ample cause to remember that moment.

Our journey down the river was long and stately, and by the time the Roman bridge at London came into view I could have jumped up clapping for joy at getting off that boat.

The people of London turned out to give us a welcome as gay as the water trip had been solemn. They crowded onto the bridge and lined the wharf below the walls, while out on the river scores of skiffs and coracles formed a procession as we headed for the quay.

Lancelot and Bedivere stood on the pier, and after Arthur asked the ranking members of the Council for permission to enter the city, trumpeters filled the air with flourishes and the two lieutenants helped us ashore.

Bedivere gave Arthur a broad grin of welcome, but the Breton greeted me with great solemnity. Instead of the courtly nod I expected, he studied me intently as he took my hand and helped me ashore.

"Are you well—not overtaxed by such a long trip?" he asked.

"A little tired," I admitted, giving his hand a squeeze of appreciation as the wooden dock firmed up beneath my feet. "If only the royal trappings weren't so cumbersome." I tugged at the cape which had caught on the rough edge of a piling.

Bending low in a gesture that might be construed as a deep bow, he untangled the corner of the offending garment.

"Your freedom, M'lady," he said lightly, and then we were laughing as he offered me his arm, and we hurried after Arthur.

Cei and Enid were arranging a splendid feast with which to conclude the oath taking, so I was blessed with several days of relaxing and catching up with bits of news and gossip from all over the realm.

In general men talk about what *happened*—who has been bravest or bloodiest and where the victory lay—while women discuss who did what and *why,* and how it will effect the rest of us. So I went to the women in order to gauge the mood of the Court.

All the Britons, both northern and southern, were basking in the victory at Mt. Badon. Our journey down the Thames was hailed as a stroke of genius, and the midsummer gathering in the old Imperial City was seen as a fitting climax of pomp and power. Only the Roman girl Augusta made bold enough to mention Maelgwn, asking snidely about his standing in the Round Table. I brushed her question aside and was glad when no one else pursued the subject. Hopefully they realized that a confrontation could lead to civil war, and we needed the men of Gwynedd as allies. For myself, I was still frightened that it would lead to Arthur's death.

The Park around the Palace was in splendid shape this year, so I arranged a picnic for my ladies, hoping to catch whatever breeze came off the river to relieve the summer heat. A fat bumblebee was making its way through drifts of flowers, the hum of its wings lying soft on the still air as the talk moved round to visiting royalty.

Our guests had begun to arrive from all over the realm. Everyone except Morgan le Fey and Maelgwn had promised to be in attendance. Even King Mark of Cornwall had overcome his fear of travel and arrived that very morning, bringing a large entourage for Isolde and the Champions Tristan and Dinadan as well.

"The Cornish Queen and her husband's nephew are never out of touch," Ettard commented, her childish voice giving the innuendo an ingenuous twist. It caught me by surprise, for I hadn't realized that royal romance had become common knowledge.

Vinnie handed round a tray of biscuits and sliced cucumbers and scowled at the convent girl, who looked away with a giggle.

"You're a fine one to talk." Augusta's patrician voice cut sharply across the mirth like the bee darting for a new patch of blossoms. "Everyone knows you and Pelleas spend all your time together."

Ettard blushed but raised her head haughtily. "It is he who seeks me out," she snapped.

"And you're no longer pushing him aside. What's the matter, is he the best you can get, after all?"

"Now just you shush," Vinnie exclaimed. "Whoever heard of such tattling in front of a Queen?"

The girls settled down after that, and the older women made a point of keeping the conversation on more steady subjects: the state of the crops, the arrival of Byzantine traders at the London docks, and the gradual growth of trade between the Saxon women and their counterparts in the city markets.

"Sometimes I think if it was left to women, we'd have long since settled the difficulties between the tribes," Enid mused, and I couldn't help but agree with her.

The men, however, went about it in their own way.

The acceptance of the Saxons' oaths took two full days. Not all were willing to pledge themselves as Arthur's men, and those who refused were led to a block a short distance away, where their heads were chopped off unceremoniously.

I winced whenever the sword fell, for while many had died in combat against us, execution was something else again. But the bloodier-minded Celts cheered happily each time a Saxon head rolled, and Arthur's standing among them rose another notch.

A small but grizzly collection began to decorate the wall over the gate, as a warning to any who might plan to cross the Pendragon again.

"This thing gets heavier every year," Arthur muttered, taking off the crown at the end of the first day and looking about for some place to put the golden circle. Our chamber in the Palace was enormous and over the centuries had become the final resting place for wardrobes and linen chests, tables and stools and couches of all kinds. Arthur finally put the crown over the stile of a chair and sank wearily onto the seat.

In the distance the crows quarreled and flapped among the heads, pulling the flesh from the recent dead and squawking in raucous victory over each bloody morsel.

I came round to stand behind my husband, trying to massage the tension out of his shoulders and commiserating on the less noble aspects of being a ruler.

"Part of the job," he grumbled, rubbing the red mark the crown had left on his temple.

"It's not always going to be like this," I murmured.

"That's up to them." He spoke curtly, the hard edge of authority cutting off all other comment.

I rested my cheek against the top of his head with a sigh. It was one thing to understand his avoidance of personal emotions, and even to put aside my own desire for support when I was scared or hurt or sad. But this callousness toward those whose lives had become forfeit to our sovereignty was something new. I wondered if empathy and compassion no longer existed for him—if too many wars and too much violence in the effort to bring peace kills the capacity to feel anything afterward.

"Time for bed," he yawned, leaning forward and away from my embrace. "At least tomorrow will see the last of it; Cei's feast can't come too soon for me."

I nodded silently, echoing the sentiments myself.

TWENTY-FIVE

The Lily Maid

"I wish Merlin could have seen it; I think he would be pleased," Arthur commented as we presided over the grand feast.

I slid my hand into my husband's and gave it a squeeze in agreement.

The cavernous main Hall of the Palace was full of light and color; everywhere you looked there were banners and sconces, flowers and fresh rushes and the bright glint of gold. It was a rich and sumptuous setting for the nobles and warriors who had gathered to do us honor.

The women ranged from the delicate beauty of Isolde to the country bonniness of Pellinore's young wife. And the Companions were just as diverse. Yet Palomides with his dark, Middle Eastern cast and Gawain, ruddy and high-spirited as they come, were but differing facets of the same jewel. They made the Round Table shimmer like a living tapestry.

In spite of their variety, the Court I now gazed on had come together with one identity; over and above all else, they were the proud followers or allies of King Arthur.

Nimue took her place nearby, and I raised my goblet in a silent toast, glad that she could see the Sorcerer's dream come true.

When the tables were cleared Dagonet called for Wehha the Swede to come forward, then paraded slowly around the inner circle of the trestles holding up a large serving vessel of silver so that the torchlight glinted off its polished sides.

I caught my breath as I recognized the Anastasius Bowl, that gift the

King of the Franks had sent to Arthur years ago. Of all the peoples of East Anglia, Wehha alone had honored his treaty with us and not joined Cerdic's forces. Arthur intended to reward him well.

"You don't mind, do you?" my husband asked in a whisper, gesturing toward the treasure he was giving away. I shook my head, thinking that if shiny cold metal would assure a peaceful future, he was welcome to all the silverware in the royal households.

Nonetheless I stared at the bowl and wondered what the barbarian would make of its classic elegance. I had a sudden picture of him parading through London preceded by his standard of feathers, strutting along with the silver basin inverted on his head like a helmet. The notion was so funny I had to bite my lip to keep from laughing aloud.

The leader of the Wolfings approached us with great solemnity, one hand holding his drinking horn and the other extended in his particular salute. Hailing Arthur as his equal, he turned to address the assemblage.

"Please to note, not all Federates and newcomers are traitors." His Latin was oddly cadenced, as though this were a speech learned by rote so as to make the rest of the Fellowship aware that he too was a man of culture. "An honorable immigrant respects the hospitality of his host King, even if his compatriots do not."

Wehha lifted his horn and after pouring out an oblation for his Gods, toasted the Pendragon and drained the wine. His men were standing at the back of the Hall, and when they began the rhythmic clapping by which these people express approval, Arthur rose and saluted them in return.

I scanned the gathering of Swedes, looking for some sign that Wehha's wife had grown bold—or curious—enough to attend a feast again, but outside of the warriors the only figure I could make out was Wehha's son, Wuffa. Too old to be called a child, too young to have been blooded, the boy stood stiff and silent before his father's men, scowling fiercely during the proceedings.

I wondered why he should be so angry, but a commotion at the end of the hall distracted all of us, and the thought was lost.

A page dodged past the crowd of peasants standing at the door and advanced upon us, breathless from running.

"A boat . . . a little skiff . . . with a lady lying across it. There's neither

oarsman nor sail . . . only a length of fabric trailing in the water
. . . and it moves by itself, as though guided by a God."

The lad's teeth were chattering, and his eyes went huge with fright
as he told of watching the little boat come floating down the Thames.
Its strange, silent cargo was borne along on a steady current, striking
fear and awe in all who saw it. Finally a fisherman had found the
courage to row out and tow it in to shore.

"It was he who sent me to fetch Your Highness," the child gulped.
"He asked you to hurry . . . said you'd know what it means."

Arthur turned to Lance, but the lieutenant was as puzzled as the
King, and the Hall filled with curious murmuring. I put my hand on
Arthur's sleeve, concerned that such an unnatural event boded ill, but
he gave me an encouraging smile and turned to the gathering.

"Something so uncanny is not to be ignored. Whoever wishes to join
me at the river may do so."

Cei called for more torches and within minutes we were trekking
through the night to the water's edge.

The fisherman was just bringing the little vessel alongside the pier
and Cei leapt forward to secure the tie-rope. The flickering torchlight
alternately hid and revealed a tragic picture, and in the hush the little
crowd of onlookers made various signs asking their Gods to protect
them from whatever magic was afoot.

A young woman lay across the boat, her face hidden by the loose hair
that floated like a shroud on the waters. There was a length of tapestry
rumpled under her, the free end of it slipping overboard, undulating
in the river like a banner on the wind. It appeared to have been ripped
unfinished from its loom, and an elaborate pattern of lilies had been
woven in the weft.

A skein of yellow floss tangled about the girl's wrist caught my eye
as they pulled her body into the boat.

"Elaine. . . ."

In death she had the same faraway look as in life, and I stared at her,
speechless, shocked by the thought that dreams were all she would ever
know of living now.

I pictured her trying to escape that island prison, creeping down to
the water's edge under the cover of darkness—only to slip and fall amid
the welter of skiffs tied by the pier.

Bedivere bent down and gently pried a wax tablet from her grasp. "Just one word," he said softly, peering at the childish scrawl. "Lancelot. . . ."

Beside me the Breton caught his breath as the crowd stirred with sudden interest. Kneeling on the pier beside the boat, Lance slowly took the girl's cold fingers in his own. The consternation on his face tugged at my heart; pity, sadness, grief and puzzlement were all reflected there, and I wished there was some way to shield him from the prying, smirking reaction of the courtiers around us.

"No wonder he's paid no court to others, with a wench like that hidden away at Astolat," someone quipped, and a ripple of knowing chuckles followed.

"I think," I cried suddenly, "I'm going to faint. Please, Arthur, take me back to the Palace."

There was a flurry of reaction as people turned from Lance and rushed to my aid. Arthur, who knows very well that I am not the fainting sort, looked at me in alarm and swung me up in his arms when I went limp beside him. I was tempted to give him a wink, but the gesture would have been lost in the press of people and uncertain light, so I just closed my eyes and let him lead us all away from the quay.

All, that is, save Lancelot.

The Breton didn't return to the Hall that evening but saw to the laying-out and Christian burial of the girl who had so thoroughly woven his presence into the web of her own fantasy. It struck me as a dear and tender thing to do.

But when he didn't come to Court the following day I began to wonder if the rumors that had risen about the pair were based on substance after all. Not, I told myself firmly, that it was any of my business; Lancelot was a grown man, with all the needs and desires of any Champion, and if he chose to hold trysts with the Lily Maid, that was up to him.

The idea didn't set well, however, and I was snappish with my women when they brought the subject up at tea.

"He's not the sort to play on a young girl's infatuation," I declared, knowing even as I said it that I sounded dreadfully righteous.

More important, I told myself, he's not the sort to dally with her and then look on me the way he had. Or at least, the way I thought he had. The old question of how much was real and how much my own imagination rose to haunt me again, and I tossed fitfully that night, unable to say any longer where the truth lay.

Fortunately Arthur didn't notice my restlessness, but too little sleep made me cross and distracted the next day, and the constant gossip grated on my nerves. So when Pelleas asked if he might accompany me for a stroll in the gardens, I was more than pleased to accept.

In spite of the efforts at restoration, the Park was still half-wild, harboring secret corners where shrines and statues lay hidden by rampant greenery. It made for an air of sanctuary, and I breathed in the greenness as I listened to the young horseman's plea.

"Now that the King has promised me holdings of my own, I've been thinking . . . I mean, maybe . . . the Lady Ettard might look on me more favorably. As a husband, that is," he added hastily.

"Have you discussed it with her?" I inquired, watching a red squirrel whisk out of sight at our approach.

"Oh no, Your Highness. But perhaps . . . if you could talk with her . . . encourage her a little . . ." Pelleas stammered out his request with earnest sincerity. "I promise to take good care of her. I never really had a family, you know, what with being orphaned and poor. But now that I'm becoming a man of substance I can take proper care of a wife and children."

We'd reached the end of the garden, and I thought we might sit on the white marble bench, but Pelleas was unaware of anything but his dream and automatically turned back toward the fountain.

"I've loved her since the first day I came to Court, Your Highness. I'm but a country lout in comparison with the fine lords and ladies here—and sometimes I pinch myself, thinking it must all be a dream and I'll wake up back in the stable after all, and the Lady Ettard too far above me to even know my name. But with a house and steading of my own I have something real to offer her . . . more than just my devotion . . . and if you could put in a good word for me . . ."

Pelleas looked over at me shyly, like a child, and I wanted to tell him that love doesn't require material props to give it value. But there was something so touchingly hopeful about the lad, I couldn't bring myself to dampen his ardor.

So I stopped at the fountain to gather herbs for the kitchen and promised to speak with Ettard at the next opportunity.

The convent girl sighed and put down the shift she was mending when I brought up the young man's request.

"How like him to ask someone else to plead his case for him," she complained. "Really, one wonders if he has any backbone at all."

"He just lacks self-confidence," I admonished her gently. "You could make a world of difference in that."

"Oh, I know he'd treat me well enough; he's never crude and boorish like the other Champions, and he's already Christian." She frowned at the fabric that lay in her lap. "That's important, now that I've become a convert."

The declaration startled me, for it must have happened while I was away.

"It makes it doubly difficult," she went on, "what with most of the Companions expecting a ready tumble in the hay . . . why, they have no respect for a virgin at all, and want to take my honor without even offering a wedding ring."

"Virgin?" I sputtered, distinctly remembering Ettard's tale of rape at the hands of the Saxons. Surely she didn't believe baptism would give her a new body as well as a reborn spirit?

"But of course, M'lady. I am, after all, a woman of worth now, and must protect myself. And Pelleas has always seen that; it's what makes him a trustworthy companion. Still," she added wistfully, "he isn't nearly as powerful as some of the other Champions are, and I'd surely never stare off into space dreaming of Pelleas as Isolde dreams of Tristan."

"Well," I concluded, "it's an honest offer well made, and a good marriage does not require romance to make it work."

It was the best advice I could think of, given to myself as well as Ettard, for sometimes even I envied the romantic cloud that surrounded Isolde and her lover.

.   .   .

Lancelot returned to Court several days later, quietly and without being announced. I'd gone to the Park in the morning to pick some flowers and came across the lieutenant sitting in contemplation under the willow tree.

"Good morning, M'lady." He smiled wanly, his voice as distant as his expression when I planted myself in front of him.

I stared at him closely, looking for some sign that he was grieving for the death of his beloved. I found a man saddened but not sorrowing and the testiness that had been building in me evaporated. I asked quietly, "Are you all right?"

He nodded slowly and making room on the bench, gestured for me to join him. When I did, he reached into my bouquet and extracting a lily, stared at it thoughtfully as he began to talk.

"Where do you draw the line of responsibility, Gwen? How you treat people . . . isn't that truly the mark of what sort of human you are? Pelagius says we could all become as enlightened as the Christ if we were willing to take responsibility for our actions. Not that *that* teaching lasted very long," he added, slowly turning the flower between thumb and forefinger. "The Roman Christians branded him a heretic and now preach St. Augustine's theory of Divine Grace instead."

Philosophy was not something I spent time thinking about, and I stole another look at the Breton, trying to fathom what this had to do with whether or not he and Elaine had been lovers.

He knit his brows, completely absorbed in the idea he was pursuing. "You can't live by another person's dream, particularly if it goes against your own nature." He sighed and shook his head slightly. "That would be as hollow as trying to live *for* another. We have so little time, surely we should cherish the chance to grow and flower in our own ways and allow others the same freedom. . . . *Oh, God, Gwen, I never meant to be the cause of her death!*"

The words burst from him with a sob, and he bowed his head to his hands while the tears streamed unchecked down his cheeks.

"But if you let her believe—if you were her lover . . ." My voice trailed off. Suddenly I didn't want to hear his answer.

Lance lifted his head and turned to look directly at me.

"I was never that. Friend, confidant . . . no, more like guardian, or even older brother. But I swear, never lover. I would not have bedded her, even if she had been fully right in the head, because I love . . . another."

The last word was spoken abruptly, as though he might have said something else and changed his mind at the last moment. And suddenly I knew, clearly and without any doubt at all, that I was the one he loved.

The very knowledge staggered me, making my head swim and my breath catch in my throat. I looked down at my hands, terrified by the prospect of meeting his eyes, of seeing all the love and tenderness I'd ever longed for in his face, of standing naked in my own response.

Through the silence that surrounded us I could feel Lance's gaze on my cheek, my eyes, my lips, as tangible as if it were a caress. Blushing, I turned my head aside.

His hand beneath my chin was the gentlest of touches, lifting, guiding, bringing my face around to his. The tension grew unbearable as I raised my eyes and stared, trembling, at the fullness of his mouth. Slowly, inevitably, our lips came together in the barest of kisses.

A long soft flutter of pleasure rose through me, surging in ripplets of desire, and I felt my breath escape with a sigh.

And then I was on my feet, running blindly for the Palace, flowers and basket and shears all scattered behind me. I fled without thought or purpose or specific goal, and when I burst into the Palace I ran right past my husband.

"What on earth?" he exclaimed, reaching for his dagger. "What's happened?"

I came to a sudden halt, my headlong dash ending as abruptly as it had started. "A snake," I stammered, knowing my talent for lying was nil. "I was clipping flowers and accidentally disturbed a snake."

"Oh, for goodness' sake, Gwen," Arthur grumbled. "I thought at the least the sky must be falling."

His reference to the familiar warning from childhood gave me a reprieve. "Not quite," I responded, beginning to get my breath. "Nor is the earth opening up, or the water receding beyond the shore. It just feels as though it is."

Arthur gave me a puzzled look before he turned back to matters of state, and I tiptoed away. Clearly I needed time alone to collect my thoughts before the situation with Lancelot got totally out of control.

But peace and privacy were not to be had, for as I crossed the patio next to the sleeping quarters, my attention was caught by the Queen of Cornwall.

Isolde sat working on a piece of embroidery every bit as colorful as the clothes she herself wore. Her dress was the same violet as her eyes, and the bands of green and blue and gold brocade that edged both neck and sleeves accented the whiteness of her skin. Even in shadow she was beautiful, and I could understand why other women were jealous of Mark's Queen.

She looked up from her handiwork with the bewildered expression of a child. From the wetness of her cheeks it was obvious that she had been weeping for some time, although she made no sound.

"Goodness sakes," I said, handing her my handkerchief, "you're going to ruin your embroidery."

She took the hanky and crumpled it into a ball in her fist, the tears continuing to stream down her face. Those eyes, dark and brooding, stared up at me imploringly.

Ye Gods, I thought, what am I going to do with her?

"Well, now," I began awkwardly, "let's go to my room and have tea, shall we? Then we can talk a bit in private; things don't seem nearly so terrible if you can tell someone."

She stared at me uncertainly before nodding her assent and we moved into my chambers, where she huddled on the window seat. I took the hanky from her, then crouched down and gently dried her cheeks. Her lips trembled, but still she didn't speak.

"There, there," I said, putting my arm around her shoulders and letting the frail form beneath the splendid robes lean against me. " 'Tis a time in every life for tears, and then a time for putting things to right. You'll see . . . we'll find some way to work things out . . . it will be all right anon. . . ."

Every word of comfort I could think of slid past her, deflected by the hugeness of her grief; in the face of such anguish they all sounded inept and stupid.

"Is it Tristan?" I inquired at last, thinking perhaps they had had a lovers' quarrel. "Has he hurt you?"

"Yes," she whispered, then hastily, "No. That is, not in the usual way. Oh Your Highness, I cannot tell you how awful it is to love like this. Sometimes I think I cannot face another day with him—yet I cannot live without him. People sneer, and snicker, and call me foul for having betrayed my King, and maybe they are right. Maybe I am the whore they say, dishonoring family and country as well as the bed of my lord. I don't know anymore . . . I don't know. . . ."

She lapsed into tears again, sobbing with a heartbroken wretchedness.

It was her cousin, Branwen, who brought the tea things, quietly setting them up on the table by the window and withdrawing discreetly to the far side of the curtain. Silently I blessed her loyalty, knowing she would guard the entrance like a mastiff and allow no one to disturb her mistress.

When Isolde's sobbing subsided I handed her a cup of tea, and for a few minutes we sipped the warm liquid in silence.

"You know Tristan and I are fated to be lovers for all time, don't you?" she asked finally, her voice full of despair and resignation. "My mother is a very powerful sorceress, and she was worried that I might not enjoy my life with King Mark. So as a wedding present she made a potion that would insure neither of us would have any interest in anyone else, ever. Tristan and I drank it on the boat, by mistake, before I even reached Cornwall, and now we're destined . . . fated . . . to love each other more than life itself."

The beautiful girl looked down into her lap, the very picture of royal tragedy. Her story was so obviously self-serving, I felt no compassion until she added, softly, "I did not ask it to be this way, and would undo it, if I could."

Her lament was sincere, and her pain undeniable, so I gave her what comfort I could. By the time she had finished her tea she was at least past the crying fit and went back to her own chambers with some composure.

. . .

There are those who say nothing happens in our lives by accident, and the visit with Isolde gave me pause for reflection; as Arthur's Queen I could not afford to fall into the trap that held Isolde. So I spent the rest of the afternoon preparing to tell Lancelot that this morning's encounter must never happen again.

At least, that was my intention before I went down to the feast.

TWENTY-SIX

Morgan

"ut where did he go *to?*"

The very notion that Lancelot would leave without even saying good-bye stunned me, and I froze on the spot.

We were midway across the center of the Round Table, and there was a sudden eddy of confusion as pages and serving children had to swerve around us, their arms laden with trenchers and tureens for the table.

"I think he's heading for the steading I gave him, the one up at Warkworth," Arthur said, reaching for my elbow.

"But he didn't mention leaving when we spoke this morning," I protested.

"I guess he'd only just decided." By now Arthur was tugging me out of the way. "He said he's been thinking about it ever since he brought you back from the convent—wants to spend more time at that Garden of his."

We'd reached our seats, and after motioning for Gawain to move his chair into Lance's place, Arthur turned to see who else had arrived.

"But why?" I asked, still struggling to understand what was happening. "Why should he leave?"

"I didn't ask—didn't think it any of my business."

Arthur turned back to Gawain and I stared into empty space. Dagonet appeared out of nowhere and greeted us with a deep bow that turned into an elaborate petting of Caesar as he tried to coax a smile from me. It was exactly what a jester should do, providing the audience with a diversion and giving me time to compose my public face. I smiled appreciatively at his efforts.

Yet for all my outward calm, chaos raged inside. The kiss in the Park this morning had been an accident, a mistake—a longing for something too dangerous to pursue. The more I thought about it, the more I knew it was true. But now he was gone, before I had a chance to tell him it mustn't happen again.

Drat you, Lancelot, I thought, grabbing up my wine goblet the moment it was filled.

The Hall was stuffy because the breeze from the river refused to rise. I found myself kicking Caesar in the ribs when he tried to rest his chin on my foot, and I downed my wine each time the glass was refilled. It was Dinadan's turn to sit beside me, and I was relieved that the Cornishman didn't notice my growing tipsiness. Perhaps at Isolde's Court he'd grown used to peculiar behavior in Celtic Queens.

Bedivere took up his harp following the meal, and a great rush of drunken affection for the whole of the Court swept over me. Wonderful people, really, those who had been with us since the beginning . . . Bedivere and Cei, Pelli and Lamorak, Nimue and Griflet, and all the others who were at the core of our Fellowship. Solid friends . . . the kind you could rely on, could understand . . . forthright sorts, who spoke up about their feelings. Nothing hidden and mysterious there . . . you always knew where you stood with them . . . even Morgan, if you overlooked her arrogance and occasional bad temper.

I stared into my empty wine cup, waiting for the server to refill it, and tried to remember what Igraine had said about her daughter. Something about her conviction that the Old Ways must be followed or the world was doomed. No, that sounded more Christian than Pagan . . . but then, there was something of the same crusading zeal in both, if I could just sort them out.

"Her Majesty, the Lady of the Lake."

The deep voice of Morgan's dwarf echoed around the Hall, and I lifted my nodding head to peer blearily at the figure in the center of the Round Table, thinking I must have slipped into a dream.

It was indeed Morgan's lieutenant, and as he stepped to one side the Queen of Northumbria swept into the heart of the circle.

"We bid you well come, Sister," Arthur called out, rising to greet her. "I'm delighted you could join us after all."

"Blessings on you," the High Priestess intoned as she turned to include the rest of the Fellowship. "It is always a pleasure to be part of your company, particularly when I bring you word directly from the Goddess."

The Hall had grown silent when an unexpected hiccup escaped me. Morgan ignored it, concentrating instead on her brother as she sent her voice floating out over the audience.

"As we all know, the Old Ways decree that a man whose wife is stolen must seek redress for that insult before his honor can be restored. It is a law made in the Beginning, and no husband can ignore it, unless the wife was complicit in the escapade."

"Now wait a minute." I started to object, but my tongue was thick and unmanageable, and the words slurred together in a groan. My knees wouldn't work when I tried to rise and Dinadan steadied me as I swayed, drunkenly, halfway out of my chair.

Morgan ignored me completely, playing to the crowd and carrying them along on that magnificent voice that swooped and soared, dipped and purred from point to point.

"How much more necessary is such action if the man is High King, and the woman is the people's Queen? Normally the rapist's life would be forfeit—but what if the Queen begs he be spared, claiming it is out of family loyalty? Even if a loving husband accepts such an excuse, how is he as King going to overcome the stigma of lost manhood? These were the questions I brought to the Goddess, seeking Her guidance, begging Her wisdom, for I cannot allow this fine young monarch to endanger the whole future of Britain by ignoring the ancient laws."

Morgan's innuendos snapped the tether of what self-restraint I had left. "Balderdash!" I exploded, planting my hands on the table and pushing myself upright.

The Lady of the Lake turned to stare directly at me, her silence drawing more attention than any gesture could have. I stared back at her fox face, hypnotized by those green eyes that burned both hot and cold until I was spinning in wave after wave of dizziness and without a word crumpled back into my seat.

"You see, even your Queen appreciates the difficulties," Morgan said as Vinnie and Ettard and Dinadan all leaned over me. I closed my eyes and swung slowly into reeling, head-spinning darkness.

Morning came hot and sticky and still, and after a horrified peek at the sunlight, I burrowed under the pillow again.

"You must wake up, Your Highness," Ettard was saying. "The King wants to see you before he leaves."

My head hurt and my mouth tasted vile, but I nodded at the girl, wondering where on earth Arthur was off to when we had a city full of guests.

By the time I had swung my feet over the edge of the bed, my husband was standing before me. I blinked up at him balefully and he laughed. "Maybe you'd better stick to cider from now on," he teased, sitting down next to me on the bed. "Thought I'd like to say good-bye before I go, just in case."

"Just in case what?" I asked, waving Ettard out the door and turning to stare at him. He was fully garbed in battle gear and wore the Goddess cape, though how he could stand its weight in this heat, I didn't know. "What's this all about?"

"I thought you'd passed out before Morgan explained about Maelgwn and the ritual."

It seemed that my cousin had had an attack of conscience and, having repented his sins, sought forgiveness from Illtud's protégé, Gildas. That young monk had arranged for Maelgwn to go live in a monastery, which put him well beyond the reach of Arthur's vengeance.

But before he went to hide behind his suddenly espoused Christianity, the Lady of the Lake was able to elicit an apology from him to Arthur. In it Maelgwn agreed to relinquish part of the Welsh Marches to us and give over that great black dog, Dormarth, in reparation for having "hosted" me at his hunting lodge.

"It's a splendid animal," Arthur concluded. "Since Cabal's death I need a new war-dog, and this one is fully trained. Quite a prize, actually."

I shuddered at the idea of having the creature in my own house but put my loathing aside as I queried what apology Maelgwn would make to me.

"Morgan pointed out how eloquently you pled for your cousin's life, and that by accepting this treaty I will be honoring your wishes as well. It restores my prestige without having to kill him."

Arthur's answer sent a flash of anger through me. This arrangement neither made amends for what I had suffered nor dispelled the implication that I had complied with Maelgwn. And far from having pleaded for his life, I would have preferred to see him publicly punished, providing it didn't pose a danger to Arthur. All of that had been left out, naturally.

Like all her strategies, it was very clever and hard to rebut. I sighed wearily. At this point I wasn't up to fighting her and Arthur was already talking about something else.

"Once the ritual is over, it will finally be behind us."

"What ritual?" I asked suspiciously.

"Morgan has devised a ceremonial combat to celebrate my victory over both opponents—Maelgwn and the Saxons. She says it will symbolically fulfill Merlin's prophesy about the Red Dragon conquering the White Dragon."

My head was throbbing as I tried to think what we would need for such an event—maybe a feast, maybe not. But if it was a ritual, we'd have to accommodate all the Round Table guests; maybe hold it in the arena. "When is all this supposed to take place?" I queried.

"We're leaving for Windsor Forest as soon as possible." Arthur gave me a wry grin. "Morgan's arranged for the druids of the Sacred Grove to officiate—says it's important that the Pagans see the Old Gods have forgiven my sacrilege in digging up Bran's head."

"But Windsor Forest is the better part of a day's ride from here," I exclaimed, aghast at the notion of my head trying to tolerate even an hour on horseback.

"There's only a few people to attend; all men, all carefully picked. Bedivere and Gawain will stay here with you, and I'll take Bors and Geraint, Griflet and Pelleas with me to the Grove."

"I don't like it, Arthur," I said, getting to my feet too quickly. "It doesn't sound like any ritual I've ever heard of, and why should it be

done so far away instead of right here where the people can participate?"

"It's new, I tell you, and it's only symbolic." Arthur's voice was
starting to show the testiness that always comes up whenever we talk
about Morgan. "The armor, the masks—even the swords will be ceremonial rather than real."

My skepticism must have been obvious, for he went on brusquely,
"For goodness' sake, Gwen, what harm can there be in it? And don't
start casting suspicion on Morgan again—she won't be anywhere near.
Women are forbidden at this rite."

"Where will she be?" A ripple of apprehension slipped down my
spine.

"Why, right here, helping you prepare the feast we'll have when we
get back."

"Oh, jolly," I grumbled, turning my back to the window and wondering if a cold compress would help my head.

"Well, you might wish me luck," Arthur concluded, coming to stand
hopefully in front of me.

I looked up at him, wondering how he could tell me there was no
danger on one hand and ask for luck on the other. The contradiction
seemed suddenly very dear, and I stood up and wrapped both arms
around him.

"Do you have to leave just now?" I asked, slipping my knee between
his legs and sliding the length of my thigh along his.

"Enough, wench!" He laughed, walloping me on the rump, then
stood back to grin down at me. "That's no way to cure a hangover."

I nodded gingerly, muttering that I knew there was some reason I
wasn't fond of wine. Arthur turned in the doorway and made the
Roman "thumbs up" sign.

I answered in return, and then he was gone.

Tiptoeing to the window, I closed the curtain, then drank half a
pitcher of water and crawled back to bed, hoping further sleep would
get rid of both my hangover and the nagging suspicion that something
wasn't right.

But the heat was oppressive and I was plagued with jumbled dreams
of danger and desertion. Finally I decided to get up and face the day,
even if it did include my sister-in-law.

. . .

Morgan was sitting in the inner court, a richly dyed fleece at her feet and the spindle twirling beside her as she spun. She greeted me with all the graciousness of a proud hostess, as though this were, in fact, her own Court. I sat down on a chunk of broken masonry and took a sip of the skullcap tea that Cook had said would help my headache.

"Such an elegant hue," the High Priestess noted, admiring the perfectly even thread she had just created. "The whelk shells from the beaches of Northumbria provide the best purple dye, don't you think?"

I nodded silently, wondering how this woman who had tried to have me killed last time we met could sit here so calmly under my roof. Perhaps in her monumental arrogance she assumed I would never call her to account for past actions. Or maybe she was confident that what Igraine used to call "good manners" would keep me from doing something reckless.

It seemed unfair that the people with manners must put up with the often unconscionable behavior of those without. Thus are gentlefolk made helpless by their ethics, I thought glumly.

"The men will be starving when they come back tomorrow night," Morgan mused, her eyes beginning to shine. "I promised there would be a fine feast, a truly sumptuous banquet for the victorious King. You don't mind if I arrange something a little special, do you?"

"Not if Cei doesn't," I murmured, trying to imagine how the High Priestess and Seneschal would get on in the kitchen. The implication that our usual fare was dull would surely rub Cei the wrong way, as he took great pride in his culinary prowess. I smiled to myself, wishing I could be an invisible presence when these two met over the menu.

"I didn't see Lancelot," she continued, her pleasant attitude never flagging. "Isn't he here these days?"

"No," I whispered, concentrating on the potted plants along the edge of the patio. I'd have to tell Lynette I'm not fond of fleshy primroses—field poppies are more my style.

"Lancelot was one of my most devoted students; remarkably talented, and so sensitive. Don't you find him so?"

"I suppose," I replied as my tea went down the wrong way, making me cough and sputter violently.

The Lady continued to spin her web, watching me all the while. "I thought you two might get along."

My uneasiness was mounting, in spite of the tea. It made me cross and testy, so I found some excuse to leave my sister-in-law and went in search of Nimue.

Merlin's mistress had taken over the bower under the willow, where Lance and I had last met, and as I waited for her to return, disquieting memories of that kiss fluttered all around me. Confused, I went back to the Palace and retired to my room.

"No, I don't want anything more," I snapped when Enid came to get my dinner tray, then apologized and asked her to sit down. "What do you know of this ceremony Arthur's to take part in?"

"Very little, Your Highness. It doesn't sound like anything I've ever heard of, but Geraint promised that he'd keep a sharp eye out for trouble, in case the King needs protection. And Geraint doesn't miss much," she added. "Never saw such a man for picking up a nuance."

I mulled over her answer, both relieved and alarmed that others were also uneasy. My headache was gone, but the apprehension remained. "And Morgan? How has she spent the day?"

"The Imperious One?" Enid snorted derisively. "Came into the kitchen like a whirlwind, and is preparing the most pretentious meal you've ever seen—more fit for a coronation than a welcome home. At first I thought Cei would put her in her place, but the man seems to be in awe of her. Have you ever noticed that he won't cross his equals or betters, particularly if they are men, but is a terrible martinet to those under him? Personally I don't understand it."

I nodded slowly, thinking there was much about Cei that nobody understood.

"Where is the High Priestess now—do you know?"

Enid shook her head but volunteered to go find out. I balked at that; it's one thing to ask what your guests have been doing and quite another to spy on them. So the matter was dropped.

During the predawn darkness Ettard slipped into my room and shook me into wakefulness.

"Come quick, Your Highness," she begged. "The Lady is prowling through the Palace, casting powders and spells all about her. She's surely up to no good, and Vinnie says you must do something at once."

"Where is she now?" I asked as I felt for my slippers and wondered what on earth possessed my sister-in-law.

"She was last seen going into King Urien's quarters," the girl whispered, and I groaned aloud.

"For goodness' sake, Morgan has a right to join her husband in bed." The idea of being wakened for something as common as that made me wonder if all my women had gone daft.

"But she was muttering curses, and looking all about furtive-like," Ettard persisted. "And it's not like you and the High King, who always end up together. . . ."

Ettard's voice trailed off as I turned to stare at her; I would have thought that servants and courtiers had better things to do than keep track of when Arthur and I retire to our separate chambers and how long we stayed there.

"Well, I'm not about to interrupt the royal pair from Northumbria," I said flatly, remembering all too well Morgan's reaction when I had inadvertently come upon her and Accolon. "And I'd suggest you go back to sleep and let our guests do likewise."

But the last word was barely out of my mouth when a terrible howling filled the building. Wild and keening, it careened through the halls like the screams of a banshee, making the hair on my nape stand up. Grabbing the lantern from Ettard's hand, I ran toward the sound.

Shadows went leaping over the walls and ceiling of the hallway as the door to Urien's rooms burst open and a ranting, wild-eyed Morgan was wrestled through it by Uwain. One or both of them had hold of Urien's sword, and when it clattered to the floor her son suddenly let go of the Priestess and took a step back, gasping and shaking uncontrollably.

The boy stared at the weapon, a look of horror slowly engulfing him. I saw the flash of recognition slide from mind to heart, then twist into the gut as his face crumpled in disbelief and tears began streaming down his cheeks. Yet though he opened his mouth, no sound came out . . . the hideous keening we were hearing emanated entirely from his mother.

The cries that spewed from her throat were barely human. She stood
with feet apart, arms taut at her sides, hands balled into fists. Her face
was contorted hideously and lifted to the Gods, but whether in anger
or fear, it was hard to tell.

Guards and household members were running in from all over the
Palace, pushing and milling among themselves as they stared at the
High Priestess. Gradually, like the dawning of the sun, Morgan realized
that she was not alone. The return of reason muzzled her frenzy until
she stood still as the henge stone at Mayburgh.

Her green gaze flickered around the hallway, and she began to
whimper. "Where's Urien?"

Every head turned to stare at the King of Northumbria.

Nightshirted and barefoot, he stood in the doorway to his room. His
face was going from white shock to red rage as his gaze moved from
the sword to the High Priestess.

"I'm right here, no thanks to you. Try to kill me with my own
weapon, will you?"

The anger behind his words swelled slowly from doubled-up fist to
full expletive as he called her every name he could think of for this
worst of treacheries.

"No, no, M'lord," Morgan cried, reaching out to him in supplica-
tion. "Truly it is not what you think. Have I ever harmed you, in all
the years of our marriage? I have naught but respect for Your Lordship,
as our son can tell you. . . . M'lord, it was a nightmare, a sleepwalking,
a case of possession by one of those Christian demons."

Her words came more and more swiftly, a garble of explanation and
defense until, in a single motion, Urien stepped across the hall, lifted
his sword from the floor, and turned to face her.

Morgan's eyes flared wide, and she threw herself against her son,
hands clawing at his shoulders, head buried against the young man's
chest. "Uwain, save me . . . stop his madness, tell him I am innocent.
By the life I bore in you, I swear I did not know what I was doing
. . . I was but dreaming and then woke to find you grappling with me
at M'lord's bedside. . . . Tell him, son . . . tell him!"

The boy put one arm around her, revulsion and desire to believe her
doing battle across his face. His Adam's apple bobbed convulsively as

he tried to swallow, and his eyes pleaded with his father. "What she says is so, Sire. . . ."

"Phawww, you puling pup! What do you know of women and their machinations? Conniving, vicious, embittered wasp, she has no love for anyone but herself and the acolytes of her precious Goddess!"

As he was speaking Urien brought the tip of the blade to a point just under Morgan's chin, and everyone froze. The silence grew long and brittle while the King of Northumbria debated what to do.

At last, with a curse, he lowered his sword.

"Good thing for you we're guests at Arthur's Court," he spat at his wife. "If we were home, I would deal with your treason in one stroke."

A little sigh of relief escaped the crowd, and the wronged husband glanced over at me. "Get her out of my sight," he commanded, then paused. "I'd suggest you hold her over until Arthur returns and learns what she has done."

I nodded silently and ordered Morgan to be sedated and bound.

Urien disappeared behind his door, and Morgan swooned in Uwain's arms, moaning incoherently. Her son carried her back to her room and coaxed her into drinking the sleeping draft, and the two of us sat beside the bed as the High Priestess lapsed into a deep sleep.

"How did it happen?" I asked, trying to keep my voice gentle, for the boy was still deeply shaken.

"Strange thing," he said slowly, looking constantly at his mother, not at me. "That dwarf of hers came and woke me, all upset and agitated; said some sort of spell had been put on her, and she was walking in her sleep. Said he feared for her life. . . . But when I got to my father's room, it was he who was about to die. She was by the bed, the royal sword held high in both hands, with its point aimed directly at his heart. I think I must have screamed, or maybe it was she who screamed when I leaped at her . . . I can't recall. I just know I could see the blood welling up out of him, could see her dripping with the stain of his death, could see her grinning . . . grinning, M'lady . . . she was grinning. . . ."

The lad began to cry silently as the horrible scene replayed itself before his eyes. No child should be caught in a war between parents, so I rose and putting my hands on his temples, let him lean against me as his shoulders shook with sobs. I couldn't change what had happened, but I could hold him safe and protected while the torrent of disbelief and despair poured from him.

At last, when Uwain had cried himself out, I bound Morgan's hands and feet to the bedposts and led the boy out of the room. A bevy of white-robed devotees kept vigil by the door, but I saw no reason to drive them away; it was clear the Lady wasn't going to go anywhere until after Arthur returned.

The sun was well risen by now. I went to the kitchen and between us Cei and I pared down Morgan's intended feast to a more manageable meal.

"Can't think what had got into that vixen," the Seneschal said, gesturing to the range of silver and fancy dishes she had ordered brought out of the cupboards. "She kept talking about the victorious King, as though this were an ordeal Arthur must survive rather than simply a ceremony he was performing."

Despite the heat, Cei's words sent a cold fear through me. The Seneschal had voiced exactly the danger I had felt but been unable to name.

"Any word from the men?" I asked quickly.

"No, and not likely, either." Cei scowled. "The mock battle was to take place at sunrise, and I'll warrant they'll be returning with the same speed as a messenger might. Peculiar business, though . . . very peculiar."

I nodded, and when the plans had been made ready for the day, I went to my chamber for a nap—we'd all been up since well before sunrise.

On the way I stopped to check on Morgan, who slept surrounded by her ladies-in-waiting. The room had been darkened with drapes and the heat was as thick as the silence that greeted me. One might think the High Priestess had died.

Most of the white-robed acolytes ignored my presence, though I paused to peer more closely at one of the women who reminded me of the matron at Maelgwn's. When she looked up and nodded civilly, I decided she was not the same.

Summer thunder rumbled across the sky, but it was no more likely to cool the air than a cuckoo is to raise the offspring it lays in another bird's nest. Staring out the window, I found nothing but the pale blue of a hot summer day and a cluster of clouds too far off on the horizon to promise much relief.

I stretched out on my bed, weary and cranky and full of oppressive gloom.

If only I'd wake to find Arthur returned, hale and happy and full of his usual energy. . . .

TWENTY-SEVEN

The Ordeal

"N̶ow see here, you heathen, you can't go in there!"
Vinnie's indignant cry brought me awake as a flash of
lightning lit the storm-dark room. A white-robed figure
burst through the door along with a clap of thunder,
followed by the matron's compact form.

"Your Highness, I must speak with you in private," the druid
croaked, panting heavily. I jumped to my feet and after looking closely
at the person hidden beneath the hood, motioned for Vinnie to withdraw and turned to face Nimue.

The mistress of disguises slipped back her hood and sank down on
the edge of the bed. "He's alive, but just barely. It was a trap, only no
one realized it until he was wounded."

Her words came out in a jumble and I sagged down next to her, my
mind going numb as I realized she was speaking of Arthur. Beyond the
window the storm clouds began spitting fire and sheets of lightning
clashed in the sky like Merlin's dragons battling for the destiny of
Britain. Gradually Nimue regained her breath, and the story unfolded.

"I was uneasy about this new ceremony, so when Arthur's party left
I followed them, unseen. They turned into the dark woods of Windsor
beyond the chalk ridge that overlooks the river, and made camp beneath an enormous oak—by the time I got there the men had put down
their shields and settled in a circle."

Nimue watched as the Champions' shields were hung amid the

branches of that spreading tree. They swayed in the moonlight like a crop of sinister fruit—and well out of reach. Then the Master of Druids collected all swords and daggers because the most ancient of Goddesses cannot be approached by anyone wearing iron. Only then could the ritual begin.

"They held a ceremony that night," the doire sighed, "keeping Arthur and his men up all through the dark with prayers and chants of purification. No food for anyone, but a dozen different potions for the High King. It's a wonder they didn't just poison him outright!"

Nimue stayed hidden in the shadows, trying to follow what was happening. Shortly before sunrise Arthur was taken aside and the witnesses made their way to the Sacred Grove, passing through woods grown dense with beech and elm, holly and yew. Gnarled oaks hung over the path, their rough bark showing the twisted faces of spirits imprisoned long ago.

The Grove encircled a clearing in which stood a single, waist-high stone. Old as time, it had served as an altar for untold Gods—sides caked with the blood of ancient rites, top worn to a cradle from centuries of heads being laid there in the final act of sacrifice.

But grizzly as the altar was, it was the tall wooden column beside it that made Nimue shudder. The post was solid and firmly rooted and so big around that two men could barely encompass it. The wood was old and weathered to a silver gray except where it too had been stained with dripping blood.

"Niches had been carved in it—niches to hold skulls. There must have been half a dozen in all, the upper ones filled with the toothless remains of long-ago victims." Nimue's voice dropped to a whisper, and I shivered, for as a child I had come across Morgan worshiping at such a shrine, using a goblet made from a skull.

"The bottom spaces held a pair of recently severed heads, bedecked with ribbons and dried flowers. The flesh had rotted from the bone, but judging by the long blond hair, they were probably Saxons. It was the middle niche that caught my attention, however—it stood empty, save for an ivy wreath waiting to crown its occupant. For a symbolic rite, it seemed excessive."

In the gloom Nimue mixed silently with the men. As long as she stayed away from the actual druids she could pass for just another acolyte, and when the ceremony started she moved to the edge of the clearing where she could see everything unhindered.

"There was much chanting and clapping beforehand, but as the first ray of the sun struck the stone altar a hush fell on the gathering. It felt as though Death had come to watch the ordeal," she said, her words shaping the picture before my eyes.

The opponents emerged from the shadows of the woodland in absolute silence. Each wore a special set of armor, complete with helmets that served as masks so that one couldn't tell who was fighting whom. Arthur's was black with a red crest and a picture of the Red Dragon worked on the cheek flaps, and the same insignia was worked on the black bull-hide shield. His opponent was covered with identical armor, though his crest and dragons were white in color. Both swords, which were the shape and length of Excalibur, had been covered with some kind of sap and smeared with soot. Like all the rest of the armor, they appeared to be identical.

The two men met at the altar, each bowing formally to the other. The warrior Morgan had found to be the Unknown Opponent was a little younger and not as adroit as Arthur—but close enough a match to be the image of the High King three years ago.

"As the ritual battle began, a druid came to stand next to me," Nimue continued. "He peered under my hood just long enough to determine who I was . . . and for me to recognize Cathbad, the druid who was your tutor when you were a child in Rheged."

I caught my breath; ever since Cathbad had gone to live and work with the Lady, I'd wondered where his loyalty lay.

"His hood was up, and under cover of the cowling he whispered, 'Beware the real Excalibur.'" Nimue looked into my face with an anguished frown. "Gwen, I didn't know what he meant, or if he was to be trusted . . . and he vanished as silently as he had appeared. I dared not interrupt the rite without knowing more, so I turned my attention back to the combatants, keeping a close eye on the swords."

Like dancers the two men move about the altar—thrust, parry . . . feint, sidestep . . . lunge. Graceful and elegant, mirrors of each other, self fighting self.

The stage broadens—beyond the altar, across the greensward, back slowly toward the column with its haunting of heads. Avoid the altar—dance around it, keep it always in mind as the pace quickens.

Time enough—the point is made, and Arthur is weary after his night-long vigil. Yet the Unknown draws the contest out, makes no move to surrender, refuses to capitulate. Impatient, Arthur brings his sword around full sweep, knocking the Opponent off balance . . . and the blade of the ceremonial sword snaps.

The Unknown rushes forward in a frenzy. Blood everywhere, running down Arthur's arms and legs, oozing from under his armor in a dozen places.

Aghast, the Companions reach for swords that are not there; Geraint swears at the memory of weapons collected the night before. Arthur's men look quickly from one to another, uncertain if they should charge across the sacred ground to the King's aid.

The Opponent is driving Arthur back, deadly, relentlessly. The King crouches, pivots, attempts to spin away. Bumping into the unyielding stone of the altar, he trips, struggles for his balance, and falls backward across the sacrificial table. Death rises above him, the blade poised for the final stroke.

Out of nowhere and everywhere comes the sound—a whispered growl, a growing roar that rushes finally into the high, piercing howl of the Morrigan—the battle-cry issues from Nimue's mouth. Unnerved, the Opponent pauses, looking around warily for the War Goddess. In that moment of distraction the High King wraps both fists around the pommel of his broken weapon and smashes it directly into the face of his adversary.

Stunned, the Unknown goes down, his weapon dropping from his hand. Arthur lunges for it, feels it fly to his grasp like a trusted friend returned at last—the High King recognizes the heft and weight of Excalibur coming home to his hand.

Blind rage rips through him as Arthur turns to savage his Opponent.

"It was all over within minutes," Nimue concluded. "When the Unknown refused to surrender, the High King smote him at the base of the neck and opened a fatal gash."

"Who was it?" I cried.

"Morgan's lover, Accolon. She had promised to make him High King once he killed Arthur."

I groaned aloud, and Nimue nodded grimly.

"Accolon confessed everything as he lay dying, begging forgiveness from his King. Arthur let out an anguished wail and slumped unconscious beside the dying Gaul. I threw off my disguise and calling up Arthur's men, raced across the field as both the druids and Accolon's followers disappeared into the woods.

"There was nothing to be done for the Opponent—his fate was sealed when he let Morgan seduce him with her dreams of power. I gave Arthur all my attention, for though he had no shattered bones, he had lost a great deal of blood . . . from wounds inflicted by his own sword."

I stared at the doire with horror as her last words registered. Memory of King Pellam and the wound that would not heal floated before me.

"Griflet knew of a deserted hermit's hut not far away, so we carried Arthur there as quickly as possible. I've begged the Mother for help in healing him—he's well sedated and watched over by his men at this point. I dare not bring him back by horse or litter for fear of opening the wounds again. I'll need a sizable troop to take back to the hermitage: some to keep a guard around him until he recovers enough to be moved and some to bring Accolon's body back to Court."

She paused finally and sighed. "Arthur's last wish before he lost consciousness was that the warrior's corpse be presented to Morgan here, in the Court she had herself expected to rule."

Slowly, I began to see the pieces of the puzzle come together. Morgan hadn't cared if Urien became Regent of Rheged because she was going to replace him with Accolon. And she had insisted on a feast fit for a coronation because she expected her lover to take over Britain as the "victorious King"—by which time she would have disposed of Urien. Morgan must have been planning this treachery for years, and even I had been too blind to see it.

"What do we do with her?" I asked, my palms going damp at the notion of confronting the Sorceress with news of her darling's death.

"Put her in irons before you tell her what has happened. Or better yet," said the doire, showing a streak of vengefulness I didn't know she had, "lead her unprepared to the Palace entrance tomorrow to see firsthand that her ambition has cost her love his life. That was, I think, what Arthur had in mind."

I nodded morosely, seeing once more the shadow of Arthur's darker, Celtic side.

"Where is Morgan?" Nimue asked, and when I told her, the doire pulled me to my feet. 'Call up Pellinore and that strapping son of his, and we'll go shackle her immediately."

It was not to be that easy. When we reached the anteroom to where the High Priestess slept, her women rushed to surround us, praying solemnly against the tattoo of the raindrops that pounded on the window. But Morgan's bed was empty, and when I demanded an accounting, her acolytes stared at me in silence, refusing to explain what had happened or how.

"You cannot go against the will of the Goddess," their leader intoned as I fumed over this new development.

I was certain my sister-in-law had not departed by herself; the brew we gave her would have her still asleep, wherever she was. Her rescuer had to be someone strong enough to carry her away, and though several of her ladies might have succeeded in such a task, none were missing. Both Urien and Uwain were accounted for, though I hardly thought they would have been involved.

"Have you found her lieutenant?" Urien asked, then nodded sourly as I shook my head. "Fanatical little man, you know. Adores Morgan and is as jealous of her as any lover . . . though knowing her tastes, I doubt she considers him more than a pawn. But if you find him, I wager you'll find her as well."

I tried to imagine the dwarf hauling Morgan, drugged and trussed, into the night by himself. It made me marvel at the power even a hopeless love can call up.

We had to leave it at that. A search of the Palace failed to find either of them, and there were two horses missing from the pasture. At dawn I sent Pellinore and Lamorak out after them, for the men of the Wrekin were followers of the Goddess who would try to capture Morgan without doing her any harm; the last thing I wanted was to give the druids reason for claims of brutality.

But I had little hope they'd be successful; the rain had washed away the most obvious signs for tracking, and the country people revered her. No doubt some would hide Morgan and her lieutenant as they made their way back to the Sanctuary at the Black Lake. At least, I comforted myself, Arthur must finally see the true nature of his sister.

Nimue remained in London an extra day, visiting the shrines of Isis and Cybele in search of ways to counteract the treachery of Arthur's wounds. I intended to go with her when she returned to Arthur, but there were so many visiting monarchs, it was decided I should stay and make sure the last days of the gathering went smoothly.

With Bedivere and Gawain at my side I was able to reassure the members of the Round Table that Arthur, although wounded, would soon be on his feet again. I presided over the last Council meeting, concluding various treaties and standing in state to receive the farewells of those Saxons who were now free to return to their homes.

Nimue reported that Arthur's wounds reopened at the slightest provocation, and it was a fortnight before she deemed it safe to move him. By then the summer doldrums had settled over London, with the river going sluggish and foul and the various leaders began returning to their own realms.

When the King of Cornwall decided to leave, the other guests from the south made plans to join his party. A sizable group gathered that morning, and Cook put out food and ale for anyone who wanted a meal for the Road.

Geraint had brought Accolon's body back to Court and stayed to help me during the last days of the Round Table. I thanked him now as we shared a bannock before he departed.

"You make serving the High Queen a pleasure, M'lady. Would that you had a sister to share my throne in Devon," the gallant replied.

"Come now, M'lord, with your charm you have the whole of Britain's womanhood to choose from." I laughed.

He sighed. "Most of them seem too busy in front of their mirrors . . . perhaps they don't make Queens the way they used to."

"Then find someone you like and teach her," I joked, remembering my own tomboy beginnings.

"Not a bad idea." The King of Devon ran an appreciative eye over my ladies. Ettard was standing near enough to hear our exchange; with a flutter of eyelashes she asked to accompany him to his horse. Grinning, the courtier bade me adieu and swept the girl out the door in fine style.

I was shaking my head in amusement when Isolde made her way through the throng and, pausing shyly, extended her hand.

"Thank you for your hospitality, M'lady," she murmured. "There's few places I feel comfortable these days, what with the Cornish people always finding fault and Mark surrounding me with spies."

I was shocked by the realization that the Cornish King would demean his wife by spying on her and looked at the girl with pity.

"It's a relief to be treated like a human being, and not just a pretty toy," she went on. "I know Mark means well, but he'd never allow me to do half the things your husband expects of you."

"Perhaps you should ask him," I suggested, but the beauty gave a derisive snort.

"I've tried. He just laughs and says I don't need to trouble my head about such matters . . . as though the only thing I'm good for is singing Irish songs and gracing M'lord's bed."

The anger in her voice surprised me, and I was trying to think how to respond when her portly husband bellied up to us.

"Now don't you go filling my little love's head full of heathen notions," he cautioned me jocularly, insinuating himself between us. "She's as pure as an angel, and I'd not take kindly to seeing her corrupted."

The man's inane twaddle disgusted me; the girl was Pagan to the core and only wore the mantle of Christianity because he imposed it on her. Besides, if he was suspicious enough to resort to spies, it seemed hypocritical to mouth such praises of her purity—unless he only wanted to reassure himself rather than discover the truth.

It appeared that Mark was a blatant example of the old saying that love is blind. I wouldn't want to be present when his eyes were opened.

After the last of our guests were gone I walked slowly through the Imperial Palace, worn out and thankful that the public ordeal was over. In the kitchen Enid greeted me with a row of picnic hampers all packed and ready to go. I grinned tiredly and told her how much I appreciated it.

Tomorrow I would finally get to my husband's side.

TWENTY-EIGHT

Recuperation

e boarded the barges and headed upriver in the cool of the morning. A flock of swans accompanied us; the white adults glided regally beyond reach, but the young gray cygnets came over to investigate when I splashed my feet in the water.

Bedivere laughed and, standing up, called out, "I hereby proclaim all the swans on the river Thames belong to Her Majesty the Queen, and are to be held safe in her name from this day forth."

"Fat lot of good that will do during a bad year," I told him, but he shrugged.

"Who knows . . . maybe someone will remember."

I grinned up at him, glad that he would be staying on at Court with us again. Faced with the losses he had known, many another man would have retreated into anger or resentment. But Bedivere had come to terms with his moira and not turned warped and bitter. It made him all the more dear.

We tied up to a stand of willows beside a meadow near Windsor's cliff, where dragonflies glimmered over the water.

"I'm surprised no one's built a fort on it, commanding the river as it does," Bedivere noted.

"Give them time," Enid commented. "If it can be turned to a military advantage, someone will find a way to do it." My lady-in-waiting took a dim view of grandiose military postures, an attitude which did not endear her to the more arrogant warriors.

"I have some new riddles," Lynette piped up. The Saxons are extraordinarily fond of riddling, and during her childhood in London the Grounds Keeper's daughter had collected quite a store. She brought them with her when she joined the Court, and now we all took turns laughing and testing each other's wit.

Some we could guess, and some not, but all of a sudden Bedivere asked, "What is rippling red, streaks across the heavens, and moves out of the forest without touching the ground?"

His gaze flicked to something over my shoulder, and with a glad cry of "The Red Dragon of Britain!" I turned around.

A small procession of warriors and healers were making their way through the trees to the water's edge, carrying Arthur propped and cushioned on a stretcher. I scrambled onto the bank and ran through the green-dappled sunlight toward him, shocked by his wasted condition, delirious with joy because he was alive. Nimue had called on every bit of medical art and magic at her command, and the treacherous wounds were healing slowly. He would continue to sleep much of the time, but she was confident he would make a full recovery.

When I reached his side my husband opened his eyes and recognized me, but before I could speak he stayed me with a lifted hand.

"The Pendragon extends greetings to the competent and admirable High Queen of Britain," he said. "They tell me you have done a fine job in my absence. Behooves me to get well before you decide you can do it all by yourself."

"This Celtic Queen has no desire to rule alone." I grinned in reply and helped to get him settled comfortably on the barge. As we cast off, Taliesin played one of his melodic songs, adding to the festive air of our voyage.

It occurred to me how odd time is, stretching and twisting in a most peculiar way. It was barely three weeks since Lance had left, yet with all that had happened, I'd had no time to think about it—and now the scene in the Park might have taken place in another lifetime entirely. On the other hand, Arthur and I had been married for seven years, and the whole of that time was as close to my fingertips as the ripples of the trout rising on the river ahead of us.

Watching my husband nap under the canopy, I tried to remember when I first knew I loved him. Certainly not when he was announced as my intended groom. Perhaps it was the night at the Wrekin, when I saw our moirai were entwined for life—or during the wild ride away from Morgan, with the horse pounding under us and the wedding lying ahead.

Or the time he'd come back from war, wounded and weak and barely hanging on to life. Seeing him so vulnerable, even as he was now, always made my heart leap up. Nimue had said once that she loved Merlin not for his magic and power, but for the humanness of the man.

I knew exactly what she meant as I looked at Arthur.

It's fine to see you proud and regal, sending shivers through the crowd and gathering the warriors to your side—or thoughtful in the quiet times, testing, searching, always trying to evaluate what will bring your Britain into its own. No one could help but love you then, my dear . . . but oh, my love, how much more we could share, if you would just . . .

I reached over and brushed the hair from his forehead, not even knowing what I wished he would do, yet still hungering for something I couldn't put into words.

I'll never cease to love you, I thought, though I may starve to death in the process.

Arthur's recovery was difficult at best, and for the next few weeks he drifted in and out of melancholy, sometimes turning snappish and sharp, sometimes just staring off into space. How much was the effect of his wounds and how much due to anguish over his sister's betrayal, I couldn't tell. One never knew when his sunny countenance would go hard as flint, and if I tried to talk with him at such times, I'd only be rebuffed. Finally I decided to wait until he himself brought up the things that were gnawing at him.

Bedivere and I had chosen Oxford because it was easy to get to by water but remote enough to provide some sanctuary. It proved to be a lovely spot, surrounded by meadows and farms as well as a rich, wild wood. Along this part of the Thames the people were as patchwork as the land, with British aristocrats longtime neighbors of Saxon Federates. They not only seemed to live in peace, they were delighted to have the High King in their midst, even if he wasn't on his feet and among them yet.

Frieda went often to visit her family, who had remained loyal to us, fighting at Cador's side to stop the Saxon drive to the midlands. And once her kin returned with her, coming to pay their respects to the High King. I watched them curiously, noting that her mother was an older, plumper version of the girl I'd come to regard as part of my family.

"We appreciate all you have done for our daughter," her father told Arthur. "Sons are companions in war and work, but daughters are special gifts from the Gods."

He smiled broadly at the girl, though he never even looked at Griflet standing beside her, and when he called down the blessing of his Thunder God, the gesture clearly did not include the Master of the Kennels. Perhaps the Saxon Gods were as intolerant of Christians as the Roman bishops were of them.

It occurred to me that with so many disparate beliefs, the Cause could founder if religious warfare ever broke out in Britain!

One afternoon as I was coming back from gathering the last of the wild strawberries at Wytham, I found a venerable old man resting under an ancient oak by the ford where they drive the oxen across. My ladies and I greeted him cordially and asked if we could share the shade. The old fellow nodded and, after looking our party over carefully, began extolling Arthur's fame and glory. I noted with relief that he left out all mention of Maelgwn, concentrating on the battles and adventures of the warriors instead.

"I'm writing 'em down," he explained, stroking the white beard that splayed out across his chest. "Learned to write back when I was going to become a monk—not much use for it since. I couldn't live holy enough to please the bishop, and the sinners I get on best with never learned to read. But the Pendragon ought to have some archives, so I thought I'd draw 'em up."

I told Arthur about it that evening, thinking he'd be pleased, but he grumbled darkly instead.

"And what will history say of King Arthur . . . that he came of a family riddled with death and treachery? Born by the grace of an old man's dying in a righteous cause, risen to the throne over the body of one sister's husband and marked for extinction by the arts of the other. . . . What will they say of Arthur in the end? That kith killing kin runs unavoidably through his days?"

He turned away from me, deep lines of despair scriven on his face. I ached to see him so tormented and sat down beside him on the bed in silent commiseration.

"My own sister, Gwen." It was the first time he had mentioned Morgan, and I held my breath. "My own sister, the very one who gave me the Sword of State. Was she plotting even then to see me dead? Has there been nothing real behind her friendship and support? I trusted her second only to Merlin. . . ."

The words were hard and harsh, forced out between his teeth with the same constrained anger as when he spoke of Morgause.

He paused, and I kept very quiet, not needing to bring forth my own record of pain and loss at Morgan's hand. At last I ventured a small comment.

"Surely it is not so much that she hates us personally as it is the old Celtic tragedy—the blood-feud. Most probably she's never forgiven Gorlois's death."

"Ye Gods, am I to be held accountable for my parents' acts?" Arthur cried. "It's the Christians, not Pagans, who saddle the sons with the sins of the fathers, isn't it? And if it were so, what hope would there be for me or my children?"

He was staring at the wall, not me, but the realization that in spite of his protestations Arthur too had contemplated raising children sent a wave of sympathy through me, and I put my hand on his shoulder.

He laid his unbandaged fingers over my mine, though still without looking at me. "Sometimes it feels as though no matter how hard I work, no matter how hard I try, I'll never quite see the dream realized. And I can't tell if it is because of anger on the part of the Gods or because I've not planned something out as well as I should have."

"Perhaps," I suggested softly, "it's not so much the fault of the potter as the fabric of the clay. You're not exactly dealing with the most malleable materials, you know."

There was a long silence during which he stroked my hand, and at last the shadow of a smile crept across his face. He looked up at me with one of those slow, sidewise glances. "You're just not going to let me lie around and feel sorry for myself, are you? In case I haven't told you lately, I'm awfully glad you're my wife."

My eyes started to brim with tears, and I looked down at our inter-twined fingers, a dozen loving words clamoring to be said. But before I could begin, he withdrew his hand and clenched it into a fist in his lap.

"Now as long as I'm facing things, tell me what happened in London while the 'ceremony' was going on," he demanded.

I stared at him blankly, wondering what that had to do with love.

"Well, go on," he said. "It's about time I hear the details."

So I swallowed my emotions and recounted how Morgan had tried to kill her husband with his own sword. Arthur winced at that, well aware that she had even managed to use Excalibur against him.

"But Bedivere said she fled after Accolon was killed."

I nodded. "It seems the dwarf managed to get her out of the Palace. Her women may have helped and simply stayed on at Court afterward so as to distract us and not slow down the fleeing couple."

"Ummm," Arthur ruminated. "Or it may have been Uwain. One can't ignore the bond between mother and son."

I glanced at him quickly, surprised he should think of that when he was so cold to his own mother. Of course, his foster-mother might have been a different matter.

"I can't believe Uwain could be involved," I said. "He was too badly shaken to be feigning surprise, and if he was complicit, he would not have stopped the attack on his father."

"Unless his gorge couldn't quite accept it at the last minute," Arthur noted. "Urien I trust; he's been a solid ally since the Great Battle. But the boy was too cowardly to stay and protect you at Penrith."

I started to explain that Griflet had sent him for help, but Gawain came to the door just then, full of tales of a wild-man loose in the Wood of Wirral, so we dropped the subject. It wasn't until a week later, when Arthur decreed that Uwain must be banished, that I realized how deep Arthur's suspicion had run.

"It's unfair, Your Highness," Gawain slung at him, storming into the room and pounding his fist on the table where Arthur and I were working. "Bloody unfair, and you know it!"

"Steady there, nephew," Arthur warned, easing himself back among the cushions that propped him up in the chair. "Regicide is not a pretty matter, and I can't afford to keep the whelp of a traitor within my den."

"But Uwain had nothing to do with the attempt on your life," the redhead protested. "He's my cousin—I've known the boy since he was a toddler—"

"And he's my nephew, just as much as you are," Arthur cut in, moving restlessly in the chair. For a man so used to action, the inability to get up and move about was tantamount to being imprisoned, and he had to struggle to keep his voice even.

"I didn't exile him from Britain, or forbid him to have contact with his mother, either one of which would have been a perfectly reasonable thing to do. I've said I don't want to see him here, within my Court, and that is that. Do you understand?"

Arthur was glaring at his nephew, and the Orcadian glared back, as stubborn and hot-tempered as ever. But he blinked and looked away first, perhaps startled to see what I was beginning to think of as "Uther's nature" overcome Arthur's usual reserve. With a curt bow Gawain turned and stalked out.

"Don't say a word," Arthur growled, not even looking at me. "I neither enslaved nor killed the Saxons last year, though they would have done as much to me without a moment's pause. Nor did I mount an army and take my revenge on Maelgwn, though I had every right and desire to. But I have to draw the line somewhere, Gwen, and this is where. If he is as blameless as you say, and keeps out of trouble for the next few years, perhaps he can come back later. But for now I say he is banished, and my word is law!"

It was clear he was deeply upset, for the last statement flew in the face of all his concepts of fairness and justice. There was no point in continuing the conversation, so I picked up the tablet with my notes on the salt centers and brought my attention back to the problem of how to get that necessary stuff to those places that were not endowed with it by nature.

Arthur continued to snarl at everyone for a day or two more, but his punishment of Uwain seemed to have lanced the rage that festered within, and he gradually settled into a calmer mood.

Finally, as we were coming up to the midwinter festival, he could look the world in the face with his old confidence again. The mark of Morgan's betrayal was there for those who knew him well to see, but our subjects rejoiced in his outward recovery.

I thanked the Goddess that her plans and the High Priestess's were not the same.

With spring and the melting of snow, the Roads opened to the west and we began to see the first straggle of visitors. One in particular had caught my women's attention, and when I came into the room for tea they were all discussing the newcomer.

"She's even brought a kitten with her!" Ettard's voice rose with astonishment, and Vinnie's eyebrows did likewise. "It's a pet, not a barn animal, and goes everywhere she does," the convent girl added.

"Well, she may be terribly pretty," Augusta said, raising her tea cup with her little finger extended, "but I'll bet she's got fleas."

There was much giggling at that, and I looked to Vinnie. "Who are you talking about?" I asked, plumping down in my chair with a general greeting to the rest of the women.

They nodded in return, and the matron explained it was the new girl from Carbonek.

"Carbonek?"

"The kingdom poor old Pellam rules." Vinnie pursed her lips primly and poured me a cup of tea. "The place that's become a wasteland because his wound won't heal."

A shiver ran down my spine, and though I couldn't blame any father for wanting to send his daughter away from such a situation, I wished she hadn't come here.

"I was sure you'd accept them, so I gave her the room at the end of the corridor. I imagine they're busy unpacking right now," Vinnie noted.

"What kind of entourage did she bring, and does she have a name?" I inquired.

"Only her chaperone." The matron sniffed. "Pushy woman, intent on catching the best husband for her charge. The girl is called Elaine."

Oh, Glory, I thought . . . another namesake for that Greek temptress of men. I hoped that this one was only a little eccentric, not mentally incompetent.

"What's this?" Gawain bellowed at dinner that night, rising to his feet in alarm. "Did I hear you right, Pelleas? Marriage, you say?"

The horseman flushed a deep red, and Gawain turned with elaborate surprise to Arthur, then back to his pupil.

"I do believe it's true. The Lady Ettard seems to have agreed to wed this fellow." Good humor filled Gawain's countenance, and he lifted his drinking horn in a toast. "To the best pupil I've ever had; he's a staunch friend, fine horseman, and only a little backward with the ladies."

Ettard was sitting next to Pelleas, and she ducked her head in embarrassment and stared at her lap. Laughter was running round the room, and when Arthur raised his goblet his nephew reached across and filled it.

"Where do you plan to live?" the King asked, and Pelleas smiled.

"In the land you gave me after the Battle of Mt. Badon." He lifted his own mug in a toast. "To the most generous King in Britain."

Bedivere was sitting beside me, and he leaned closer. "That young man has grown up rather nicely, hasn't he? And going to be landed gentry after all."

I nodded, remembering the thin, ragged youth who had come to Court after the Irish campaign.

Ettard was looking imploringly at Arthur. "Perhaps we can stay on here?"

"Of course, you'll both be welcome whenever you wish to return," he responded kindly.

I wondered how she would fare out on a steading when she'd grown so used to being in the heart of the High King's Court but reminded myself not to borrow trouble; there was plenty enough around without looking for more.

Gawain was teasing Pelleas about his lack of experience as a lover, and soon the Companions were convulsed with laughter.

But just when Arthur's nephew tired of the subject and was getting ready to sit down, a peculiar expression crossed his face, and he bent to peer into the shadows beneath the table.

"By the Horned One!" he exclaimed, lifting something up for all to see. "We have a new kind of varmint, and it's mistaken my shin for a tree trunk!"

He was holding a small mottled kitten by the scruff of the neck, turning it from side to side at arm's length.

A young woman scrambled to her feet and rushed to rescue the animal without so much as pausing to acknowledge Arthur or me.

"Oh, Sir," she cried, "be gentle with Tiger Fang, I beg you."

A roar of amusement filled the Hall as Gawain mimicked the cat's name and brought the homely little thing up to his face with a grimace of mock fear. The kitten had more spirit than size and, flattening its ears, hissed boldly at the stocky warrior. Gawain laughed all the harder as he turned to its owner.

"And who may you be?" he asked, cocking his head to one side and keeping the pet well beyond reach. The entire Hall had gone silent, watching to see what would happen.

"Elaine . . . Elaine of Carbonek," the girl answered, her bright gaze traveling from the little cat to the Orcadian.

She was very pretty in a saucy way, and the hair that flounced about her head was as red as Gawain's own. For a long moment the two of them took each other's measure. There was no question of her deferring to his size, nature, or status.

"Have you met the King, Elaine?" he asked casually.

"Not yet." She dimpled, never taking her eyes from his face. "Perhaps you should introduce me . . . after you return my pet."

"Perhaps I should." He nodded, watching her shrewdly. "Why are you here, my dear?"

"Because my chaperone is," she shot back, blithe as milk.

"To find a husband?" he inquired.

"Only if someone extraordinary comes along."

Agravain and Gaheris burst out laughing, and Gawain himself started to grin. It was the first time he had met his match since Ragnell, and it occurred to me that Elaine could do far worse.

With a grand gesture the Prince of Orkney restored the kitten to the young woman, then formally presented her to us. She made a deep curtsy, clutching her golden-eyed kit to her breast, but I noticed that when she looked up, the long, slow sweep of her glance went only to Arthur, not to the both of us.

After she rejoined her chaperone my husband turned to me. "Now that's a pleasant breath of freshness, isn't it?"

"Mmmm," I responded, thinking she had a good bit to learn about life in a High Queen's Court.

"Oh, M'lady," Ettard wailed, "Pelleas's holdings are so far away. Whatever am I going to do there?"

"Make a home for your husband," I answered, not altogether kindly. It was clear Ettard had been crying, and I wondered again how pretty women manage to weep without their eyes getting red and puffy as mine did.

But later, when Nimue and I were in the pharmacia taking stock of which herbs we would need to replenish this spring, the doire reproved me for my brusqueness with Ettard. "Be a little gentle with her—she's not got long to live."

Her words brought goose bumps to my skin, and I looked up sharply. "How do you know?"

"I'm not sure." She shrugged slightly. "It's just a feeling. But the girl thinks she should have everything, and is caught betwixt too many desires. She wants to be married, but she also wants to stay at Court. She wants a fancy husband, but she's afraid to wait much longer for fear of getting old. She can't fill one need without being at cross purposes with another, and the strain of that conflict is likely to be her downfall."

I tried to be more patient after that, and the day Pelleas left to go to his holdings and make them ready for his bride, I made a point of asking Ettard to serve tea with me.

"Oh, but Your Highness, I distinctly remember yesterday you promised you'd teach my Elaine how to pour," the chaperone Brisane announced as Ettard set up the silver service next to me.

"I was so much looking forward to the lesson," the girl from Carbonek put in hopefully.

I sighed ruefully, reminded that Brisane was right. "You can serve next time," I promised Ettard as she moved away silently.

After that Brisane began pushing Elaine forward to garner attention or honor whenever possible. Often the woman sought special favors for her charge, explaining that the girl's hands were too delicate for gardening or her nature too exuberant to spend hours spinning.

"It's fine for an old lady like myself," the chaperone would conclude, cheerfully taking over the girl's chores, "but Her Ladyship isn't used to such things."

I wondered what, beside play and frivolity, the young lady was used to, but Elaine's high spirits made it hard to blame her for her chaperone's behavior. The girl could invest anything with an air of fun, conjuring up pranks and games that delighted everyone. Before long she had usurped Augusta's place of honor among the girls, but while the Roman beauty fumed, Ettard simply withdrew more and more into herself.

One day in the full flush of spring I brought an armload of flowers into the Hall as my ladies got out the silver to be polished.

"Well, I don't know who he is," Elaine said as she dragged a piece of string across the floor for her homely kitten. "But he's certainly the most exciting man I've seen yet."

"Exciting?" Augusta made the term sound unbelievable. "What sort of emblem did he wear?"

"None at all that I could see," Elaine answered, lifting the twine into the air when the kitten pounced. The little animal was all eyes and claws, thrashing its tail wildly as it looked about for the string. In spite of its diminutive size there was something so single-minded in its actions, one couldn't help being amused by it.

Elaine scooped up her pet, bringing it in to snuggle under her chin. "He has black hair, and is as lithe as a cat," the girl from Carbonek added, still thinking of the stranger she'd seen.

My heart leapt in my ribs, and I instinctively glanced out the window toward the courtyard, sure she was talking about Lance.

"Where did you see him?" Enid asked, sorting through the blossoms.

"At the stableyard. He was attended by a blond page." The girl

sighed extravagantly. "I can't remember a more splendid fellow.
. . . Surely he has a name?"

Augusta was buffing her fingernails with a strip of lambskin usually
used on the silver, and she paused to admire their shine. "He didn't
tell you?" she queried, baiting the new girl.

"No, he didn't," Elaine flared. "We weren't close enough to speak.
Besides, he and the boy went off toward the Hall."

"Still, he should have noticed you," the Roman vixen opined, "what
with your being so pretty, and having such gorgeous red hair."

"Oh, for heaven's sake!" I stormed. "Can't you do anything but stir
up trouble?"

I'd risen without even thinking about it and ran out of the room,
leaving my women speechless.

It was coming up to the anniversary of our midnight ride, and though
I tried not to remember the occasion of that rescue, Lance had been
more and more in my thoughts of late. I hadn't the slightest idea what
to do or say, but I moved toward the Hall as though drawn by a magnet.

"Ah, Gwen, there you are," Arthur called as I came into the room
we used as an office. "The Queen's Champion has returned."

Lancelot was leaning against the window frame and he came to
attention as I moved across the room. His smile was pleasant but
serious, though the full lips never parted, and he greeted me with a
cross between a nod and a bow. I extended my hand as I would have
to Bedivere or Gawain, relieved to discover I could look him fully in
the face without a qualm.

"He just now got in from Warkworth." Arthur's voice was more
cheerful than I'd heard in months. "And he brought this young fellow
with him."

A blond boy of about the age of twelve came forward and gave me
a full formal greeting. His pale, silky hair was cut in the short style of
the north and even the motion of his hands was graceful—a rare thing
for a lad barely out of childhood. From his actions it was obvious he
was familiar with court protocol, and I wondered who he was.

"We met on the Road," Lance explained. "He prefers not to go into
his family background, but I thought he might find a place as a page
until he's old enough to train as a squire."

The lad inclined his head slowly. "I haven't much in the way of credentials, but I'm willing to work," he allowed.

"Lance's recommendation is enough," Arthur answered. "Do you have much experience with horses?" The newcomer shook his head, and Arthur shrugged. "Well, no matter. We'll find something for you to do while you learn. Now," he went on, turning back to Lance, "tell us about the north."

The three of us settled into chairs while the boy sat tailor-fashion on the floor and we began catching up on news and gossip.

Lance had spent most of his time in his garden by the sea, developing the fort and getting to know the people of the nearby fishing village. He'd made several trips up the coast, meeting with settlers and making sure the area was free of brigands. And there'd even been a brief visit to the Lakes, where he went to see Morgan at the Sanctuary.

Arthur stiffened at the mention of her name, so I asked when Lance had visited her.

"On my way north, actually, but she wasn't there. Someone said she had gone to London after all."

"Indeed," I answered, realizing that Lance knew nothing of her involvement with Accolon or how close Arthur had come to death. So I told the tale as simply as possible, wanting for Arthur's sake to get it behind us.

"Ah," the Breton sighed when I had finished. "Do you remember what I told you when you were accused of murder? There will always be those among the Cumbri who will plot and scheme for Arthur's ruin, and you would do well to keep your guard up."

Arthur nodded curtly. "Neither of my sisters is welcome at Court," he said flatly. "They are banished, exiled, forbidden to come to Logres or wherever I may be visiting, and there are to be *no exceptions.*"

I had long since given up trying to figure out why Arthur harbored such hatred for Morgause. Whatever she had done following the Great Battle, I thought it should be remembered that she had just been widowed, and grief can make us all say hasty, ill-thought things. I had hoped that time would mellow Arthur's attitude toward her, particularly since she continued to send her sons to serve us. But it seemed unlikely the rift would ever be healed now that Arthur was lumping both her and the Lady together in one prohibition. Morgan clearly deserved it, but I still wasn't sure that the Queen of the Orkney Isles did.

Lance's homecoming caused a flurry of excitement and some distress at the Hall that night. Arthur simply reinstated the Breton in his old position at the King's side without mentioning it to Gawain before-hand.

I saw a look of surprise and then hurt cross the Orcadian's face as he found his chair had been moved away from the King's.

"Come, now," I suggested, "no one's spoken for the seat next to me, and I'd be delighted with your company."

The Champion gave me a scathing look, then carefully scanned the Hall. "Thank you anyhow, Your Highness," he said coldly. "But I see that the Lady Ettard is all alone, and I promised Pelleas I'd look after her until he returned."

He picked up a handy goblet of wine and, downing it on the spot, sauntered across the room to where the convent girl sat. I watched him go and saw the sudden radiance that lit Ettard's face when she realized he intended to join her. Oh, dear, I thought, she'll never be willing to go live on a steading now.

It was Cei who sat beside me instead, and when Lancelot introduced the boy he'd found on the Road, the Seneschal looked him over through narrowed eyes. "I'd say he's never done a day's work in his life. You can see from his hands; they're far too well kept for a workaday lad. What do we know of him?"

When I explained that he didn't want to go into his past, the Seneschal gave a snort. "Could be a runaway slave escaped from some Middle Eastern merchant—I hear they like young boys." Cei absently swirled the wine in his goblet and passed it under his nose several times while his eyes continued to appraise the youth. "He's very pretty . . . one might almost say effeminate."

That hadn't occurred to me, and I turned to look at the newcomer more closely. He caught my glance and came to stand before me.

"I appreciate your hospitality, Your Highness," he said, then nodded to Cei.

"What would you like to be called?" I asked, realizing he had not given us his name.

"I for one will call him 'Beaumains,' because his hands are so fair," the Seneschal announced, abruptly leaning forward and taking one in order to examine it. Clasped in Cei's bejeweled fingers, the boy's hand looked almost delicate.

The lad gave a start but didn't pull back.

"Have you and the King decided what you should do here at Court?" I inquired.

Beaumains shook his head, and Cei smiled tightly as he studied the lad's palm. "I can use him in the kitchen," the Seneschal decreed as he let go of the boy. "Have you any experience in cooking?"

"Not much, Sir . . . but I'm willing to learn." The lad laughed in an open, friendly response. It was clear he was not going to let Cei's abrasive style disturb him.

So it was arranged. Beaumains walked away with a kind of instinctive ease and pleasure that was at total odds with the brooding, secretive Cei and I wondered how long the lad would last in the kitchen. At least I was sure that Cook would see he was treated fairly.

The evening went comfortably from then on, and after Arthur had gone to sleep I lay wakefully beside him, studying his profile in the moonlight and thinking about Lance's return.

The Breton seemed very much at home with Arthur and me together, and the Companions were glad to have him back. For my part, I welcomed the return of Arthur's enthusiasm and the easy friendship that flowed between the three of us, just as it had in the past.

Whatever Lance's feelings were, he seemed to have dealt with them while he was at Warkworth. There was nothing in his manner to indicate that the encounter under the willow had changed anything. One might almost believe the kiss had never happened—and with care it would never be repeated. As long as I had Arthur to focus on, to stand between me and Lancelot, I was comfortable.

The notes of a wakeful thrush filled the night—rich-throated and exuberant, there is no other bird song so splendid, or so unselfconscious. By its very nature it made me think of Arthur.

I looked at my husband one last time and smiled before going to sleep.

TWENTY-NINE

The Lovers

ith the return of Lance, Arthur's recuperation was complete, and it wasn't long before we were all involved in developing plans for the new headquarters at South Cadbury's hill-fort.

"It'll not only be a good headquarters for keeping track of the Saxons," Arthur mused, "it's also big enough to hold the entire Court. I've been thinking I'd like to put a fine Hall up here on the ridge, and the stables over there. . . ."

Bedivere and Lance were so engrossed in the sketch Arthur was making, they didn't notice Dinadan's arrival at the door. The Cornishman was one of the most easygoing people I knew, but now he was travel-tired and haggard, and an alarming tension radiated from him. Tristan was nowhere to be seen.

"He cannot stay away from her!" Dinadan exclaimed, his voice full of exasperation. "The new priest lectures him—to no avail. I point out the folly of the thing—to no avail. Even the swineherd has warned him—to no avail. The man is deaf to reason!"

"Swineherd?" Lance queried.

Dinadan sighed wearily. "Tristan's been living with a swineherd in the forest, and he sends the man to Castle Dore to learn when it's safe to meet Isolde. I swear that Tris thrives on the dangerous part of this mess—even though King Mark has banished him from Court, he still creeps into her garden at night."

"Banished?" Arthur's reaction was one of shock. I thought of Uther and Igraine—perhaps there are some lovers for whom the element of danger is part of the excitement.

Dinadan gave another nod. "The Lady of the Lake sent Mark a letter saying straight out what everyone else already knew, and the old King flew into an absolute rage—made all kinds of fuss, swearing he'd give the girl over to bandits and brigands for their pleasure, threatening to have Tris executed. . . . At least that made some impression on the lad; that's when he went to live in the forest."

"What happened to Isolde?" I asked.

"The wiles of women never cease to amaze me!" Dinadan made an apologetic nod in my direction. "Your Highness is one of the more exceptionally honest of the sex I've ever met, you understand. Isolde claimed that the accusations were only spiteful rumors started by people who were jealous of Tristan's standing in his uncle's Court."

To prove herself blameless Mark's Queen offered to undergo any test her husband might demand. One of Illtud's pupils, a monk named Samson, had recently come to Castle Dore, breathing fire and brimstone. He convinced Mark to hold a Trial by Ordeal at the bank of a nearby stream, where all could see how the guilt or innocence of the Queen was resolved.

"I may have reason to question my bride," Mark declared, "but I have faith that the God of Christ would not let harm come to an innocent party."

As the day of the Ordeal approached, Isolde grew pale and tense, weeping through the nights and spending her days railing at her husband for believing more in his God than he did in her. Mark, meanwhile, lived with the misery of doubting both his nephew and his bride.

"I do not know which pained him more," Dinadan said softly. "Tris is the son of Mark's sister, who died in childbirth, leaving him to raise the lad as his own. So the idea that Tristan would betray him like this cut doubly deep." The Cornishman shook his head in bewilderment, sorrowing equally for his friend and his King. "Mark dotes on his wife as though she were the sun in his heaven. He may be grossly selfish and not always an honorable leader, but he's honest and true in his love for the girl, however misguided it might be."

Early on the morning of the trial the Cornish Queen accompanied her husband to the chapel in Lantyne, carrying in outstretched hands a beautiful altar cloth that she had embroidered herself. Slowly and reverently, with downcast eyes and bent head, the Irish beauty walked into the little church and laid her offering on the communion table. There were ohs and ahs from the parishioners, and even the fault-finding priest had to acknowledge that the girl had done a fine bit of handiwork in the service of the Lord.

During Mass she and Mark sat apart, for the issue of her innocence was still to be proven at the river's edge and he dared not weaken in his resolve.

When the praying was over the whole congregation followed the King and his lady as they set out for the stream. On the far side was a forge, and the smith had been ordered to have the coals well banked and cherry red.

People came from miles around, both Pagan and Christian, to see the outcome of this test, and there was much muttering and craning of necks by those who wanted to watch the nobles.

"Tris had gotten us both up in the habits of novices from a monastery," Dinadan recounted. "You know how he loves to play games and tricks on people . . . one would have thought this was just another prank, although both his life and Isolde's would be forfeit should the coals prove her to be false."

The two warriors waited in a willow clump beside the brook, and as the royal party approached, Tristan pulled the hood of his habit up over his head. Hitching his robe up to his knees, he edged out into the waterway. Slack-jawed and stooping, he gawked at the King's party like any country yokel.

Isolde and Mark were riding in a cart, and when they paused midway in the ford, Tristan moved closer, staring at the portly monarch, mouth open and eyes squinted as though to see him better. It appeared he did not even notice the Queen.

Pointing to the fire, King Mark cries out, "There, my dear. If you can honestly swear you have not committed adultery, God will allow you to carry a burning coal from the forge to the river without so much as blistering your hands."

The young Queen gasps and casting a stricken look about her, falls from the cart in a faint. Lunging forward, Tristan made an awkward job of catching her, and lifting her above the water, carries her to the other side of the ford.

Drenched from the knees down, the novice stands on the bank, stammering stupidly as he looks around for help as to what to do with the Queen. All can see he's a pious country boy, struck dumb by the nearness of so much royalty.

Isolde's eyes flutter, and she begins to moan. Everyone's attention shifts to the fragile beauty, and having put her on her feet, the novice laboriously wades back across the water to watch the proceedings— unnoticed—from the farther bank.

In a stentorian voice the new priest commands God to judge this matter, then asks the Queen to swear to her innocence.

"By the White Christ," she cries, her voice lifting with conviction, "I swear that the only two men to hold me in their arms have been my husband, Mark, and the novice who carried me across the stream just now."

With great dignity she holds out her hand as the smith takes his tongs and carefully lays an ember in the center of her palm.

Dinadan shook his head in amazement. "She received it with neither twitch nor wince, and walked to the stream in a kind of stately trance. The coal hissed and sputtered when she dropped it into the water, but there was no sign that she had felt its heat. If I hadn't heard Tris boasting of their times together, even I would have thought her to be blameless. I swear a beautiful woman can make men believe anything!"

I snorted and glanced at Arthur and Lance. The High King was watching Dinadan, but Lance's gaze was far off, and neither noticed my reaction.

"Where do things stand now?" I asked, getting to my feet and stretching. There had to be some reason why Dinadan had come to us.

"She's returned to Mark's good graces, but he watches her like a hawk, and she's begun begging Tris to take her away." Dinadan turned to Arthur. "Can we count on you for sanctuary?"

"We?" Arthur noted, and Dinadan looked hard at his own hands.

"I've long wanted to become a member of the Round Table," he said bashfully. "Perhaps if I bring the finest warrior from Cornwall, I will have earned a place in the Fellowship myself?"

"Of course, my friend." Arthur laughed. "Both you and Tris have always been welcome, whenever you chose to come." But he paused and shot Dinadan a more serious look. "What will Mark's reaction be if she leaves him?"

"I don't know. Anger, or sorrow . . . or maybe relief."

"Do you think he'll come after them?"

"I'm not sure." Dinadan rubbed his chin diligently. "It would take a lot for him to mount a war against you, particularly with his best warrior in your camp. But I cannot altogether swear he wouldn't."

Arthur was pacing the room, weighing the probabilities. "Well," he said at last, "it won't make any difference in whether I take the lovers in or not, just where we keep them. How would it be, Lance, if they joined you at Warkworth for the summer?"

"But what about the work at Cadbury?" the Breton exclaimed, obviously surprised.

Arthur frowned. "I don't really need you for that—Bedivere can handle it. But I do need someone to give Tris and Isolde a safe haven. And Mark isn't likely to march an army all the way up to Warkworth just to claim his wife."

"True," Lancelot agreed, though it was clear that he'd prefer to spend the summer with us. "Couldn't Pelli put them up at the Wrekin?"

"With that great brood of children he's produced, and all the warriors and family members that have collected around him? He doesn't have room," Arthur answered, then grinned. "Besides, royal guests expect royal accommodations."

Dinadan noted that anything would be an improvement over the swineherd's hut, and he for one thought the whole subject of love was hugely overrated, especially if it interfered with one's housing arrangements.

We all laughed at that, and when he left the next day to return to Tristan we assured him we would give the Cornish lovers sanctuary.

It was an unusually beautiful spring, and a number of romances began to blossom among our courtiers. Pages and squires stared calf-eyed after flocks of giggling household girls, the newest warriors boasted and strutted before my younger ladies-in-waiting, and even the seasoned Companions responded to the beguilements of the season, though not always with a light heart.

"Griflet wants us to make our pledge and begin our own family," Frieda confided one morning as we checked on the newest batch of pups. We had procured another bitch after Cabal's death, and the kennels were now full of Caesar's progeny.

"Sounds very sensible," I commented, watching the little ones nuzzling blindly for their mother's teat.

"But it means I must choose—between my family and him, that is." A catch in the Saxon girl's voice reminded me how closely she was tied to her kin. "Oh, M'lady, I love them both. I can't imagine giving up either one for the other . . . or why they should demand it. Why can't loving just be loving, without all kinds of decisions?"

Why, indeed, I thought, gently commiserating with her.

Fortunately not all our lovers were caught in conflicts; Ettard, for instance, seemed suddenly very happy.

"This morning she was singing to herself." Augusta paused meaningfully. "I tell you, something has changed."

I coughed pointedly, and the Roman gossip looked down at her lap. At least she'd control her poisonous tongue while I was around.

"Maybe," Elaine suggested, "she's simply excited about her wedding. Didn't you say she was to marry Pelleas as soon as he comes back? I'll wager she's just full of good spirits because of that."

The redhead was on her hands and knees retrieving her kitten, and she looked up at me with a grin. I nodded, thinking that while the girl from Carbonek might be every bit as spoiled as Augusta, she at least had a habit of looking on the best side of things rather than the worst.

The conversation veered to other things: the abundance of lavender blossoms in the garden this year, and what fine sachets they would make when dried; a new recipe for using the ashes of bracken in making soap, and the most recent stories of strange happenings in the Wood of Wirral.

"I've a cousin who lives there," a new girl from Chester noted, "and she says it's the Green Man who goes stalking through the Wood at night. That Old God ain't been seen for generations, you know." She made the sign against evil, for the Green One was feared and revered by all.

"What we need is one of the traveling saints to banish the wretched thing," Vinnie said firmly. "I could write to my friend the Bishop of Carlisle and see if he's got someone to send down that way."

Vinnie had badgered the hierarchy into sending a bishop to refurbish the old church in Carlisle when I was a girl, and to this day she took a proprietary interest in his activities.

" 'T'ain't wretched," the Chesterite said quickly, fairly bristling at Vinnie's assumption that what was non-Christian was evil. "He's the most ancient one of all, God of the Beasts and Field, who commands the whole of life . . . excepting maybe what the Goddess controls."

"I'll wager he challenges all comers," Elaine speculated, her eyes wide with awe. "Just like the great warriors at the river fords of old; 'Present arms, Sir, or you shall not pass!' " She grabbed her kitten and held it up as the challenger, making us all laugh.

The little animal put its ears back and glared about, then, reaching out a silken paw, patted the girl's cheek until she brought it under her chin and let it scramble onto her shoulder. They made a charming picture.

I've never had time to be jealous of beautiful women, but if I were to be piqued by such things, this bright, lively girl might stir me to envy. Instead I grinned at her ingenuousness and put the thought aside.

Two nights later I awoke to her shaking my shoulder and whispering, "Come quickly, M'lady . . . come quickly."

"What on earth?" Arthur mumbled, sitting up and opening the shutter of the lantern.

The girl was all soft and tousled from sleep, her hair a halo of wild waves and curls and her young athletic figure softened by a white bedshift. When she saw she'd wakened the King as well, she dimpled prettily and bobbed a curtsy.

"Whatever is the matter?" I asked, thinking the child had far too much nerve.

"It's Ettard, M'lady. She's so distraught, the matron said I should fetch you."

"Mmh," I responded, wondering why Vinnie hadn't sent directly for Nimue; in the end, it was the doire who would fix things with a sedative, anyway.

But I came wide awake when I walked into the room where the convent girl huddled in a ball of misery on a stool. White and pale as death, she sobbed silently, her head sunken between her shoulders and her arms wrapped across her chest in a protective embrace. When I tried to talk with her she simply shut me out by closing her eyes.

"What in the world . . . ?" I asked, turning to Vinnie.

"I don't know, M'lady. She won't speak at all now, but when I first heard her sobbing, she was crying for Gawain."

"Gawain?"

"Yes, M'lady, Gawain." The matron knelt beside the weeping girl and tried to comfort her with an embrace, but Ettard didn't respond. "You know how fond she was of him, always talking about him before she decided to marry Pelleas. Maybe he can help."

I was running back to our chamber to ask Arthur if he'd fetch the Orcadian when I heard voices coming from the Hall.

"By the Gods, what made you do such a foolish thing?" Arthur was clearly angry. "There's a hundred single ladies who'd be delighted to ease your night's sleep, Nephew. Why did you have to pick Pelleas's fiancée?"

"She's been asking for it for years, Arthur," Gawain shot back. "And now, what with Pelleas gone and all . . . well, she was willing and I was needful. And it's not as though tonight was the first time; we've been romping regularly for the last few weeks. Besides, who was to know Pelleas would come back this early?"

Oh, Glory, the groom-to-be was also involved! I squared my shoulders and crossed through the shadows of the Hall.

Gawain flushed as I came within the circle of the lantern light and had the decency to look away while I watched him. "Where is Pelleas?" I asked.

"Who knows?" The redhead shrugged. "After he found us together, he drew his sword and threatened to behead me on the spot. You better believe it was a sticky moment, and I had just rolled away from the wench when the blade of his weapon began to shake and he drove the tip a full handsbreadth into the floorboards next to me. After that he turned and ran, and I decided I'd best be getting back to my room."

"Leaving your conquest to fend for herself?"

Gawain hung his head for a moment, then shrugged again. "I assumed she'd find her way back to her quarters, though I admit I didn't wait to find out. An outraged fiancé isn't that different from an outraged husband, you know."

"What did you tell her when you bedded the girl?" I demanded.

Gawain lifted his head proudly. "I never promised her anything, Your Highness. I don't deal in lies."

The old pride of honesty flamed across his red face. Cut off your head, ruin your marriage, make war over a broken tea cup he would, but never, never lie! The Celt in me responded fondly even as I shook my head in reprimand.

"And you never talked of love, or marriage, or the fact that she was a virgin?"

"Virgin? Oh, come now, she may have called herself that, but she had no objection to being bedded. As for love, they all talk about that. But I never promised her anything," he repeated, his voice rising with belligerence. "She knew perfectly well what this was: a fling, a last lark, a time for play before the marriage vows took over."

Arthur was watching his nephew closely, and now he sighed heavily. "There are many girls who go hunting husbands among the Companions, using fair means or foul. But the point of the Fellowship is a bond of trust with one's brothers. How do you defend your actions where Pelleas is concerned? You were his mentor, his idol, and his best friend, after all."

"So what's a little—" Gawain clamped his mouth shut on the crudity with a glare at me. "If you're going to snoop and pry and worry over each person's ethical behavior, perhaps you had best begin by looking to your own, Uncle."

His voice was full of indignation and I suddenly thought how much he sounded like Morgan when she gets upset.

"You who prate about law and order, and fairness for peoples . . . and then send away a loyal and blameless lad because of a personal grudge. What sort of honesty is that within yourself, Your Highness?"

Gawain spat the words at Arthur, and I saw my husband blink with surprise and lack of comprehension.

"I'm speaking of Uwain, damn it. Exiled from the one place he felt at home, by a man he revered. Don't you dare sit in judgment of me, you . . . you Roman hypocrite!"

For a moment Gawain's hand rested on the hilt of his dagger, but a loyalty deeper than all the anger in the world restrained him. Without another word he spun on his heel and marched into the gloom.

Arthur and I both let out a long breath and looked at each other in amazement. Neither one of us had any idea Gawain was harboring such a grievance. My husband spoke first.

"Do you suppose he's right about hypocrisy?"

"Ye Gods, Arthur, this is no time for soul-searching; we've got a woman in hysterics and a cuckold young man lost somewhere in the dark. Have you any idea where Pelleas is?"

Arthur shook his head but went off to look for him while I went back to Ettard. She may well have brought it on herself, but that didn't mean she wasn't in desperate straits.

Nimue had already fixed her a cup of cowslip wine by the time I arrived, and although the convent girl was still pale and teary-eyed, she had at least begun to talk. She rambled on about her fear of leaving the Court and how Gawain owed it to her to make "an honest woman" of her now that he'd enjoyed her favors. Her voice had the same flat tone as when she'd told me of her childhood, and I wondered if there was any love and caring for anyone behind the pretty facade.

As she drifted into sleep Nimue and Vinnie and I sat in vigil beside her—the Christian crone, the Pagan priestess, and, somewhere in the middle, the Queen who was determined to hold things together. We could not have been more different in outlook or temperament, yet we gathered protectively around one of our own who was too hurt to protect herself. Men may deal in active blows, but it's women who bind up the internal wounds.

All three members of the miserable affair left Court within a week. Pelleas crept away in the early dawn following his discovery of Gawain and Ettard together, having spoken only to Palomides.

"I do not know what will happen to him," the Arab told me sadly. "The one saving grace is the land Arthur has given him. If he can face going back there without Ettard, perhaps it will eventually bring him life and hope again. The land is always healing, M'lady."

I agreed but wished there was something I could do or say to the young horseman—he was the one most deeply hurt by this twisted, stupid mess.

Gawain also departed, ostensibly to check on his lands in the north. I hoped that was all it amounted to; we could ill afford to have the Prince of Orkney turn on Arthur as his father had.

With the strange, quixotic sensitivity that marks the Celts, he sought me out the morning before he left, precisely to allay my fears.

"I own I lost my temper, M'lady, and laid a harsher tongue on the two of you than I meant. Arthur's said he understands, and I hope you'll accept my apology as well."

"Perhaps the change of scenery will do you good," I replied, looking fondly at the redhead. "We'd hate to see you leave full of black rage . . . or feel you couldn't return."

He smiled disarmingly. "Arthur and the Court are still my home and family. But it's been years since I've seen my kin. Mordred and Gareth must be so big by now I wouldn't recognize them. And Mother . . . well, it's time we made up our differences."

I nodded, hoping that both of them had mellowed enough to patch up the old wounds. If so, there might be some way to affect a truce between her and Arthur as well. With that in mind I asked Gawain to give her my regards, and tell her that I would like to meet her someday.

Gawain shrugged and said he'd tell her. It was a casual remark on both our parts, but I hoped it might bear useful fruit.

Before the week was out Ettard announced that she was going to move to the Cornish holdings Igraine had left her. Clearly she had no future with Pelleas, and word of her involvement with Gawain had become the tattle of the Court, so I didn't blame her for leaving. I wished her well and gave her the litter Igraine had used, as she seemed much more comfortable with it than I ever was.

Silently I commended her to the Queen Mother's care, for even in spirit form I was sure Igraine had more patience than I did. Besides, with the imminent arrival of Tristan and Isolde, I had no time to worry about Ettard.

The party from Cornwall reached Oxford a week later and Isolde retired immediately to the quarters I'd put aside for her. I inquired if she and Branwen wished to join us at the table for dinner but was told she would be ready to face the world no sooner than the morrow, so I went to the Hall without them.

"You made very good time," Arthur was saying to Tristan. "We weren't expecting you this soon, or Gwen would have been packed."

"I would? What for?" I asked, caught totally off guard.

"Why, to accompany Isolde this summer." My husband seemed equally surprised that I hadn't foreseen this new development. "She'll need a chaperone, you know."

I started to laugh aloud, the idea of protecting Isolde's virtue being blatantly ridiculous. But Arthur was looking at me with his "don't you dare" expression, so I stifled my laughter and glanced at Lancelot. Our eyes met for a moment, and I realized suddenly that he was as disconcerted by this development as I was.

"But I don't want to go to Joyous Gard," I protested to Arthur as we prepared for bed. "I thought we were going to work at Cadbury together."

"I did, too." My husband sighed. "But until we see how Mark is going to react, we have to take all possible precautions. The last thing I want is war with the man—it could easily involve Ireland as well. With you accompanying Isolde, it will look like a summer frolic for two Queens."

I groaned inwardly, knowing there was no way to tell Arthur that I was afraid to be alone with Lance for weeks at a time. It was one thing to enjoy his company as part of Arthur's team and quite another to come face to face with . . . with what? I noticed I couldn't even finish the thought.

"It will take weeks to get the Court ready to move," I countered.

"Then take a smaller retinue," came the answer. "I'm sure it really doesn't matter how many there are, as long as we can tell Mark that the needs of Christian propriety were served."

My husband came over to stand in front of me and putting his arms around me, pulled me to him. "I don't look forward to being separated all summer, either," he said. "But the needs of Britain come first, and right now that means giving Mark time to calm down before he decides what to do about his wandering wife."

I looked up at him, loving him, hating him, wanting to scream, "Can't you ever think of anything but Britain!" and so torn inside that tears welled unexpectedly to my eyes.

"Come now, is my favorite Celtic Queen going to cry over something as small as a three-month separation?" he teased, wrapping me in a bear hug.

I threw my arms around him and clung for dear life, all my words of doubt and uncertainty heaped on that great pile of silence where the sharing of love and hope and sorrow also lay.

Someday, Arthur, I told him silently, someday they'll find a voice, and then you're going to get such an earful, you'll never never be able to ignore them again!

THIRTY

The Garden of Joy

o we went to Warkworth: Lance and I, Tristan and Isolde, Palomides and Griflet—who coaxed Frieda into coming, too—and most of the women of the household because at the last minute Arthur looked at me in dismay and said, "What on earth am I to do with them while you're gone?"

After miles of travel across the Cheviot Hills with their high, windswept reaches rippling with purple moor grass, the vale of the Coquet River was a wonderful relief. Winding down into its lush shelter, I understood why Lance loved it—green and sweet, it has the air of an enchanted kingdom.

When we dismounted to rest the horses beside a rocky pool, the flash of a kingfisher caught my eye like a streak of blue lightning. For the first time in years I stopped to savor my surroundings—gray lichen on the gnarled trunk of an oak; mosses, rich and plush, clinging to damp rocks; the silver dance of water as it dropped from ledge to ledge. The smell of the woods and the coolness of spray-drenched ferns offered a peace and tranquillity I didn't even realize I had lost until it was restored.

My life at Court had become a dizzying round of decisions and diplomacy. It amazed me to think that all the while I hurried from duty to duty, trotting from cobbled courtyards to tower chambers, the earth continued to pour forth her silent strength for any who had sense enough to seek her out. I drank in the beauty of it like a parched traveler who stumbles on a hidden spring, slaking my thirst with wonder and gratitude to the Gods. With a sigh I promised myself that for this summer, in this joyous garden, I would not let affairs of state keep me from being part of the world around me.

Lance's new Hall was both comfortable and homey. Perched on its knoll in the loop of the river, it was more a farmstead than a military center, and though a ditch and bank encircled it, there were no ramparts. The overseer and his wife were warm and friendly, and I woke the first morning to the smell of bacon sizzling on a country hearth. It was so much like my childhood, I could have cried for pleasure.

Our sojourn quickly turned into a summer idyll as we worked and played together like a large family and I reveled in the freedom from protocol and propriety. Even Isolde responded to it, gradually dropping her reserve and taking part in whatever we were doing. I was glad, for it gave me a chance to get to know the girl better.

"Are you very homesick for Ireland?" I asked one morning as we were digging clams for dinner on the golden beach.

"Not really," she answered, energetically poking about with a pointed stick and scattering wet sand everywhere. "Castle Dore's on the track between Ireland and the Continent, so there's caravans and boatloads of people coming and going all the time. That was one of the things I was charged with in this marriage . . . making sure that Cornwall continues to be hospitable to Irish traders."

The matter-of-fact way she spoke of trade needs and geography didn't fit my picture of a spoiled darling only interested in pretty clothes. Perhaps she was better equipped to be a working queen than I had thought.

"I often wondered why your family married you off to a man so much older," I said, deciding that if we were going to become friends over the next months, we'd better start with honesty. "Had you no say in the matter?"

"Not much," she admitted, sitting back on her haunches and looking thoughtfully at the rocks rising beyond the surf. "And by the time I found out my mother had tried to salvage some happiness for me, it was too late. Don't ever drink wine from an unmarked flagon," she cautioned ruefully.

"Ah, the love potion," I responded, and Isolde bobbed her head in response.

"Actually, I'm sick of thinking about it." She shrugged and stared at the wheeling birds that filled the air with their cries. "Just look at those black-headed gulls! We have them in Ireland, too, and I used to love to run through the dunes where they nested in the spring, and see them all rise up in a great cloud of flapping wings around me."

I grinned in reply, for many were the times when we were children in Rheged that Kevin and I would do just that. I shared the memory with the Cornish Queen, silently wondering what had happened to the boy I had loved so long, so early in my life. Perhaps we all have our secret loves; it's just that some, like Isolde, are more public about it than others.

"Wasn't the bonfire on the beach wonderful?" Elaine asked the next day, sitting beside Vinnie and carefully pouring out cups of herb tea. "Did you see how elegant Lancelot looked in the firelight? I couldn't keep my eyes off him, really. I always thought bucked teeth were homely before, but his make his mouth look fuller and richer, somehow."

She had developed a serious crush on the Breton, and though the rest of the women teased her about it, she continued to insist that he would someday return her affection.

"You wait and see," her chaperone butted in. "It's just a matter of time until he recognizes their moira."

Not likely, I thought to myself, glancing at Lance, who was playing chess with Tristan. We'd taken a picnic to the grove beside the river, and once the board was set up he'd become immersed in the strategies of the game. He's much too deep for the likes of you, I thought, looking back at Elaine . . . though I had to admit she was attractive in that flashy, pert sort of way.

"Oh, look, Tris—a swing!" Isolde cried. Someone had flung a thick rope over the main branch of an oak, creating a pendulum that swung out over a pool in the river. "Do come here, Lover, and give me a push."

"Not now, Pet," Tristan replied, too engrossed in his game to pay her much mind. "Maybe Palomides will help you."

Palomides was busy trying to get Elaine's kitten down from the tree where it had fled at the first sight of Caesar. The estimable wolfhound was getting old and slow and had shown no interest in the cat at Court, but it was no good trying to explain that to a feline that seemed to take delight in scaring itself.

"Someone call me?" Palomides inquired, returning the kitten to its owner with an elegant bow.

"Take care of Izzy, will you, my friend?" Tris responded, not even looking up from his game.

The Arab turned and gave Isolde such a dazzling smile, I almost choked. There was love and adoration written all over his his face, and his beautiful dark eyes seemed to drink her in, as though he could absorb her very soul through them. I looked away hastily, wondering what sort of spell the Irish girl put on men.

"Is Palomides as smitten by Isolde as I think?" I asked Lance later, when we took Caesar for a walk by the stream. "He looks to be wearing his heart on his sleeve."

"He is, indeed. And hopelessly so. Sometimes I think the Greeks were right about love being sent as a punishment from the Gods. Not only does Isolde ignore him completely, Tristan is his idol. We talked about it last week—the man is very sensitive and the whole thing is terribly hard on him."

"But he could have his choice of many other women," I mused. "They flock around him almost as much as they do around you."

"Ah," answered the Breton, "but what is easy to hand isn't necessarily what you want."

The perversity of human nature made me laugh. "Maybe he just can't resist Isolde's beauty."

"Maybe," Lance agreed. "Some men don't realize that true beauty comes from within."

I glanced at him quickly, wondering if he was really that impervious to women like Isolde and Elaine, and caught him watching me with a secret smile that threatened to burst into a grin no matter how hard he struggled to hide it.

"You don't know, do you?" he asked obliquely, and I shook my head.

"Know what?"

"How beautiful you are."

I stopped dead still, unsure whether he was teasing or not.

"To think, Caesar, that she had no idea how the sun gets tangled in her hair, or that her neck is as white and elegant as a swan's. . . ."

His tone was light and playful as he talked to the dog and the blush that had overtaken me when he first spoke began to fade as I realized he wasn't going to confront me directly.

"Nor does she know how graceful her body is, like a birch tree swaying beside a stream. Even her feet are wonderful, planted firmly on the ground, and altogether I could stare at her for hours and never tire of seeing the moods that move across her soul. Yet it is amazing how oblivious she is to all these things."

"And how determined to remember that we are each of us bound to Arthur, in our different ways," I said firmly, directing my reply to Caesar and patting the top of his head as I spoke. The wolfhound stood between us, delighted to be the center of so much attention.

"Now will you look at her." Lance gently tugged the animal's ear. "You must tell her I would have neither of us do anything that would hurt the King . . . but surely to laugh a little; to catch a moment of beauty and know there is another who sees it, too; to look with trust upon each other as well as Arthur . . . that need not be treacherous or deceitful."

I watched in silence as Lance's hand slid over to mine, and then we were holding hands and staring directly into each other's eyes. "You see, it isn't so terrible, is it?" he said with a grin.

A wild, free laugh welled up inside me like a great cartwheel of joy that wanted to leap forth in singing and dancing. I had no more idea of where it came from than I knew where the crushing weight that lifted from me had gone to . . . it was simply coursing through me in a fine fierce flow of love and living.

"You're right," I acknowledged, lifting my chin and still looking him full in the eyes. "It isn't so terrible."

And so we made the vow—the promise to share without fear this one magical summer while still keeping faith with Arthur.

After that the days became a gathering of rainbow hues and star-filled nights. Never had I seen so many flowers, or whistled so many tunes, or laughed so much for the sheer pleasure of being.

The whole world came alive, lovers and houseguards and ladies-in-waiting all taking part in this season of delight. I couldn't tell if everyone was touched by the enchantment or only seemed so in my eyes, but the result was a time so rich and vibrant, it surpassed even my most splendid dreams.

Racing the horses along the shore, we laugh and jest when Griflet's mount throws him in the surf. Staring into the coals after the flames die down and the embers turn to molten gold, we point out castles and towers, dragons and other shapes from childhood fantasies. Frieda regales us with Saxon folk-tales, while Palomides recalls scraps of stories he remembers from before his parents' death—and we all wonder aloud about what Arabia is like. Both day and night Tris plays his harp, making up music and songs to fit the mood.

And always there is the magic of sharing with Lancelot; humor or triumph or sympathy flowing between us without words, our eyes meeting in silent recognition above the group. Like dancers in a dream, both responding to the same music yet never touching, we skipped and leapt and spun apart through the firmament of gay times; lifting each other with laughter, guiding each other with a smile, turning slowly, soft and tender, into each other's sphere as we drew together in the quiet times.

. . . It was security and freedom at the same time—a flowering of all the things I'd missed for so long, and I luxuriated in the fullness of it.

One misty morning day we went together to meet the shepherds who looked after his flocks, our hair growing spangled by the fog as we trudged through the heather.

We rarely touched, but on that day I slipped when climbing down from a stile and Lance caught me full against his body.

"Steady there," he cautioned as we leapt apart like guilty lovers, laughing awkwardly at the desire that suddenly flared between us.

Neither of us spoke of it, but after that we were careful not to do things alone and always took at least one other person wherever we went.

So it was that Elaine accompanied us to the hermitage. Lance often visited the holy man who had dug out a cave beside the riverbank; this day he was bringing the fellow a portion of oats.

The hermit was out when we arrived, no doubt gathering herbs or communing with his God, but Lance carried the bag of grain into the grotto. When he didn't come back I peered through the doorway to see why.

The cave had been made into a tiny chapel, hardly big enough for more than two people. There was no altar for sacrifice—only a table, simple and unadorned. A bowl of oil held a floating wick and its tiny flame cast soft shadows into the corners.

The air of sanctity was oppressive, as though the clean winds of heaven had never touched the place, and I was surprised to see Lance kneeling before the table, offering a prayer to the Power it represented.

When he rose, his face bore that strange, inward look that had mystified me during my convalescence at the convent. Now, as then, his spirit was engaged in some inner quest, and even though our eyes met when he came out, there was no spark of recognition and sharing. It was clear I had no place in this particular experience. A chill slid over my shoulders, and I followed after him in silence.

"Dreary old place," Elaine averred when we were mounted and riding away. "Can't imagine why you keep coming back here."

Lance made no effort to reply, and Elaine began to natter at him. "You aren't planning on becoming a Christian, are you? My father converted after he was wounded—spends all his time praying for a miracle to heal him. That's all very well for him, but I'm not interested—there's so much a Christian can't do, on pain of sin or something. And I wouldn't want to marry one. . . ."

She cast a lissome glance his way, but the Breton might as well have been deaf for all the attention he paid.

I watched her covertly, amused by her reaction because it could have been my own. She had yet to realize, however, that there was something between Lancelot and his Gods that brooked no interference. It was a part of his nature that would never be accessible to any woman—herself, or me, or any one else.

.   .   .

The strand where the river meets the sea holds a small settlement of fishermen. Shanties of all kinds and shapes cluster there, for the surf washes the doorstep of Saxon and Celt and Pict with equal ease. Yet no matter how scattered their origins, the people fit into this miniature world with a peacefulness and pleasure that touched my heart. It was one of the reasons Lance took to calling his steading Joyous Gard.

Palomides was as fond of the town as Lance and I, and we invited him to come along when we went to buy fish from the men who hauled their little boats up on the shore.

"I just wish he would treat her more kindly," the Arab said as the three of us rode home one afternoon. "It's none of my business, but I hate to see a man take advantage of a woman."

I had not thought of Tristan and Isolde's romance in those terms, and I paused to reconsider the matter.

"Yes, I know they've been blessed—or cursed—by the Gods to love this way . . . but that doesn't mean he has to be a such a boor. I suppose one doesn't have a right to tamper with another person's moira, but they got into another row last night, and I was hard-pressed not to step in. Not," he added humbly, "that she would have thanked me for it . . . fated to love forever, indeed!"

"It's awfully convenient, that love potion, isn't it?" Lance remarked. "I can't really think of an easier way to get around one's own responsibility." He brought the back of his hand to his forehead, feigning distress. "After all, the Gods made us do it."

I burst out laughing, and even Palomides smiled before Lance turned to him, suddenly serious. "What do you know of the Arab Gods?" he asked.

"Not much . . . not much at all," our Middle Eastern friend responded. "In fact, there's a great many things I don't know about my mother-country. I sometimes dream of going there to see what it is like; I might find it more home than Britain, after all."

It was a chance remark, one of thousands in that flower-strewn summer, and it passed without notice or thought. Who could have guessed that within the year we would all be scattered on very different paths, and the summer at Joyous Gard would be only a lovely memory?

THIRTY-ONE

Isolde

hat's it. I've had enough!" The child-bride of Cornwall flung herself into my chambers with the energy of an angry Goddess.

"Just because I've given over everything in the world to be with him doesn't mean I deserve to be treated like a dog. Worse than a dog, even," she added hotly. "At least he speaks to his dogs when he comes in."

I was hard-pressed not to grin; how often had I wished Arthur would look on me with half the tenderness and concern he used to show Cabal.

"What's Tris done this time?" I asked. The lovers' quarrels had gotten louder and more frequent as the summer ripened, and there was no way not to notice them.

Isolde moved around the room restlessly, finally coming to a halt at the open window. "Oh, it doesn't matter." She sighed. "I mean, it isn't just this time. It's the whole situation: his lack of interest now that we're away from Mark . . . my guilt . . . our mutual shame. There are times when loving him so much is what the Christians would call sheer hell."

"Maybe," I ventured, "it isn't whether you love him or not that matters so much as it is what you do about it."

I wasn't sure the Irish girl would brook any criticism, being convinced that her love was destined by the Gods, but to my surprise she turned to me and lifted one eyebrow in query.

"Like you and Lance?"

I flushed furiously, and she laughed. "Come now, you don't think

I could miss the signs of another clandestine love, do you? But I would guess you haven't bedded yet, have you?"

I was so stunned by her directness, I simply shook my head.

Isolde leaned against the window frame and stared pensively out along the river to where the little estuary glimmered between the dunes, and the fishermen's boats bobbed beyond the breakers. Her voice grew dreamy.

"Do you know what it is like, to lie cradled in the arms of a god? All passion spent, and still held close and dear by the man who holds your soul in his hands? I do not know if other women . . . if it is the usual way of things. All I know is that it isn't like that with Mark . . . not like that at all. With my husband it is a duty, a kind of bumping, squirming athletics where I try to be as accommodating as possible to the mound of flesh that huffs and puffs above me, like a walrus scratching off barnacles. And when he's finished, he just rolls off me with a grunt and goes to sleep. I've lain beside him, sleepless, night after night, wondering what is wrong, what I could do to make things better. I've even tried to talk with him about it. . . ." She glanced over at me, searching my face for understanding.

"Did he listen?" I asked hopefully.

"Listen!" Isolde snorted, the fire coming back into her voice. "Listen? Only enough to decide that I was belittling his prowess as a man. Gwen, I tried so hard to be tactful. I even suggested that there was something wrong with me . . . that maybe I wasn't built like other women, because I needed petting and touching and caressing a little. But that only made things worse. Oh, sometimes after that he'd fumble around a bit with my breasts, or even put his hands between my legs, but there was always something so . . . so furtive about it. It was as though he were afraid of being caught, or was placating me, half hoping I wouldn't notice, like some nasty little boy who prays the girl he's rubbing up against won't realize what he's doing."

She shuddered violently and looked down into her lap.

"Perhaps, if Tris and I had not . . . come together . . . if I didn't know what it could be like . . ." Her tone was low and vibrant, and even her averted gaze bespoke a kind of ecstasy. "Sometimes it's fire and fury and a kind of immolation, and sometimes it's gentle and tender and soft as the lapping of a wave on the shore of a lake, but always afterward there is that floating, expanding, indescribable beauty, and we hold each other in an embrace of pure joy. Oh, not the laughing, bantering play, though that's there in the beginning, usually. No . . . this is something else. There is nothing I would not do for him, could not be for him . . . or him for me at those times."

She shook her head and looked back at me, eyes alight with wonder and awe. I caught my breath, sure it was what Lance and I would have were we to bed—and knowing I mustn't even think about it.

"So I put up with his boorish behavior, and become the fishwife myself, screaming at him with no better manners than he shows me. . . . Ah, well," she sighed, "no one promised it would be easy."

Something in her voice brought back the memory of Igraine saying much the same thing. Perhaps it is the very nature of grand romances to be difficult.

That afternoon Lance and I walked slowly down to the grove, each of us quieter than usual.

The late August sunlight shimmered on the water and dappled the ground beneath the trees. The days were growing shorter, and before long we must decide what to do for the fall, for I doubted that Arthur intended to leave us stuck up here so far away from Cadbury through the winter months.

A thrush was singing, clear-throated and rich from the top of a nearby tree, its song the very essence of this summer past.

If only there was some way to capture this peacefulness forever . . . to wear it as a talisman around my neck, to dip into it like an elixir and refresh my soul when times are trying.

"At least we have the memory," Lance said softly.

"And a beautiful one it is, my friend," I replied.

Of a sudden all the beauty of our stay at Joyous Gard welled up within me: companionship and understanding, playfulness and the simple, silent reassurance that had filled every day, graced every night. I'd even known what it was to feel beautiful, here in this enchanted retreat. Tears of gratitude and pleasure filled my eyes, and I turned away hastily, determined to avoid a scene.

"I have yet to try the swing," I announced.

"Well, we'll make up for that right now." Lance grabbed my hand and we ran to the swing where he plopped me in the seat. "Hold on, M'lady," he cried, releasing the guy-rope that kept it tethered to the shore and giving me a push.

And then I was flying, soaring, sailing out over the water, with the wind in my hair and those silly tears drying on my face. A rook in its acrobatics, an eagle in its soaring, even a Goddess in her majesty, were no more free than I was, and I pressed into the wind as though against a lover, letting the overflow of all the summer's emotions sweep out and away on the rushing air.

Slowly the exhilaration faded, the arcs diminished, and I returned, content to be earthbound again. Lance reached out to stop me, settling his hands on my hips and holding both the swing and me safe against him. Defenseless, unguarded, I leaned back against him in sheer trust.

"You are my love . . . you, and no other," he whispered, resting his cheek against my hair. "God knows if I shall ever get another chance to say it, and I want you to hear it at least this once."

My spirit rose up, dancing, light-headed, enthralled. All the years of loving in silence, of never hearing, never really knowing how the other felt—all that uncertainty fled on the instant. Desire and rapture and a great surge of delight coursed through me, and I raised my arms to turn into Lance's embrace, only to run into the ropes of the swing.

Laughing, I left the seat and came around to stand before my love, lifting my heart as well as my arms to his embrace. But he grasped my wrists firmly and put them back down at my sides.

"I will not play the Tristan to your Isolde," he said softly. "The lovers from Cornwall may have their 'love potion,' but we must live with our own consciences."

I stared at him uncertainly, knowing I'd just been rebuffed but not sure why. He led me to a rock where we could sit and look out over the pool as he tried to explain.

"Call it honor, pride, responsibility—whatever term you're most comfortable with. Tris and Isolde have sacrificed every ethic they've ever had in order to live out their love, until they've been corrupted from inside. I'll not let that happen betwixt us, ever."

We sat in silence for a bit while I thought about what he'd said.

"And when we return to Court both of us will be able to look Arthur in the eye," he added slowly. "Gwen, I would give the world to have it otherwise . . . but not my honor."

"Spoken like a true Celt." I sighed, half-relieved, half-furious that now the assurance of love had been won, there was nothing we could do about it.

"Sir Agravain of Orkney," Frieda announced, her guttural voice filling the kitchen.

I turned from the berry cobbler I was making, thinking how preposterous it was to introduce Gawain's brother so formally in this setting. But one look at the handsome Orcadian showed me why Frieda had presented him so; he was scowling at the people in the kitchen with total contempt.

"There must be someplace we can speak in private," he demanded as I wiped the flour off my hands and came forward to greet him.

The youngest of the three close-born sons of Morgause, he was also the most abrasive. Gawain flashed fire and ice while Gaheris sulked amid gray rain clouds, but Agravain was as barbed and stinging as sleet.

We settled at a table in the room next to the garden. The late morning sun was gilding the hips on the rose vine, and I made a mental note to harvest them next week.

"King Mark of Cornwall has announced that he will declare war on Logres unless Arthur can affect a reconciliation between him and Isolde. There isn't much room for negotiation, and the High King wants you to convince the Irish whore to go home."

Agravain's tone and choice of words were unnecessarily harsh, and I was hard put not to show my aversion. Hopefully I could send him quickly back to Arthur. "Does His Highness want an immediate reply?" I asked.

"He's my uncle, too, M'lady . . . not just Gawain's," Agravain noted obliquely, then shrugged. "I guess I can stay around for a few days . . . if the Queen's Champion doesn't mind, that is."

The innuendo wasn't lost on me, but I stared at him with as bland an expression as I could muster. It was one thing to deal with Gawain's explosive nature and quite another to rile Agravain, who, I suspected, had a broad cruel streak.

"Sir Lancelot will no doubt find a place for you," I suggested smoothly. "And I'll take up the matter with the Queen of Cornwall as soon as possible."

I found Isolde seated by the window, sewing. Her face turned ashen and her eyes filled with tears when she heard Mark's threat, and she stared at me in misery, her fingers unconsciously smoothing the seam of the shirt she had been working on for Tristan.

"I knew we would bring trouble to you," she whispered. "I knew we should not have come . . . but Gwen, there is nowhere else we could go. And now . . ."

"Are you willing to consider going back to Mark?" I put the question as gently as possible, but it jolted her nonetheless.

"Willing . . . ?" She drew the word out slowly and was silent for a long minute, the shirt lying forgotten in her lap. At last she turned and looked over the oak grove toward the little river and the heather-clad hills that shield Joyous Gard from the rest of the world. "I don't want to go back," she mused, "but that doesn't mean I won't, if necessary."

"What would make it necessary?" I was trying desperately to remember the political realities and not get tangled in emotions, though my heart went out to her now as it never had before.

Isolde's answer was far more practical than I anticipated.

"If Tris wants it. If his life is in danger if I don't. If we have nowhere safe to go from here. If we'd have to go back to living in huts and hovels with swineherds and such. . . ."

Her voice trailed off, and she shot me a quick look from under those lovely winged brows. "It's hard to forget you were born and raised a Queen when your stomach is empty and you're stiff and cold from sleeping on a dirt floor."

"Have you discussed the possibility of returning to his father's people?" I queried, trying to find a solution.

"They don't want him." She grimaced. "He has no standing there. And besides, the climate is terrible."

The girl should have been a horse trader, given the rapidity with which she assessed and dismissed the options.

She straightened on her cushion and, carefully folding the shirt, spoke her peace with a strong, regal voice.

"I will return to Cornwall on two conditions: that King Arthur must order it, and that he agrees to accept Tristan as his own Champion. . . . Tris must never be left without a country, a king . . . someone to guide him."

"And Dinadan," I added almost automatically.

"Yes, and Dinadan. He doesn't care much for me, or I for him, but he's good at looking out for Tris."

She sighed deeply, as though giving in to something inevitable, then looked up at me with a sudden urgency. "It must be done as soon as possible. I dare not think about it, worry over it, prolong the pain of it, or I won't be able to give him up. Help me, Gwen—help me to break out of it now, before we do more harm, dole out more pain."

There was such anguish in her voice, I reached out to her instinctively, putting my arms around her and promising we would leave for the High King's Court as soon as she was ready.

"This afternoon," she whispered. "I'll be ready in an hour."

"But Tris and Lance are out hunting; they'll probably not be back until dark," I reminded her, and got a wan little smile in return.

"Gwen, if I try to tell him—if I have to face a farewell—I'll never leave at all. Surely you can understand that."

So we agreed to pack immediately, and I left her chambers with infinite sadness. My respect for the child-bride had grown immensely. Weighing the options, protecting her lover, accepting her moira . . . all this within the space of half an hour by a girl barely past the age I was when I had married.

The fact that I knew so clearly what she was giving up made it doubly poignant.

It took some doing, but we were riding away with Agravain by midafternoon and were well beyond the rugged Simonside Hills before the men came home for supper. Isolde said never a word, either that day or the next, but her eyes grew swollen and blotched from crying, and my heart broke for her all over again.

THIRTY-TWO

The Priest

e reached South Cadbury on one of those smoke-smudged days when the stubble of the fields was being burned. A misty gray veil hung over the land and the setting sun was a copper disk.

The tiny village at the base of the fortress's hill was crowded with the tents of craftsmen from all over Logres who'd come to work on Arthur's stronghold—carpenters and smiths, stone workers and plumbers, carvers and painters, all eager to take part in creating the King's new home.

The hill itself rises from the lowlands as suddenly as the Tor at Glastonbury, though Cadbury is more rugged and lacks the lake and marsh that lap the feet of the Tor. During the days of the Empire, when all hill-forts lay deserted, bramble and scrub had grown thick over the banks and ditches. Arthur had removed all trace of tree and vine lest they provide a handhold for attacking Saxons, and now the rock foundations of the fortress towered over the plain in four steep tiers.

I caught my breath as I stared up at it. A wooden parapet had been built atop the rockwork wall, and lookout towers pointed in each direction of the compass. Large double gates, bound with iron and boasting huge hinges, opened on a steep cobbled road that led upward to the broad plateau inside the ramparts.

It was here, on the highest ridge, that Arthur had constructed an amazing Hall. Double-storied, with a peaked roof like that of the Great Hall at Appleby, its walls of newly planked wood shimmered palely in the afternoon light.

Pennants fluttered on the lookout towers, and the Banner of the Red Dragon floated over the roofbeam of the Hall, proclaiming the High King's presence. Craftsmen called back and forth to each other or paused to survey their work before hurrying off for more materials. Altogether it had the life and sparkle of a miniature city spun into reality by the arts of the fey.

I sat tall and proud in the saddle as we drew near. Thanks to Lance I was returning to my husband without a trace of guilt, yet there would be a difference. Never again need I hunger for words Arthur couldn't say. Never again need I think of myself only as that competent but childless Queen. No matter what else the summer at Joyous Gard had brought, I knew I was loved, and even seen as lovely, by a man I admired and loved in return. That knowledge wrapped around me like a charm.

When we reached the gates Agravain called out to the sentry in the tower, announcing that he had the Queens of Britain and Cornwall with him. There was something childishly boastful in his voice, as though he were unused to filling a position of importance. I wondered what his childhood had been like; too young to keep up with Gawain and Gaheris, too old to enjoy playing with Gareth and Mordred, perhaps he had never found a niche of his own in Morgause's family.

Once inside the walls we were surrounded by a fever of activity. Workers and soldiers were laying out drainage ditches while over at what I took to be the stables a cadre of men were hoisting the roofbeam into place. And all of it to be part of our new home.

I stared about me, thrilled and impressed.

"Almost ready for its Queen," said a familiar voice, and there was Arthur standing in front of my mare. Featherfoot nickered and brought her nose down to be patted as he grinned up at me. He was wearing the leather apron of a laborer and was hot and sweaty from working with the builders, but the pride of accomplishment and welcome in his voice was unmistakable.

Staring down at him, I felt the summer past slip suddenly away. I fairly leapt off my horse and then Arthur was lifting me in one of those high, wild embraces he does so well.

A cluster of workmen cheered and clapped approvingly, and when we'd shared a long, full kiss I threw back my head and, looking up at him, announced firmly, "Now that is more like a welcome home."

For a moment I thought he was going to drop me, he laughed so hard.

Once Isolde was settled, Arthur and I sat down to exchange news.

"Tristan didn't know she was going to leave," I explained. "I wrote Lance a note, asking him to detain Tris at Warkworth until Isolde reaches Cornwall—with all the rest of the women to move as well, it will take them some time just to get started. What have you heard from Mark?"

Arthur frowned. "Nothing so far, but he should be satisfied now that his wife is returning. How did you get her to agree so readily?"

"I think," I answered carefully, "she's simply had enough of grand romance. . . . She and Tris paid a very dear price for their love." I paused, not wanting to discuss the subject. "Now tell me, what's been happening at Court?"

"Everyone here's been working on the buildings. Between Bedivere's engineering and Cei's ability to find materials, we've made wonderful progress. Elsewhere, the Saxons are quiet. Sir Ector reports that Cynric is settling in well—says he's a bright lad who seems to have accepted the loss of his father's cause. Only time will tell if he's willing to accept me as his overlord, so we'll wait and see. Haven't heard anything about Pelleas—or Gawain, for that matter. Mostly," Arthur concluded, coming to stand in front of me, "I've spent the summer missing you."

It was such a surprising admission, I threw my arms around him in a hug, and then we were kissing and stroking and groping for the bed, everyone and everything else forgotten.

I woke next morning to the cheerful whistling of a carpenter hammering away in the next room and, squinting in the sunshine, was surprised to find Arthur still abed.

"I think waking up with you is what I missed most," he said casually, grinning down at me. It was the kind of comment he never used to make and I wondered if I should go away more often. Whatever accounted for my husband's change of habit, I was delighted.

By comparison, the mood of the Cornish Queen verged on despair. I found Isolde lying on her bed, staring silently at the ceiling. "Yes,

yes—I know I must make plans," she acknowledged. "And I won't be going back on my word. . . . It's home to Mark I go, and that's all there is to that. But not yet, Gwen . . . I'm not ready yet."

I was loath to press her further—who knew what memories and sorrows she was grappling with. I just hoped a few days' rest would revive her spirits.

Later, when Arthur took me to see the new kennels, memories of my own rose to haunt me. Coming through the doorway, I ran right into Maelgwn's hound from the Otherworld. He raised his head and stared directly at me, as he had in the hunting lodge, eyes glowing red, throat full of growls.

"What's he doing here?" I cried, clutching my husband's arm in panic and turning away from the brute.

"He's well chained, Gwen—can't possibly hurt you. Giving over Dormarth was part of Maelgwn's reparation. I've always wanted to breed up a strain of black dogs, you know. . . ."

I began to shake uncontrollably, a cold sweat covering my skin. Quite apart from the fact that it seemed a small payment for the grief my cousin had caused, I simply could not face the idea of living with that constant reminder under my roof.

"Please, Arthur—I haven't asked for many things over the years," I begged, still shaking. "Please get rid of him. I don't care how, just make him go away."

Arthur stared at me, confusion and surprise in both his voice and face. "I had no idea it would upset you so. . . ." From the way his voice trailed off I knew he hoped I'd change my mind, but the very presence of the creature made my stomach turn, and I held firm.

Fortunately Gwyn of Neath, who had indeed built a small Hall of his own on Glastonbury's Tor, arrived that evening to welcome me home, and Arthur gave the devil-hound to him. The gnarled little man was immensely pleased and promised to breed the dogs for Arthur but not bring them here, so everyone was satisfied.

Isolde's problem was not so easily remedied, however—she continued to lie on her bed without tears or words, as though uncaring about either life or death. While I conferred with the builders about small additions and amendments to the kitchen—including a dovecote like the one at York—I tried to think how to encourage the Cornish Queen to continue her journey. Castle Dore was only a few days away, and I didn't want Mark to come haul her home when she'd already made the trip this far. Besides, there was no telling how long Lance could keep Tris in the north.

I was debating the matter as I carried out a rack of fresh bread to cool. For a moment I paused to stare down the cobbled roadway, still marveling at the citadel the workers were constructing.

A swarm of people had gathered around a traveler who was making his way up the hill, and as they came nearer I cried out in surprise.

"Lance, what are you doing here?" I couldn't imagine why he was on foot, and there was no sign of Tristan.

He glanced up at the sound of my voice and I called out again so he could see where I was. As the little crowd opened to let him through, I realized he was wearing the habit and cross of a Christian priest. My heart began to pound, and I shook my head in disbelief. Mouth open, eyes all but popping out of my head, I stood there like a ninny, gaping at the man who limped toward me.

"Your Highness." His blue eyes twinkled as he made a formal bow. "Allow me."

He took hold of the rack just as I was turning to put it down, and for a moment we engaged in a little tug-of-war.

"Oh, Kevin, is it really you?" I exclaimed, finally finding my voice as Beaumains rushed to relieve us of the loaves.

"Aye, 'tis me in the flesh, my dear, and more than glad to have found you!"

The people watched in astonishment as we hugged and cried and laughed like moonstruck children until I explained that Kevin was the closest thing I had to a brother, who had been lost and long thought dead.

"But I never believed it," I rejoiced once we were seated in a quiet spot under the loft that runs around all four sides of the Hall. "You know I made Rhufon send Ailbe after you, don't you?"

"Ah, so that's how the wolfhound came to join me." Kevin smiled. "I did wonder about that."

"He was moping so badly, we thought he'd die," I explained, remembering that no one could get the great dog to eat once his master was gone. "But everyone said you'd be eaten by wolves or bears, or worse yet, captured by outlaws and sold as a slave. I was counting on Ailbe to keep you alive."

Kevin inclined his head, his tone light but his words serious. "Then I owe you my life, for I did come close to starving, and the weather was bitter that year. . . . Without Ailbe for help in hunting and warmth in sleeping, I might well have died."

There was a pause while I struggled not to blurt out the question that had haunted me for so long: Had you loved me, Kevin? Did you run away because you couldn't stand to see the emissaries of kings come courting? Or was it only my own childish dream that kept me waiting for you, clinging to the belief that one day you'd return right up to the point when I married Arthur? Now that he'd come back, even belatedly, I needed to know the truth of it.

"Why . . . why did you leave?"

The priest stared off into space, searching for some inner truth with the same strange intensity I'd seen in Lance. At last he cleared his throat, but he spoke without meeting my gaze.

"Father Bridei would say it's because I had not yet found my calling. Remember the Pictish priest we met at Loch Milton—the hardy little man with tattoos all over and the love of God in his eyes? It was he who found me lying sick and feverish in the summer house that's perched on the edge of the waterfall's chasm. If he hadn't happened by, I would have perished, but he took me to the monastery at Whithorn, where I grew whole and healthy again."

Kevin finally met my gaze and smiled. His voice and manner were much as I'd remembered, but I was sure it was no accident that he wasn't answering my question directly. Maybe it was because he hadn't felt all those emotions I'd ascribed to him—maybe that had only been a reflection of my own feelings. Maybe, in truth, all we can ever know of loving is our own part in it—all the rest must be taken on faith and trust.

It was an idea that made me distinctly uncomfortable, and my mind veered away from it. "You weren't Christian back then, were you?"

"Umhuh. Took me a while to admit to His Grace. I hear that Brigit is in a convent now?"

"Aye, up in the Welsh Marches." It struck me odd that so many of the people I loved were involved with the White Christ: Brigit and Igraine, Vinnie, and now Kevin.

"Good heavens, Lance, when did you get in?" Arthur called, hastening across the Hall, then slowing abruptly when he realized his mistake.

"It's Kevin, whom I've told you so much about," I explained, and my husband stepped forward with a grin of welcome.

"We'd be pleased to have you stay over," he announced.

Kevin accepted gladly, and by the time we had all shared the evening meal it felt as natural to have him there as if he had never been lost.

But for all that I was excited to have him returned and Arthur was gracious to him as a host, it was Isolde who truly responded to the priest's presence.

I told her about his arrival the first evening, and the next morning she asked shyly if he would hear her confession. He spent much of the day with her, and by nightfall she joined us for dinner.

Two days later Isolde left for Castle Dore, after Kevin blessed her and the warriors who would escort her home. I gave the young Queen a hug, and we waved her on her way, hoping that the most harrowing part of her loving—and leaving—Tristan was finally over.

"Whatever did you say to her?" I asked, never thinking it was an invasion of privacy.

The priest gave me a reproving look, then grinned. "I reminded her of the litany of Celtic Queens, just as I used to remind you."

I laughed, hearing in memory the many times he'd coaxed me through something I didn't think I could face, didn't want to do, wasn't sure I could—"What kind of Celtic Queen says, 'I can't'? Of course you can!" If anyone could give Isolde the necessary courage to do what had to be done, it was Kevin.

As the days shortened, the new larders filled with apples and cabbages, turnips and salt beef; smoked hams and haunches of venison were hung from the rafters; even a fair supply of salted butter was put aside to see us through 'til spring.

Lance and Tris arrived in time for Samhain, and Kevin agreed to winter over with us on the condition that he be allowed to say Mass regularly for those who were Christians in our Court. Many, both Christian and Pagan, grew very fond of him, but Tris was not among them, for he held the Irish priest responsible for Isolde's leaving.

"I don't care whose wife she is, the holy man had no right to steal her away from me," Tris complained, distorting the facts entirely. He glared around the Hall, drunk enough not to care what he said, still sober enough to best any man who challenged him.

Lance, who was the only one Tris would listen to these days, talked him into taking up the harp, and he serenaded us with wonderful music until the wine got the best of him. Laying his instrument aside, Tristan sobbed himself to sleep with his head pillowed on his arms on the table.

It was a scene that was repeated more and more often as Tris wallowed in self-pity, holding everyone but himself accountable for his misery. Then one night he went too far, turning his anger against Isolde, claiming she had played him false, led him on, deluded him with dreams of love when at heart she was a faithless bitch.

Palomides rose to his feet and stalking purposefully across the Hall, stopped in front of the Harper. "How dare *you* besmirch her reputation," he spat out contemptuously. "Everything she did was what you wanted. So take back that slander or meet me in single combat tomorrow morning."

"Why wait for morning?" Tris snarled. "I can whip any man in the Hall right now, yourself included."

Palomides lifted his chin and stared disdainfully at Isolde's lover. "I am a man of honor and do not fight people who are drunk," he announced. "Tomorrow, at dawn."

"There will be no feuds within the Round Table," Arthur bellowed, intent on stopping a senseless letting of blood. "Tristan, it's time for you to let go of this passion of yours and get on with your life."

"You don't understand," cried the big Champion, turning furiously in a circle as though to dare all comers. "She is mine, forever. My life and my death. Fated we are, and no one, not priest or Cornish King or Arab, shall come between us."

He pounded his fist on the table, sending a clatter of plates and glasses to the floor, then whipped around and launched himself on Palomides like a whirlwind.

A gasp ran through the Hall, for Tris was the best wrestler in the realm. The Arab crouched to defend himself, and as Tris leapt at him, the smaller man twisted away.

Palomides fought only to restrain Tristan without hurting him, though they both came up with massive bruises in the end. But in spite of his drunkenness Tris was the victor, pinning the Arab to the floor and hooting his triumph before passing out.

Lance and Dinadan carried him to his bunk while the rest of the men gathered around Palomides, praising him for his courtesy and grumbling about the Cornishman's unruly behavior.

Next day Arthur asked Bedivere to take Tristan to Brittany when he went to serve as an emissary to King Ban's Court. "Surely Tris can make a place for himself with one of the local Princes," Arthur added. "With any luck, he'll start a new life there as well."

After that we settled into a winter dazzling in patterns of gold and white, *full of love and laughter and so much hard work. Riding through the frosty days with Lance, laughing and playing and glorying in the fullness of life while candlelight pours through the doors of the Hall and we dance with the people on nights of festival and merriment... working with Arthur every day, snuggling together at night beneath the comforter while the stars glitter like flashing ice in the night sky above Somerset. And every morning the two men make the rounds of the fortress, checking with the sentries, discussing the plans for the day, deciding what is to be done.*

Often I'd watch them tramping across the courtyard, matching stride for stride in the pristine whiteness of a new snowfall. Heads bent in conversation, oblivious to all else, they work together to guard and shape our world. Arthur was well filled out now, ruddy and solid and full of direct energy, while the lean, dark shape of Lancelot moved with sinuous grace beside him; they made me think of good sturdy wool and glimmering sealskin.

I could not imagine not loving them both.

We put our energies not just into the development of the citadel, but on the Cause as well. It was that winter we found the solution to making the Roads safe again.

"Everyone needs salt," I said one blustery day as we sat at the long table with maps and charts, records and tables spread before us.

"There're so few places making it, compared with the inland settlements that need it. And transporting it is so dangerous. . . ."

Lance looked up from a scroll that contained a Roman tax collector's report. "The Empire taxed the salt wagons, and used that money to keep the Roads clear. If only we had coins, we could do the same. . . ."

I was wondering how hard it would be to establish a mint when Arthur spoke up.

"We could barter for the service—offer to make sure the salt gets to those towns and war-lords who keep the Roads safe and free of obstacles. What do you think?"

"I think it's a capital idea," Lance concurred. "And everyone would benefit—travelers and merchants, and the royal messengers as well."

We all rushed to look at the map, tracing the routes the tax rolls had shown and debating which client kings would be cooperative, which resistant. In the end the system worked well and was one of the best ideas we ever had.

With the first hint of spring Frieda decided, at long last, to become a Christian and marry Griflet, and they asked Kevin to perform the ceremony. Much to everyone's surprise her mother and sisters came for the wedding, which led to great rejoicing. There was pain as well, however, for Frieda's father disowned her entirely. It was an act that hurt the both of them deeply, for she had been his favorite child.

Palomides was as courteous as ever at the festivities, yet there was an air of sad withdrawal around the man. Later he confided to Lance that while he wished the newlyweds every happiness, their joy only made his own loneliness harder to bear. "It seems," the Breton added, "he still grieves over his hopeless love for Isolde."

As the bluebells bloomed beneath the beeches and the cuckoo filled the night with longing, the Arab grew more and more restless. So I was not terribly surprised when he asked permission to leave Court.

"The Irish priest and I have been talking a lot lately," Palomides explained. "And I've decided I'd like to go to Arabia . . . to find out what it's really like, and if I have any kin there. Besides, I've always had an itch to see new places—the remnants of Rome, the city of Constantine . . ."

Arthur's consternation at the notion of losing one of his best Companions showed clearly on his face, but he was never one to hinder the fulfillment of another's moira. "I've heard some interesting things about the Byzantine laws—things that might be useful here. Perhaps while you are in the East you could look into them for me?" he asked.

Palomides agreed readily and began preparing to go to Exeter where he hoped to catch a ship for the Mediterranean. We provided him a letter of introduction to various Kings across the Continent and a special note for the Emperor Anastasius.

The day before the Arab was to leave, Kevin came to see me, asking if we could have a private chat.

"Let's take the horses out," I proposed, remembering how often we'd raced and ridden over the fells of Rheged.

We headed along the track that leads to Glastonbury. Featherfoot was growing old but was still strong and ready for a run, and it was only after a pounding gallop through the forest rides that the animals settled into a casual walk.

When we reached the edge of Gwyn's pastures, we paused to admire the mares that were grazing in the meadow. The man from Neath had ponies as well as large horses, and for a few minutes Kevin and I compared notes on the animals.

"I think I'll join Palomides on the trip to Devon," Kevin announced casually as we turned for home. "I'd like to visit Castle Dore and see how Mark and Isolde are getting on."

It had taken a while to get used to seeing my childhood love in the garb of a holy man, governed by spiritual tenets that set him apart from the flow of everyday dreams and desires. Yet once I accepted the change in him, it seemed so natural to have him at Court, I assumed he would remain with us indefinitely. The idea of his leaving jolted me from my complacency.

"How strange it will be," I mused, "with Tristan and Bedivere, Pelleas and Gawain—now even you and Palomides—all off somewhere else."

"And Lancelot, too, I think," Kevin allowed.

Shocked, I turned to stare at him. He was watching me intently, and I blushed and looked away hastily.

"You don't think I could have missed the fact that he's in love with you, do you?" Kevin asked. When I couldn't find the words to answer, he went on gently. "The Breton and I have spent a fair amount of time together, discussing many things. He's badly torn between his love for you and his love for Arthur, so I advised him to leave your side and go in search of the Almighty."

"You did *what?*" My voice found itself with a vengeance, and I rounded on Kevin with a surge of emotion in which anger and disbelief rode high. "How dare you interfere with my life this way? You, who ran away when all our future lay before us; you, who left me to be married off in a political union whether I chose it or not; you, who now spouts pious oaths and lectures on duty and have no more idea what it's like to carry the mantle of royal responsibility than Elaine's cat does! What right have you to advise Lancelot to leave me?"

"The right of a man who knows how futile it is to love a woman who is destined for another," he shot back, his eyes never leaving mine. "The right of a man who understands his brother's pain. For God's sake, Gwen, you don't think Lance can come to you and pour out his misery at watching you sit daily next to Arthur, move nightly to your chambers together, rise every morning refreshed and renewed, together? He can't tell you how much he longs for you, needs you, worships you. And he certainly can't tell your husband."

He paused, and I lowered my eyes, no longer defiant. I had never considered how Lance must view those things, and the recognition that it could be so painful for him pulled me up short.

"I . . . I didn't realize," I whispered.

"I thought not." Kevin heaved a sigh. "I'm not sure he will go on a spiritual quest, but I've suggested he think about it. He's a man who needs a cause to believe in. . . . Arthur has Britain, you have Arthur, but Lance needs something of his own. Surely you would not deny him that. Not if you love him . . . and you do, don't you?"

I looked up slowly, remembering how close Kevin and I had been when we were young, and suddenly the whole story came tumbling out. "But I don't see that there has to be a conflict," I concluded. "I simply love them both in different ways . . . they are, after all, very different people."

"I don't suppose it would do any good to counsel you to put aside your love for him, would it?" Kevin asked, as though not even hearing my last words.

"No, it wouldn't," I flared. "As long as we are discreet in our behavior and don't hurt Arthur, there's no reason why we should deny our feelings."

"You know better than that, Gwen . . . that kind of reasoning sounds like Isolde."

His tone was firm and unbending, and I turned to glare at him, sorry I had taken him into my confidence. He hadn't understood after all.

But instead of Kevin, it was Lance I saw. He sat his horse in silence, a prim, proper, Christianized shadow of the man I loved. The sparkle of humor, the touch of tenderness, the joyful sharing I had grown so used to, were gone, replaced by a righteous rigidity, as stifling as the sanctity within the hermit's cave.

It made me ache to see the free-spirited Celt so leeched of life, and I wheeled my mare around in blind terror. Leaning forward on Feather-foot's neck, I screamed in her ear and lashed her shoulders with the reins. She leapt forward like a yearling, neck extended and nostrils wide, and I clung to her for dear life as she carried me through the forest shadows.

So I went flying back to Cadbury, trying to leave that sad, dried, empty shell of a vision behind. But Igraine had been right—no one can outrun the Gods.

THIRTY-THREE

Camelot

ance didn't say anything about leaving that week or the next one, either, but by early May the strain on him was evident. I could not look up but what his gaze was on me, and sometimes, having caught each other's glances, it was impossible for either of us to look away. Within me a tension of desire began to build, and there were times when I turned to Arthur in furious lovemaking although it was Lance I longed for. Typically, Arthur didn't seem to notice either my passion or my distraction.

But if Arthur didn't notice, Elaine of Carbonek did. Ever since we had included her in our activities at Joyous Gard she assumed the right to join us anywhere we went, and if she wasn't watching Lance, she was watching me. It was particularly irritating because I wanted to talk with the Breton alone but dared not call attention to that fact by driving her away.

"Lancelot, I swear you're not listening," Elaine pouted one afternoon as we rode back from judging a cattle show.

"Sorry," he murmured, turning to the pert redhead on the other side of him. "What were you saying?"

"It's about Tiger Fang. She's been lost for three days, and I'm worried about her. Won't you help me look for her when we get home?"

"Can't do it this afternoon," he responded. "I have sword practice with Beaumains. Maybe this evening, if she's still missing. The kitchen boy is an apt pupil," he noted, turning back to me. "He has a natural talent for the sword, and it's a pleasure to be his teacher. Whoever his father is, he can be proud of the lad."

"Ohhh, I feel so faint," the girl from Carbonek moaned, lowering her eyelids and swaying in her saddle. "I'm afraid I'm going to fall. . . ."

I looked away in exasperation as Lance turned his attention back to her. He dismounted to help her off her horse, and Elaine went limp in his arms. He paused for a moment, adjusting the girl's weight as though to sling her her over his shoulder like a bag of grain, then gave me a mischievous grin.

"She can ride in front of you, can't she?" he asked, and when I grinned in response he prepared to hoist her over Featherfoot's withers.

Recovering abruptly, Elaine protested that there was no need to inconvenience me this way, but Lance and I insisted it was not safe for her to ride without someone to balance her, in case she actually did lose consciousness.

So we rode into Cadbury with my arms around her instead of his. But even though she sat upright before me, when Lance helped her dismount she whimpered about being unable to walk, and he was forced to carry her into the Hall. A pang of jealousy cut through me at the sight of the young beauty held firmly in his arms, and I turned away, blinking back unexpected tears.

Featherfoot was favoring one foreleg slightly, so I led her to the stables and stayed to fix a poultice for her leg. All the pain and vexation I felt toward Elaine came out as I pounded the herbs in the mortar, and I was so intent on what I was doing, I didn't realize Lance had entered the stable until he was stood next to me.

"Surely the little baggage isn't worth that much fury?" He grinned good-naturedly.

"That's for you to say, not me," I muttered, ducking my head away lest he see my anguish.

"Oh, my love, don't tell me you're jealous?" Suddenly Lance's arms were around me, and I crumpled against him with a sob. "She's only a chit of a thing—a child. What interest would I have in her when I'm the Queen's own Champion and privileged to love the finest woman in the realm?"

"But she's so pretty . . . and free to give herself to you," I gulped.

"Listen to me, Gwen," he demanded, his voice turning deep and serious. "I don't want her. I don't want anyone but you. I do not know how to tell you more plainly. . . ." His hands were moving along my back, caressing my sides, coming to rest on my hips. The desire so long held in check flared up between us, and we trembled in its fierceness.

Surrounded and sheltered by his body, reeling from the nearness, the warmth, the very smell of him, I lifted my face slowly and deliberately into the waiting kiss.

The world spun around us, full of the fragrance of fresh hay and springtime, love and fulfillment. Featherfoot nickered in her stall, but I barely noticed, for there was a pulse beating between Lance and me that was deep and sweet and gathered all my senses into that one focus. Never would I have thought a single kiss could say so much.

"It is good-bye, as well," he said slowly, pulling away at last. "I cannot stay here any longer, M'lady. I'll tell Arthur I want to take Beaumains and go up to Joyous Gard—maybe check on the Caledonians at Loch Lomond . . . anything, really, to leave this temptation behind." He held my head between his hands and stared into my eyes. "You do understand, don't you?"

A terrible ache lodged in my throat, blocking a torrent of protest. I shook my head frantically from side to side and drew back from him. He might be free to leave as I was not, but I would make him spell it out, each and every reason, before he upped and trotted off.

Yet his expression was so baffled, so hurt and sorrowing, I could not bear to make it worse, and with a sigh I gave a faint nod. "Go with my love, and blessing," I whispered, closing my eyes in resignation. "And know you take my heart with you."

We were no longer touching, but I felt him plant the softest of kisses on the top of my head, and then he was gone, as silently as he had come.

Numbly I knelt in the straw, trying to apply the herbs to Featherfoot's pastern. She swung her head around and blew against my hair with a warm, sweet breath of concern, and when I finished applying the poultice I stood up and threw my arms around her neck, bawling like child.

At last, worn out and drained of all emotion, I sank down on a pile of hay and stared across the barn toward the door. No doubt they would be gathering in the Hall already, and I wasn't even dressed yet. Ah, well, this night I'd let Enid make my excuses and take my meal in my chambers.

I was trying to find the energy to rise when Tiger Fang slipped through the crack of the open door. She disappeared behind a manger, and as I squinted into the shadows I heard a small, weak chorus of meowing kits.

It made me smile in spite of my grief, and I went out to face the world thinking that we all grow up eventually—even Elaine's motley little cat.

If last year's summer was a time of love and romance, this year's season was full of domesticity. Arthur concentrated on finishing the men's quarters and forge while I began sorting through the debris of the temple that the Romans had built on Cadbury's heights.

"There's plenty of good tiles," Cei pointed out. "We used the building blocks in other places, but some of the smaller things might come in handy in the garden."

The new Hall was growing into a splendid place. My women worked constantly at loom and needle, making cushions and bolsters, pennants and draperies, to grace the raw interior and give it a softer, lived-in look.

I moved between the two worlds, helping to run the realm as always but overseeing the furnishing of the Court as well. Yet time dragged endlessly; each day I found myself looking at the sun, wondering where Lance was, when he might be heading back, if the night would ever come. There was an emptiness, a hollow in my very soul, that nothing seemed to fill. Arthur was too busy to notice, and I had no way to express it, so in the end it too became part of that sea of silence that separated us.

Geraint arrived with his usual panache on midsummer's eve, sending a flurry of speculation through the ladies, who rushed to the courtyard to see his colorful entourage. Arthur greeted the King of Devon with such gusto, it occurred to me that with so many Companions elsewhere, my husband might be feeling lonely, too.

"My, but it's a remarkable stronghold you're building here." Geraint nodded appreciatively after making the rounds of the hill-fort. "Have you a name for it?"

"The village down below is known as South Cadbury," Arthur allowed. "Any better suggestions?"

"There was a place in a story I heard last time I was in Brittany." The elegant southerner stroked his mustache and thought for a minute. "It was a special land, full of magic and wonders and the finest heroes. Camelot, I think it was called." Geraint closed his eyes and savored the sound of it, then nodded. "Yes, that was it, Camelot. I say, Cei, what is that you've found?" he asked as the Seneschal marched proudly forward displaying a glass decanter and four matching goblets.

The wine turned out to satisfy the discerning palate of both Cei and Geraint, so we all toasted the new name of our headquarters. I drank my first glass slowly and switched to water immediately thereafter.

During dinner we caught up with much news, for Geraint had been traveling extensively. Everything was quiet along the Saxon Shore, and life at Castle Dore had gone back to normal now that the Queen was home. The only sad news was that Pelleas was not tending his lands but languished in bed, beset by nightmares and fevers. It seemed a wretched fate for the skinny horseman, and I wished we could do something for him.

"I've been on a special quest," Geraint suddenly confided with a devilish smile. "Looking for a Queen. And after ruling out a number of other ladies, I've come to ask Enid to marry me."

"You've what?" I sputtered, putting down my water glass.

"Now, Your Highness, I have excellent credentials," the bachelor announced glibly. "But I wouldn't think of stealing your best cook without your permission."

He was so blasé about the matter, I laughed in spite of my surprise. Of all the women Geraint might have chosen, Enid was the last I would have picked.

"And what does my lady-in-waiting have to say about this?" I inquired, wondering how such a romance could have gone on under my nose without my noticing.

"Let's ask her." Geraint grinned broadly as I called Enid from the kitchen, where she was overseeing the food for the evening.

The dark-haired young woman arrived with her apron in hand, frowning slightly at being singled out this way. "Is something the matter, Your Highness?" she asked quickly.

"I don't know. It seems this gentleman wants to steal you away from me. . . . What say you to that?"

A mischievous smile flashed over Enid's features, and she turned to look the King of Devon eye to eye. "Have you improved that kitchen in Exeter? Last time I was there the oven was cracked and the well was too far away."

"Indeed, M'lady." Geraint sighed. "The masons have built an entirely new oven, and we've piped in water from the aqueduct and paved the kitchen court besides. Now will you accept my offer?"

I was staring at the two of them, watching the playful teasing of lovers—and suddenly feeling middle-aged and stodgy.

"And a cow. Wouldn't consider a husband who doesn't give me a cow," the girl bargained.

"Three cows; white with red ears, even . . . provided, of course, you bring your recipe for clotted cream."

"Done," she announced, throwing aside her apron and rushing into his arms.

"You drive a hard bargain, miss," he allowed, tousling her hair and planting a kiss on the tip of her pointed nose.

"You'll find me worth it," she promised, spinning out of his arms and grabbing up her apron before heading back to the kitchen.

So much, I decided, for trying to guess the moira of lovers.

Ettard also came to Camelot that summer, looking dreadful. She'd developed a racking cough and roughed her cheeks in an effort to hide their pallor. The lodge Igraine gave her had contained a small chest of jewels, and she was decked out as though going to a grand occasion. The sight of her made me think of some macabre corpse.

"I just came back from visiting Pelleas," she explained, shaking her head woefully. "I had heard that he was very ill, and wanted to make amends. . . ." The childish voice trailed off uncertainly while her fingers moved from bracelet to necklace, ring to brooch, as though taking some silent inventory. "He refused to see me, but sent me away with a curse on my head. Oh, M'lady, I know I treated him poorly, but I used to be so scared that unless I married a big, powerful warrior the Saxons might . . . might could come again and . . ."

A violent coughing fit overtook her, and I found myself remembering my own fears. Perhaps the hidden scars of rape reach more deeply than even those of us who have gone through it know.

"As it was, I never even got a chance to tell him I was sorry," she whispered.

I hadn't the slightest idea what to say to the girl, for though I might understand why she had behaved so abominably, it didn't make me like her. Only her terrible condition and Nimue's prophecy of an early death kept me from sending her packing from Camelot.

"Has Gawain come back to Court yet?" she asked casually, all the time twisting one of the rings on her fingers.

"No," I answered. "Nor do I expect him . . . at least, not for some time." If she was hoping for a further encounter with Morgause's son, I intended to head her off immediately.

Whether it was the news that Gawain was not available or her own mortal timetable that drove Ettard away, I never learned. She departed for her own lands the following morning, riding proudly in the litter I had given her. Brittle and superior, she went to her death two months later, flaunting the wealth the Queen Mother had left her. It seemed a pitiful end, even if she did bring it on herself.

The summer began to wane, and the time of harvest arrived. Everyone worked that year, in the fields, at the barns, in the spinning loft and kitchens. I saw the leaves turn to gold and realized with a start that it was a year since Isolde had ridden off to Cornwall; a year since Kevin had come back; a year since Lance had told me that he loved me. Time, which dragged on its belly day to day, flew without a backward glance from year to year.

Gawain returned from the Orkneys, cheerful and glad to be back with us. The difficulties with his mother seemed to have been resolved.

"She's mellowed a good bit with age, though she's still a lively lady in most respects." He cocked a knowing eyebrow and grinned. "She specifically sends her greetings to you, and says she hopes to meet you one of these days."

Unfortunately I saw no danger in her message at the time.

Bedivere came back from Brittany, full of news and chatter and a whole new supply of songs and riddles as well.

"You can keep us entertained on the way to the fair," Arthur allowed. "I'm holding Court and a tournament at Winchester next week to celebrate three years of peace."

Bedivere allowed that a harvest big enough to have extra for bartering at a fair was a sure sign of prosperity. "Sounds as though you've secured the south," the lieutenant said, beaming.

"Let's hope the whole of Britain," Arthur amended.

I was looking forward to the fair—it was ages since we'd put aside royal duties and danced in the meadows with our people. Besides, this would be my first visit to Winchester, and memories of Igraine's story came often to mind. I took her golden torque from my jewel box, admiring once more the little pop-eyed animals at the ends of the twisted rope of gold. Each time I put it on I wondered about the many moments in the lives of royalty they had seen or heard—Ulfin had said she'd been wearing it the night of the feast, when Uther first began their courtship.

During the summer I'd made a concerted effort to overcome my aversion to Shadow—it was one thing to ask Arthur to get rid of Dormarth and quite another to let the handsome white mare go unridden because I refused to face down my fear. Arthur had bred her to one of Gwyn's Welsh Mountain ponies, and the resulting foal was a fine chestnut filly with flaxen mane and tail. I had named the youngster Etain and turned my attention to the dam as soon as the little one was weaned.

By the time our entourage was ready to leave for Winchester, I was astride Shadow once again. Pennants fluttered in the morning breeze, bells on bridles jingled, and the brass rondels on the Companions' halters gleamed in the sunlight. It promised to be a lovely outing. And to add the final touch, Lancelot rode into the courtyard just as we were leaving.

"What wonderful timing," Arthur called, hailing the Breton with good cheer. "Your horse fresh enough to carry you on to Winchester?"

Lance reined in before us, gave me a formal nod, then turned his attention to the High King. "I can't stay long—sent Beaumains on to Joyous Gard already. But I had an encounter with Morgan and thought I'd best come back to warn you."

"Does it require a military response?" Arthur's smile had faded at the sound of his sister's name, but when Lancelot shook his head my husband began to grin again. "Then let's be off to Winchester. You can tell us about it on the way to the fair—surely you've time enough for that. If you want to leave from there, you can head directly for London and pick up Ermine Street."

Arthur swung aside his stallion, insisting that the Breton ride in the middle. Clearly uncomfortable with the situation, Lance cast me a helpless look but took his place between us.

"It seems," he began once we were through the gate, "that the Lady still has designs on the High Throne of Britain. I would have thought that the experience of losing Accolon would have tempered her desires, but she's convinced herself that her lover betrayed her by being faint-hearted. The whole thing has only served to make her more determined."

He went on to describe his visit to the Sanctuary. Listening to him, I shivered as though the cold, dark water of the Black Lake itself were pouring over me.

"Morgan is twisting the Old Ways into something bitter and narrow—she's become a fanatic on the subject of the Goddess. There's no more recognition given to the Mabon or Cernunnos, or even the Green Man of old. She's proclaimed a new kind of Paganism, based on the most ancient of wisdoms, and it centers entirely on the female principle."

I shook my head in disbelief that the power of the Great Gods should now be perverted into such a shallow concept.

"She lives in virtual isolation, the Academy having collapsed," Lance went on. "Half the old families have converted to the teachings of the Irish saints, the rest are put off by Morgan's stridency. It would be pitiful, if it were not so dangerous."

"Dangerous?" Arthur questioned.

"Morgan has nothing else to concentrate on now. When I first arrived she was both surprised and gracious. We dined and chatted amiably enough—she was particularly anxious to hear about you, though later I realized she never once asked about Uwain."

I thought of the boy Arthur had banished so summarily and wondered what had happened to him.

"Anyhow," Lance resumed, "as the evening progressed Morgan

began spinning out dreams and hopes for the future of a unified Britain, much as we do here. But there is one major difference; she wants to see a monarchy powerful enough to dictate that all people worship her Goddess. *All people,*" Lance added emphatically. "Pict and Scot, Roman and Cumbri, the Ancient Ones and the new Germanic immigrants . . . all people must be made to bow before the Great Mother."

"But surely she knows I won't allow such a thing," Arthur burst in, his hackles rising at the very notion. Of all the things he has always believed in, freedom to chose one's own gods was one of the strongest.

"She knows that." Lance nodded. "Knows it all too well. But she has no scruples about overthrowing you if she can find another to take your place. That was the offer she made me," he added slowly.

Arthur turned in the saddle to stare at his lieutenant, shocked in spite of himself.

"She came right out and suggested . . .?"

"Indeed," the Breton confirmed. "Stressed how I was raised within the precincts of the Sanctuary; that the Goddess had loved me for years, giving me skills and talents most other men lacked. How together She and Morgan had groomed me for this position, and now just waited for my answer. It's a very flattering argument, and she can weave a wondrous web."

"What did you say?" I asked, remembering how she had seduced Accolon.

"I told her flat out that I wasn't interested. For a few minutes I wondered if I'd made a mistake, if I should have gone along with the scheme enough to find out what she would do. But her dwarf sat beside her, methodically sharpening his dagger on a hand stone, and I don't take well to an implied threat. She knows what I think of her plans, and will have to look for other means to disrupt your reign. There's one further thing I noticed, however. . . ."

We were both watching him closely, and he turned to face Arthur directly. "Of all the men she spoke of, you are the only one she accorded any respect. Indeed, there was even a sense of affection and attachment. Perhaps the very fact that you are not attainable makes you that much more special to her, for I would swear the Lady loves you not as a brother, but as a consort—and seeks other men to replace you because you are inaccessible to her."

I shuddered involuntarily, for incest is an ancient taboo, and repugnance at the very idea runs deep and strong.

Arthur turned his face away, disgust and a kind of blind fury twisting his features.

"That is basically all I have to report," the Breton concluded. "She let me go without any fuss, and I came to warn you immediately. Though she couldn't woo me away from you, she may well try another . . . or at the least stir up trouble among the Companions."

"Obviously," Arthur said with a sigh, "I will have to keep up my guard. Can't say that's anything new, however." He looked at Lance and grinned. "I am well blessed to have a lieutenant so true and trustworthy; may your loyalty be sung of for years to come!"

The compliment fell into a well of silence. Lance flushed, staring at his horse's withers and biting his lip while I squirmed inwardly. The love Lance and I shared had nothing to do with disloyalty to Arthur, yet for the first time I felt awkward and uncertain, as though the ground I was riding on were shifting fearfully under Shadow's hooves.

The conversation swung to other things—Geraint's having named our stronghold Camelot, Enid and Geraint's forthcoming marriage, and the news that Tristan had become lieutenant to a Prince of Brittany.

"Howell's a good man, and steady," Arthur allowed. "Tris's life should be more manageable now."

And so we rode blithely on to the Winchester fair, through a countryside where peasants in the stubbled fields and swineherds by the oak groves, smiths who'd set up forges next to stream crossings and hurdle makers carrying home loads of hazel rods, all turned to wave a greeting to their rulers. No doubt they thought our lives one long parade of splendor, without the cares or worries of the common man.

Arthur waved back to them, cheerful and good-natured, exuding confidence in all the ways the world wanted to see, while Lance and I rode in silence, each wrapped in our own discomfort.

And all the time Isolde's words floated in my thoughts . . . no one promised it would be easy.

THIRTY-FOUR

The Declaration

"**G**wen, you know I love you . . . and I want you to come away with me."

Lance's voice was husky and low, and I stared at him in astonishment. We were standing in the birch grove atop Winchester's hill, the sounds of the market drifting up from the greensward below, carried by the barest of breezes. Here, hidden in the shade of the trees, Lance had turned and taken me in his arms.

"I thought that leaving Court, that putting you and Arthur behind me, would make things better," he went on. "But oh, my dearest, it doesn't help at all. Not a day goes by but what I think of you, miss you, want you with me. I didn't intend to come back—it was the urgency of Morgan's action that drove me to it. And now that I have, now that I see you again . . ."

He was staring into my eyes so that my knees went weak and my spine seemed to melt until the only things that held me upright were his hands and voice.

"But I can't face Arthur, loving you like this, knowing you love me as well. I cannot play him false, Gwen. He is my friend as well as my King, and one of the finest men on earth. Better to be open and honest about it and make the break clean so as not to drag us and him through half-truths and duplicity. We both saw what that did to Tristan and Isolde. But if we tell Arthur outright, explain what's happened . . . We'll go to Joyous Gard, or Brittany—or even Arabia, if necessary. Away where we can love openly and without guilt. The whole of life is there to share, if we but reach out for it."

The breeze freshened, lifting my hair and tugging at my shawl. Lance slid an arm around my shoulders, and we began to walk—slowly, aimlessly—through the trees. The idea of going to live with him was so new, I couldn't take it in all at once.

"What kind of future would we have?" I asked. "You know I cannot have children."

He nodded, slowly and thoughtfully. "Aye, I accept that. It is worth it to me to have you beside me."

I heard the words but saw in memory the many times I'd watched him stop to play with the youngsters, helping a young lad mount a horse for a lesson in the stableyard or pausing to console the tot who'd fallen and scraped a knee. Lance's way with children was wonderful to behold, and to condemn him to a life without any of his own seemed dreadful.

The sounds of merriment and celebration drifted up from the vale below, led by a piper's quick, lilting tune. We had reached the edge of the grove, and I peered down at the fairgoers, as though by diverting my attention I could put off answering him.

The green was full of tents and booths, stalls and blankets where the peddlers spread their wares. I could make out each band of merchants, each clan of farmers, each laughing, colorful group of celebrants who had come to frolic as well as trade. They were my people, my subjects, the ones who called me Queen.

And in the midst of them was Arthur. Arthur Pendragon, a King of majesty, a man with a hidden heart. My own heart ached suddenly to see him there and find myself here.

"That is," Lance whispered, "if you are willing to leave him."

The very thought brought a physical pain and I turned to look at the Breton, to tell him no, it could never be.

Yet it was with Lance that I had found love and tenderness and all the joyful sharing of the spirit that makes life sometimes wonderful. With Lance it was enough that I be just who I was, without struggling for crown or children or the strength and courage of all those Celtic Queens.

The idea of a life based on my own desires rather than the needs of others danced dazzling before me, as sweet and poignant as the nightingale's song. "I don't know," I stammered. "I . . . I've never considered such a thing. I must . . . must think about it."

Lance was stroking my cheek with the back of his hand, gently pushing back the wisps of hair that had escaped my shawl. I turned into the caress, kissing his palm, letting him cradle my head in his hand. "I will think about it," I promised, and he nodded.

"I know it's abrupt—it wasn't until he was praising my loyalty that I realized I cannot carry this secret any longer. Take your time, my love. You'll have the whole winter to think it through . . . in the summer, when the hedge sparrows have returned to the gardens, I'll come back for your answer. Then, if you want, if it would be easier, I'll talk to him first. I'll have to do that sometime, anyhow."

"No," I cried, remembering how well we'd all worked together, how deeply hurt Arthur would be . . . maybe more by the loss of his lieutenant than his wife. "I'd rather tell him myself."

I stared up at my love, torn no matter which way I moved, and he smiled gently. "Until next time," he whispered, lifting my fingers to his lips.

And then we were running pell-mell down the path to the green, mixing with the crowds who had gathered around fire eater and shaman, prize bull and prancing pony. Lance bade a noisy farewell to Arthur and galloped off toward London while I turned back to my husband and my subjects.

By autumn the construction of Camelot was virtually complete. Below the hill the workers' tents at Cadbury were replaced by solid houses filled with people come to be part of the dream: merchants and craftsmen, vendors and artisans. Signs were hung, gardens were planned, fancy horses filled the stalls, and there was a new influx of youngsters coming to Court.

Sometimes I worried about what would happen to my women if I left with Lance. But at other times I could not get away from them fast enough, particularly the redhead from Carbonek, who spent her time crying because the Breton had not come back to Court. One or another of the warriors had attempted to distract her; even the Orkney brothers each tried their luck at courting, but she brushed them aside, saying only Lancelot would do.

Gawain appeared to be philosophical about it, casting his attention elsewhere, and Gaheris shrugged it off as well, but Agravain made snide remarks and brooded darkly on being rebuffed.

Elaine herself ignored them, continuing to praise the virtues of her "one true love," and I tried to avoid her whenever possible. The only other thing she spoke of was the disappearance of her cat, who had, I suspected, gone off to produce another litter of kittens.

But one evening at dinner the girl let out such a scream that the entire Hall fell silent.

"Tiger Fang . . . my Tiger Fang," she gibbered, pointing at Agravain with a trembling hand and fainting dead away.

The handsome warrior from Orkney never paused in his strut across the room, but his hand moved to the sporran he wore at his belt. Along with the other northern lairds he liked to carry his things in a fur purse, and the one he presently sported was made from the mottled skin of Elaine's cat. The little creature's skull had been removed, but the face was ghoulishly plumped out with stuffing and formed the flap of the purse.

"How could you!" I cried, enraged that he should kill a harmless pet and flaunt it in this stupid, senseless way.

He flicked me an insolent glance and kept on going, as cold and heartless as any Saxon I could imagine.

"Arthur, can't you do something?" I begged, deeply shaken by the man's cruelty.

"Nothing that would bring the lass's pet back," he answered. "I can't banish him for it, vicious as it is."

I was on my feet and moving toward Elaine as she came round to consciousness. Bedivere reached her at the same time, and between us and Vinnie we got the sobbing child upstairs.

As Arthur said, there was little one could do about the cat, but I vowed to keep a good distance from Agravain in the future.

Frieda's brother and sister-in-law had joined us at Camelot, adding their skills as barrel makers to our household. Now that we had a fine supply of wooden kegs, I intended to fill them with that famous Somerset cider, scrumpy. Nimue was helping me check the goat-hair mats we'd filter the apple juice through when I told her about the demise of Tiger Fang.

"None of the Orkney boys are easy to get along with." Nimue sighed. "Poor Pelleas is still recuperating from Gawain's treachery."

"Have you seen the horseman?" I asked.

"Ummmh," she answered, holding up the end of a mat and scanning it for tears. Something in her tone caught my attention, and I paused to consider her more closely.

The doire had a newly solid look; more than the dignity I'd seen at the cave or the gracefulness and majesty that happened when the Goddess spoke through her. It was as though she had ripened, somehow.

"Are you pregnant?" I asked, absolutely without preamble.

"No." She laughed good-naturedly at my lack of tact. "But I think I am in love. That is, we are . . . maybe."

"Sounds like an awfully cautious, one-foot-out-the-door commitment," I joked, and she grinned. "Do I know him? Has he been at Court? How did you meet?"

A hundred other questions leapt to mind, for I couldn't imagine the sort of man Nimue might choose after having loved the great Magician—she and Merlin had seemed to be the God and Goddess incarnate.

"I grieved for Merlin for several years—seeing his face in the swirl of bark on a tree, hearing his voice in the murmur of wind through grasses. At night I'd grow dizzy watching for him in the stars, and sometimes he'd come to me in dreams. I even went to Bardsey Island, back to the cave where I had lain his body. I spent an entire night at the foot of his bier, but found I was no nearer to him there than in my sleep at home. It was then I realized Merlin no longer had any use for the physical plane. He could reach me spiritually any time he chose, and it was up to me to go on with my own living."

Nimue lifted a small yellow apple and began tossing it absently in her hand. "So I made a tour of Arthur's realm, and eventually came to Pelleas's holdings. I had heard how devastated he was over the matter of Ettard, but even so was surprised to find the poor fellow had lost all will to live. I stayed with him a while, and together we began to put our pasts behind us in favor of the present . . . and here we are."

"But isn't he a Christian?" I queried.

Niume nodded and lifting the golden fruit, sniffed it reflectively. "He doesn't want to renounce it, nor would I ask it. Somehow, when we are together we are just who we are—partners with a world of difference in our individual ways of doing things, who each hold sacred the haven we have made. He gives me a balance, and a wholeness I never knew was possible."

"Like Lance," I murmured, and the doire looked up sharply.

"So it is true?"

I nodded and put down the mat I was holding. "I suppose there are all sorts of rumors?"

It was her turn to nod. "Morgan seems to have started them, after your summer at Joyous Gard. Is that why he's left the Court?"

"Yes. And he's asked me to come away with him."

"What are you going to do?"

"I don't know . . . what *should* I do?"

The doire stared into some unfathomable distance before speaking. "For the love of Britain, I would say stay here, for you are the Queen and the people need you. For the love of Arthur, I would say stay with him, for whether he knows it or not, he needs you. For the love of life . . . for that, I would say go with Lance. You will never have a better chance, a deeper love, a richer future. And for the love of you, my dearest friend, I would counsel that you are the only one who can make the decision. It cannot be to please anyone else, but must come truly from what you need to do."

There was a long pause during which she searched my face, after which she shrugged. "Not much help, is it?"

"No," I admitted miserably. "Sometimes I think it will all be decided on the day Lance comes for his answer . . . that I won't know what I'm going to say until he's standing in front of me and the words simply come out of my mouth."

But, in fact, the future was decided not in the summer, but in the month of tears, when Morgause came to the Hall at Camelot.

THIRTY-FIVE

Morgause

"S he's standing in the rain, Your Highness, soaked clean through," the Gate Keeper said urgently. "Knowing the King's feelings about his sisters, I dared not let her in, but since he's not here . . ." Lucan's voice trailed off uncertainly.

"Take me to her," I answered, rising immediately and signaling for Lamorak to come with me. I had no idea what I expected to find—half ogre, half woman, wronged by a brother's anger for which I saw no justification. At least now I would have a chance to judge Morgause for myself.

She stood in the middle of the cobbled court, making no effort to hide from the storm. Cloak and clothes, shoes and luggage ran with rivulets of water; her own hair and that of the boy she sheltered under one arm were plastered flat by the rain, and her skin had the clammy, cold look of one who is chilled to the bone. Yet she had not crept to the protection of the threshold when Lucan came to fetch me; Celtic pride forbade that she go where she was not wanted.

"You must be my brother's wife," Morgause announced as I came through the doorway. "We in the north have heard much about his Cumbrian bride."

Her tone was pleasant, as though she were greatly pleased to meet me, and her voice sounded remarkably like Igraine's. A playful smile lit her features while she looked Lamorak up and down. "But you are certainly not Arthur."

The big warrior flushed as I hastened to explain that the High King had left on a hunting expedition that morning and was not expected back for several days. "What has brought you here, and on such a night as this?" I asked. April is a chancy month for traveling, with the weather being so changeable, and I was puzzled that she had not waited for milder conditions.

"Why, I had to keep my word to Mordred," she answered, her eyes shifting for a moment to the boy. "When the older children went off to join their uncle at his Court, both Gareth and Mordred felt terribly left out. I promised each of them that when they were old enough to become pages I would bring them to Arthur so they might serve him as well as Gawain and Gaheris and Agravain have. Mordred will turn eleven next week, on May Day—and one doesn't break a promise to a child, not for weather or politics or any other reason," she added firmly.

I smiled at her reasoning, sure that if I had been a mother, I would have felt the same.

The rain was pelting down, driven by a cruel wind, and remembering the stew in our pots and the warmth by our fire, I invited her inside. In spite of Arthur's edict, I could not bring myself to leave the woman and child shivering in the cold.

"But only for one night," I cautioned. I didn't know how to explain that my husband had left orders to drive her from his gates, but since she would be gone long before he returned, I decided not to worry about it. Under the circumstances it was the only humane thing to do.

They followed me into the kitchen, steam rising from their clothes like druid's mist. It wreathed them in mystery, reminding me that Gawain had once boasted his mother was every bit as powerful as Morgan le Fey. But when they'd changed into the dry garments Lynette fetched from my wardrobe, they looked like any other travelers stranded on a wretched night.

Lamorak brought in their baggage, then waited around hoping to be useful. He beamed with pleasure as Morgause thanked him for his help, and the Orcadian Queen cast him a coquettish look while she toweled her hair.

Bigger and much fleshier than Morgan, she must once have born the mark of Igraine's beauty. Now she was overblown and voluptuous, and both her lips and eyes were painted. She made no effort to hide the strawberry mark on her cheek, but it didn't detract from her looks. Certainly Lamorak found her attractive.

Watching their flirtation, I began to wonder if this proud, passionate woman who ruled alone in the cold northern islands was starved for male attention. Or perhaps, like her sister, she simply had a taste for younger men.

Mordred was a quiet, shy boy and looked, as Igraine had once told me, far more like Morgan than Morgause. Like his aunt, he was slight of build and his eyes moved quickly and restlessly everywhere. But at least they were brown in color and not the eerie green of the Lady's.

"He's such a good lad," Morgause said fondly as we went into the Hall. "Learned everything I ever tried to teach him. Children are such a treasure in one's older years, don't you think?"

When I nodded silently she gave me a puzzled look and putting her hand on my arm, stared into my face.

"Oh, my dear, is it possible you don't have any?" Pity and compassion flooded her voice, and I looked away hastily. I would have thought everyone in Britain knew I was barren, but perhaps the Orkney Isles were so remote, not even Court gossip reached them. "I'm so sorry," she apologized. "I had no idea. . . . Well, there's bound to be other pleasures in your life, if not offspring." Her gaze slid over to Lamorak.

Seated next to me at the table, Morgause and her son ate as eagerly as young foxes.

"Did Gareth decide to stay home with you?" I asked, for he had never come to Court to be a page.

"Gareth?" The Orkney Queen's voice quavered slightly. "Gareth was lost to me two years ago . . . drowned in the killing sea near the Old Man of Hoy. I thought Gawain would have told you. You know Gawain came to visit for the first time in more than a decade," she confided, pushing away her empty bowl and brushing the crumbs from her lap. "Such a flamboyant fellow; like his father, one never knows what he'll be up to next."

I laughed, beginning to enjoy our visit. She had none of her sister's tautness of spirit but exuded the comfort and blowsy good nature of a tavern-maid. One would never guess her husband had been a powerful king who had opposed mine, or that her bitterness had been so strong, she had disowned her firstborn because he espoused Arthur's cause.

So far I had found nothing to account for Arthur's hatred of the woman and wondered how to make amends for his rudeness.

But there was no time for conciliatory gestures. Just as she was finishing the third course of the meal the High King burst into the Hall and we all froze on the spot.

Lucan must have warned him of Morgause's presence, for Arthur strode immediately to the center of the Hall, glowering like the Master of the Wild Hunt. Stopping to gather himself to his full height, he extended one arm and pointed directly at his sister's forehead.

"Were you not told to stay away from my Court, on pain of banishment?"

The Queen of Orkney stared at her brother without blinking, then slowly reached over and ruffled Mordred's hair.

"I have brought you a gift, M'lord," she said, her voice going every bit as silky as Morgan's did when she was pleased. "I shall leave by tomorrow's first light, as long as I know he has been delivered safely into your hands."

Arthur let out a string of profanity that was shocking in its virulence, then clamped his mouth shut as he wrestled with his anger.

"You will leave now, this very moment, and take your child with you," he ordered finally, his voice shaking.

"Oh, Arthur, it's so wretched out there," I burst out, only to have my husband turn on me with equal wrath.

"Stay out of this, Gwen. You know nothing of what has happened here." Turning back to Morgause, he clenched his fists until his knuckles went white. "You will leave *now*, I say!"

The rejected Queen gathered her skirts together and rose with as much dignity as possible, but it was the boy who caught my attention. He stared at Arthur with a combination of wistfulness and fear, and I wondered what was going on behind those large, liquid eyes. Only when Morgause tugged on his sleeve did the child leave off watching the High King and follow his mother toward the kitchen.

"Out," Arthur bellowed. "Out of this Hall, out of Camelot—out of my life, forever!"

"At least let me give her something for shelter," I pleaded, scrambling to my feet.

My husband turned and glared at me but didn't forbid it, so I ran after them, calling for Lamorak to fetch one of the leather tents from the soldiers' supplies.

"Find a sheltered meadow on the other side of the hills," I ordered, wanting to get her out of Arthur's sight. "Make sure she's safe, and as comfortable as possible under the circumstances."

"That's very dear of you." Morgause gave me a look of bemused resignation, as though we were fellow conspirators against the unreasonableness of men. "I understand Uther was hotheaded as well. But it is a pity we had no chance to get better acquainted. Perhaps you can join me at the tent tomorrow? I'll give you back these clothes, and we can have a talk . . . there's so much I would like to catch up on. They say you were with my mother at the end?"

I nodded and against my better judgment, agreed to visit her the next afternoon, provided that the rain had stopped.

"If not, then the next nice day," she suggested with a touch of gaiety as she and the boy followed Lamorak out the door.

Sighing deeply, I turned back to the Hall, suddenly very tired of the strange conflicts and convoluted hatreds within Igraine's family.

By tacit agreement Arthur and I stayed in different rooms that night; he was enraged at my going against his dictum, and I was chagrined that we, the most civilized Court in the West, should refuse shelter to a woman and child during a torrential storm.

It was the first time we had gone to bed with ill will between us since we'd married, and I lay awake a long while, listening to the blustering wind pound against the shutters.

The dawn was gray and soggy, but no actual rain fell, and by midday I was trying to convince Bedivere to escort me out to the place where Morgause's tent had been raised.

"Lamorak came back this morning with the directions," I noted. He'd spent the night with the Queen of Orkney, who was, he said, a lady of many talents, but I didn't think the lieutenant needed to know that. Lamorak was Pellinore's son, after all, so no one was surprised that he found his way into so many warm beds.

"Just because you know where she is doesn't mean you should be going out to meet her," Bedivere responded gruffly.

"What's this?" I fumed. "Does Arthur now forbid *anyone* to have contact with her, even outside of Camelot's walls?"

My longtime friend was looking at me gravely. When he finally spoke, his voice was firm and his words emphatic. "Guinevere, I have never told you what I thought you should do, but if I were to do so, I would say stay away from Morgause."

"Well," I temporized, ashamed at having snapped at him, "I realize your loyalty lies with Arthur. But the woman was treated very rudely last night, and I promised I'd visit today. It doesn't have to be you who comes with me—I can get someone else."

The lieutenant sighed heavily and rose to his feet.

"No . . . if you're intent on doing this, I'll escort you." He reached for the rain cape that hung on the peg by the door. "I'll get the horses ready."

Even though she hosted me in a military tent, Lot's widow had dressed in her finest clothes and was made up as though for a grand occasion. She gave me an extravagant welcome, elaborately shooing her servant out of the tent, and asking that Bedivere look after Mordred while we visited. The boy declined the lieutenant's company, however, preferring instead to explore a nearby creek.

"I am so glad you came," Morgause assured me, her tone just on the edge of gushing. "I haven't had a good chat over tea for simply ages. You do take tea in the afternoon, don't you?"

I grinned and told her that Igraine had introduced me to the custom when I first came to Court.

"Ah, yes." My hostess nodded, carefully pouring out two cups of blackberry tea. Her hand shook slightly, and she added a dollop of brown liquor to her own from a flask like the one that Bedivere keeps handy for when the stump of his arm hurts. "Mother used to say there's nothing that couldn't be settled over a nice cup of tea," the Queen of

Orkney commented. "You know, I lost contact with her after Uther's death. I'd like you to tell me what happened to her."

So we sat together quietly at the folding table while I recounted the convent years of the great Queen's life. Morgause drained and refilled her cup several times.

"And Morgan?" I asked. "Have you been out of touch with her also?"

"Oh, no, Morgan and I have always been close," she said quickly. "She's my little sister, . . . the one I looked after until the Pendragon came. It was the two of us who were banished, once Uther entered Mother's bed."

Her voice had turned nasty, with a cruel, cutting edge, and she leered at me knowingly before taking a swig directly from her flask.

"You know, it's a wonder I speak to Arthur at all," she went on, her manner shifting abruptly to a half-jocular vein. "His father killed mine, and then he killed my husband. . . ." Her voice deepened, and she studied the flask, whisky and self-pity thickening her words. "Lot was a good husband, and now that he is dead, I am widowed and bereft . . . and the youngest of the boys soon to be gone. Arthur is going to accept his son at Court, isn't he?"

Like a drunken warrior who has reached the maudlin stage, Morgause was unable to focus clearly but was very intent on trying. She peered at me closely, obviously expecting some sort answer.

"Arthur has never held the fact that they were Lot's children against your other sons," I pointed out. "There's no reason to think he'll treat Mordred any differently."

Morgause's face went blank, and she let out a short bark of laughter.

"You think Mordred is Lot's son?"

"But of course," I responded, remembering Igraine's comment that the boy had a difficult moira, having been conceived so close to his father's death. "Who else's would he be?"

Slack-jawed, the woman across the table stared at me in astonishment. It was becoming clear that this whole visit had been a mistake, and I was sorry I had come.

"So Arthur never told you?"

Having no idea what she was referring to, I shook my head.

The painted mouth snapped shut as a spasm of giggles overtook her.

They started from her toes and rippled upward in riotous bursts of glee so strong that her whole body shook. But she kept her jaws firmly locked, as if guarding a delicious secret. Her eyes were scrunched shut with the effort.

I drew back in alarm, thinking she was going into a fit. I glanced at the tent flap, wondering if I should call for help, but a strangled sound brought my gaze back to my hostess.

She was slumped in her chair, tears of laughter streaming down her face. Squeals of delight squirted out from between her clenched teeth like piglets escaping a sty. At last she opened her mouth and spewed out a raucous, tent-filling bellow.

"What a sly one he is, not to tell his own wife," she guffawed, fighting to catch her breath.

I was beginning to think she was deranged as well as drunk. Gathering my skirts, I prepared to rise.

Guessing my intent, my sister-in-law drew herself together. Hastily composing her features, she looked me full in the face.

"There's never been a question of Lot being Mordred's father. . . . That boy is Arthur's son."

The words registered slowly, and I shook my head in disbelief. Obviously the woman was mad.

But Morgause narrowed her eyes and leaning across the table, thrust her face into mine.

"So you never guessed? And he never mentioned it! But then, why should he . . . few people brag about incest."

Drops of spittle stung my skin as she flung the word at me. She was cold sober now, her faculties drawn into focus by the power of contempt and scorn. There was no question of insanity in the cold, hard eyes that stared at me in triumph. Her voice went very soft, and I began to tremble.

"Oh, yes, my dear . . . incest. Carnal knowledge of his sister. I'll wager you never thought of that, much less pictured it; the boy-King begging, groveling, slobbering at my feet . . . the whelp of Uther rolling on the floor, panting with the heat of his bursting cock, moaning to lick my breasts, my fingers, any part of me he could touch . . . while I prodded him with my toe."

Her face loomed before me, leering and twisted into a lewd grimace. I clapped my hands to my ears and, leaping to my feet, fled from the tent.

Bedivere was waiting just outside. I crumpled against him, fighting down nausea and disgust.

"She claims . . . that Mordred . . ."

My voice deserted me, and Bedivere supplied the words I could not say.

"Is Arthur's son?"

Nodding mutely, I pulled away from him in order to see his face. But instead of outrage at such a lie, I found resignation, and my stomach twisted into a knot. Turning from the lieutenant's arms, I bolted for the horses and sent Shadow galloping back down the trail before Bedivere had finished untying his own.

I raced into the hard gray wind, wishing it could scour the very flesh from my bones, cleanse my world of the slime that crawled over everything—Arthur, our marriage, the fact that I had loved him so long and patiently with so little response . . . no wonder, if his heart had been given over to Morgause all those years ago. Even her name brought bile to my lips, and when the nausea grew too strong I slowed Shadow to a walk and turned off the Road beside the ruins of an old temple. Slipping from the saddle, I fell to my knees, vomiting until I had no more strength to rise and simply crawled away into the grass.

It was there Bedivere found me, racked by dry heaves and too miserable to care about anything but death. He hauled me to my feet and, wrapping me in the warmth of his leather cape, sat beside me on the cracked steps of the temple.

"Why, Bedivere? Why did he bother with this marriage if he already had a family in the north?"

"Family?" The lieutenant grabbed my chin and lifted my face to look into his own. "Ye Gods, the presence of a child doesn't by itself make a family, Gwen . . . particularly when it came into being through the hatred of a mother who saw it only as a chance for revenge. Surely after all these years you know Arthur holds no love for Morgause, so don't go tormenting yourself with such ideas. That Mordred is his son is unfortunately too true—it is the great heartbreak of Arthur's life. But he has never thought of them as family . . . and heaven knows he had no notion of fatherhood at the time. I was with him that night, I know what happened."

I stared up at Bedivere, seeing compassion and sorrow in his craggy features, and thought of all the years we'd shared together since he'd come to Rheged to take me south for the wedding. Loyal, honest, and steady as he was, I was desperately glad he was here with me now.

"Tell me about it," I whispered.

"Are you sure you want to hear? Wouldn't it be better just to accept the boy's presence and not . . . go into details?"

I shook my head violently. "I must know. I can face anything as long as I understand what it is . . . you know that."

There was a long silence while he searched my face, and finally with a sigh, he looked off into the trees and began.

"Well, you've got to remember the situation. The whole of Britain was racked by civil war and many sided with the northern kings who didn't want to accept Uther's son. It took all of Merlin's skill and the help of Brittany's King Ban to turn the tide. And in the end, King Lot was dead and Urien conquered.

"Once the Great Battle had been won, Arthur had to be accepted as High King. A boy . . . ah, Gwen, we were all boys back then. Barely old enough to be blooded, much less leaders of the country. . . ."

Numb from the gore-spattered sight of carnage, with echoes of death screams twanging their nerves, the sobbing aftermath of war poured from victor and vanquished alike. In the midst of the tumult Uther's son stands silently on the field, accepting Urien's surrender in the blood-soaked mud, afterward helping the older man rise from his knees. Slinging an arm around him, in the exhaustion of victory the boy calls him "Uncle."

Some say it is a shrewd political move by Merlin's puppet—others see it as the human gesture of a great leader yet to come. The term would never be used again, but voiced this once it binds up many wounds.

In York the nobles paused in their preparations for flight, gaping at the news their King is forgiven. Panic in the face of ravagement revolves slowly on its axis—turns, spins, wheels into joyful welcome. Hoards of silver treasure are hastily recovered from their hiding places, the dust of packing straw barely wiped off before food for the feast is piled within. Tables groan with the weight of repast, courtiers swing between fear of a trick and the wild giddiness of reprieve.

In her chambers Lot's widow narrows her eyes at the news that her half-brother is now High King. Raised separate and apart from his Orcadian relatives, there is no familial tie, no blood loyalty to assure the future for her and her sons . . . at least, not yet.

The mingled armies marched across the bridge at York into the waiting arms of revelry. The youngsters from Sir Ector's Court whirl from bathhouse to banquet—toasted, feted, petted, sated. Young Cei cannot resist sampling every delicacy; stationing himself at the most sumptuous table, he makes his first discovery of gastronomic delights.

Merlin hurries from conversation to conversation, mending fences, playing diplomat; had he but played chaperon to his fledgling King, the history of Britain might well have been different.

Morgause is indisposed and stays sequestered in her rooms, unwilling to meet the new High King except on her own terms.

Arthur rode on a crest of exhilaration with Bedivere always at his side until, stumbling through the throng-packed halls on their way to bed, a note is pressed into Arthur's hand. "Come quickly," it pleads, though there is no signature. The new King shrugs and telling Bedivere he'll rejoin him shortly, disappears in the wake of Morgause's servant.

Bedivere notes how long his foster-brother is gone and grows concerned. As the night wanes he goes in search of Arthur, padding through silent halls with only a rushlight to guide him. There are people asleep everywhere—on couches, under tables, sprawled on beds or curled in corners. But none are Arthur, and the one wakeful servant Bedivere finds has no idea where the High King is or who would have sent for him. At last the lieutenant returned to the royal chamber, telling himself there was nothing to fear from the revelers.

Hung over and groggy, the boy-King made it back in time to prepare for the oath swearing. As Bedivere helps him dress, Arthur marvels at the reception he is receiving . . . to say nothing of the insatiable appetite of a beautiful, painted woman who has a strawberry birthmark on her cheek. All night long she'd flirted, taunted, teased and roused him to passion over and over again—frequently chuckling about nothing at all.

The young Pendragon shakes his head in amazement, wondering aloud to Bedivere how city women could be so different from country girls.

Bedivere's voice had grown hard and cold. He took out his flask of Irish brew and, removing the cap, offered it to me. The strong, dark liquid scalded my throat, and I coughed and sputtered while he took a long drink himself before going on with his story.

"He had absolutely no idea who she was, Gwen. Young, naïve, unused to thinking that others might mean him harm . . . his very innocence left him open to her scheming."

I thought of my own early blunders as a monarch and how easily they had been turned against me. Then, as now, innocence and lack of knowledge had led me into cunning traps.

"When did he find out?" I inquired, determined not to be ambushed by ignorance again.

"At the oath swearing." Bedivere sighed. "The very day that assured his reign also cast a pall over it. I saw the darkness descend."

Color and pageantry filled the Hall, splendid enough to be sung of by the bards for generations to come. On the dais, Arthur sits in Urien's chair with the loyal client Kings ranged on the steps below him. Soberly the rebels come forward, kneeling to put their hands between their sovereign's palms and swear fealty to the Pendragon. Arthur speaks graciously to each, quietly, privately, forging a personal alliance for the future. He is tired and worn with exhaustion but already solidifying his Kingship.

Only when the royal women approach does he lose his composure. Bedivere hears him catch his breath, sees him go pale as death. Before him stand his sisters: the petite Morgan, dark and feral, and next to her a beautiful woman with a strawberry mark on her cheek. Tawny, smiling Morgause, newly widowed, just bedded.

Merlin was standing well to the side, lest anyone accuse him of prompting his protégé in what to say or do. Smelling danger, the Mage tenses—probes the air, seeks the source as Morgause carefully makes her face blank.

"We throw ourselves on your mercy, my children and I," she murmurs silkily. "And pray you will remember I am your oldest sister, so it is the sons of my loins who stand closest to your throne—until you beget one of your own."

The new King's knuckles whitened as the implication strikes home. The rest of the world would assume she was speaking of Gawain and his brothers, but Arthur and Bedivere both knew the deeper, more terrible implication.

"Merlin guessed immediately," Bedivere concluded. "Before the day was out he'd sent the Queen of Orkney packing back to her islands—but there was no way to erase the small, smug smile she took with her. She guarded the growth of that child with every precaution, even missing Arthur's King Making at the Black Lake for fear of the travel involved. But she made sure we knew as soon as the infant was delivered alive. Her message was cryptic—promising she would raise the boy to become 'a sword at his father's side.' Exactly what she meant has never been clear."

The lieutenant fell into a sad silence while I mulled over the story.

"Who else knows about Mordred?" I finally asked, bracing myself in case I was the only one ignorant of the truth.

"Only Arthur and myself, and Merlin, of course. . . . But unless the Magician told Nimue, that is all." Bedivere smiled bitterly. "In that one night's work she laid her mark on Arthur for the rest of his days. I think he despaired of ever having a normal life . . . until he found in you all the openness and honesty his sisters lacked. . . . It was the first thing that attracted him to you."

I let the comment pass, remembering instead his reaction to the loss of our child at Stirling. No wonder he didn't worry about having more, with a son already hidden away up north!

My shock was turning to anger and I stood up abruptly. "It's time to go home," I announced.

"Yes, I suppose. At least now you understand the shadow that lies over Arthur. It began long before he met you, Gwen." Bedivere got slowly to his feet. "He has regretted it from the moment he learned of its nature, and rued the existence of the boy since Morgause first gloated over the possibility. Try to remember that, and not be too severe in your judgment."

I heard the words but found no solace in them, and we continued on our way in silence.

We were so absorbed in our own thoughts, a trio of horsemen almost ran us down before we were aware of their approach.

They loomed out of the shadow of oncoming night on great galloping warhorses and passed too fast for me to note their badges. Perhaps they were the spirits of the Wild Hunt, doomed to ride their nightmarish nags across the dark heavens in search of unprotected souls. The notion sent a chill down my spine, and I made the sign against evil just in case.

But the Gods paid no heed, for more devastation lay ahead.

THIRTY-SIX

Mordred

oo shaken to make an appearance at the Hall that evening, I went to my chamber and sent Lynette to find Nimue. The doire entered silently and came to sit down next to me.

"Did Merlin ever warn you about Mordred?" I asked.

"Not specifically . . . only that there was treachery in Morgause, and it could extend to her youngest son. It must be something pretty grim to make you look like this," she added, sliding her arm around my shoulder.

Sitting quite still, dry-eyed and empty, I told her the entire tale from Arthur's victorious entry into York through my discovery of Mordred's parentage.

"It is as grotesque as any of those stories about the old Greeks," she whispered.

"And ironic beyond belief," I noted savagely. "To have spent all those years desperately trying to give Arthur a child when in fact he already had one by her. . . ."

My own bitterness threatened to choke me and I leapt to my feet, beginning to pace around the room like an animal in a trap, fuming helplessly. Nimue sat silent, letting me spew forth the hurt and anger.

"At least it clears away any doubts I had about leaving," I concluded. "I'll go back to Rheged, and decide about the future with Lance from there."

"And Arthur?" she asked softly.

"Arthur can stay inside his nice safe shell of silence. He had no thought about what sort of wretchedness I've gone through—why should I care about his feelings now? Let him go talk to his precious dogs if he doesn't like it."

"So you haven't spoken with him yet—about Mordred or Lance?"

I shook my head vehemently. "What is there to say? He chose to leave me naked, to let me blunder into that awful truth without any warning . . . the least he could have done was *tell* me, Nimue. Surely you can see that. Instead of a wife confided in and trusted, I was a wife betrayed right from the start!"

"Good heavens, Gwen," the doire exclaimed, "you're not going to call something that took place years before you married adulterous, are you?"

"Of course not," I snapped. "It isn't that he slept with Morgause, or even that she is his sister, dreadful as that is. What he did before we met is between him and his Gods—and the other people involved. But he didn't tell me! I can handle anything, as long as I know what it is . . . but not to be told, not to be trusted in something as major as this . . . Nimue, if only I had known, I'd never have been at the mercy of that woman today. I was undermined by my own partner's silence, and that I can't forgive."

"Of course you can."

The doire's words stopped me in my tracks.

"It's your pride that's hurt, Gwen . . . your pride."

"When pride is the only thing you can count on, you guard it jealously," I shot back, remembering the thousands of times I'd put aside my own needs to stand with dignity before my people. Like Ragnell, pride was the only armor I had.

"If you wanted to, you'd swallow this hurt and find a way to piece together the future. You just don't want to, and the least you should do is admit it."

I stared at Nimue in silence, suddenly so exhausted it didn't matter if she was right or not. Unable to put one coherent thought after another, I crawled into bed and pulled the covers up over my head. All I wanted was to go to sleep and wake up far away, preferably in the safety of Lance's arms.

But it was Lynette who woke me to a dull gray sunrise and Bedivere's asking—begging—that I see Arthur.

I clutched the covers under my chin and stared at the wall while the lieutenant waited for my answer. Finally, with a sigh, I agreed to the meeting. It had to be faced sometime, so I rose and put on my robe, then sat by the window to wait for my husband.

The man who stood in the doorway had aged a decade in one night's time. Gray, haggard, eyes bloodshot and cheeks stubbled, Arthur paused on the threshold as if asking permission to come into the room. Without a word I nodded and he closed the door, then leaned back against it.

"Bedivere told me what happened," he ventured. "I . . . I don't know what to say. . . ."

"That seems to have been a problem for some time," I lashed out, waiting for him to advance into the room.

But he neither moved nor spoke. Instead he stared at me, face impassive, eyes miserable. As the silence lengthened I got to my feet and began to pace, trying to stir up enough energy for both of us. Someone had to break this impasse, and when I did, the words burst forth in a torrent.

"Why, Arthur? Why by all that's holy didn't you tell me?"

He watched me mutely, head turning as I made my rounds, hands hanging limp at his sides. I wanted him to move, to stomp across the room, to begin pacing—anything to leave behind this sad, empty husk of the man I had loved. Desperate for both of us, I tried to goad him into action with words.

"Did you think it would stay a secret forever? Did you think that woman would just let time pass and no one would ever find out? Or maybe it didn't matter to you that one day I would walk into the truth and have no defenses at all against her? Didn't you think? Didn't you care?"

"It was because I cared so much," he said softly, a spark of life finding voice somewhere deep in the hollow cavity of him. "I've dreaded this moment from the first time we spoke of Morgause, back before you became my wife. At first I hoped it would never come, that you'd never hear of it. Then later, when I started to believe you might understand, I cared too much to risk bringing it to light."

As though the words gave him a kind of impetus, he began to move. Slowly, woodenly, he advanced across the room toward the window. I sank down on the bed now that he was at least in motion.

"I came close to telling you several times, but the words always stuck in my throat. It's a hideous story, and I wouldn't blame you if you chose to have done with me entirely. But the very thought of your leaving . . . Oh, Gwen, I couldn't face losing you. It is the most terrifying thing in the world, the idea that you might go away, forever."

His voice had gotten very quiet, and he stared out across the roofs of Camelot, a vast gulf of misery opening around him. Finally he turned and looked at me.

"You have both the right and reason to leave, but I love you, and need you . . . and beg you not to go."

They were words that I had ached to hear for years, words I had despaired he would ever apply to me. Yet instead of delight, of hope and fulfillment and all the joy they might have brought, I felt only pain and sorrow. And an overwhelming sadness.

Without willing it I was on my feet, coming to stand before him, reaching up to take his face in my hands. I tried to smooth away the aching lines that furrowed his forehead while tears coursed down his cheeks and fell on my own. Wrapping my arms around him, I held him close as he bent his head and sobbed.

I too began to weep, silently, mournfully. I could not promise Arthur that I would stay, but neither could I tell him I was leaving. All my resolve to go to Lancelot was melting away in the presence of my husband's anguish, and I was back once more in the limbo of heartbreak, despairing at the loss that either choice would mean. So we stood there entwined, sharing separate pains that neither one of us knew what to do about.

There are times when tears are more healing than either words or actions, and this was one of them. When the first flood had passed, I settled on the window seat and Arthur sat on the floor, his head against my knee as he told me about Mordred. It was the same tale Bedivere had told, and as long as he felt the need to put it into words, I hoped they would help dispel some of the horror of it.

I ran my hands through his hair, brushing it back from his forehead as he talked, noting it was not as thick as it used to be. Age was taking its toll on all of us.

By the time Arthur finished, the day had begun to blossom. Down in the village the dairyman whistled as he went out to milk his cows in the pasture, while out by the barn a rooster crowed raucously. My flock of pigeons rose fluttering from their cote, disturbed by a commotion in the stable, and a cluster of exclamations drifted up to us. When Bedivere banged urgently on the door, I had a chilling premonition that something else had happened.

"It's Gawain," the lieutenant blurted out the moment Arthur let him in. "He's downstairs with Morgause's head in a satchel."

"What?" we chorused, as alike in our response as a pair of twins.

Bedivere glanced at me. "The riders we passed on the Road yesterday were the Orkney brothers, all in a race to go visit their mother. But it seems she wasn't expecting them, and they arrived to find her in bed with Lamorak. Rutting bitch had to pick the very warrior whose father had killed her husband," Bedivere muttered, sinking down on the chair. "Gawain let out a scream of recognition while Agravain drew his sword and, either by accident or design, cut off his mother's head."

Arthur groaned aloud, and I turned to stare unflinchingly out the window. It was a gruesome but fitting end for a woman who so often used others' passions against themselves.

"In the pandemonium that followed, Lamorak got clean away, scrambling out of the tent without even stopping for his breeches. When Agravain realized what he had done, his mind snapped. Sitting on the floor, he cradled the head in his arms, crooning and talking and singing to it as if to a baby. I gather Gaheris is now taking him north, hoping that his sanity will return once he's back in the Orkneys. Gawain spent the night digging a grave and burying his mother's body, and now asks leave to take her head back to the one place where she was happy—to Edinburgh where she and Lot spent the early days of their marriage. You have no objection, do you?"

"No, I suppose not," Arthur said wearily, regret and relief mingled in his voice.

A pall was spreading over us, filling the room with a thick, gray silence. Agravain would bear the mark of matricide for the rest of his life—cruel, vicious Agravain, whose frustrations had no doubt been honed on the stone of Morgause's own bitterness. Now even in death the woman would dominate her son's life.

I gasped suddenly. "Mordred! What's happened to him? Is he all right?"

The two men looked at me blankly, as though the name had no meaning.

"I think he's with Gawain," Bedivere replied slowly. "I suppose he'll go back to the Orkneys. Unless"—the lieutenant turned to Arthur—"he stays at Court with you."

"Ye Gods, what would I do with him?" the Pendragon cried.

The question balanced on the air for a long minute. Glimpses of the future floated before me with Arthur and Queenhood on one side, Lance and love on the other. And in the center, Mordred became the fulcrum.

The price, Igraine had said: the price of a love that left the children motherless. . . . Was it not that which started Gorlois's daughters' vendetta against us? Now it threatened to be repeated again, in the next generation.

Not this time, I vowed silently. Not this time.

"We'll take him in."

My words were simple and firm, but the two men stared at me as though I had just uttered some dire prediction of doom instead of the world's most basic law—first you take care of the children.

"He's old enough to become a page—that's why she brought him here. So we'll take him in, and give him the kind of family he never had in the Orkneys. I'd rather his background not be known to begin with—you can decide later whether to recognize him as your son or not."

Arthur shook his head slowly. "Are you sure you're willing to do this?" he asked.

The dreams of life with Lance glimmered before me, poignant as the reflection of the new moon on a lake, then dispersed when the ripple of my voice broke the silence.

"Of course I am. You know I've always wanted a son." My words were light and cheerful, skittering across the aching void of my own pain like a water beetle running over a pond. "And now we have one. I may not have raised him from birth, but a child is a child no matter who its parents are. And the boy is in need of reassurance and acceptance, particularly after what's happened to his mother."

So the men agreed, soberly and hesitantly, and I set about trying to rescue some sort of future from the chaos.

Nimue was less than sanguine about the matter, however, and she intercepted me on my way to find the boy, trying to dissuade me from my decision.

"If he isn't a viper now, he'll become one, Gwen," she warned, determined to keep me from going into the commitment blind.

"He's only a child," I retorted. "He needs a family, a place of his own. Maybe he's the son the wicca promised Arthur and I would raise."

The doire scowled, sure it would bring disaster to us all. But for good or ill, I would not see it that way, and I ran down the steps to look for my stepson with a growing sense of excitement.

I found him in the kitchen, half-hidden in the shadows between the cooling cupboard and the oven, his back to the wall, his eyes downcast.

The people in the busy room ignored him, a fact that surprised me until I remembered that they didn't know he was Arthur's son. Then, too, they had no doubt heard some hint of his mother's death and were staying as far away from him as possible.

"Mordred?" I asked, coming to stand in front of him, but not too close. There was no way to tell how upset he was, and I didn't want to crowd the youngster.

He looked up at me without a word, neither denying nor confirming his identity. The level gaze, so like his father's, held me at a distance.

"Do you know who I am?" I queried, wondering how to bridge his silence.

"You are the lady who took us in out of the storm; the High King's wife, Your Highness." His reply was courteous enough, but his defenses were clearly up.

"You may call me M'lady, if you wish," I offered, moving a step or two closer. He was at that in-between age where going down on my knees would put me below him, but standing left me speaking across the top of his head.

"Here," I said, reaching for his hand. "Come sit on the bench with me while we get acquainted."

The brown eyes regarded me solemnly as I led him to the table. "Are you hungry?" I asked.

He shook his head, never wavering in his observation of my face.

"When did you eat last?" I seated myself on the bench and patted the spot next to me.

The shrug was noncommittal, as though food had no meaning, but he sat down nonetheless.

In the early morning sunlight I had a chance to study the boy more closely. He was thin and pale, with a childish, undeveloped body offset by the quick, foxy look of Morgan. But his gaze marked him unmistakably as Arthur's offspring. It surprised me that others didn't see it as plainly as I did.

"Is there anything special you would like?" I persisted.

"To know what has happened to my mother."

The words were measured, carefully rationed out in a tone that contained neither hope nor fear, and I stared at him with consternation, having no idea what to tell him.

"What do you think happened?" I hedged, trying to find out how much he already knew.

"I had terrible dreams last night . . . nightmares, with my brothers arguing and yelling over a pool of . . . of something black. And then, this morning, Gawain brought me here. But he refuses to talk to me, to explain why Mama isn't with us, or where she is now." Suddenly the dark eyes were full of life and concern as he scanned my face. "Do you know where she is?"

I swallowed nervously, not wanting to lie to him but unwilling to drop the whole weight of the tragedy onto his frail shoulders at once.

"Gawain is taking your mother back to Edinburgh." I picked my words carefully. "He's left you in my care. She was bringing you to meet the High King, wasn't she . . . now that you're old enough to join the Court?"

Mordred nodded cautiously, perhaps as loath to pursue the truth as I was to bring it forth.

"I understand you have a birthday coming soon," I went on, hoping to move the conversation to less difficult ground. "That you'll turn eleven . . . old enough to become a page."

There was a further nod of the head, and for a moment his mouth relaxed into an almost smile. Lynette was lifting hot bannocks from the hearthstones, and I caught her eye and motioned toward our table.

"What would you like to do, now that you're at the High King's Court?" If I could reach some hidden dream, it might help fill the void of his mother's absence.

"Why, become a warrior, of course." The lad answered without hesitation, in a tone that reminded me vividly of the young Gawain. "The House of King Lot is famous for our Champions, and I want to be the best of all."

It seemed that Mordred assumed Lot was his father. Certainly this was not the time to bring up the question of his paternity, so I accepted his statement with a smile.

"And here, for the future Champion of the Round Table, is a fresh-baked bannock," Lynette announced, curtsying impishly as she set the plate down before us. Her gamin face was full of mischief, and she looked barely more than a child herself. "Perhaps, just for the young lord, I can find some butter."

Mordred's eyes widened at that, but whether it was because of her acceptance of his status or the fact that butter so late in winter is a rare treat, I couldn't tell.

"In honor of your birthday," I interjected, gratefully following Lynette's lead. "Maybe we can also find you a horse as well. You do ride, don't you?"

"A little."

He paused, eyeing me thoughtfully as I broke off a piece of bannock and began to eat. I was trying not to push him; strange youngsters are like strange dogs—if you stare them down they cower away, but if you appear unconcerned and give them a chance to sniff all about you, eventually they will make up their own minds about being friends. So I looked around the room, nodding to the servants and smiling at the very pregnant Frieda when she waddled in from the kennels. Only now and then did I bring my gaze back to Mordred.

"At home Mama makes me stay inside, practicing with our scribe," he volunteered. "She is most keen that I learn to read and write."

"Very handy things to know," I concurred. "But if you'd like to do more riding, there's a pony in the stables that could use some exercise.

Did you know that Gawain and I rode together when we were children?"

Mordred shook his head, so I launched into the tale of our escapades when King Lot and Gawain had come to visit my father in Rheged. I didn't mention that I had bested the young Orcadian in horse racing, however, as I wanted to give Mordred as much pride in his family as possible.

"We've been friends ever since," I concluded, noting that the boy had buttered a chunk of bannock and consumed the whole thing while I talked.

"Will I have time to learn to ride, if I'm to be a page?" he asked.

"Of course. And in a couple of years you'll become a squire—and from there a warrior. I have no doubt you'll make your family proud." I watched him lick the butter from his fingers and, after dusting the crumbs from my hands, grinned over at him. "Want to go down to the stable and take a look at that pony?"

The boy gave me another thoughtful appraisal, then nodded, so we pushed away from the table and headed for the horse yard. By the time I'd introduced him to Whitenose and showed him the King's stallion and my own two mares, he was asking questions and volunteering comments like any other youngster. I heaved an inner sigh of relief, glad to have found a common ground between us.

It was not so easy with Arthur, however.

Mordred and I entered the room with the long table early that afternoon. Arthur and Bedivere were going over a list of the hostels where royal messengers could stop for lodging, and they both glanced up when we entered.

Exhausted from the ordeal of the night before, my husband barely glanced at the lad before turning to me.

"This is Mordred, brother of Gawain of the Orkney Isles," I announced as the youngster made a proper bow. Morgause may have been a hellcat, but at least she had taught this youngest child good manners. I thought of how pleased Igraine would have been.

Arthur nodded curtly and immediately went back to studying his list. It was Bedivere who smiled at the boy.

"Well come to the Court of King Arthur," the lieutenant said. "May it prove to be a happy home for your new life."

The boy looked at both men, observing them from behind that silent guard.

"We've been down with the horses," I explained. "Mordred took a fancy to the pony, Whitenose—I thought I'd give him the animal so he can learn to ride."

Arthur grunted noncommittally, and Bedivere rose to his feet. "Why don't I take Mordred round to find a place to sleep?" he suggested. "What say we give him Beaumains's place since the kitchen boy is north with Lance?"

Mordred moved to Bedivere's side, though his eyes were still fastened on Arthur. I glanced up at the lieutenant and smiled gratefully as he put an arm around the lad's shoulder, and they moved toward the door.

When the leather curtains had flapped shut behind them, I marched over to the table and stood in front of my husband, arms folded and hackles raised.

"What sort of greeting is that to give the child?" I demanded. "Why, the poor boy has gone through all sorts of horrible things, and you didn't even smile at him."

Arthur looked up wearily from his work. "I never said I would help you raise him, Gwen. You know I've no fancy for youngsters—I've told you you can take on as many as you wish, but don't bring them into our personal life. That holds as true for Mordred as for any street urchin."

We stared at each other across the work table in silence, and finally he gave me a tired, crooked smile. "Ah, lass, don't ask me to be everything to everyone"—he sighed—"and I won't ask it of you."

"Fair enough." I grinned with understanding of his plea, and coming round the table, planted a kiss on the top of his head.

Whatever Arthur might or might not be as a father, he was still the husband I loved and admired.

THIRTY-SEVEN

Motherhood

hen the need to provide Mordred with a home came up
so fast, both my heart and mind knew full well what I
was giving up. Still, I dreaded having to tell Lance that
I would not be coming with him.

Certainly it was not for lack of love I'd made this choice, yet I had
no idea how to explain it or what his reaction would be. How could he
possibly understand, not having been with me at Igraine's deathbed?
A hundred questions and memories rose to haunt me, and I finally put
the problem aside by telling myself I'd find the words when Lance
arrived. In the meantime I concentrated on getting to know my stepson.

I gave Mordred daily riding lessons and arranged a small celebration
of his birthday in the midst of the May Day festivities. And Bedivere
agreed to tutor him in Latin, picking up where his teacher in the
Orkneys had left off.

The boy was bright and willing to learn, and while neither reading
nor writing were among my favorite pastimes, he was very good at both.
He enjoyed showing me how proficient he was and offered to help me
get through one of the scrolls he was working on.

It turned out to be about the Trojan War, and we had great fun with
it—I explained the background of Gods and people that Cathbad had
taught me about years before, while the boy sharpened my Latin
vocabulary and syntax. I wasn't sure anyone in Logres would understand a reference to the "wine-dark sea," any more than they cared how

many boats a Greek war-lord had called forth on his expedition to
retrieve his brother's wife, but Mordred and I enjoyed it, and that was
enough.

Lance returned to Court during the lovely month of May.

"Good afternoon, M'lady."

He had entered the kitchen unannounced, and I whirled around to
find him smiling down on me. It was the moment I'd been trying to
put off, and it caught me totally unprepared.

I stared at him, speechless, the spoon in my hand forgotten as it
dripped eggs and milk onto the floor. Flustered, I put it back in the
bowl and handed the whole thing to Cook with the admonition, "It's
a custard for Mordred's tea."

Taking off my apron, I motioned for Lance to follow me out the
door. My heart was pounding in my ears, and all I could think of was
the need to find someplace private where we could talk.

But it was Lance who chose the setting.

A huge, solitary oak stands between the courtyard and the stables,
the lone remnant of what had once been a thick grove of trees. He
guided me toward it without a word—its lack of privacy should have
told me he already knew.

One of Tiger Fang's offspring, a large orange-and-white tabby, was
sunning herself at the base of the tree. She watched us curiously as we
approached.

"I've been talking with Arthur," the Breton said, his manner pleasant but constrained. We had stopped beside a stump and he gestured
for me to sit down. "He told me about Mordred . . . all about Mordred."

I looked up at him sharply; was this, then, to be the public and
courtly conclusion of a dance that should have been for life?

"There's no need to explain, Gwen," he went on, staring down at
his hands as though by not looking at each other we could maintain
the formal distance of the moment. "Nor did I say anything to Arthur
that either of us might regret."

My ears heard his words but my mind refused to accept them.
Instead, my eyes devoured him.

His face was brown from months of work outside, no doubt at Joyous Gard. Memories of our summer mingled with the sudden realization that he had been fixing it up in preparation for my joining him. It was then my heart rebelled.

All the wild, sweet magic of the love we shared shimmered in the air between us, like a joy that has no idea how fragile it is. The fact that it might have continued, might have flowered into something even more splendid, yet now could not, brought a savage ache to my heart, and my eyes began to brim.

I reached out to him, struggling to find my voice, wanting to tell him how much I loved him, how deeply I cared, and how unable I was to do anything about it.

Tears were glistening in his eyes, too, but he took my hand in his own and the smile he gave me was full of tenderness.

"It seems you've finally found your family."

The words were simple, said gently and with more acceptance than an hour of explanation could have elicited. I stared up at him, weak with relief and gratitude that he understood.

He was looking deeply into my eyes, as though to touch my soul, and my heart began to soar with the pain and beauty of knowing that nothing was really changed between us.

In the tree above, a nightingale burst into song.

Lancelot dropped my hand abruptly and straightened up.

"I left Beaumains at the Garden," he said, his voice going husky. "So perhaps I'll just keep traveling for a bit."

"Oh. . . ."

My elation stumbled on the reality of the situation, for nothing had changed at Court, either. Only the chance to fling ourselves into a life together had been altered—the love remained.

"You aren't going to stay?" I whispered, knowing it was a foolish question.

He shook his head. "Maybe next year I can come back to Camelot. But not this summer. . . ."

"How long before you leave?"

"As long as it takes to tell you that you'll always be the lady of my heart, and if you ever need me, I'll come. Wherever you are, and for whatever reason, I'll come as soon as you send word." He reached out and tilted my chin up so that I was looking at him again. "Promise you'll remember that?"

I nodded mutely, fearful that if I opened my mouth, my heart would lay the whole of our careful composure in shreds. It was enough to know the love was still there, even if the future was not.

The cat had padded over to us and now began to rub against our ankles, weaving back and forth between us. Lance bent down and picking her up, put her in my lap. Unlike her mother, this one was calm and friendly, and she settled under my hands, purring contentedly.

"Don't get up," he said. "I'd like to remember you here, just like this."

So he backed away from me while I petted the cat and fought to keep my tears in check. When he was well into the courtyard, he turned abruptly and strode away as wave after wave of anguish washed over me.

I stayed on the stump, blindly stroking the animal, until I heard the sound of hoofbeats going down the cobbled drive and Lance called farewell to the sentry. Scrambling to my feet, I raced up the steps of the rampart and threw myself against the parapet, shading my eyes and peering into the sunlight.

The plain below was golden green, rich with new grasses and the sweet smell of spring. Buttercups bloomed in the meadows, and larks flew up singing as Lancelot rode past.

He sat his horse with the ease of years in a saddle, letting his mount set the pace but never looking back. Only when the trackway disappeared into the forest did I lose sight of him and the life we might have had together.

A torrent of tears flooded down my face, and I stayed crying against the wind until there wasn't a single drop left to shed. After the breeze had dried them, I turned slowly back to Camelot.

The sounds of the Court began to drift up to me: the smith at his forge, the girls in the kitchen, the stable hands talking to the horses in the barn. Down in the practice field the men were giving lessons to the squires and I walked slowly along the parapet, drawn toward the cries of warning and encouragement.

Bedivere was demonstrating a particular thrust—one-handed or no, he was still one of Britain's finest warriors. The boys went through the motion over and over, until they could accomplish the move in one fluid sweep. But it was a small dark head at the sidelines that caught my eye. The helmet in his lap lay forgotten, and the polishing rag, too, as Mordred drank in everything Bedivere was telling his pupils.

I grinned to myself—recognizing Mordred in a crowd was coming as easily to me as if I were his natural mother, just as his eagerness to learn swordplay was as natural to him as to his father. The slow, sure knowledge that I had done the right thing welled up beside my heartbreak.

Mordred had a natural aptitude for riding, and by the time the bees were gathering nectar in the lime trees he was ready to go on extended outings. It was fascinating to see what the boy responded to. He loved to watch the golden eagles gliding high and free above the earth, for they reminded him of the Orkneys, and when I took him to Stonehenge for the druids' midsummer gathering, it brought out just as much superstitious awe in him as the Standing Stones at Castlerigg had in Gawain years before. The lift and swell of the downs made him smile, especially when we galloped through the long grass with the wind in our faces—but the dark, untamed woods filled the boy with dread.

"We don't have forests at home," he said one day, scowling into the trees that encircled us. "The Orkneys are all open and free and windswept."

"Are they bare?" I asked, trying to imagine such a place.

"Not really; there are lots of fields, and a few groves of trees twisted by the winds from across the sea. But nothing as dark and scary as this. I sometimes dream Mama's lost somewhere in here," he whispered, glancing nervously from side to side. A shudder crawled across his shoulders. Then, with a visible effort, he lifted his head and spoke more clearly. "I don't think the High King likes me. Perhaps I should return home."

"Right now the King is very busy," I interjected. "Maybe come fall we can coax him into doing more things with us. Oh, look"—I pointed upward, thanking Providence for the timing—"there's an eagle circling. . . . Let's see if we can spot its aerie."

Mordred's spirits perked up at that, and by the time we reached

Camelot his fears were no longer evident. I couldn't do anything about his mother, of course, but his fear of the High King might be allayed. Later that night I brought the subject up to Arthur.

"I know you don't want to get involved, but if you'd just give him a chance, you'd find him likable enough. And eager to please," I concluded.

We were in that quiet state after loving, and I ran my fingers through the hair on my husband's chest, noticing the occasional white ones that were beginning to sprout there.

Arthur sighed and propping himself on his elbow, looked down at me. "You really are determined to bring him into our lives, aren't you?" he queried.

"It was you who brought him into being—doesn't that count for something?" I asked gently. "Besides, there is so much of you in him. I'm not suggesting that you recognize him to the rest of the world or anything like that; just give him the chance you would give any other youngster coming to Court to serve you."

"Does he know . . .?" Arthur made no effort to finish the sentence.

"I'm not sure. What I am sure of is that your coldness worries him." I put my hand on Arthur's cheek. "He spends all afternoon at the practice field trying to learn the heft and hand of a sword, studying the way the warriors move, trotting after Bedivere in the hope of being useful. It would make such a difference if you encouraged him a little."

My husband shifted his gaze from my face to some far, lonely place of his own, then nodded slowly. "I hear you, Gwen . . . and I'll try," he promised.

I didn't expect it to happen right away but smiled quietly, satisfied that he understood how much the boy needed him.

After that we settled into a kind of informal routine. In the morning I had charge of the lad—teaching him about horses and history and diplomacy. In the afternoon he joined the younger boys down at the practice field, where the High King occasionally came to observe the lessons. Arthur neither said nor did anything special, but he no longer avoided the child, and that was a start.

The girl from Carbonek, on hearing that Lance would not be returning to Court this year, packed off home, still prattling that one day he would recognize her as his fated love. By then I was more than glad to be rid of both her and her pushy governess.

As the summer ripened Frieda gave birth to a pair of twins, healthy and sturdy as their mother. We teased the Kennel Master about having a litter of his own, and he was so excited, for a minute I thought he was going to name the babies Caesar and Cabal.

Gwyn of Neath came to visit frequently, bringing his brother Yder with him. Together with Arthur they went over the breeding charts, checking the new foals and sending off the yearlings to Llantwit, where Illtud began the process of breaking and training them.

Below our ramparts the village of South Cadbury continued to grow as peddlers and merchants made it a regular stop on their travels. I tried not to ask, not even to think about Lance, but every visitor to town or fortress brought a new story of his adventures. His reputation for honor and bravery was sung of everywhere he went, and the people soon counted him their favorite hero.

"Sir Lancelot bested a bandit who was holding a merchant caravan for ransom," one fellow reported.

"Came to the rescue of a girl whose uncle was trying to claim her lands, now that her father had died," said another.

"Spent some time with a hermit in the Brecon Hills," announced a monk. "Very devout man, that Breton."

I nodded silently, remembering our trip to the hermitage when Elaine had chided him for being so spiritual.

In the autumn, when the haying was over and the days were growing cool, Gawain returned from the north. He reported directly to Arthur, then came to find me in the garden where I sat making a corn dolly wreath of the last shock from our fields. Laying aside the ancient symbol of fertility, I rose to give him a kinsman's embrace before stepping back and looking him up and down.

The Prince of Orkney was lean to the point of stringiness, but he'd developed an unusual air of calmness. His movements weren't so sudden, and even his voice had gentled.

"Our family is deeply appreciative of your taking Mordred in hand, M'lady. I hope he has not been a bother."

Startled by the realization that everyone else in the world thought

Mordred belonged to Gawain's family, not to mine, I sat down abruptly and busied myself with braiding the wheat stalks.

Gawain took a seat on the bench across from me and putting his fingertips together, stared thoughtfully at them. "Does the lad know what happened to Mother?"

I shook my head slowly. "If so, he never speaks of it. And Bedivere has made sure no one, from noble to stable hand, has breathed so much as her name, on pain of banishment."

"Aye, best we keep it that way—I'll find something to tell him to quiet his questions until he's older." The redhead sighed. "It's been a long summer—a very long summer. Sometimes, one has to stop and take stock. Maybe the old days of reacting to the moment without any thought are just as well past. It's fine for the young men—they're always eager to die in glory so as to live forever in song. But when you've seen almost three decades out—when your reflexes start to slow, and you know you're a fraction of a moment off, even if no one else realizes it—then you have to draw on experience, not just bravado."

I watched him in silence, amazed that the most hotheaded of the Round Table Champions was turning philosophical. He stroked his beard absently and frowned as he chose his words.

"I've been thinking maybe life itself is like that—maybe honor, like experience for the warrior, comes in to give you the edge where instinct once guided you. It was instinct for Agravain to draw his sword, instinct for me to take Ettard—and just look at what happened! You know," he added earnestly, "I made a point of going to see Pelleas on my way back here; wanted to apologize. He heard me out, at least, and didn't run me off on sight. But that's a companion I've lost for life because I didn't honor the trust of friendship."

I smiled and reaching out, put my hand on the Champion's arm. The old impish grin creased his face.

"Not that I'll ever be as renowned for 'honor' as Lancelot is—everywhere you go someone is singing that man's praises." Gawain snorted, half in derision, half in envy. "Well, give the Breton his due—he's as close to an equal in arms as I'll ever see! Meanwhile, it's time to start thinking before I go leaping into a fray—or a bed."

He was concentrating on his hands again, his voice dropping even lower. "I thought a lot about women . . . about Mother, and Ragnell, and some of the other women I've known. There's been many hurtful things done without thinking, but I'd like to change all that . . . or at least try to in the future."

There was a flicker of blue as he glanced up at me and then away. He made me think of a roughneck child trying to remember to say "please" and "thank you," and I wondered what was causing this unexpected shyness.

"I've taken a vow to come to the aid of anyone in need—but particularly women—as a matter of honor."

"Oh, Gawain, I think that's splendid!" I cried, deeply touched by his seriousness. "And I have no doubt you'll soon be known as the most courteous and trustworthy of knights, as well as the bravest," I told him.

Arthur's nephew blushed, then squared his shoulders and looked me full in the face. "I hope so, M'lady. I do hope so. Well now," he concluded, getting to his feet, "think I best go find Mordred. Arthur says he's most likely down at the practice field."

"Probably." I nodded, then added hastily, "You know, I've been giving him riding lessons, and tutoring in the morning. I do hope we can go on with that."

"Sure." The redhead grinned. "Maybe teach him a bit about honor and courtesy as well—wouldn't hurt to start a little earlier than I did."

We both laughed at that, and I watched him walk away, shoulders swaggering, muscles taut. He brought the most amazing zeal to anything he went into, and I shook my head in bemusement.

Thus always with the Celts, I thought, forgetting that I was one myself.

THIRTY-EIGHT

The Face of the Future

s the year moved toward Samhain, the other Companions who had gone off on their own business over the summer began to return to Camelot. There was much exchanging of news and jests, and the Hall filled with familiar faces.

Bors arrived from Brittany, bringing his brother Lionel for the first time. Lionel proved to be less boisterous and outgoing than his sibling, but with just as much humor, and between them and Dagonet our meals were kept merry.

Pelleas and Nimue returned to Court, having made their vows at the Sanctuary of Avebury on the night of a blue moon. I watched them together, as comfortable and settled in their partnership as Arthur and I were in ours. The delight of romance might be missing, but the sturdiness of a solid marriage made up for it. If one had to chose between the two, I told myself I had the better part of it.

Then, in the height of winter, we heard that Tristan had married a girl in Brittany. I froze, wondering if Isolde knew, hoping she didn't. But what if it was Lance who had wed . . . wouldn't I want to know? The very notion shattered my composure, and excusing myself from the table, I fled the room, white and shaken.

Grabbing Igraine's cloak, I made my way upstairs to the lookout tower atop the Hall. The young sentry on duty nodded respectfully, then left me alone to pursue my own thoughts. Pulling the hood closer about my chin, I leaned against the window ledge and stared out over the land, waiting for my heart to quit racing and the tears to leave my eyes.

A full moon had breasted the snow-covered hills, and in the glittering blueness of the night only the biggest of the stars remained to be seen. Down below both forest and wildwood lay black against the land, while here and there the little golden glow of a steading's light offered a warm touch of humanity.

I focused on one in particular, wondering about the people who lived there. Were their lives happy or sad, lonely or fulfilled? What had they known of grief and loss, hope and wonder? Had they ever been deeply touched by love—were they among the blessed whose lives were shaped by love? Or is it that we shape love to fit our lives?

The idea was new to me, and I puzzled over it, seeing it both ways. Take Morgan, for instance, with her impulse toward love and ambition so tangled together, not even she could undo the skein of her scheming. It seemed impossible for her to think of one without the other.

By contrast, there were Griflet and Frieda, stolid and quiet in their feelings for each other but just as committed as Morgan would ever be. I thought of the Kennel Master and Saxon girl with a special fondness and prayed their lives never became as complicated as Lance and mine had.

Or Tristan and Isolde. Now there were a pair of tragic lovers for you! The very memory of their willful, selfish ways brought pain and aggravation in equal measure, and I turned my thoughts to Pelleas and Nimue. Like Enid and Geraint, the story of their marriage was only just beginning to play out, and I wondered how such different partners would fare over the years. Or, for that matter, whether durability and length of contact is the true measure of love. Maybe in some couples it denotes more stubbornness than long-lasting affection. . . .

Nor does love have to be shared to reflect one's moira—the Lily Maid's was both brief and unrequited, yet I could not say it was not beautiful, at least for her. Or Palomides, who cherished an ideal of Isolde that had little to do with the real woman. The pain of knowing he could not have her was real enough, however . . . it had sent him off to the unknown East, searching for something to take her place.

And what of those who were rejected outright? Bedivere, quietly absorbing and accepting Brigit's choice; Gawain, turning cynical and

dissolute after losing Ragnell . . . all reflections of loving, in one way
or another.

Indeed, it seemed to me we had each of us been altered by it. The
how and why, in which way or for what reason, were still beyond my
ken—maybe always would be. But the power and universality of it was
both amazing and faintly ludicrous . . . after all, it was my love for a
man who made me feel beautiful and vulnerable and worthy of protecting that had me led up here to sit under the moon and freeze!

You're likely to come down with pneumonia if you don't stop this,
I told myself, and with a rueful smile to the sentry, slowly made my
way back down the stairs.

Clearly the subject of love was bigger than I knew what to do with;
it was enough to know it existed, and was lodged firmly in my heart.

"I think," Arthur announced one evening in April, "that we should
hold a tournament next summer—combine it with a horse fair and give
Gwyn a chance to show off his new stock. Might as well convene the
Round Table then, too."

It would be the first time we'd officially hosted the Fellowship at
Camelot, and I smiled at the prospect. I could think of no more fitting
way to show that our home was finally complete.

"Besides," Arthur added, giving me one of his sidewise looks, "it's
been ten years since we married, and I'd like to celebrate."

The very fact that he'd stopped to count made me laugh with
pleasure.

They came streaming in—heroes and Champions, Kings and nobles
and representatives of all our allies. A large contingent from the south
and west arrived: Geraint and Enid, Mark and Isolde, and Constantine
of Cornwall. His father, Cador, would not attend, having fallen from
a horse and broken his collarbone. The son was fully accepted in his
father's place, however.

Even Pellinore came, though I noted that Lamorak remained behind
at the Wrekin, where he now lived. With Gawain having come back
to Court, I thought it a wise choice.

Pelli had grown grizzled and graying, though his back was still as
straight and his eyes as merry as in years past. He strode through the

Hall with a toddler on his shoulders, basking in the pride of paternity. Considering that his grown children had made him a grandfather many times over, I found his adoration of this youngest child to be both amusing and touching.

"I've finally given over the quest for the perfect woman, M'lady," he offered by way of explanation. "The Goddess is a hard mistress, and I'm not getting any younger. Now that I've got this little fellow, I'm going to raise him to be the best knight of all. Say hello to the Queen, Perceval," he prompted as the tyke crowed happily and tugged on his father's ears.

We housed our guests everywhere—in the Great Hall, in the village, even in camps scattered through the open woods. Pavilions popped up in the meadows around the base of the hill-fort, and Cei erected a reviewing stand beside the field at the foot of the hill that had been set aside for the lists. It looked to be one of the most splendid gatherings we'd ever had, and Cei was well set and organized for it.

On the first morning Arthur and I stood hand in hand and waited for the trumpeter to call the tournament open. As gay as any gathering at Caerleon, as grand as London, it was the flowering of all we'd ever dreamed to do. I only wished that Lance were here to share it with us.

"Would you believe," my husband marveled as the silver notes lifted in the bright air, "that it would come to this?"

"No . . . yes. . . ." I laughed, remembering how young and unknowing we had been and thinking that as long as Arthur lived, anything was possible in Britain.

The opening of the tournament began with Gawain leading a procession of Champions across the field. Single file they came—warriors dressed in splendor, horses sleek and shiny, the rondels on their bridles glittering gold and crimson in the morning sun. Each had a page riding beside him, holding aloft the standard of his house. Bright as a May Day dance, the flags and pennants streamed out on the breeze when they formed a circle around the edge of the green.

It was then that Bedivere brought forth the Banner of the Red Dragon. At the lieutenant's side, riding smartly at attention, was Mordred. When they reached the center of the green they paused while the trumpeter gave out the notes of assemblage. Then slowly, majestically, the two of them turned their horses to each quadrant of the compass. As they did so the pennants and house flags of each client king dipped in salute, like a run of field poppies bowing before the wind.

Once the motion was complete, Bedivere and his page came directly to the foot of our reviewing stand. With grave precision Mordred led the salute to us, black hair gleaming in the sunlight, the badge of Orkney flashing on the sleeve of his yellow tunic.

Arthur saluted the child in return, and for a moment father and son stared into each other's eyes. When Bedivere wheeled away and raced the Banner back across the green, I gave Arthur's hand a squeeze and he grinned cheerfully.

The first three jousts went well, with much partisan shouting as the audience cheered on the combatants, but about midday there was a commotion at the edge of the green, and an Unknown warrior rode onto the list.

He wore no badge and his shield was without device. His helmet was unlike any I'd ever seen before—more conical than a Roman round-hat, with nose guard and cheek flaps that all but covered his face and a veil of chain mail protecting the back of his neck. Even the new-comer's horse was unfamiliar, and a ripple of curiosity spread through the gathering.

The Unknown rode deliberately into the center of the field and, turning slowly to face all four sides, threw down a challenge to the men of the Round Table.

Nothing like this had ever happened before, and Arthur narrowed his eyes thoughtfully as he scrutinized the stranger.

There was much hooting and jostling as the Companions vied for the chance to meet the challenge, until Gawain claimed his right as the King's Champion and rode out to face the newcomer.

The two men met silently in the center of the green, nodded for-mally, and wheeled their horses away to opposite ends of the field.

When the lances were couched Arthur muttered something about the man's technique being similar to Palomides's. But we had recently received word that he was leaving Ravenna for Constantinople, so it surely wasn't the Arab.

The competition between Gawain and the Unknown began well enough, but they made pass after pass with neither able to unseat the other. At last, showing signs of tiring, the stranger's horse veered slightly, and Gawain's thrust sent his opponent to the ground.

Wheeling his own steed around, the redhead bore down on the newcomer, lance lowered as though to skewer the fallen man. I caught my breath, wondering if, in the heat of competition, the Orcadian had forgotten this was only a tournament. At the last possible moment he raised his lance and hauled back on the reins so hard that his mount came to a crouching, rearing halt. By then the Unknown was on his feet, sword drawn and ready.

The contest resumed on foot, with the advantage going now to one, now to the other. Each was wearing a chain-mail tunic, and though they received minor cuts, there was little bloodshed.

Then suddenly it was over. Gawain slipped in the trampled grass, and the stranger was on him in a second. Astride the Champion's chest, the victor leaned down and said something to him, then carefully stood up and extended his hand to his adversary.

Gawain hesitated only a moment before accepting the help. There was a flurry of back slapping and congratulations before the two of them turned to us and stripped off their helmets.

"Lance!" Arthur cried as my heart leapt into my throat and the audience let out a roar of acknowledgment.

Surprise and relief were coursing through me, and I leaned forward intently as the Breton went down on one knee before us.

"Indeed, Your Highness . . . I find I cannot stay away from Camelot after all." Devotion sparkled in his blue eyes, and the joy of reunion on his face was matched only by that on Arthur's. "No matter where I have gone, it is the Pendragon's Court that calls me back."

He turned without hesitation to smile at me, and we stared at each other with unabashed delight. Neither qualm nor guilt clouded our joy.

"You are my King and Queen, and I belong at your sides," he said simply.

"But why come incognito?" Arthur queried.

"Just to keep them on their toes." Lance shrugged and looked at me. "Besides, I wanted to surprise you."

Arthur threw back his head with a laugh. "Can't think of a nicer way to celebrate the completion of Camelot. Now come on up here and tell me where you got that helmet."

So Lancelot joined us, seating himself on the other side of Arthur just as he had in the past. Handing over the strange headpiece, he explained he'd found it at the Saxon market in Canterbury—bought it with one of those gold coins you gave me when I first came. The peddler claimed it was in common usage among a Continental people called the Burgundians.

The two men immediately fell to examining the thing, oblivious to all else. Seeing them together again sent waves of joy and contentment through me. At last my dream was complete; everything I had ever longed for was gathered here—a child to raise, a love to share, a husband to admire, and a Court to serve.

I looked slowly around the green at the Fellowship. . . . Men who saw themselves as members of the Round Table first, Merlin had said. Civilized men of law, Arthur had said. Champions of honor and courtesy, according to Gawain. The finest Court in the world, Cei called it. My own family, I thought with wonder.

My glance traveled up to many-towered Camelot, rising in splendor on its hill, then swept back down to the two men of my heart.

Clearly the best of all futures still lay before us.